Virgin
at the
Rodeo

Virgin at the Rodeo

Sarah Bird

DOUBLEDAY

New York London Toronto Sydney Auckland

PUBLISHED BY DOUBLEDAY
a division of Bantam Doubleday Dell Publishing Group, Inc.
1540 Broadway, New York, New York 10036

DOUBLEDAY and the portrayal of an anchor
with a dolphin are trademarks of Doubleday,
a division of Bantam Doubleday Dell
Publishing Group, Inc.

Library of Congress Cataloging-in-Publication Data

ISBN 0-385-41124-3
Copyright © 1993 by Sarah Bird
All Rights Reserved
Printed in the United States of America
September 1993
First Edition

Dedication

To Casey Fuetsch, daughter of a cowboy,
for always believing.

Acknowledgment

The author would like to thank the Godfather of Black Rodeo, Rufus Green, the Godmother of Women's Rodeo, Jan Edmondson, master *charro* Juan Montoya, Dean Jackson of the All-Indian Rodeo Association, and all of the women and men who rope and ride in the "other" rodeos for sharing their lives and their love of rodeo with me.

I could tell that Stephen was deeply impressed by the Apache. But then anyone else would have felt the same. Winnetou was the ideal figure of the Indian and seeing him would have delighted any man of the West.

I have always seen him as he now stood before us, immaculate, a commanding presence, every inch a man, a hero.

Winnetou
Karl May, 1876
A small village near Dresden

Yeah, I've heard about the dying West, the vanishing West. Like that. I don't know. There's always gonna be some fool wants to be a cowboy. Like me.

Gaylynn Sabrowski, bullrider
Women's Professional Rodeo,
Hereford, Texas

Chapter 1.

Dark, half moons of sweat formed beneath the armpits of Sonja K. Getz's Mercurochrome-colored bridesmaid's gown. It was only the eighteenth of June in Dorfburg, Texas, not even close to the thermal core of summer, but the First Lutheran Church already felt like a sickroom with a giant vaporizer steaming away. Sonja glanced over at the sixty-six-year-old groom, Earl Walp. Walp, recently retired owner of his own Color Tile franchise, attempted to radiate an air of dignified joy. In fact, the bridegroom wore the transfixed-by-terror look so frequently captured by driver's license photographers and taxidermists.

Sonja K. Getz's mood darkened further.

Only the gaudy horror of a wedding could penetrate her gloom. She would actually have found the proceedings interesting from an anthropological standpoint if she could have hovered at the back of the church, steno pad in hand, jotting down field notes the way she usually did at other Dorfburg social rituals, such as the Lions' Pancake Supper. But notetaking was not possible if you were a bridesmaid clutching a wad of rosebuds and baby's breath, waiting for the bride to appear.

Especially when the bride happened to be your mother.

Sonja had always found her height, five foot eleven, to be a particular advantage in field work. She surveyed the rest of the crew flanking the altar. Ah yes, the merchandising monolith was in a gruesomely high gear, what with the proliferation of cummerbunds, ascots, nosegays, and dyed-to-match *peau de soie* shoes among the wedding party. If one single event could encapsulate all that Sonja found most loathsome about American consumer society, it would have to be the full-bore, small-town wedding. Why couldn't her mother and Earl have simply joined hands around a hickory marriage stick in the profoundly elegant manner of the Cherokees? For that matter, they could have gone down to the courthouse and filed an Informal Declaration of Marriage for $27.50. But, no, her mother *would have* her baby's breath.

Sonja turned to the crowd filling the pews and studied the turkey wattles, liver spots, and blue hair.

For their part, the attendees studied Sonja's heavy, unplucked eyebrows, the freckles of mascara left around her eyes by her unpracticed hand, the lack of foundation garments of any description so obvious beneath the clinging fabric, and how, even on this joyous occasion, Tinka's daughter's solemn face refused the benediction of a smile. How different she was from her mother! Already taller than anyone else in the bridal party, Sonja pulled herself up even taller, tilted her chin even farther upward, all with the hint of an arrogance that those assembled found only too characteristic. The popular bride's many friends and admirers stared at her hulking daughter, and were, as always, perplexed by the vagaries of genetics.

The father? the assembled Dorfburgers wondered. What must the father have been like?

Sonja caught Miss Delfel scrutinizing her. Of course her mother had invited the despised Delfel. Sonja glared at her archnemesis until the now middle-aged P.E. teacher dropped her gaze. Delfel wasn't quite so fearsome without her reflector sunglasses and that whistle round her neck. Without her band of shin-guarded harpies whining about who would "have to take" Getz for their volleyball or field hockey teams, she seemed almost pathetic. In spite of the daily gang-bangs on her dignity that the woman had orchestrated back at Dooley Kleinholz Junior High, Sonja felt something close to pity for the stringy woman in her ill-fitting suit. Delfel had done her a service, really, by illustrating so dramatically that the common herd was a lowbred, snarling pack that would maul anyone slightly different from themselves unless their target kept herself very aloof indeed.

As she'd done so often in the past, Sonja erased Miss Delfel and imagined herself to be Hester Prynne, standing on the scaffold of the pillory before *her* narrow-minded neighbors, wearing the scarlet letter of her Indian heritage as proudly as Hester had borne her mark of shame. Sonja shrugged. Who could expect these Dorfburgians, these pawns of the merchandising monolith, to understand her people?

As bad as the actual ceremony was turning out to be, Sonja reflected on an even more dismal prospect: the nonalcoholic reception to follow. It wasn't often that she felt the need for alcoholic sustenance, but when one's fifty-two-year-old mother pledged her troth to a fang-toothed linoleum salesman with alarming born-again tendencies, bubbly was in order. Sonja suspected that it was Walp's extreme cheapness rather than the Christer religious beliefs he claimed that was to blame for the absence of champagne.

The bridesmaid next to Sonja, Schatzi Allbright, shifted position. The accompanying popping and snapping of joints sounded in the silent, expectant church like a volley of small-arms fire. Given that Schatzi had just celebrated her seventy-third birthday, a few joint explosions had to be excused.

What could not be excused was Sonja's mother's insistence upon a "theme." While most brides contented themselves with simply choosing a couple of coordinating colors, Tinka had embraced a far grander vision: Hawaiian Sunset. Through many fights, Sonja had failed to make her mother understand that simply because she and Walp had eaten Spam and pineapple chunks off skewers at that first fateful meeting, at Luau Night at the Dorfburg Senior Activities Center, was no reason that five grown women should now have to dress up as giant fish eggs.

"Flame, the color is flame," her mother had argued.

"Roe," Sonja countered. To no avail.

"Woe?" Tinka had repeated in her lisping German accent. When Tinka fell back on her Deutscher-cutie incomprehension, Sonja knew that the discussion was over. It was the strategy her mother used to abort any topic she found unpleasant. Tinka used it whenever Sonja brought up the topic that her mother found the most unpleasant of all: Who is my father? ·

The answer Sonja invariably received through all the days of her deadening Dorfburgian girlhood was "Fazzer?" If pressed, Tinka would study her bewildering daughter over the tops of her half-frame glasses and add testily, "Fazzer? I am telling you already all what I know about your fazzer."

All what Tinka purported to know was that Sonja's male progenitor was an Indian, a trick roper, and a louse. A red man lost in the white man's America, he must have been even more of an outsider in Germany, where he met Tinka. Knowing that her father was a Native American had been almost enough to sustain Sonja. It explained and made bearable her being an outsider, too.

Standing now in front of *tout Dorfburg*, reflecting upon Hawthorne's stouthearted heroine, Sonja was convinced that a modern-day Hester Prynne, one who talked back, would be very much like herself. Growing up, Sonja had scoured the library for other tales of noble social outcasts rising above the petty, benighted communities that ostracized them, but none was ever as inspiring as *The Scarlet Letter*.

Several bald heads nodding sleepily onto bony chests jerked up when Ferne Duff, organist, hammered out the first booming chords of "Jesu, Joy of Man's Desiring." At this signal, Irma Krepel's three-year-old granddaughter, Honey, minced down the aisle, sprinkling rose petals from her basket.

As little Honey paused to grind a few particularly inviting

petal clumps into the carpet, Sonja imagined her future in the Earl Walp household. Adjustments would have to be made; she accepted that. Once Earl was her mother's husband, she would learn to overlook his vampirishly prominent bicuspids and stop calling him the Count. Still, even with the most open of hearts, Sonja could not foresee any genuine rapprochement with a man who waxed the floor of his garage.

Sonja experimented with "Earl," "Mr. Walp," and the nickname his cronies at the Activities Center used, "Sarge." She feared, however, that use of the nickname might trigger yet another round of stories about Fort Riley, where Walp, in the pivotal role of supply clerk, had won World War II. Sonja resolved simply to avoid direct address for as long as possible. If the syrup happened to be at his end of the table, for example, she would just have to eat her waffles dry. The one bright spot in this whole, miserable affair was Walp's house.

No doubt the primary attraction for her mother, Walp's house was immense. Though Sonja herself cared little for any but the barest of shelters, Walp's acres of rooms presented her with an unprecedented opportunity for expanding her business, Son's Pest Control. Sonja planned to offically start calling herself Son once the business caught on. The cramped quarters of Tinka's tiny house on Schwarzwald Street were severely limiting her new enterprise's future.

A hissing like the rustle of a snake through dry leaves caught Sonja's attention. The snake image invariably preceded Sonja's perception of the word being hissed, *Scheisse*. She knew instantly where it came from and refused to look toward the vestibule at the back of the church, where her mother waited in the wings.

"*Scheisse*," Tinka hissed again. As always, Sonja was impressed by Tinka's ability to project a hiss that apparently no one other than herself could hear. Of course, the German word for "shit" was made to be hissed. Sonja's earliest memories were of Tinka branding an endless number of things American as *Scheisse*—puffy bread, thin shoelaces, clumping mascara, watery coffee, powdery chocolate. For Tinka, everything about her adopted country, from the man who had brought her to it and the sperm he had left planted in her body to the horrible, gas-producing American cucumbers—"I am never having this gazz back home in Germany"—had been a disappointment.

"So why don't you just go back?" Tinka's precocious, unfathomable daughter asked when she was not quite four years old, already understanding that she might or might not be included in her mother's travel plans.

"I can never go back," Tinka would always answer, sighing mysteriously in a way that communicated to her daughter that she, Sonja, was the cage trapping her mother.

"But why not, if everything is so much better in Germany?"

"You think you are so smart. Big American girl. You think you know everything. You don't know nothing."

But Sonja did know some things. She knew that Tinka, Dorfburg's smiling, apple-cheeked darling, despised Americans. That her mother believed them to be lazy, spoiled, stupid babies. That her own intelligence was purely because of the German blood she was privileged to have in her veins.

So her mother's lesson for her daughter was that she was better than anyone else in Dorfburg, but that she was also American and therefore *Scheisse*.

It was enough to make a little girl who loved books anyway do things like memorize "Gunga Din" to recite as her Show and Tell offering in second grade the week her class studied Peoples of the World. With books there was no confusion. Sonja was simply, unequivocally better. Better than anyone. She was, in short, not shit.

"*Scheisse!*"

When at last Sonja gave up and faced Tinka, she found her mother's laser beam of disapproval fastened on her feet. Sonja slid them under the long skirt, but Tinka had already spotted the moccasins she had worn as a gesture of solidarity with her father's people. Sonja had told her mother that the dyed-to-match heels were not only an affront to her feminist beliefs, but a threat to her skeletal integrity. Tinka had nonetheless ordered her daughter to wear them "or else."

Sonja did not understand why her mother could not be content with her many other concessions. The use of a deodorant, so antithetical to her father's people. The surrender to a smear of Tinka's lip gloss, sitting even now upon her lips as heavily as an oil slick. And the ultimate submission to the hairdo Tinka had prescribed. She had endured what seemed to be hours of having the long dark hair she usually wore in two braids tortured into something called a French braid that clutched the top of her head and left her looking like a stegosaurus.

Ferne, the organist, cued the bride that launch time was upon her with a short break in the music. When Ferne boomed out "The Trumpet Voluntary," the future Mrs. Walp, a proud size three petite, started down the aisle. Sonja detected no discernible bodily motion beneath the iron confection of her mother's dress. The leg-of-mutton sleeves, the heavily beaded, re-embroidered lace bodice, the sweetheart neckline, the Basque waist, the cathedral train chugging along behind, all seemed to move forward on their own. Even the headpiece, a flapperish affair dripping strings of pearls and sprouting the kind of ostrich plumes favored by Las Vegas showgirls, appeared to waft down the aisle independent of the tiny human beneath. Tinka was like the driver of a giant, white parade float peering out of the porthole beneath her headpiece.

She had been taken hostage by her bridal finery.

Sonja marveled how, in the midst of powering this snowy mountain down the aisle to join her life to another's, her mother still had enough awareness left over to notice her footgear. But notice she did. Tinka continued staring icily at the moccasins while simultaneously beaming at her betrothed and inching forward at a laborious pace. Tinka had perfected this double-channeling skill over the years she owned Edelweiss Optical and Sonja had worked as her assistant. There, Tinka would stare adoringly as she adjusted some male customer's earpiece while berating Sonja at the same time for leaving salt, still warm from the heating pan, on the frame.

Pastor Buzboom, a frail man exhausted by a lifetime of holding up a big, round head on his spindly, wattled neck, waited for Tinka to take her place beside Earl before he spoke. The eighty-three-year-old pastor liked to say he was "semi-retired," but this day he appeared to have only semi-emerged from that state to perform this ceremony for his "little Tinka." The powder blue sleeve of his flannel pajamas poked out from beneath his surplice, and stripes of dried shaving cream marked the erratic path his razor had taken.

"Friends, we have all known . . ." The pastor waved a finger in the air several times, waiting for the names to come to him. He finally gave up with a disgusted snort and turned to the note cards the church secretary had thoughtfully placed on the pulpit to spark the old clergyman's spotty memory. "Tinka! Of course, little Tinka and Earl." The pastor wagged his big head from Tinka to Earl with a professionally fond gaze for each one. "Earl was baptized, married, and buried the first Mrs. Walp right here in this church."

He paused for a mischievous look at the bride. "We haven't known Tinka as long. She's a newcomer to our community."

The congregation chuckled appreciatively at Pastor Buzboom's scampish wit. Three decades in Dorfburg! A newcomer!

"We first met little Tinka when she stepped off the San Antonio bus, speaking no English, and carrying within her the baby of her husband so recently deceased in that tragic accident with the half-track tank out there at Lackland Air Force Base."

Sonja rolled her eyes when Tinka lowered her head. That was one other reason she disdained Dorfburg and all Dorfburgians. By the age of six, she had been able to see through the story about the deceased husband. Yet no one ever questioned "little Tinka" about what an airman was doing getting killed in tank maneuvers. She, however, found herself grilled, then ridiculed, when she could not supply concrete details the few times she had attempted to spread the truth that her father was Native American, a trick roper, and alive. It was her first lesson in the sad truth that entirely different standards apply to the cute.

"Thank the Lord for the Krumhoffs' good bakery!" Pastor Buzboom exploded. "For it was Lotte's *Pfeffernussem* and *Lebkuchen* and her warm words in Tinka's mother tongue that kept her in our town."

More chuckles for the story that had become part of the town's mythology: how the little German girl, more homesick than morning sick, had tottered off the bus from San Antonio right into a luscious German *Willkommen* of *Lebkuchen* with pink icing and *Pfeffernussem* dusted with powdered sugar. Of how little Tinka Getz had found her own tiny chunk of the Fatherland right there in Dorfburg, Texas.

With her pink cheeks even more rounded and glowing with pregnancy and her head of honey-blond curls, Tinka slipped easily into the role of town mascot. Sonja's mother had spent her life being the apple of aging eyes. Born a change-of-life child to Lobegott Getz, dairy farmer in Schweinfurt, Germany, and his tearfully grateful wife, the tiny pink doll kept even a war and subsequent famine from intruding on her parents' delight. When all the other children of the village had nothing but an extra piece of bread spread with pig lard on Christmas morning, Tinka found perfect marzipan angels and elves to pop into her rosebud mouth.

Her parents laid what they had of the world at her feet. But the war ended, the rubble was cleared away, and Tinka's world suddenly expanded dramatically when an American Air Force base was opened on the former site of the Luftwaffe's largest training facility. All the good parents of Schweinfurt forbade their *Kinder* to go near the *Americanische* base. And all the good children obeyed. Tinka's parents forbade her as well. But the darling girl was not pulled to the Yankee outpost by a simple love of Snickers bars or Coca-Cola, though little Tinka did love nothing more than eating Hershey's chocolate syrup with a spoon out of a cup. She could have given all those things up. What she could not forsake were American movies. Westerns.

Since little Tinka had already developed a will that terrorized her aged parents, she was back on the base after less than a dozen tears. Besides, Herr Getz felt his daughter's attraction was his own fault, since he had made the tragic error of infecting her with his love for the works of Karl May. May was a German novelist who, though he never traveled west of the Rhine, was responsible for infatuating millions of his countrymen with his mythologized vision of an American West inhabited by noble savages with exceptional pectoral definition and the Yankee greenhorns who learn from them.

Like her father and countless other enthralled readers, Tinka believed that her life in Germany was but a pale shadow of the vivid adventure it could be in the country of Winnetou, one of May's well-built Indian heroes. Described by the writer as "a commanding presence, every inch a man, a hero." Little Tinka swooned as she read and reread about the Indian prince's "graceful yet muscular form."

Dreams of Winnetou came to life on the screen for the German girl just as puberty hit, at the relatively late age of fifteen. The meeting of her hormones and Hollywood's magic was a fateful one. The sight of some big-screen brave's rump pumping, bare and muscled beneath a flapping breechclout, on the back of a pinto pony charging forward to tomahawk a white woman caused a sexual thrill within little Tinka so deep and so complicated, it planted a time bomb that would one day detonate not just her level-headed world but, decades later, her daughter's as well. Before that happened, or rather, in order for that to happen, Tinka found a job at the base as an assistant at the optical dispensary, where she worked for several years before Sonja's father entered the picture.

At this point, the story became a bit hazy, but Sonja had been able to piece together that the dispensary is where Tinka and her Native American father had met. Or maybe it was at the exhibition rodeo, where he performed feats of Indian roping skill. Sonja wasn't exactly sure, because her mother's selective grasp of English weakened and inevitably slipped altogether whenever Sonja brought up the subject of her father.

What Sonja did know was that Tinka had ended up in San

Antonio six weeks pregnant and gasping from heat so hellish, it left her too weak even to wonder where the pinto pony she'd dreamed of might be. Though Sonja regularly begged her mother for information about her father, Tinka swore that the man was a mystery to her, separated by vast gaps of both language and taste. For reasons that Tinka refused to specify, but which Sonja figured were due to immigration irregularities, Tinka didn't return to Germany when Sonja's father abandoned her. Instead, she found a near-perfect replica of her homeland in Dorfburg, a small German settlement near the outskirts of San Antonio populated by former farmers who were growing moderately wealthy selling their land to subdivision developers.

Tinka, answering a classified ad for an optician's assistant that she had found in the *San Antonio Express-News*, entered the communal life of Dorfburg at precisely the moment when its citizenry had the time, the means, and the need to cherish a petite visitor who embodied their most sentimentalized visions of the lost ancestral home. Taken up primarily by the older residents, who still spoke German and cherished all things Teutonic, she was only too happy to become their little Tinka.

Little Tinka's daughter, born seven and a half months later, was another matter entirely. Named after Tinka's idol, the ice-skating princess Sonja Henie, she embodied all of Dorfburg's worst fears about the mongrelization of their precious genes, and even deeper fears about an unnameable blending of the sexes. By the age of nine she stood two inches shy of her ultimate height of five foot eleven. Big-boned and thickset, Sonja, with her lank brown hair curtaining a wary brown face, thick black eyebrows brooding above deepset eyes unacquainted with twinkling, was everything her mother was not. And since Tinka had already claimed blond, delicate, and adorable, Sonja was left with dark, dense, and difficult. The only other thing Tinka, sweetheart of the Rhineland, had left for her daughter to claim as her own was the English language.

And claim it she did, for Sonja turned out to have a natural genius for language that had her reciting "Jabberwocky" by memory at the age of four and finishing off *The Narnia Chronicles* by the age of five. Before she was ten, Sonja had read her grandfather Lobegott Getz's entire Karl May collection, shipped over after his death several years earlier, in the original German. She plunged so early and so completely into books that it would have been hard to say if living in a world of words made the little girl unacceptably strange to her Dorfburg playmates or if she chose to escape to the printed page in search of the friends she could find nowhere else. Whichever came first, books or the bookworm, very early on Sonja discovered that the only shield she had against a world that wanted nothing except to change everything about her were words and, eventually, a manner that a New York maître d' would have envied.

"By the power vested in me," Pastor Buzboom declared, his freshly shaven cheeks glowing pink beneath the stripes of dried shaving cream, "I pronounce you man and wife. You may now kiss the bride."

"You have stepped over the camel's back!" Tinka exploded, the instant the photographer put down his camera and joined the few guests who had not already stampeded directly into the Fellowship Hall. The reception was potluck, and those who didn't step lively would be left with nothing but Hildie Uldabatt's vat of macaroni salad. Only Sonja remained outside in front of the church with the bride and the groom.

"You're confusing your homilies," Sonja informed her mother evenly. "One either steps over the line or one refers to the straw that broke—"

"Moccasins to a wedding! Never am I hearing such a thing as this."

"You're having trouble again with the present progressive. A not uncommon linguistic pitfall of the native speaker of Teutonic—"

"What are you gassing on about now?" Earl asked Sonja.

Tinka gestured dramatically. "Look, moccasins to a wedding!"

She collapsed against the chest of her new husband. It was a pose Sonja found all too familiar. She was used to seeing her mother take refuge in the arms of someone, usually male and considerably older, whom she could make feel stronger, wiser, richer by rescuing little Tinka.

"What happened to the shoes that go with the dress?" Earl asked.

Sonja stifled a hasty response. It was fence-mending time, time to lay down a solid foundation upon which to build the new family the three of them would be forming. It was up to her to make the initial overture.

"Earl—"

"Call me Pa."

Sonja blinked three times. "Pa." There, she'd said it. "Earl, do you think I could borrow your trailer to start moving some of my things over to your house?"

Tinka's buried head rose off Earl's chest and she glanced up at her new husband. Earl lifted both bushy eyebrows as he looked down at Tinka.

"I thought you talked to her about the new living arrangements."

"Not yet, Earl." Tinka's heavy accent and accompanying lisp turned "Earl" into "Oowoe."

"What 'new living arrangements'?"

Earl glared now at his new bride. "Tink, I told you there was no way on earth that . . . All three of my kids were out of the house the day they got that high school diploma. They all had jobs from the time—"

"Your one-man fight to repeal the child labor laws is well known, Pa," Sonja said.

"Look, I don't have to put up with—"

Tinka silenced Earl with a soft finger across his lips and turned to her daughter. "Since four years now the shop is not doing well. Everyone is wanting fast, fast, fast. They go now to the mall. The big operators. 'Glasses in about an hour.' Glasses that *last* about an hour, yah. But you Americans, quality you don't care. Is only fast you care."

"Tinka, the first words I learned at your knee were 'the shop is not doing so well.' "

"*Scheisse!*" Though long used to her mother's favorite expletive, it unnerved even Sonja a bit to hear a bride hissing "Shit!" just moments after exchanging the holy vows of matrimony. "It is only since I have no one to help me that the shop is not doing so well."

Tinka paused to let that particular blade sink in. Sonja had worked by her mother's side in Edelweiss Optical since she was old enough to take a base curvature reading. Which, given Tinka's concentrated tutelage, the little girl could do shortly after her seventh birthday. Since that time, Sonja had spent every afternoon after school and every day of summer vacation in her mother's shop until the fateful moment seven months ago when she had announced she was quitting to start her own business.

Sonja was a superb optician. "Better even than I am at your age," Tinka had to admit. Though Sonja could nail the cylinder power on an astigmatic correction for Mr. Magoo and pinpoint the pupil distance on a pair of Coke bottle bottom trifocals, she always hated optical work. Tinka, on the other hand, loved it. Her two greatest desires—making money and being the belle of the ball— dovetailed perfectly in the hothouse atmosphere of Edelweiss Optical, with its predominantly male clientele. Though her customers claimed their loyalty was due to the Germanic precision Tinka lavished on their eyewear, it actually owed much more to her coquettish laughter and lingering touch. To the "spontaneous" outbursts of "*Ooo, das ist schön!*" when she seated a finished pair of glasses. To the way she lovingly whisked sideburns and stray locks of hair away from the stems of the new glasses.

With Tinka's flirting heading the list, every aspect of the eye business repelled Sonja. She couldn't understand how her mother, who spritzed her shoes out with Lysol spray every evening of her life, could tolerate such an occupation. Sonja, so willing to live life in harmony with all of nature, in keeping with her aboriginal heritage, was daily revolted by some facet of vision correction. The gym sock odor that wafted off the tray of hot salt when she had to swish a misaligned frame through it was, in itself, enough to turn her stomach.

"So now I close the shop," Tinka continued, having given her daughter ample time to reflect upon the ruin she had caused with her announcement seven months ago that Sonja K. Getz would not turn thirty working in an optical shop. "So now Earl sells his big house what he don't need no more."

"Sell his house?" No one had informed Sonja of this decision. "Where will we live?"

"The house on Schwarzwald Street, *naturalich*."

"Tinka, our house is eight hundred and fifty square feet. There is barely room enough for the two of us." Tinka looked up at Earl and a sudden wave of nausea gripped Sonja. "You're turning me out! I'm to be a complete orphan now, abandoned by my mother as well as my real father!"

"Jiminy Cricket!" the bridegroom said. "You're thirty years old."

"I'm twenty-nine."

"You can live with us until you get your own place."

"Earl says it is time you are living on your own. Earl says that from always living with your muzzer, your social development is retarded."

Sonja caught the breath that had been knocked out of her by this stunning announcement. "I cannot tell you how devastated I am by this critique from a man whose favorite family activity was Dumpster diving. So it is on the advice of this child-care expert that you will be rupturing your family ties?"

"No, we don't rupture the tie. We maybe are stretching them a little bit."

"Gads, you *are* turning me out. Abandoning me to fend for myself. I shudder to think of the depravities that shall be visited upon me. The depths I shall be forced to descend to simply to keep body and soul together. The chubby fake fur jackets and red satin hot pants I shall have to purchase. The unnatural demands I shall be called upon to satisfy. The drug-depraved pimps I shall have to—"

"Where's my violin," Earl broke in. "Sonja, you're young, you're strong—"

"A few nights at the Trailways bus station plying the trade you are reducing me to will break me." ,

"For crying in a bucket, you have enough college credits for half a dozen degrees in, what is it? Sociology."

"Sociology? That refuge of the woolly-headed? Anthropology," she corrected him. "An arcane field unvalued by a mercantile society. I cannot depend upon it for sustenance when I am abandoned."

"Abandoned?" Earl turned back to Tinka. "How do you put up with this?" To Sonja he said, "Look, you make enough from that, that, crazy pest control business to cover bills."

"Business! Hah! Business. I have the rumblings of a class action lawsuit."

"Okay, okay." Earl held up his hands. "Like Tink says, you can stay as long as you like. We'll be gone for three weeks on the honeymoon. Take as much of that time as you need."

"Three weeks! Three weeks! I am to fabricate an entirely new life for myself while you two are despoiling yourselves upon your pleasure barge?"

"We rent a houseboat on Lake Powell, Arizona, for three weeks," Tinka said. "This is not Cleopatra on the Nile."

"Hey, you two work this out." Earl tightened the knot of his tie around his corded neck. "I got a wedding reception to go to."

Sonja stood in silence with her mother for a moment as Earl walked away. A hot breeze ruffled the feathers in Tinka's headpiece.

"Earl says if you are not now leaving the nest, maybe you are never leaving. Maybe if you leave the nest, yah, you will be speaking like normal people. Not always these big words. Earl says these big words all the time are a defense mechanism, a wall you put up to keep people away."

"Given that the monosyllabic Earl couldn't scale a verbal curb, I can understand why he might be put off."

When Tinka failed to take the bait of her last comment, Sonja had to play her trump card. "Well, I suppose, I'll just have to"—she turned toward the far horizon and paused for dramatic effect—"go look for my father." She glanced down at Tinka to see if mention of the redskin renegade who ruined her life might have thrown the bride into some sort of cardiac crisis.

But no. Tinka was straightening the stargazer lilies and baby's breath in her bouquet, preparing to toss it to one of the widows in her Aqua Nuts Water Fitness class waiting inside the Fellowship Hall. "*Naturalich*. It is time. Again the rodeo is in town. You go every year now to look for your father, who did not want you. You think you will find him in his Indian paradise. You have always this idea that whatever is Indian is better. Maybe I have this idea once too. It is a wrong idea. But I cannot stop you. I am never making you change. What you do, you do."

For twenty-nine years mother and daughter had been locked in a grip that was half dance, half homicide. Suddenly the soundtrack of their squabbling was sputtering to a halt.

"*Scheisse*," Tinka muttered with sad annoyance, resigned now to how it had all turned out and ready to take her second chance at happiness. The new Mrs. Walp shrugged, tucked twelve feet of train over her arm, and walked away. She had a bouquet to toss.

Sonja watched her mother leave and tried to calm herself with wisdom from her father's people. Her mind turned instinctively to one of the stories that had sustained her through her long exile among the pink people of Dorfburg, the Navajo creation myth. She thought of the Hero Twins, the sons of Woman Who Changes who search for their father. Taking a holy trail, a rainbow, the boys zipped along until, soon after sunrise, they saw smoking rising from the ground. They looked down the smokehole and saw Spider Woman, who bade them enter.

"Where are you going?" Spider Woman asked the fatherless boys four times. And four times they refused to answer her.

"Perhaps you seek your father," guessed Spider Woman.

"Yes," they answered, "if only we knew the way to his house."

"Ah," said Spider Woman, "it is a long and dangerous way to the house of your father, the Sun."

Sonja thought of Earl installing his television set in the house where Tinka had, for Sonja's entire life, banned this ultimate expression of *Americanische Scheisse*. She thought of the horrific home video programs Walp had entertained them with on the rare evenings she had been invited to his immense house. Of the fat men, boxer shorts flapping, pants dropped around their ankles, of the wives, bums aloft, with their heads caught in the dishwasher, of the braying laughter soon to boom unceasingly through the tiny house on Schwarzwald Street, and she shuddered.

The sound of clapping came from inside the Fellowship Hall. Tinka had thrown her bouquet. She had not asked her daughter to join her friends in trying to catch her wedding lilies.

Sonja weighed the lure of Hildie Uldabatt's macaroni salad against the aggravation of facing Earl, her mother, Pastor Buzboom, and Miss Delfel.

"*Scheisse*," she whispered to herself.

She turned toward her truck out in the unpaved lot, reached down, pulled the skirt of the long coral dress up through her legs, and held it gathered at her waist to make a serviceable pair of pantaloons. She strode off toward the dusty lot, pleased that she had not surrendered to the high heels.

The sun beat down, making sweat pour from her dark hair and run into her solemn face, her Indian face. But the heat didn't bother Sonja. It felt as warm on her shoulders as the embrace of a long-lost father.

Chapter 2.

Prairie James shook some Tabasco sauce and squeezed a lemon wedge into his beer. El Marinero had taught him to drink his cerveza that way and, after scorching out his throat a few times, he'd gotten to almost like it. Basically he hated beer. He had a hard enough time as it was, traveling around in a converted chip truck—not even a truck; a converted step van—with a flatulent horse. He wanted to order a Brandy Alexander spicy with nutmeg. Or a Grasshopper minty with crème de menthe. Or a King Alfonse creamy with half-and-half. Or a Tequila Sunrise sweet with grenadine. He'd have liked anything sweet. Preferably sweet and creamy.

But a back booth in the Broken Spoke Saloon and Dance Hall outside Dorfburg, Texas, was just not the place to sing out for a Pink Slipper. Especially not at four in the afternoon, when you'd been driving all day and most of the night before. Especially not when you had to perform in a few hours at the Dorfburg Pioneer Days Rodeo at Deutscher Downs. Especially not when you were greasing up the moves on the waitress who'd just taken your order.

"Jo Lynne, darlin'." He consciously used the shitkicker pronunciation he hated so much. When in Rome. The waitress, clearing empty Shiner longnecks at the next table, let a good three beats go by before she turned to him. That was an excellent sign. She wanted to show him that she didn't care, which meant, of course, that she did. Prairie's mood lightened at the glimmer of hope that he might sleep in a bed and take a shower, a bath even, after tonight's performance.

Jo Lynne tucked the big round tray loaded with bottles onto her hip, tilting her pelvis into his face, and asked, "What *else'd* you like for that beer? Some Dee-john mustard?"

"No, babe, hold the Dijon." A trace of his native Detroit accent—staccato, big city, functioning brain in his head—crept into his answer. He switched quickly back to cowboy dumb. "This lemon wedge you all gave me, though." He held up the desiccated sliver of citrus. "It's dry. See?" He squeezed the petrified bit of fruit. "Nothing. I like 'em dripping with juice. Y'know what I mean?"

He was pretty sure old Jo Lynne did. Two things Prairie James could do in life with an uncanny, God-given excellence: spin a rope and spot a dirty-legs.

Jo Lynne swung her tray farther out to the side so that she could move closer to him. Close enough so that he could smell, *yes, Lord,* Vitabath Green pumping out of the waitress's pores. Which one of his wives had used the stuff? Hope? Sheila?

"Well, maybe," she purred, tilting her tray-bearing hip even further into his face. "You just ain't *ska-weezin'* in the right places."

Caramba! Thank you, Jesus. He wouldn't be bunking with the nag tonight.

Jo Lynne reached out sweet, plump fingers with thin half-moons of dirt beneath nails painted a pearlized melon color. She had a silver ring with a tiny silver heart dangling from it on her little finger. Now, if he could just concentrate on those sweet fingers and forget her stumpy teeth and chapped lips, he wouldn't have to put up with Domino farting in his face all night. That possibility provided powerful inspiration.

She touched the lemon slice, and Prairie drawled for all he was worth, "Jo Lynne, darlin', you just show me the right places and I'll *ska-weeze* until the juice runs."

Did he just imagine the greedy tip of her pink tongue peeking out from between her frayed lips or could he already feel a feather pillow under his head? Possibly a neck bolster for that crick he'd had since last week?

"I'll run gitchew 'nother lemon. A big. Thick. Long one. That's the way I like 'em."

I just bet you do, Prairie thought as Jo Lynne sauntered away. He was in! He was in!

A long Vitabath soak just might make life bearable again. Prairie wasn't looking forward to tonight. That pigporker Casey Dakota had slotted him in at the last minute. Again. This time his scheduled "big name" performer had decided that she'd rather stay shacked up with the pool boy at the Abilene Holiday Inn rather than fulfill her contractual obligations to play the Dorfburg Pioneer Days. If Prairie had had more than fifty dollars in his wallet, he would have told Dakota to screw himself. In point of fact, he *had* told Dakota to screw himself, but he'd also taken the gig. What choice did he have?

Dorfburg? Dorfburg? Prairie tried to remember if he'd ever played Dorfburg. It rang a distant bell. Couldn't recall whether it was a roping town or not. Probably not. Hardly any of them were anymore. Dorfburg? There was a name meant to be forgotten. Not like some of the great city names with which he'd been intimately acquainted. Not like the greatest of them all, not like Bangkok.

No, he wasn't looking forward to Dorfburg. The crowd wouldn't be there to see him. They'd be expecting some yodeling twat singing that lonesome-me C and W shit. He despised country and western music only slightly less than the people who listened to it. If he was going to listen to music, save the sap. Give him some Miles. Some Coltrane. Give him the best there ever was. Give him the Bird.

Sheila. It was Sheila who'd first introduced him to the delights of Vitabath, he now remembered. Hope might have squirted a shot of Lux liquid into her bath water every now and again, but it would just have been to cut the tub ring. Hope had never held much with pleasures of the flesh. Particularly when it was his flesh being pleasured.

Jo Lynne came back with the thickest, juiciest slice of lemon Prairie had seen since the Okay Joe Bar in Singapore, where the bartender hung what looked like a quarter of a grapefruit on the side of your drink. She put the drink down and slid into the booth next to him.

He was tantalized by the chemical floral scent of hair conditioner mixing with Vitabath. Prairie had found that he could overlook any number of physical shortcomings if a woman smelled good enough.

"You sure you're a cowboy?" Jo Lynne asked. "You're too pretty to be a cowboy."

Too fucking smart is more like it. But Prairie just gave Jo Lynne his patented bashful smile, complete with downcast eyes. The real entertainer always gave the crowd what they wanted.

"You look like, what's-his-name? That TV actor? Troy Galloway."

Clu Gulager, Prairie mentally corrected her. The marked resemblance was to Mr. Clu Gulager. Prairie had taken a proprietary interest in the actor's career ever since he first unveiled his smoldering cowboy-without-a-cause persona in "The Virginian." Only women noticed the sleepy, sexy quality he shared with Clu. Prairie felt that the actor had never gotten his professional due.

"When's your shift end, darlin'?" he asked.

Before Jo Lynne answered, she locked his gaze to hers, leaned in real close, and *ska-weezed* that hunk of lemon with her surprisingly powerful waitress fingers until it was milked dry and shriveled as a raisin. She left no doubt in Prairie's mind that whenever her shift ended, his would just be beginning. Prairie flinched and rolled back his shoulders. He didn't mind paying the wages of sin; he just wished they weren't so damned hard on the lower back.

"I'm pullin' a double shift tonight," Jo Lynne answered. "I'll be here right through to quittin' time. When can I expect to see your shinin' face again?"

"Let's see, allowing for the usual encore or two. And, oh, shit, I just remembered, they're going to be doing that special Prairie James, Roping Legend, tribute. Allowing time for the award ceremony, it'll probably be close to eleven before I can make it back. Listen, Jo Lynne, darlin', if you were to give me the key to your apartment right now, I could go on over, maybe sack out for a few hours before the rodeo. Be rested and . . ." Prairie paused to work in a dirty wink. "Ready to go tonight."

Jo Lynne appraised him from beneath lashes clumped with Maybelline mascara. There weren't too many men she'd turn her apartment key over to directly after meeting them, and a Yankee trick roper faking a country accent, no matter how cute he was, definitely did not make that short list.

She pointed a pearlized nail down to the maroon vinyl of the seat. "Why don't you just stretch out and get your beauty rest right here where I can keep an eye on you?"

Prairie picked up his beer and drained it in one long theatrical gulp. He hadn't liked asking for the key, but he positively detested being turned down. There once were days when women, good-looking women with lips like candy apples, had slipped their keys into his pockets without one word being exchanged. It had happened. And not that long ago, either. He slammed down the mug and stood up.

"Catch you later," he tossed over his shoulder as he sauntered toward the door.

He even walked like a Yankee, Jo Lynne observed—in a hurry. She caught a flake of lip skin between her front teeth and chewed. Cute butt, though. Very cute.

Prairie knew he'd be back, but he wasn't going to leave Jo Lynne with that distinct impression. Give her a few hours to miss him, then see if she was going to be suggesting he curl up in a back booth like some lapdog.

He pushed open the scarred door of the Broken Spoke and the sun hit him like ground zero at Bikini Island. The prospect of the Vitabath soak and Jo Lynne's bed waiting for him at the end of the night cheered him a bit as he walked toward the chip truck. But he couldn't help worrying about Jo Lynne herself. Those chapped lips. He hoped she had rubbers. He'd pick some up. Babes that eager, you just had to wonder. Nowadays. Of course, with those teeth, he doubted she got that many offers. She wouldn't have gotten his if he weren't so hard up for a place to sleep. It depressed Prairie to be dogging pillows now instead of pussy.

It was no life for a man pushing fifty years of age. Not when he was the best trick roper left in the world today. And also looked like Clu Gulager.

Chapter 3.

Sonja drove home, still reeling. She almost missed the turn she had made every day of her life onto Schwarzwald Street. The street where she had grown up was dark. It was always dark. Sonja's neighbors had tried to transform their tiny corner of America into a little slice of the Black Forest. Dense stands of pecan, sycamore, hackberry, live oak, magnolia, crepe myrtle, Chinese elm, and tallow trees blotted out both sun and moon.

Of course, Tinka's Buick Skylark was not in the carport. She'd parked it at Earl's so that there would be a car in front of his house for the three weeks they were going to be bobbing about on Lake Powell. Sonja claimed the spot for her small Mazda truck. The vehicle's allegedly revolutionary Wankel engine backfired explosively as she pulled into the carport. The struggle for possession of the shaded area beneath the canopy was but one of a continuing series of skirmishes between mother and daughter. A series that appeared to be ending.

Sonja unlocked the door of the two-bedroom frame house. It suddenly felt like a motel room, a familiar place she was entering for the first time. She walked through the kitchen, where a half-eaten bowl of Uncle Sam cereal wilted on the table, and into the living room. Across the room, on Tinka's glass-shelved étagère, trembled delicate Hummel figurines that captured her mother's deluded visions of the Fatherland. A little shepherdess leaning on her crook and blowing a curl off her pink forehead danced to Sonja's heavy tread across the hardwood floor. As did a family of dachshunds—mama, papa, and baby—their xiphoid snouts and tubular bodies rendered with an unsavory accuracy. Sonja Henie, Tinka's ice skater figurine, jittered across the glass as well. The famous skater's cheeks were forever red from the cold, tiny hands thrust into a muff of white fur, head arching back daintily to meet one upflung skate, short, fur-trimmed skirt furling from her frozen turn. Sonja Henie. Her mother's girlhood idol. The petite paragon whose name she was cursed to bear. She'd hoped that her business would provide a means of escape from the name. That Son's Pest Control would seize the Dorfburgian consciousness so strongly that any memory of Sonja K. Getz would be obliterated and she could be reborn under the far more robust, more elemental, more *hozro* name, Son. There appeared little chance of her wholly owned concern surviving now, let alone galvanizing Dorfburg.

Sonja picked her work uniform off the recliner and slumped into the chair. Even in her dispirited state, she couldn't but admire the handsome logo she'd embroidered on the back of the khaki uniform. Beneath an eye-dazzling rainbow, she'd stitched the motto of Son's Pest Control: HOZRO. The word meant "peaceful state of union with nature" in Navajo and reflected Sonja's desire to live in harmony with all life, including cockroaches.

Of course she had been misunderstood when she had listed the business as Son's Pest Control in the *Thrifty Nickel Shopper's Guide*, where she spent the bulk of her advertising dollar. A majority of her calls came from Christers who thought that Son was aligning herself with *the* Son. She found them to be the most resistant of all her clientele to an organic, herbal-based approach to pest control.

The Christers wanted to rain chemical death. They were unimpressed when she puffed boric acid over their living rooms to bring a nontoxic end to roach complaints. They were less than appreciative when she gathered, at great effort, the white berries of the myrtle evergreen and distributed them around their houses to urge fleas to move on. And they were positively abusive when she misted their rugs and upholstered furniture with a meticulously concocted brew of oil of wintergreen to abort unborn ant plagues. Sonja tried to explain to her clients how Christianity glorified death and alienated modern man from his natural surroundings and how they would have to overcome their philosophical limitations to appreciate the methods grounded in her aboriginal beliefs, but she met with limited success.

Now she punched on the message machine she had purchased for her business at a "slightly damaged" sale. The machine tweeted and squawked. Sonja had to finish rewinding the tape manually. She planned to return the machine as soon as possible and argue that it was more than slightly damaged. Her messages started.

"This is Anita Sturgel again."

Sonja winced at the whining, pinched tones of the long-suffering Christer.

"Those wasps? The ones you turned loose to eat the roach larvae for 'pre-emergent control'? Well, they're turning out to be a lot worse than the roaches. They're building a nest in the breakfast nook and Jamie refuses to go in there anymore so he's been eating his cereal on the bunk beds and yesterday—"

The Sturgel account had been nothing but headaches. Of course there were going to be a few wasps. Sonja fast-forwarded.

"—but I guess Jerry swung a little too hard so now there's this big hole in the Sheetrock over the nook. And now Jerry thinks we ought to talk to a lawyer. I told him I was sure you would make this right. So give me a call. You have the number. In His name do we—"

Sonja sped the tape past Anita Sturgel's blessing. Why hadn't she had the foresight to select the type of message machine that cut callers off after a specified time? Say, ten seconds. It disturbed her to listen to the complaints of tract-home buyers who demonstrated no ability whatsoever to live in harmony with nature. She caught the next message *in medias res*.

"—damn lizard's worse than the damn mice. Come and get it out of our house."

It was Mr. Capelli. Not one of her believer clients. She resented the tone he was taking. In any sort of negotiation, there was always room for basic courtesy.

"I did not pay thirty-nine ninety-five to have my house sprinkled with lizard turds. And I'm damn tired of talking to this machine. You call me back *today* or expect a personal visit."

There were three more messages, precisely the number of remaining clients. Sonja wondered why she had been condemned to dealing with such seriously *Koyaanisqatsi*-type individuals. Man out of balance, as she'd learned from the film of the same name, described her client roster to a T.

From her extensive anthropological studies, she knew that a Native American, a man in balance, in *hozro*, one of her father's people, would have welcomed any of the creatures she was paid to exterminate. Would have welcomed and known some life-sustaining recipe for putting the tiny being back into the cycle of life. The phone rang. Sonja quickly switched her machine to the monitor mode.

"You know who this is."

Indeed she did. She found Mr. Capelli's tones of borderline psychosis to be unforgettable.

"In addition to the lizard, I want you to clear out all the other crap you crapped our house up with. Especially those fuzzy, lumpy pieces of shit you dumped all—"

Sonja reached for the machine. At the last moment, she stopped herself from breaking into Mr. Capelli's demented tirade to inform him that those "fuzzy, lumpy pieces of shit" were *bois d'arc* apples widely known throughout a more enlightened world to be a highly efficacious flea repellent.

Mr. Capelli raved on. "And that diastolic dirt you threw all over the—"

Sonja lunged forward and grabbed the phone receiver. "That's diatomaceous earth.

"Ah-hah! So you been there all the time. I don't like that. Don't like being listened to."

The man's paranoia was limitless. "As I told you earlier, diatomaceous earth is not dirt at all but the siliceous remains of millions of diatoms."

"Ask me if I care. If it's in my house and I don't want it in my house, it's dirt."

"Mr. Capelli, I will happily refund every cent you've given me if we can consider our dealings terminated."

"Nothing is terminated until you get all your crap outa my house!"

"That language is not necessary."

"Don't give me your high-and-mighty crap. I know where you live. I'm gonna be over there soon as my shift's through tonight. I'm gonna get satisfaction on this—"

Sonja depressed the receiver button, cutting off Mr. Capelli's deranged ramblings. She wondered briefly if the genetic exigencies of his Mediterranean blood might drive him to hot-blooded sorts of behavior involving the breaking of thumbs. These reflections caused Sonja to feel intensely just how *Koyaanisqatsi* her own life was. Her efforts to educate a clientele addicted to comfort and chemicals were not going well. She was twenty-nine years old and four years behind in her Life Plan. She'd intended to be living on her own by the age of twenty-five. Close to the land. Preferably in a locale sacred to her father's people, in a hogan opening to the east.

It seemed that she was on her own now, but just as far from the land as ever. She looked around Tinka's house, tidy, dainty, delicate, really more a *haus* than a house. For as long as she could remember, the little bungalow had been pushing her out. Tinka was its voice, constantly telling her not to touch, put it down, don't run, don't yell, don't get it dirty, don't break it, don't bring that in here.

Sonja sat in the recliner, thinking, for over an hour, then hauled herself up and went to her room. Just as Sonja herself was everything that Tinka was not, Sonja's room was everything that

Tinka's perfect, pastel *haus* was not. She had painted the walls a
peanut butter tan, then covered them with posters calling for the
release of Leonard Peltier and a halt to the destruction of the
golden-cheeked warbler's habitat. The speckled linoleum floor was
strewn with dirty pants and T-shirts. Her brick-and-board shelves
were crowded with books, rocks, and birds' nests. A stranger would
have guessed that the room belonged to a twelve-year-old Eagle
Scout.

A closer inspection of the bookshelves would have turned up
little to change that impression: *Will Rogers' Favorite Rope Tricks*,
Ropin' Plain and Fancy, *Lassos, Lariats, and Legends of Roping*. In
addition to several yards of scholarly tomes on Native American
anthropology, the shelves were filled with the sorts of books that
had indeed thrilled many a twelve-year-old boy: *Twenty Years
Among the Pawnee*, *The Horse-Eaters*, *Geronimo: Warrior-King*, *I Rode
with the Mustangeros*. And, of course, her grandfather's fateful collection of the complete works of Karl May, including an especially
well-thumbed copy of *Winnetou*.

Sonja flopped onto her narrow bed covered by a worn quilt.
Once pink, now fuzzy and gray, the twenty-two-year-old quilt rep-
resented Tinka's last effort to feminize her daughter. Sonja considered her future for several moments as she stared up at the faint
tracings of the constellations she had painted on her ceiling.
Abruptly, she jumped out of bed and rushed to her closet.

She fumbled with the combination lock she had installed on
the door to keep Tinka out. In her agitation, she overshot the last
number three times before the lock fell open. Inside hung the few
garments Sonja had picked up at Betty's Bargain Barn: a couple of
sturdy blouses, work pants, a particularly ill-advised dirndl skirt.
Her rodeo outfits, the Western get-ups she saved for Dorfburg
Pioneer Days, were the only possessions Sonja had ever paid retail
for. They hung apart from the other clothes, carefully encased in
dry cleaner's bags to preserve them for their annual outing.

She pushed the bags back to reveal a shrine set against the

closet wall down on the floor next to a pair of sneakers that dated back to Miss Delfel days and a pair of "leather-look" vinyl cowboy boots Sonja had purchased at Tiny's Western Wear. The shrine resembled a picnic basket–sized cosmetics kit, which, in fact, it had been until Tinka threw it away and Sonja retrieved it for alternative duty. Sonja turned on the battery-operated lights ringing the mirror that flipped up from the top of the case, then pulled open the tiered drawers, fanning them out like stairs on either side.

Taped over the mirror was the shrine's centerpiece, a photograph dating from the late fifties. Mass-produced on the cheapest paper available, it was the sort of black-and-white, eight by ten glossy that actors sent out by the thousands. Except that this photo did not depict a movie star. It featured an Indian wearing a feathered headdress, moccasins, and beaded buckskin shirt and pants. He held a rope. The caption read "Gray Wolf, Greatest Redskin Roper of Them All!" Booking agents were urged to call a phone number that had been scratched out long before Sonja found the photo in her mother's lingerie drawer.

Like so much else that went unspoken between mother and daughter, Sonja's removal of her father's photo was never mentioned by Tinka.

Not that the photo held that many clues. Though she had researched the matter assiduously, Sonja could not even uncover her father's tribal identity from his costume. It was a hodgepodge. The beading on the shirt was Pawnee by way of Hong Kong. The moccasins were a Creek design as interpreted by Sears, Roebuck. The only remotely authentic item was the blanket thrown over one shoulder. Definitely a Navajo motif.

The rope Gray Wolf held was the standard Sampson's Spotcord, which nearly all American ropers had used since Will Rogers.

The photo, overexposed to begin with, had never been fixed properly, and the parts that were not turning pinkish brown were disappearing altogether. Gray Wolf's face, which Sonja had caressed so often, was vanishing even faster than the rest of him, and it was impossible to tell what color her father's skin had been to begin with or even to guess at his age. What the photo did convey was a nobility of spirit, an indomitability that spoke directly to Sonja and comforted and sustained her through the long years of the Dorfburg exile.

In a drawer beneath the photo was a pair of men's sunglasses. Sonja had found them in the trash, and three clues led her to deduce that they had belonged to her father: the frames were a clunky, government-issue style, the edges of the temple pieces had been beveled in Tinka's precise Germanic fashion, and the lenses were both flat and photochromatic. The flatness of the lenses dated them at least thirty years, back to the days before all lenses were ground with a marked convexity. But they were also photochromatic—they darkened in response to the amount of light they were exposed to. Sonja knew from Tinka's many lectures on the subject that, as in most fields, the Germans had led the world in photochromatic technology. A pair of lenses both thirty years old and photochromatic could have been made only in Germany.

Of course, Sonja had checked the prescription at her mother's shop. There was no correction; the lenses were plain glass. Sonja imagined Tinka going to the roping exhibition starring Gray Wolf. Perhaps the featured performer had picked the lovely *Fräulein* out of the crowd. A discreet conversation had followed in which Tinka had revealed that she worked at the base optical dispensary. Gray Wolf then invented the need for a pair of sunglasses as a pretext for seeing Tinka again.

In the largest drawer was the medicine bundle Sonja had gathered for herself. Unable to obtain the buffalo calfskin she would have liked, Sonja had substituted a car wash chamois to construct a pouch, which she filled with several of her own baby teeth, a chunk of fool's gold in the shape of a dog turd she'd found at a construction site, and several marijuana joints, procured from her Field Work Methodology lab instructor at Central South Texas University, which she intended to smoke at the appropriate moment to induce her personal vision.

Other drawers contained construction-paper Valentine hearts, a glitter-sprinkled toothpick holder, and a plaster of Paris ashtray. All gifts that Sonja had persisted in making at school for her father. When well-meaning teachers suggested that it might be hard for Sonja to give those presents to her father, she took it as further proof of how little any of them knew about her, of how limited their imaginations were.

Sonja turned from the shrine and found the World War II mess kit that she used as a purse. She carefully packed the sunglasses, the photo of Gray Wolf, and her medicine bundle, then dug through the inside pockets of the yellow rain slicker that she used as a safe-deposit box and pulled out what remained of her savings. Ninety dollars. She stuffed the bills into the mess kit and turned next to her rodeo outfits.

She tore open one of the dry cleaner's bags and removed a pressed pair of jeans that featured orange panels running up the inside of both legs. She put them on and added a blue blouse with snap buttons and ruffles up the front. The scarlet sash from her Dorfburg High marching band uniform completed the ensemble. Sonja had always liked the jaunty cavalryman's look made by the long sash's fringe dancing beside her knees. When she freed her long hair from the French braid, it fluffed out nicely around her head in a crimped, pre-Raphaelite way that Sonja thought quite handsome. She added some Flame-Glo Partyline Pink lipstick, which she'd picked up at Betty's for fifty cents a tube, and her toilette was completed.

She shouldered her olive green mess kit purse and stepped outside. The heat was still at blast-furnace level. As she drove slowly to the rodeo grounds, she half-expected her mother's Skylark to appear in the rearview. Sonja decided that if her mother begged, truly begged, she would agree to live with her and Walp, with the stipulation that the carport must be converted into a hoganlike addition opening to the sacred east so that she could have a modicum of privacy.

At the gate to the Deutscher Downs Fair and Rodeo grounds was a hand-scrawled sign, PARKING $2. Sonja whipped the truck back into traffic and drove several blocks until she came to a side street, where she turned off and parked for free.

During the hot, dusty hike back to the rodeo grounds, Sonja noticed that through the vinyl of her boots might "look" like leather, it certainly didn't behave like any substance that had ever been alive. Besides crackling when she walked, each boot had turned into a personal sauna, making her feet sweat until they sloshed. The poly-blend fabric of the two-toned jeans also displayed some remarkable heat-retention properties. Sonja was dripping with sweat and dying of thirst by the time she reached the downs.

A sunburned man stationed on a lawn chair beneath the PARKING $2 sign scowled at Sonja. "Still got to walk back," he informed her sourly, thrusting his hands into the carpenter's nail apron tied around his waist.

Sonja did not dignify him with a reply. Someone who would turn churlish just because he'd lost a two-dollar parking fee did not merit her courtesy.

The Dorfburg Pioneer Days Rodeo was just beginning its run, and the fairgrounds were crowded with gaudy attractions: rides where pubescent females shrieked, booths where cheap stuffed animals could be won, and concession stands.

It was the last that interested Sonja most in her parched condition. Normally, she would have made a reconnaissance tour of the entire area to comparison shop the various vendors. Given, however, that each step she took cracked the unyielding uppers of her boots against her increasingly tender insteps, she stopped at the first booth she could limp to. In the windows she could see trays of candy apples, both glossy red and caramel with nuts on top, sitting on sheets of wax paper, sticks dug into them. The smell of burned sugar testified to the freshness of the pink clouds of cotton candy.

Bottles of Sno-Kone syrup in neon blue, nailpolish red, stoplight green stood on end in a dispenser rack.

Outside the stand, a black man with a slightly receding hairline, wearing a faded work shirt with the sleeves torn off and blue jeans with the name JACKSON tooled on the back, hunched over a thick orange extension cord he was attaching to a generator.

As she drew nearer, Sonja saw that there was another man working inside the dark booth. This man was white, short, and scrawny, one of these unreadably aged sort who could have been anywhere from his early thirties to late fifties. He wore a gimme cap with the bill flipped up in front; a white apron was tied over his short-sleeved plaid shirt; and he had both of his arms up to the elbows in a pan of sudsy water.

Suddenly all the lights inside the stand blasted on, the cotton candy machine started twirling around, and popcorn began pushing out of a stainless steel tub hung inside a glass case painted with red letters asking "$1.25 a bag."

The man pulled his hands out of the water, each fist filled with quarters, dimes, nickels, and pennies, and yelled out a side window, "Ith on now, Jack-thon! We got power!" He was missing both of his upper front teeth.

Jackson, clearly the owner of the booth, yelled back, "I thought that might be the case, Mickey! Judging from the lights!"

Mickey stood thoughtfully for a moment, suds dripping from his fists, then nodded and crimped his empty mouth into one word, "Oh." He plunged his hands back into the water and proceeded to jangle the silver.

"Excuse me," Sonja said through the screened order window. Mickey jerked his head up, noticing her for the first time. "Could I trouble you for"—she studied the bill of fare, searching, as always, for the most healthful selection at the best price available—"an 'icy cold glass of fresh lemonade'?"

Mickey studied his customer for a moment before asking, "Are you in the Marine Honor Guard?"

"Marine Honor Guard? No."

"Oh. I had an uncle who had a thath jutht like that one you got there." He pointed to Sonja's band sash. "And he wuth in the Marine Honor Guard. But you ain't."

"No. The lemonade?"

Mickey dried his hands on a towel and looked around anxiously. Jackson had gone to the back to hook up a tank of propane. Mickey reluctantly turned back to his customer. "Well, the change ain't through gettin' wathed yet."

"I think I can give you the exact change," Sonja answered, her mouth getting dryer by the minute.

"Well . . . the lemonade ain't made up yet."

Sonja felt the booth tremble; then the back door opened and Jackson stepped in. Sonja had not noticed how large Jackson was, bent over the extension cords outside, but he filled the small concession stand. Surprisingly, his dark skin did not appear darker inside the shadowed booth. To the contrary, Jackson seemed to have brought the sun in with him.

"You taking good care of our customer, Mick?"

Mickey looked balefully at his boss. "She wanth lemonade and there ain't none made up and the change ith all wet." He sighed from the desperate hopelessness of it all.

"That's all right, Mick. You go back to getting the change ready." Jackson turned and spoke to Sonja through the screened opening between them. "That's one lemonade?" He held up a single finger, long and brown as a cigar.

"Yes, please. Preferably before I wither to a crisp," Sonja said with a gasp.

"Most certainly," Jackson agreed readily. "Well in advance of that dire circumstance."

Sonja was taken aback. Hearing Jackson's highflown response was like being in a remote land and hearing a countryman speak your native dialect. Jackson turned his back to her and Sonja noticed that, though the concessionaire was well into his forties, he had an athlete's body. She suspected it came from muscling around tanks of propane and hitching and unhitching the concession stand on wheels that was the source of his livelihood. He pulled toward him a five-gallon, square plastic tank with a spigot on the front, popped off the lid, and filled it with water. Lifting the filled tank out of the sink caused all the muscles north of Jackson's tooled belt to come to life, putting Sonja in mind of Winnetou.

She immediately squelched her attraction and searched for a more fitting focus for her attention. She found it when Jackson ripped open a commercial-sized packet of Country Time Lemonade powder, dumped it in, and proceeded to stir it.

She stood on tiptoes to speak more forcefully into the screened opening. "What, might I ask," she inquired, ever the consumer watchdog, "of the 'fresh' lemonade?"

Jackson continued stirring. "Fresh, made up this very second."

"In my crippled condition, I suppose I have no choice. I'll take the reconstituted fraud."

Jackson handed her a cup stingy as a movie theater's. Sonja gave him two dollars. She wasn't going to dig for the exact change at those prices.

"Wash this lady up three quarters, Mick."

His tongue sticking out the tiniest bit between his lips, Mickey grubbed through the slurry of change at the bottom of the dishpan until he came up with the correct coins. With a long-handled brush, he scrubbed away at them. When he had rinsed and patted them dry, he started to put the coins into Sonja's palm, but she withdrew her hand.

"Does either of you have a communicable disease?" Sonja asked.

Mickey looked at his boss.

"No. No communicables," Jackson answered. "Mickey just likes handing back shiny pennies, sparkling dimes, gleaming quarters, and the occasional glittering Kennedy half. That's just the way he likes to do it."

"That's it?" Sonja probed suspiciously.

"Yeth, thath it," Mickey confirmed, handing over her change. "Thath jutht the way I like to do it," he added with stubborn pride.

Jackson, pouring kernels into the popcorn kettle, added, "Some things we do my way and some things we do Mick's way. It all gets done."

Sonja closed her fist around the damp coins. "You have a very enlightened viewpoint for a member of management."

Jackson bent down to study his customer through the screen. As he tilted his head up, the light caught his hazel eyes and turned them into wild things glittering in a jungle night. The damp quarters squeezed in Sonja's hand grew a bit damper. She forced herself once again to stop thinking of the admirably endowed Winnetou.

"Thank you," Jackson said.

His courtesy caused a great wave of fellow feeling to well within Sonja and buoy her up. As always when reaching out to other humans, whether to parry thrusts or to offer a misguided hand of friendship, Sonja ended up speechifying. Intending to further the rapport that had sprung up between them, she said, "I'm sure your sensitivity has resulted from your being a man of color. I know that being a woman of color has heightened my awareness of the variously challenged."

Jackson's brow creased in barely perceptible puzzlement. " 'Woman of color?' Now, what color might that be?"

"Red. Indian. That is to say, Native American."

Jackson nodded. "Uh-huh. Well, enjoy the fair."

"Thank you, I shall." Sonja, warmed by the encounter, waved, then stopped, not wanting to break off this highly satisfying exchange. She hoisted aloft the paper cup of lemonade. "Really quite refreshing. I wouldn't switch to fresh. Too labor intensive."

"It is that," Jackson called back to her.

Sonja grinned.

Jackson flagged another wave at her.

Sonja waved back. After Jackson held up his hand in one final, definitive good-by, she turned and wandered off to the Agricultural Hall.

Even after she'd viewed an extensive selection of prize peppers, read all the literature about the *What Is the Edwards Aquifer* exhibit, and spoke at length to the representative of the Hydro-Tron Electronic Water Treatment System, it was still not even five-thirty. The rodeo didn't start until eight. Sonja figured that if she was in the bleachers by six-thirty, she'd still be in plenty of time to beat the ticket seller and save herself the four dollars admission.

By walking well back on her heels, her toes pointed up to the sky, Sonja discovered that she could make relatively painfree, although stiff-legged, progress. She headed for the midway, which turned out to be an even more than usually offensive carnival of consumer rip-offs. She couldn't believe the pathetically credulous teenagers waiting in line to pay a dollar twenty-five for a ride on the Screamin' Meemie.

Back outside the arena, she stopped to kill time by looking through a display of bumper stickers. They were spread across a folding table set up next to a pickup with a camper shell on top. No one was minding the table. Not surprisingly, Sonja noticed, along with the usual *Honk If You're Horny* and *Don't Laugh, It's Paid For*, a strong rodeo motif:

ROPERS HANDLE ANYTHING HORNY
TEAM ROPERS CHANGE POSITIONS
STEER WRESTLERS GET IT ON THE SIDE
I'M A LIAR, A DRINKER, AND A WILD FILLY RIDER

Sonja held up one that proclaimed *Bullriders Ride The Wild Humpers*. She was appalled by the infantile braggadocio and double-entendres.

"That right there's one my biggest sellers. I'm just now introducing it this season." A compact woman in her mid-thirties came out of the camper, a stack of bumper stickers in each hand. She had red hair going gray at the temples, blue eyes going fuzzy around the edges, and pale, freckled skin that had been in the sun too much. She also had hands like an oil field worker's and a body and voice like those of a thirteen-year-old boy. A thirteen-year-old boy about four foot eleven whose voice was changing. The woman's reedy voice cracked on every fifth word.

Sonja found the raspy quality of that voice oddly appealing. There was something in general about the woman that disarmed her characteristic prickliness. She pretended to read over the bumper sticker again. "Yes, it's very clever."

"Wrote it myself."

"You did?" Sonja was slightly impressed. So few people ever showed even this minute spark of creativity.

"Sure enough. This one here, that's mine too." She pointed a calloused finger, and Sonja picked up a sticker and read, *For Sale Ex-Husband, Take Over The Payments.* "That's my feminist one."

"Normally, articles and prepositions aren't capitalized in a title," Sonja said.

"They ain't?" The woman seemed genuinely interested.

"Of course," Sonja continued, "the question now is, do the punctuation rules for titles apply to bumper stickers."

"That would be the question," the woman said thoughtfully, putting down the stacks of bumper stickers and pulling out one of two lawn chairs from behind the table. She positioned her narrow backside carefully on the three remaining webbed straps of the chair and gestured for Sonja to take the other one.

"Of course, when you think about it," Sonja said, settling into the frail chair, "you're the supreme sovereign here. You could make up any rules you want to." The woman's friendliness made Sonja unusually expansive.

"Damn straight." The red-haired woman nodded in ferocious, comradely agreement. "We'll just make up the rules as we go along. How 'bout that?"

Sonja liked her attitude. She seemed a person in harmony with the earth. The kind who wouldn't resort to chemicals at the first sign of roach infestation. "That is exactly what I've always proposed doing, though it hasn't been easy around my mother, who's a demon for doing things by the book."

"Mothers'll do you that way and I should know. I been one five times."

Sonja had difficulty imagining the prepubescent body spawning once, much less five times. "You have five children?"

"Last time I counted. Course, they coulda all murdered themselves by now or someone else done it for them, one. They's all out terrorizing the midway. They know if they hang around here, I'm gonna put 'em to work. They hate work, every doggone one 'em. They get that from their daddies."

"So you've been married more than once?" Sonja, who normally loathed being privy to the domestic details of anyone's life, was flattered by the way this woman opened up with her. She suspected that the "hen sessions" she'd heard about were like this, and she wanted the cozy, clubby feeling to continue.

"Never been married at all."

"You haven't?" Hester Prynne in the flesh!

"Nope, not a one 'em worth keeping. All made good babies, but they woulda made rank husbands. They's all in rodeo. Just like my daddy was and his daddy before him. I just got rodeo in the blood and I keep passin' it along." She laughed a Huck Finn laugh that ran from crystalline to cackle and back again. "You married?"

"Me? Married? Hah! That'll be the day. My mother, now she's another story. Calling caterers and tossing garters at the drop of a hat."

The woman shook her head at the wonder of it. "How'd you get your hair to go like that? It looks like a palomino's tail after it gets unbraided."

"Well, that's precisely what I did. Braided it."

The woman touched one of the crimped strands fluffing out around Sonja's head. "I might do mine thataway sometime. Where'd you get them pants? They're real cute. They have any other color combinations? I'm not partial to orange."

As Sonja was explaining to her about the restrictive return policy at Betty's Bargain Barn, the woman stuck out her weathered mitt. "I'm Tuffie Branch."

Sonja shook Tuffie's hand and, realizing that an introduction was in progress, stammered out, "I'm Sonja . . . I'm Son. Son Hozro."

" 'Hozro?' What is that? Czech?"

"No, it's Navajo." Son tried to sound modest.

"Indian? My meemaw's daddy was full-blooded Cherokee!"

"I sensed a wholeness about you." Son was so delighted by the unprecedented acceptance she had received that day that she did something she almost never did. She asked for help. "Tuffie, have you followed the rodeo circuit for a long time?"

"If you consider twenty-five years long, then, yes, I have."

"Tuffie, I'm looking for someone, for a trick roper."

"Trick ropers! They's all gone practically extinct. You looking to hire one?"

"No. I . . ."

Tuffie tilted her head in the friendly collie way she had, and Son surrendered. "I'm looking for my father. My father was a trick roper. An Indian trick roper. That's almost all I know about him."

"You know how old he is? That'd make a difference. That'd narry the field some."

"No. My mother refused to talk about him."

"Now, I know that feeling. Oh, yes. I'm with her there." Fine lines crinkled around Tuffie's Malamute blue eyes as she studied Son. "So your daddy's an Indian trick roper name of Hozro."

"Well, that . . . Hozro. That's more an homage. I don't really know what his last name is. He performed under the name Gray Wolf."

"Okay, okay. Now we're getting somewhere. Gray Wolf. Gray Wolf." Tuffie studied a cumulus formation building up in the north as she considered the name. "No, no, can't think of any Indian trick roper name of Gray Wolf. Now, Cootie, Cootie Ramos used to poke some feathers in his hair. Dab on a little warpaint."

"Cootie?" Son repeated, excited. "How do you spell that?"

"Cootie. Like a cootie."

"Where would I find this person?"

"Cootie? Lord, it's been, what? Ten, fifteen years at least since I bumped into old Coots."

"Cootie Ramos." Son filed the name away.

"Got to be Indian, huh?" Tuffie stuck the chewed-off stub of a thumbnail in her mouth and gnawed at the cuticle while she thought. "I never saw him, but Prairie always said El Marinero, the Sailor, was the best there ever was. Course he was Mexican, too. Retired now for some time."

"Well, naturally, the aboriginal peoples of Mexico would qual- ify."

"Yeah?" Tuffie pulled the thumb out of her mouth and pointed it vigorously at Son. "I got it! I know just what you need to do. You need to go down to the Sailor's. He has some big reunion every year for all the ropers still flinging floss. If your daddy's alive, that's where he'll be."

Son was thunderstruck at the bonanza. "Where do I find him? Where is this sailor?"

"Now that's the tricky part. I'm sure if he wanted to, Prairie James could find him. All them trick ropers pretty much wet around the same stump."

"Prairie James? Who is Prairie James?"

"Biggest loser and best trick roper you'll meet this side of the Rio Grande."

"Where . . . where might I find him?"

"You *might* find him in just about any old cow's bed. But he's supposed to be performing tonight."

"Tonight? Here? There's a trick roper tonight?" Son panted with excitement.

"Now, don't get lathered up. Prairie and the Sailor have been having a frothy spell. Been a few years since Prairie was invited to one of the Sailor's fandangos."

"Prairie James," Son repeated, feeling a path open before her. She was about to ask Tuffie if this felicitously named individual might not have a drop or two of indigenous blood running in his veins, when a boy of about three, in tiny Tony Lama boots and a pair of stretch-waist jeans that had fallen halfway down his bottom, charged up to Tuffie and butted his head into her lap.

"You're about to lose your britches, son." Tuffie tucked both her thumbs into the boy's waistband and ran them around, pulling him backward and forward about a dozen times until his pants were snugly lodged up beneath his armpits.

Four more children followed their brother. From the looks of them, Tuffie could have been a hermaphrodite, so stamped were they by her genetic impress. As they swarmed about their mother, Son felt overtaken by a tribe of red-haired, freckled pygmies all whining, chattering, badgering, and jabbering in the same reedy, cracking tones of incomplete recovery from laryngitis that characterized their mother's speech. They each delivered urgent messages that boiled down to one basic communication: "Can I, Mom? Huh? Huh? Huh? Can I? Please? Please?"

Son reflected that children got away with behavior that would have resulted in bench warrants for taller individuals.

"Settle down!" Tuffie shouted. "Next one talks, I'm going to thump his gourd. I want all y'all to meet my new friend, Son Hozro."

One of the sad facts of Son's life was that she had been called "friend" by far too few. Hearing Tuffie bestow this title on her affected Son so deeply that two unprecedented impulses seized her. The first was to think Tuffie's children so adorable in their miniature, freckled bodies with their squeaky voices that she wanted to hug them.

"Son, this is my oldest, Boots." Tuffie pointed to a pretty girl Son took to be about eleven. "She helps me out full time now that she graduated high school." On second glance, Son detected dwarf breasts. "And this is Spur." A girl in pigtails smiled shyly. "And them's my twins, Lasso and Latigo." Two identical children, one male, one female, each with identical oversized Bugs Bunny incisors poking out of their grins, flagged Son shy waves. "And this here's my baby, Jonathan. I was kinda wore out on rodeo names when it came his turn."

The little boy with his head buried again in Tuffie's lap rolled over to study the visitor. "If you're the sun," he piped up in his tiny Tuffie-esque voice, "why ain't you up in the sky?"

His jibe broke the spell of shyness that had momentarily settled over his siblings, and they laughed uproariously.

Wanting to be a part of the good time, Son joined in, asking the little boy, "If you're a Jonathan, why aren't you up in a tree?" She smiled warmly, but the laughter stopped abruptly.

Jonathan looked up at his mother. "Whud she say?"

"A Jonathan," Son repeated, only too familiar with the dead silence of communication gone wrong, and determined, this time, to overcome it. "Like an apple. A Jonathan apple." She looked at the older children. Lasso and Latigo were screwing up their noses at each other and raising upturned palms as they shrugged their small shoulders in incomprehension. She turned to Boots. Surely the American public education system covered apple varieties at some point in twelve years of mandatory education. But she was as blank as the twins. Son felt the cement of alienness setting up around her fast. It was Spur, the second oldest, who broke her loose.

"I get it! A Jonathan apple!" Much to Son's relief, the girl laughed and the twins joined her. At last the light had flicked on! "Yeah! A Jonathan apple! Get it? Like a Latigo peach. Or a Lasso orange. Or a Boots cherry."

Soon the whole crew was laughing merrily at the madcap wit of their mother's new friend and, caught up again in the warmth of belonging, the second of the two unprecedented impulses struck Son: she wanted to spend money unwisely. This novel impulse sprang from a deep, irrepressible desire to contribute in some way to Tuffie's rough-and-tumble family. Without further thought, Son pulled some bills from her mess kit, laid them on the table, and started shuffling through the bumper stickers. "I've just got to have some of these. They're just so good." Forgoing her usual close scrutiny, she grabbed one that read *BUCKLE BUNNY.*

As Son was searching for another selection, she noticed out of the corner of her eye a woman heading for the ticket seller's booth. A pulse of alarm beat through Son when she saw this woman carrying a metal box undoubtedly filled with tickets and change. She jumped up from the folding chair.

"I've certainly enjoyed meeting you," she said, watching the ticket seller fumble with the lock of the booth. "But I have to be running along now to claim my reserved box seat at the rodeo."

"Well, y'all come back and visit with us some more." Tuffie choked the words out, for her youngest, little Jonathan, had climbed his mother and was now hanging off her neck. She tried to say more, but his stringy arms were clamping her wind off.

"I will," Son promised, breaking into a slow trot to beat the ticket seller.

"Hey!" Tuffie yelled, peeling her son's hands from her neck and plucking up the bills Son had left on the folding table, "we owe you some money here!"

And then, words that Son would have sworn only hours before she would go to her grave without uttering passed her lips: "Keep the change!" The experience of largesse was surprisingly exhilarating. Son nimbly slipped past the ticket seller at the precise moment the woman unlocked the door and opened it so that her view of one unticketed spectator was momentarily blocked.

Son selected the best seat in the house and sat down to warm herself with the magic of the trinity that had just entered her life: Cootie Ramos, El Marinero, and Prairie James. One of these men would lead her to her father. One of them might even be her father.

"Pa," she snorted to herself, recalling Earl Walp's request that she address him as such. She'd show the fang-toothed linoleum salesman. She'd show them. She'd show them all.

Chapter 4.

Prairie James dreamed. He was back aboard the *Sugar Islander*, a 523-foot freighter. Built as a World War II troopship and redesigned to carry heavy cargo, she had a dead-weight tonnage, a carrying capacity, of 11,187 tons. They got the cargoes other ships couldn't handle: landing craft, locomotives, planes, artillery pieces. It was 1960. Prairie was sixteen years old. His ordinary seaman's card was two weeks old. He was scared shitless.

He and El Marinero, the able-bodied seaman from Veracruz who'd come aboard with a tin can full of ropes and a four-foot machete, were once again riding out that Force Eight blow off Pentland Firth when all the tiedowns holding the load of tractors they were hauling on that run snapped in the cargo bays. The chief mate, a bad drunk, ordered him and El Mare to go below and secure them. Prairie knew for a fact they would be crushed to death.

The noise below deck was worse than an iron foundry at full tilt, with the gale pitching the ship around like a toy in the bathtub and John Deere tractors caroming from one side of the dim hold to the other. The grizzled veteran had taken one look and put his hand on Prairie's arm to stop him.

"Time for a butt break," the Sailor had announced. He had

the best English of any Mexican that Prairie had ever known. The two men had spent the next couple of hours smoking and watching the tractors roll around while El Mare put the greenhorn wise about when to risk his life and when to lay back. To pass the time, El Mare pulled off the maguey rope he wore coiled around his chest, like Zapata with a cartridge belt, and spun Wedding Rings around the tractors' exhaust pipes.

The dream fell apart when the tractors all turned to bulls and he and the Sailor tried roping them with winching cable. One of the bulls pinned Prairie to the deck and pressed its snout against his neck. He waited for El Mare to save him, but all he got was hot breath and bull slobbers. Prairie was missing his old friend before he was even fully awake.

"Get away from me!" Prairie reached around and shoved aside Domino's whiskery muzzle. Domino snorted loudly. Prairie did not want to open his eyes. It felt as if an iron ski cap were crushing his skull. He needed about eight more hours of sleep to feel anything close to right.

Domino leaned back in and snuffled wetly on Prairie's neck. "Goddammit!" He sat up and looked into the horse's pale face. Domino stamped his hooves and the former Lay's potato chip van, now converted to combination horse trailer–mobile home–truck, swayed and creaked uneasily.

"Yeah, yeah. Walksies." Prairie stroked the horse. "You've been a good troop." A lance of pain shot from his neck to his fingertips the instant he raised his arm. He rotated his shoulder, trying to work the stiffness that thirty years of slinging a rope on top of five years as a merchant marine had set in all the way to the bone. Thirty years? Prairie shook his head. He could not believe it was that long since he and the Sailor had waltzed down their last gangplank together, ready to amaze and astound a waiting world with miracles in maguey.

"Domino, I got two words for you and heed them well, lad: desk job." Prairie tapped his head. "Use the brain, not the back. It lasts longer." Domino blinked. That was one of the few things Prairie liked about the horse. He knew good advice when he heard it.

Prairie heaved himself off the foam-covered plank he'd installed in the back of the truck, purely for the odd catnap now and again. He'd always put the rope tramps he'd known back in the old days—who lived in their trucks amidst a welter of rusty spurs, dirty underwear, and cheeseburger wrappers—only half a step above a hobo. Having dipped regularly into the practice himself over the past few years, he now rated it dead even and falling fast.

He put his feet down on a crunchy carpet of Tom's Snack bags and crushed Big Gulp cups. Nests of stiff jeans, salt-rimed tack, and discarded copies of Tom Clancy novels mixed with bottles of Corn Huskers lotion, tins of Mentholatum Deep Heating Rub, and flattened tubes of Blistex.

Okay, Prairie admitted, it was a pit. Still, anything having to do with him as a performer was preserved in a vertical sanctuary high above the roiling chaos below. He'd put up a pegboard just like the one his dad used to have in his garage back in Detroit with special hooks for each of his tools. But Prairie didn't use his pegboard for crescent wrenches and needle-nosed pliers; his were for ropes.

Fifteen precise coils hung from fifteen pegs. He had his cottons, the all-purpose 12-gauge Sampson's Spotcord, he had his everyday shitwork nylons, and then he had the silks of roping, the magueys, made from the Mexican maguey cactus. He was the only roper working north of the border who still used magueys. Coming as they did from a close cousin of the plant that supplied mezcal, it was not surprising that magueys were wild and unpredictable. For Prairie, magueys were true Mexicans. They turned balky and hated to work when the weather was wet. But then, if it was too dry, they'd go limp and useless on you. With all that, though, only a maguey could give you the flights of pure ecstasy, of passion and beauty, that he'd only known south of the border.

It was El Marinero who had taught him how to pull poetry out of the air with a length of rope during their years together on one ship after another. First the *Sugar Islander*, then the barge carrier *Tusitala*, the tramp *Orinoco*. The ships changed, but El Marinero, the roping seadog, was always there with a new trick, betting everything he had that this one, *this one*, the gringo could never do. The only trick the Sailor refused to show him was El Zopilote, the Buzzard. Priarie never found out exactly how old the Sailor was. He was one of those tough, sinewy men who, Prairie felt, your more equatorial-type countries were so good at producing; they stayed children until puberty, when they abruptly turned into burnished mahogany guys of an indeterminate age.

Chingao! they'd had some good times. While all the other losers, twistos, and alkies on board were drinking, reading stroke rags, or pounding each other's faces, he and the Sailor roped. Prairie had always been good with his hands. It was the Sailor who told him he was *de talento*. That he could be good. One of the best there ever was.

That cruise on the S.S. *President Wilson*, their first passenger liner, the captain saw them work, asked them to perform. Prairie's mentor was already an old hand at performing. Back home in Mexico, the Sailor grown up on *estancias*. Spent more time on horseback than on foot. Then graduated to the charro circuit, working as one of the few paid professionals in what was becoming, increasingly, a rich man's sport. He'd been making quite a name for himself, right up until the moment he was half-shanghaied by a heavy-drinking crowd of "new friends" onto a tramp steamer loaded with pineapples, bananas, and avocados bound for Hamburg.

Prairie and the Sailor had been buddies for more than a year before the Sailor told him the whole story of that first tour. About how he had nearly died of seasickness, then homesickness. But that a stroll down Hamburg's notorious Reeperbahn had opened his eyes to new worlds where women wrestled in mud and a handsome Latino in a cowboy hat and boots who could rope a lighted cigar from a man's mouth at twenty paces was a bigger draw than Cantinflas. The one other discovery the Sailor made that first trip was this: he was probably the best trick roper in the world. Outside of Mexico.

Prairie examined the frayed cuff on a midnight blue satin shirt with real mother-of-pearl snaps that hung in plastic on one of the pegs in the pegboard. His first performing shirt. El Marinero had taken him to his personal tailor on Kowloon Bay in Hong Kong. He'd gotten the midnight blue, a white brocade with the yoke outlined in fringe, and a maroon silk with red piping. He still had the maroon silk, but some floozbo up in Ardmore, Oklahoma, had stolen the white brocade. The remaining shirts floated in their dry cleaner's bags like angels above the mess below.

Prairie rarely wore them anymore. As worn-out as they were, though, the Hong Kong shirts could beat anything else a paying customer would see in an arena these days. As he dropped the cuff, Prairie noticed that the wrist snap had been pulled loose.

"Damn cheap shit Amarillo dry cleaner," he muttered. Looked like the guy had taken his best shirt out and beat it on a rock in the river. Fucking best shirt in the world and some anvilhead does this to it. Prairie was disgusted. A shirt like that deserved better. It deserved some respect.

Respect: the word made him reach for the key he wore on a leather thong around his neck. Prairie realized that the chip truck was about as secure as a bread box, so anything he really cared about he kept stashed away in a gray metal school locker bolted onto the interior wall. He fitted the key into the commercial-grade, brushed-chrome Schlage lock and opened the louvered metal door. He patted Miss April's buns taped on the inside of the door. But it was the scrapbook, which he reverently lifted out of the locker, that he hoped would bring him luck. Or, at least, remind him of the luck he'd once had.

He had barely opened the book, just started to glance at all the old clippings, the old interviews, to relive the days when a visit from Prairie James, inheritor of Will Rogers' mantle, rated a full-page spread in the paper, when Domino snatched his head back and forth, then bumped Prairie with his muzzle.

"Yeah, yeah, walksies. I'm coming." Man who lived in the past wasn't going to have much of a present to worry about and no future at all. Prairie put the scrapbook back into the locker and clicked the Schlage shut.

Outside, even at six in the evening, it was high noon hot. He led Domino through the tent town of rodeo contestants' trucks and trailers that had sprung up in the empty field next to Deutscher Downs. Fifteen, hell, even ten years ago, he'd have known all the ropers and most of the rough stock riders. He'd have been a celebrity, with young girls trailing behind him, hiding their braces with their hands like geishas when they giggled. Now all he got were hostile glances when he wandered close enough to the trailers to glimpse a family seated around a miniature table eating their beanie wienies and watching "Wheel of Fortune." It caused Prairie to wonder if the whole world was less friendly than it used to be or if he had reached the age when a single man started giving off geezer derelict vibes.

Prairie sucked in his gut, stood up a little straighter, and put a springy purposefulness in his stride. Whether anyone knew it or not, he was tonight's featured performer and he was out exercising the wonder horse, Domino, and limbering up his talented muscles. At the next trailer, he cranked up a sincere Jimmy Stewart vibe, touched a friendly finger to the tip of his hat, and plastered on a smile.

"Evening, folks."

The no-neck man, his wife in tourniquet jeans, and their whey-faced kids all went from surly to sunny in the beat of a heart and chorused back, "Evening!"

Prairie strode off like the legend he knew himself to be. That was it; you had to put out that positive energy to get it back. He unloosed powerful bursts of just such energy. They buzzed around

him like happy protons and electrons until they all came to a careening halt at the sight of Prairie's two least favorite people in the
world, Beau Beaulieu and Casey Dakota.

This prize-winning pair was standing in front of Dakota's lux-
ury liner of an RV. Actually, Beau Beaulieu, rodeo announcer and
the man who taught Vaseline how to be greasy, was only a minor
burr under Prairie's saddle compared to the colossal hemorrhoidal
pain that was Casey Dakota, rodeo producer.

Dakota's six feet two inches were bumped up to about six-six
by his boots and trademark black hat with the wingspan of a ptero-
dactyl. A bullrider's hat. It suited Dakota to give the impression
that he had been a bullrider, to have that air of suicidal surliness
floating about him. Particularly when he was negotiating contracts
with rodeo committees. But Prairie knew the truth about Dakota,
and for him the producer didn't need to wear any swooping black
hat to earn his nastiness stripes. In one hand, Dakota carried a
piece of radiator hose. In the other was an electric cattle prod. Both
were for hurrying and hurting his livestock, two- and four-legged.
The radiator hose was for saving wear on the hotshot's batteries.

Beaulieu's hair was as black as Dakota's hat. Prairie figured the
announcer must have stepped up from Grecian Formula to the
hard stuff. He was obviously mainlining Clairol now. The natty
announcer wore a tan Western suit, starched white shirt, a scarlet
string tie, and his customary ass-kissing pucker. Even from half a
football field away, Prairie could feel the suction. Dakota accepted
the brownnosing as impassively as a feudal shogun.

Prairie jerked the lead line to turn Domino around, but it was
too late. Dakota's nostrils were already twitching. He smelled an
opportunity for subjugation. He turned his shogun face to Prairie,
eyes dark and intensely focused, cheeks cut by the rivulets of a
constant scowl, and bellowed, "James!"

Prairie turned his back to Dakota and walked away. He could
feel Dakota's black eyes on him and wondered how he, Prairie
James, could have sailed four oceans, seven seas, any number of
major inland waterways, how he could have walked every continent

on the globe, and ended up working for the biggest son of a bitch to ever produce a third-rate rodeo. Prairie knew that Dakota kept him around like a cat keeps a mouse around he hasn't finished mauling. And why did he stay around? Easy question. Easy answer. Casey Dakota was, literally, the only man alive still willing to hire a trick roper now and again.

Life! What a whore.

"James! Get your sorry ass over here."

Prairie's carotid artery throbbed and he kept on walking. A few seconds later came the rapid scurry-scuffle of Beaulieu's polished Tony Lamas getting dusty as he ran after Prairie.

"James! James!" Beaulieu tried to use his richly resonant announcer's voice, but the wheezes and gasps for breath cut the effect. Finally he gave up and squawked, "Goddammit, James, wait up!"

Prairie stopped. Domino didn't. At least not until the horse had plowed into his master.

"He . . . He . . ." Beaulieu caught up to Prairie. "The boss wants to talk to you."

"Beau, you're wearing make-up. Pancake, isn't it?"

Beaulieu swatted away the finger that Prairie held out to touch his cheek. It was pancake, all right. Sheila had smeared it over her face with a sponge the size of a vanilla wafer every morning before she went to work at the phone company. Obviously, pancake was not good for running in the hot sun, as it was now dripping down Beaulieu's face in muddy rivulets.

"The dermatologist prescribed it." Beaulieu mopped up what he could with a handkerchief that quickly turned a brownish orange. "I've got precancerous malignancies I need to keep covered up from the sun. The boss wants to talk to you."

Prairie started walking again. "Well, fine. Tell him he can find me in the Lay's potato chip truck. Should be the only one. He won't have any trouble."

Beaulieu let him walk away. "You'd better get your ass over to the motor home, you want to work this summer, smart boy!"

"Chip truck," Prairie repeated. "I'll put the teapot on."

"The market ain't improving for broke-down trick ropers, James!"

"Then I'd better wait for the Avon lady to come visit with her make-up kit, so I can start up a career in rodeo announcing!"

Prairie was humming as he broke down a flake of hay for Domino to eat, and his shoulder didn't hurt quite as much. He was almost ready to go spin a loop or two.

Chapter 5.

For the first hour, Son sat alone in the stands, contemplating her prospects. She almost believed that she could take Dorfburg on as Son. Son Hozro. If her mother was giving up her old name, why couldn't she do the same?

Son had selected the perfect seat: directly opposite the bucking chute, second row up so that the fence top would not be in her line of vision. She was three years old the first time she'd sat on the creaky wooden bleachers, and even then they'd been caked with decades of new coats of green paint industriously defaced by carved initials. Three years old and now she was almost thirty, and still the biggest thrill she got every year was coming to the rodeo to fantasize about her father.

Son sighed. She supposed that lack of male companionship was the price she would have to pay for opting not to be a pawn of the merchandising monolith. Oh, sure, if she'd allowed herself to be blown about by every breeze exhaled from the gaping maw of the monolith, if she'd rushed out over the years to purchase bell-bottom pants, platform shoes, Nik-Nik disco shirts, body suits with snaps at the crotch, wraparound jersey dresses, she surely would have had her pick of young men as well formed as Winnetou.

But she had sternly resisted the gaudy blandishments of Madison Avenue. If no man had been independent-minded enough to accept her as she was, without being packaged to fit that moment's fashion, then so be it. She would not submit to the deranged dictates issued by the Sodomites of the merchandising monolith. Let her mother stoop to such tactics in her desperate bid to snag a mate; she would not.

Her mother. Son's momentary exhilaration leaked away as she contemplated her life's upheaval. Not a thrilling life, granted, but one she had become comfortable with.

"Hey, Getz! Getting any?" A hearty clap on her back jolted Son out of her reverie. She revised her earlier thought; there was one man who was attracted to her and had been since they'd marched together in the Dorfburg High band, Walter Dittlinger.

She turned and faced the loosely packed 250 pounds that were Walter Dittlinger. In one hand Walter held two sausages on skewers. With the other he gripped a couple of tallboys of beer.

"Hello, Dittlinger." She greeted him coolly, hoping to head off the blustery bonhomie he'd affected since taking over his father's meat shop and attendant persona as the jolly fat butcher. A role dear to the hearts of Dorfburgers. Son had found Walter far more bearable as a fat, introverted piccolo player.

"Here. Take one." Walter poked one of the sausages in her face. "Eighteen inches of pure, pulsing Dittlinger pleasure."

Son parried his sausage thrusts. "Get that compensatory device for your own phallic inadequacies out of my face." For her whole life, Son had been at odds with a town that had taken as its symbol of highest good a wad of ground animal byproducts encased in intestine and impaled on a stick. A town that actually glorified stuffed tripe with its own annual celebration, Wurst Days, when men felt free to expose their bony knees in lederhosen.

The bleachers groaned as Walter lowered his bulk onto the aging boards directly behind Son. A spray of grease rained down on the back of her neck when he bit into his sausage. In his new bumptious butcher manner, Walter asked, "So, how's the bug biz? Making a killing?" He glanced around, spotting neighbors and customers in the crowd. Each *har* of his Falstaffian *har-har-har* hit

Son between the eyes like a ball-peen hammer. She was prepared, however, to remain civil, until, with a mighty *ka-whoosh!* Walter opened one of the tallboys and drenched her with beer.

When Walter leaned forward to mop her off with the spotted handkerchief he reeled out of his pocket, Son jumped up and pivoted out of his reach. Facing the stands now, she recognized familiar faces making half-hearted attempts to conceal familiar smirks: Miss Delfel in her reflector sunglasses. Gussie Patton, president of the Girls' Athletic Association and inevitable captain of the field hockey team. Rema Kleine, her henchman.

"Hey! Son-jay!" Walter's oafish voice boomed out. "Nice pants!" She glanced back at him, stung by his betrayal. His newfound acceptance had corrupted him. He basked in the chuckles of their former tormentors.

With all the élan she could muster, Son marched away, the fringe of her scarlet sash vigorously whisking her knees. The effect of her noble retreat on the puerile minds of the gut gobblers was weakened somewhat when her proud stride was reduced again to an elf-toed hobble as the cursed boots gouged into her feet.

As soon as she reached a set of stairs, Son escaped from the lighted stands and made her way down to the shadowed area in back of the arena fence. This was better anyway, Son decided. She could see far better from her new position clinging to the chain links than she ever could back with the common herd.

At precisely eight o'clock, a voice as practiced in its mellifluous richness as any funeral director said, "Ladies and gentlemen, this is Beau Beaulieu. I'd like to welcome each and ever one a you to the thirty-eighth annual rodeo here at Deutscher Downs."

Son, long an aficionado of the form, noticed that this announcer's creamy tones were peppered with just the right mixture of twang and illiteracies to butter up a rodeo crowd.

"You know, ladies and gentlemen, they say we don't have heroes no more. But I dispute that claim. I say we're going to see so danged many heroes out in this ring tonight that we'll just plumb lose count."

Son feared that Beaulieu might have overreached himself with the "danged" and the "plumb." But no, the crowd was still with him.

"These rugged individualists that we're going to be seeing tonight travel the highways and byways of this great land of ours asking no quarter and giving none. No sponsors support these men. No government handouts aid their quest to do the best and be the best the good Lord and this free land of ours will allow."

Son's head reeled at the new heights of smarminess being achieved in a field noted for its unctuousness.

"So, ladies and gentlemen, won't you rise now and join me in this evening's invocation dedicated to rodeo's future and the future of this great land of ours, the Youth."

A sound like a great wind stirring high branches swept the stands as the good people of Dorfburg dutifully stood. In the arena all activity ceased. Hats were pressed against chests and eyes downcast.

"Lord, it's me again, Timmy." Beaulieu put a pitiful, plaintive edge on his words as he took on the simpering voice of Youth. "I just wanted to say, Lord, that my life was mighty empty until you sent me heroes. Oh, there was the booze and the pot and the pills. But there was that big ole empty space too, Lord. I just wanted you to know that it started to go away the first time one of those heroes put a piggin' string in my hand and a set of spurs on my . . ."

Son momentarily tuned out Beaulieu's soliloquy to watch a tall man in a wide black hat jab a cattle prod into the backside of a steer coursing through the chutes into the holding pen. When the animal didn't move fast enough, the man swiped at him with the length of radiator hose he gripped in his other hand. When she tuned back in, Beaulieu's gassy stemwinder was still going strong.

". . . thank you also for my other heroes, o Lord, those brave fighting men who died in defense of this great land of ours. I know they're with you up there now, Lord, the ones who gave their lives battling communism from the burning sands of Iwo Jima to the steaming jungles of Vietnam . . ."

The only motion in the entire arena was the occasional swish of a horse's tail. That and the compact, practiced movements of the bareback bronc riders scrambling over the chutes, rigging up whatever beast they'd drawn to ride that night. Son crept closer to the chutes.

The cowboys were silhouetted against the light of the arena as each one straddled a green metal chute containing nearly half a ton of disgruntled horse. After a quick perusal of this year's crop, Son zeroed in on an especially well-grouped specimen she calculated to be eighteen years old.

Like nearly all of the rough stock riders, he sported a preponderance of fast-twitch muscle fibers, the kind that crowded up so nicely in shoulders and buttocks. One boot planted on the chute on either side of the animal, the bronc rider put his mouth to the wrist of his right hand and pulled his glove ties tight.

When the scratchy sound of a familiar recording swelled up behind him, Beaulieu dropped the simpering Timmy and, in chest-rumbling tones of full oratorical tumescence, asked, "Oh-oh, say can you see?"

As the national anthem came to a close, Beaulieu choked out, "Kinda makes your collar get a little tight." A second later, he was all bounce and pep again. "Without further ado, let's get our grand entry under way. Okay, cowboys and cowgirls, let's head 'em up, pull 'em out, and let's us rodeo!

"Down in Chute Number Three, ladies and gentlemen, we got a tough cowboy, a local boy, Duane Yearout, on the bad horse Crybaby!"

Crybaby burst out of the chute, bucked twice, and dumped Duane precipitously onto his head. Duane jumped up and scowled at Crybaby, who was cavorting merrily about the arena with a couple of mounted pickup men in hot pursuit.

"We go now to tie-down calf roping," Beaulieu announced as the last bronc was being herded off to the holding pen. "In the box, we got Dewey Dakota. Dewey's the boss's son, but even if he weren't I'd have to tell you that Dewey is one of the best young ropers we got. He was last year's National Junior Rodeo calf-roping champion and looks strong for this year. So let's go rope us a calf, Dewey!"

Dewey Dakota was a giant of a boy. Son wondered if it was the way his hat was squashed down tightly on his head, making his ears stick out, that gave him the slightly vacant look he wore. But it was more than that. He moved and carried himself like an android programmed to fling a loop around a running cow's neck. With mechanical smoothness, Dewey backed his mount into the corner of the box, nodded for the calf to be turned loose, and spurred his horse out after it. The calf shot out of the box. But Dewey zinged out a lasso with robotic precision and caught the fleeing animal.

The instant the calf hit the end of the rope, it bounced back as if it had smashed into an invisible rubber wall. Dewey leaped off his horse, ran to the calf, tied three of its legs, and threw his hands up in the air. The judge dropped his flag and the clock was stopped.

"Now *that* is how you rope a calf!" Beaulieu announced as Dewey Dakota's time of 3.5 seconds flashed on the computerized scoreboard. Dewey didn't even bother to turn around and check his time. He knew he'd won. He always won. He'd already picked up his cattle prod so that he could help his father hurry a knot of balky calves into the chute.

The saddle bronc riders were followed by a "kids' calf scramble." Son recognized four of Tuffie Branch's five red-haired dwarves. The oldest, Boots, five years beyond the age cut-off of twelve, was out ahead of the pack from the beginning, tearing through the plowed arena dirt in her bare feet. She was the first, by a wide margin, to reach a calf and pull off the tag taped to its rear.

After the prizes were awarded, Beaulieu announced, "And now, what you've all been waiting for. The evening's entertainment."

Son hugged the chain link fence. Her pulse throbbed in her ears.

"I'm sorry to have to tell you that we've had a last-minute cancellation. As you know, Charmayne Susen was scheduled to entertain us all tonight. It saddens me deeply to inform you that some emergency oral surgery is going to keep Charmayne from being here with us tonight."

A gigantic "Aw-w-w-w!" was exhaled by the disappointed crowd.

"In Charmayne's place, however, we are honored to have Prairie James, the Boss Hoss with the Twirlin' Floss!"

The announcement of the fill-in precipitated a mass exodus as spectators flowed out of the bleachers toward the food stands.

Behind Son a small boy asked, "What's he saying, Mommy?"

A voice sharp with irritation answered, "He's saying we paid extra to hear Charmayne sing and now we have to watch some stupid rope tricks."

"What's road tricks, Mom? Mom!"

"*Rope*, Jason. Rope tricks. It's something people used to like to watch before television. Come on, let's go get you a Big Red."

Son took advantage of the chaos to slip around the fence into a dark corner beside the bucking chutes.

A scratchy recording of the theme music from "Bonanza" boomed over the p.a.

Son waited, heart thumping, for Prairie James to come charging out. For the man who could lead her to her father. Instead, there was a foul-up with the lights. First, they went off and it was pitch black for a few seconds. Then half the lights came back on. Then they all went off again and a spotlight beamed through the darkness. The beam of light zigzagged crazily over the arena until it focused on the gateway. The second time "Bonanza" came on, right at the duh-duh-duh-duh, duh-duh-duh-duh, Buh-*nan*-zuh part, a man on a snow white horse shot out of the gateway.

But Son caught only a glimpse of the roper before the spotlight operator lost him entirely. When the spotlight finally caught up to Prairie James, he was scowling dangerously. The scowl disappeared the instant the light hit him, and Beau Beaulieu burst out, "Prairie James and his good horse Domino!" Son pounded her palms together, never noticing how loud her clapping was in the polite patter of applause.

Prairie James and Domino, bleached by the spotlight, frozen in the middle of the arena, appeared to be made of plaster of Paris. They both looked bone white, from the tip of Prairie's Stetson down to Domino's hooves. Only a few black shadows defined them: a ring under the rim of Prairie's hat, clefts beneath eyes, nose, mouth. A cobra head's shadow on the roper's thigh cast by the horn of his saddle. The inside of the horse's ears, his nostrils, and the thin seam of his mouth were black.

What Son focused on, though, were the roper's cheekbones, his nose. They were unmistakably Indian. She told herself to be calm, be objective. Wouldn't the estimable Tuffie Branch have mentioned it if this Prairie James were Indian?

When even Son had stopped applauding, Prairie raised his right arm with a slow elegance, whipped it twice, like a crewman starting a propeller, and a rope Son hadn't even seen was sent spinning above his head. Though Prairie appeared not to move his hand, the rope whirred faster and faster until it was a continuous blur hovering above his head like a halo. Son gasped from the unexpected beauty of it.

Prairie ran quickly through the catalogue of Will Rogers' tricks. He started off with a Flat Spin, went into the Wedding Ring, then got a little fancier with a Tornado, pulling his buzzing rope into a twisting spiral that funneled higher and higher up above his head until he was dancing in a dust devil of rope. Then he tilted it like a ten-foot top that rotated all the way around his head. When he'd swept the rope dust devil all 360 degrees around his head, Son clapped her palms red. Her applause echoed hollowly against a general murmur of conversation and bursts of laughter from Walter Dittlinger's crowd.

The laughter made Prairie James set his jaw in a grim line.

Domino, also annoyed, cocked his ears back. He turned his regal profile away from the unappreciative audience. Though it was clear both horse and rider were stung by the lack of attention, Prairie kept on.

Still twirling, he stepped off his horse. His fancy-tooled boots sank deep into the plowed earth of the arena. He lowered his loop from above his head until it opened out directly in front of him wide as a shimmering tunnel. Prairie cranked the loop still wider, put the opening in front of Domino, and clucked his tongue. The horse looked the other way.

"Hah!" Prairie yelled.

Domino swung his head around, stared at Prairie, glanced back over his shoulder at the crowd of boobs in the stands, looked away again, and didn't budge.

Down in the middle of the arena, Prairie felt the spotlight burning on his back. He looked back at the audience and saw that most of the crowd was watching a blubber boy shoot a tallboy of beer.

"Haw!"

Domino knew Prairie was genuinely pissed-off this time and so, heaving a lip-flapping sigh of bored exasperation, he stepped through the spinning rope.

As his snowy tail passed through, Son exploded again into rapturous applause. Prairie squinted into the dark area by the chutes where the only sound other than the pounding chords of "Bonanza" and hee-haws for the fat boy's antics was coming from. He feared a repeat of the last time he'd gotten such an enthusiastic response.

That was over near Brenham at the Half-Pint Rodeo Finals. Every trick he'd done had gotten a standing ovation. Only after he'd gone through his entire repertoire twice did he find out that the Civitans had sponsored a busload of residents from the state school. His fans!

Still, there was something decidedly "present" about the dark figure's clapping that cheered him. His apprehension disappeared completely when he rolled the great circle of the rope back and forth in front of himself and an unmistakably female voice screamed out, "Yeah! Wagon Wheel!"

Prairie couldn't remember the last time a civilian had identified a trick, and never a female. Not since Twirlin' Twyla Calhoun died back in the seventies. He rolled his Wagon Wheel over a bit closer to the fence and followed it to the far edge of the spotlight. He could just barely make out a female figure there in the darkness. Hair looked good. That was a big plus. Kind of crimpy wavy. Waist seemed to tuck in at the right angle. But, whoa, hold the phone! Check the keister on this one. Ah, what the hay, he didn't mind 'em a little broad in the beam. A little ballast never hurt in high seas.

Inspired, Prairie flicked his wrist and the Wheel stalled, kicked up a puff of dust where it whisked the arena, then switched back and rolled the other way.

"A Reverse!" the Dark Lady yelled. Prairie was liking her shape more and more. He pushed his hat far back on his head so that she'd have a clear view of his face; then he shot her one of his patented babe-destroyer winks so she'd know the next one was going out especially for her. He dragged his wrist on each revolution until the spinning rope flattened down from a circle to an oval, to a long, low caterpillar crawling along the dusty earth.

"The Rattler!" Son yelled.

Prairie bobbed his head. Chalk one up for the little lady. Next, he took the squashed circle and whipped it up over his head so fast that it left a blurred arc shimmering in the air.

Son scrambled for the name and provenance of this radiant trick. When it came to her, she squealed out loud, for this was a trick that had supposedly died with the last of the ropers from Buffalo Bill's Wild West shows. An Indian trick!

"Blowing Bubbles!" She screamed the name the cowboys had given the trick of her father's people. Those Wild West ropers had stolen the trick from the Indians, who'd called it Rainbow Parting

Clouds and had performed it only during solemn ceremonies as a symbol of their solidarity with all of nature. A rare Indian trick on top of those cheekbones. What further proof did she need?

With his free hand, Prairie made a gun and shot her a you-got-it-babe *Ky-y-y-ew*. Maybe he wouldn't have to face Jo Lynne's flaking lips tonight after all. He didn't know when he'd started grinning, but he stopped abruptly when the dorkhead on the lights threw them all back on, making the arena blaze like a football field. Irritated as he was, Prairie kept on twirling. He wasn't about to stop his act just as he was building to the grand finale.

"Okay! How 'bout a big Dorfburg hand for Prairie James and Domino!" Beaulieu led what was left of the crowd in the biggest hand the roper had gotten all evening, and even that could only have been described as a smattering.

Beaulieu cut in again. "Moving right along, folks. We got the girls' barrel racing up next! Some of our fine young riders'll be out here tonight competing for over three-hundred and fifty dollars in prize money!"

Although Prairie's loop had never dropped, Beaulieu had obviously decided that the "entertainment" was over. The pickup men in orange vests rolling padded beer barrels into the arena for the barrel racers obviously agreed with the announcer. As did the petite barrel racers in their pastel hats and matching boots fighting their skittish mounts to the entryway. The audience swarming back in also agreed that Prairie James was through. Even Domino, trudging riderless toward the exit, agreed that the act was over. The only ones who didn't agree were Prairie—and Son.

Prairie felt the hairs at the back of his neck prickle at the nerve of Dakota's butt boy giving him the hook like that. Not in front of the Dark Lady, who was still pounding her palms together over in the shadows next to the chutes. No, sir, he was not about to be run off for any prisspot barrel racers packing more weight in hair mousse than gray matter.

Furious, Prairie narrowed his Blowing Bubbles loop tighter and tighter as he fed out more rope. He was, by God, going to finish his act. Twenty-five years in show business and he'd never blown a crescendo yet. He'd give these yahoos a grand finale they would not soon forget.

By the time he'd choked his loop down to the eye of a needle, he had forty feet of hemp standing straight up over his head like a telephone pole. It vibrated there until enough of the jabonies in the stands had punched enough other jabonies and pointed in his direction that, for the first time that night, the house was with him.

When he could finally feel the crowd's attention on him, Prairie let his rope drop. It fell like a giant redwood, pitching straight over 45 degrees to stop dead, directly above Son's head. Prairie goosed his wrist and shook action even he didn't know he had into that rope. A bump of energy shimmied along the outstretched hemp. When it reached the end it jerked the tiny loop into a parabola so elegant that the numb nuts on the lights shut everything off for a second, plunging the arena into darkness.

Prairie felt invincible. It was his night. He could do anything he wanted. He could even do the one trick he'd been forbidden to do. The trick that had driven a wedge between him and the Sailor. El Zopilote, the Buzzard. The one trick the Sailor had ordered him not to perform because he was saving it for his "real son," Heriberto. Prairie had stopped doing the Buzzard, not because the Sailor had forbidden him to, but it usually just made him too sad to try it. But not tonight; tonight he would do El Zopilote for the grand finale.

In the moment of darkness, Son heard nothing other than the whirring of the rope over her head. She thought nothing other than finally, *finally*, she was getting the attention she deserved. Like a Baptist coming forward to be saved, Son stepped out from behind the chutes for her moment of recognition. When the spot came back on, it shone on the hovering loop until it was a halo revolving above her head, singling her out for admission to the elect. She stood up straight, sucked in her tummy, and prepared to yell out what had been in her heart for twenty-nine years waiting to be shouted to the world.

Then Prairie saw her lips move. Not a bad mouth. He still liked her hair. It was taking him a while to get over her face. It had been a jolt when that spot had hit her. He'd had something a bit softer, more feminine in mind for his cheerleader. But his Dark Lady was a hunker. Tall and rawboned as a plowboy, she was one seriously substantial chick. And he wasn't entirely sure he enjoyed the way she was crowding out of her dungarees. But the jeans were not a fatal flaw. None of it was fatal as long as she smelled good enough. He'd educated other women about how he liked them to dress. How to undress. How to straddle that all-important area in between.

He noticed that she was still yelling, but as he'd finally gotten some crowd action going, a little chatter in the backfield, he couldn't hear what she was saying. He knew she couldn't be yelling any trick names. The loops he was twirling now weren't in any book anywhere. They came straight out of pissed-off and pushed-to-the-limit combined with moves no one else on earth ever had. Not even El Marinero.

Prairie switched to a plain Flat Spin smooth as a ring around Saturn while he walked across the arena, closer to his number one fan. The halo above her head widened with each step he took as he fed more line into it. He wanted to hear what she had to say. She had a look on her face like a teeny-bopper watching the Beatles, Elvis, his man Sinatra. It had been a long time between groupies, and he was ready for the drought to end. He got close enough to see the orange inner panels on her jeans before he could finally make out what she was saying.

"Daddy! It's me, Sonja! It's me, your daughter!"

The rope halo dropped to the earth like a python falling down dead out of a tall jungle tree. The Buzzard would not fly tonight.

Chapter 6.

Prairie James sat in the farthest back booth the Broken Spoke had and sipped his Pink Slipper. Of course the bartender, a smirky, short man with sloping shoulders and arms long as an ape's, had been forced to look the drink up in his Mr. Boston's and tell everyone in hearing distance, including Jo Lynne, how he didn't get many requests for *Pink Slippers* and how his *Pink Slippers* technique was a little rusty. After that little testimonial, Prairie had left his stool at the bar, taken his cocktail as far from the bartender as he could get, and sat with his back to the little monkey man.

Screw him. Screw him and screw Jo Lynne. After the night he'd had, he'd drink any damn thing he wanted, and what he wanted was a Pink Slipper. A dull headache buzzed across his forehead as he considered what he should have done.

The minute, the second, the *instant* that spot hit her and he saw what he was dealing with, he should have cleared off. Just run like sixty. But no, he had to keep spinning a halo over her head like she was the g.d. Virgin Mother herself. Right up until she yelled out, "Daddy!"

Daddy? Christ.

Prairie gulped half his drink, hoping the alcohol would dim his memory. It didn't. *Daddy*. He'd stopped cold the instant he'd heard her. But that jagoff Dakota, with his abnormally honed appreciation for another man's humiliation, had ordered the light man to stay on her. When he'd seen her coming at him, he'd beat it over to Domino and mounted up fast. But, damn, she could cover ground. What was he supposed to do when she ran over and threw her arms up to him?

Jesus Christ on a crutch, he'd about herniated himself hauling her lard ass up into the saddle in front of him. After that, what else could he do but ride around a little with her on his lap waving and smiling like the frigging Queen of the May?

The Daddy routine didn't stop when they got out of the arena and he finally unloaded her. She genuinely had some cockamamie idea that he was her father.

"Look, babe," he'd had to put it to her, "you're too old for me to date, so let's forget me being your father."

"I beg your pardon." The wacko had gone straight from calling him Daddy to icing him with this highbrow tone. "I am twenty-nine years old. You appear to be at least fifty."

"Hey, 'appear' anything you want, I'm no fifty years old." That stung. He knew for a fact that he looked younger than his forty-nine years. And she was one to talk. He'd have put her at thirty-six, thirty-seven, easy. Not that a few years would have made any difference in her case. Maybe he should touch up his hair a little. Fuck that. You could always spot a dye job, and the only thing worse than looking old was looking old and vain.

It had been a major headache, shaking loose of that lard-butted loony. Then Dakota stiffed him. Not that that was any surprising novelty. Only gave him seventy-five for the night; said he'd get the rest if he worked a black rodeo way the hell and gone over in East Jesus, Texas. What *was* the name of that town? Jordan? Prairie wanted to know how the hell he was supposed to get down the road to a rodeo in Jordan, Texas, on seventy-five dollars. Dakota laughed. The producer had built a thriving business out of marrying a rich woman who promptly died, leaving him her first husband's rodeo company, and then cheating anyone who couldn't afford a lawyer. It had proved to be a winning combination.

All Prairie wanted after the show was to be on the road and gone, but he had to cool Domino down. Not that the piece of shit had worked worth a damn. So they had a little walksies; then when he went to load the horse up, there she was again, lurking out by the truck, the Duchess with her high tone and haughty manner. She told him her whole story. As if he cared that her name was Sun Cornrow or whatever and her father had been the greatest Indian roper of the century. He had never heard of any great Indian trick roper and he had heard of them all.

Did not faze the Duchess in the slightest. She'd rambled right on about how they needed to team up and search together for her father. It was like talking to Stuie the Archangel, the messman who was never quite right again after he took that header off the observation deck back aboard the *Sugar Islander.*

He'd finally been forced to say, "*Hasta la vista, señorita,*" and leave her standing there, still nattering on. He would have liked to hang around and read the light man the riot act for stepping all over him, but he wasn't going to give Dakota a few more dozen chances to call him Daddy.

As soon as Domino was loaded, he had hit the road. He drove by the Broken Spoke a couple of times before he decided to stop. He wasn't exactly panting for Jo Lynne. He doubted she even had cable. But he needed a bath. A bath and maybe a gentle touch.

His empty cocktail glass sat in front of him, coated in pink as if he'd just put back a double of Pepto-Bismol. He contemplated the most pressing concern of the evening: how was he going to get to his next gig on seventy-five dollars? After gas, feed, and a couple of hamburgers he would be close to broke, and he still needed a new set of tires and some clutch work just to keep rolling. He'd been sticking to back roads because he hadn't been able to pass a safety inspection in two years. Brake lights didn't work, headlights were cross-eyed, all four tires were balder than a porpoise. He needed an infusion of some serious cash or he'd have to be looking into the purchase of a ski mask.

Jo Lynne's hand appeared around the stem of the glass. "Buy you another one of those, cowboy?"

In spite of himself, a little bounce knocked Prairie's heart. "I'd be much obliged, ma'am." Jo Lynne slid another foamy pink drink in front of him and glanced up at the bar. Her drink orders weren't up yet, so she slid into the booth next to Prairie. "How'd the tribute go?"

"The—? Oh, the tribute. Touching. Really very touching. They sort of hit on the highlights of my career, you know. The command performance for the queen. Talked about how I'd single-handedly kept a dying art alive. Stuff like that."

"I think that's real exciting." Jo Lynne scooted over close to him and squeezed his arm. Prairie sat up a little taller, sucked in his gut, and puffed his chest out.

A man, a woman. Prairie felt he momentarily understood again why this combo had been such a winner throughout history.

Jo Lynne patted his hand and stood. Her order was up. "I can't wait to hear all about it. I know you won't spare me any of the details."

"Darlin'." He favored her with his shitkicker drawl again. "I won't be sparin' you nuhthin'."

That little pink stub of a tongue poked out of its hole to flick lasciviously over her fuzzy lips. She gave a gravelly titter and left.

A nice warm buzz worked its way up from Prairie's gut and left a soft glow, easing the pain in his shoulder and salving his wounded pride. He nestled into it, and the evening's humiliation began to float away from him like a bad port he was shipping out of. Prairie was picturing the frozen gray stinkhole of Vladivostok, slipping away in the mist, when a voice from somewhere above his head said, "I do not appreciate your complete lack of courtesy and pro- fessional demeanor."

Prairie hoped he was hallucinating those crabby, imperious tones, but didn't think that was possible on two Pink Slippers. His worst fears were confirmed when he raised his gaze just enough to take in that capacious can stuffed into those orange-paneled jeans.

"Jesus, lady—" was all he got out before she shoved into the booth next to him.

"I followed you. We don't have to immediately address the issue of you being my father—"

"Don't even get—"

"Prairie, I know you feel that an unbridgeable chasm separates us, but I sense an empathic link. I think you too know what it means to be an outsider, to be ostracized. Haven't you ever dreamed of standing before the high school P.E. teacher who persecuted you and the piccolo player who marched beside you in band and being revealed as completely out of their league?"

The dull headache sharpened abruptly to an icepick poking directly into Prairie's eye. "I dropped out."

"Oh. Well. Don't let your lack of education embarrass you. I sincerely believe that there is a wisdom in the common man that can often surpass that of many a degree holder in the social sciences."

"Thanks a mil."

"No, really, you cowboys especially—"

The icepick stabbed down again. No way was he going through the shitkicker charade for her. When he opened his mouth the words machine-gunned out high octane, fuel-injected. Pure Detroit metal. "*Cowboy?* Did you say *cowboy?* Let's get one thing straight. I am not a *cowboy.* Never have been, never will be." It felt good to talk natural. Just the way it felt at night when he pulled off the cockroach-killer boots.

"Well, certainly, all right, have it your way. I just naturally assumed that if it dresses like a cowboy, and walks like a cowboy, talks like a cowboy, and smells—"

"*Smells!*"

"Don't be offended. I'm not one of your typical microphobes."

"Great! Good. Fine. Listen, I don't give a rat's ass what you think about the way I smell, but I've never in my life talked like a cowboy when it didn't suit my purposes. And it sure the hell don't suit them with you, babe."

"Don't take such umbrage at what was an innocent assumption. Most men would be complimented to be cast in the Marlboro man mold."

That was it. She had pushed him too far. "Look, I'm an entertainer. Get it? I don't go charging out there and jack up baby cows for a big eight-second thrill like that ding-ding Dewey. Cowboys've got one trick with a rope—catching a cow—and there's a million of them all trying to do it just one way—faster. Faster, that's all it is with cowboys.

"I, on the other freaking hand, can make a rope do things you couldn't pay a Filipino whore to do, and every trick, every single trick, I'm trying to do slower. For the audience's entertainment. Not to win any tin buckle the size of a frigging license plate. You getting this? I'm an entertainer, not a calf strangler."

"Yes." She tilted her head to the side so that her hair fluffed out in an all right kind of way against her neck and studied him. "Yes, I do hear the harsh tones of an urban accent."

"Damn straight. Dee-troit born and bred. Motor City through and through. I'm no hick off the farm and I don't talk like one. I'm no cowboy and I don't talk like one of those either. I've got every port of call in my logbook you can name: Glasgow, Rota, Subic Bay. I've got fugging Kompong Som, Lisbon, Nassau, Naha. I spent my life on the big water, babe. I'm no calf strangler. Just in case you missed it the first time, allow me to repeat. What *I* am is, *I* am an entertainer."

Prairie noticed that his headache was gone. He rolled his shoulders. It felt good to set the record straight once in a while.

"You'll get no argument from me. I'm something of a trick-roping aficionado, given my inherited interest in that art form."

"Art form. I'm glad you said that. I like that. Art form."

"I believe that most sincerely."

"That's the problem with performing for cowboy crowds, they have no appreciation. You're up there busting your hump and they could give a flying frap. Just my luck to be the absolute best at something that doesn't draw enough paying customers to fill a toilet stall. One show out of a dozen you get an old-timer who even knows a Cyclone from a Wagon Wheel. It's not worth doing half my act. Only another roper understands how hard they are."

"I suppose that's why you're looking forward to the gathering at El Marinero's."

Prairie backed away. "How'd you know about the Sailor?"

"Oh, just around the circuit. So where's the reunion to be held this year?"

"I'm not telling you that."

"Because you don't know or because you don't like me?"

"Hey, it's not like you're knocking yourself out being Miss Congeniality here."

"Wanting to be liked is a trap. A woman's trap. Wanting to be liked is tantamount to letting down the castle drawbridge. The Visigoths will overrun you with their hockey sticks and wrist corsages. If they know you care, they'll maul you."

"Hey, glad I didn't go to your school."

"So where is the reunion to be held? Will Cootie Ramos be there?"

The name was a sucker punch out of nowhere. Cootie Ramos. Christ, the guy could wrap his half-Apache legs around a galloping pony and pop off tricks most ropers couldn't do standing on solid ground. Old Coot, could he raise hell. That time down in Reynosa with the Sailor . . . Prairie fell into a reverie thick with the scent of the Rosas de Oro talcum powder the whores dusted themselves with and the sound of the Sailor's laugh ringing down onto the zócalo when Cootie, standing on the balcony, roped a bunch of gardenias right out of the vendor's hand three stories below.

Prairie thumbed away a bead of water rolling down the side of his glass as he thought of the loop men who were gone. Where had all the wild ones and all the wild times gone?

"Wonder how many of the boys'll be at El Marinero's." Prairie was surprised he'd spoken his thought out loud, especially to her. He was getting windy. He never thought he'd be one of those geezers who blabbed away whenever someone slowed down long enough for them to get a word in. He'd have to watch that. Now that he was pushing fifty.

"Isn't El Marinero Spanish for the sailor?" Son asked as if she weren't able to read *Don Quixote* like the Sunday comics. "Who is he?"

"Who's El Marinero! I thought you said you knew ropers. The Sailor was just the best that ever was. We sailed together. Put together a little roping act. They knew us in every port from here to Haiphong."

"In the navy?"

"Swabbies? Are you kidding? That's the second time you insulted me. Merchant marine, babe. Able-bodied seamen."

"So this El Marinero is having a reunion for trick ropers?"

Prairie sagged and the headache came back. For the fifth year in a row, the Sailor hadn't tried to get in touch with him. Hadn't sent an invitation to the P.O. box he'd maintained in New Orleans ever since he'd gotten out of the merchant marine. The Sailor sure as hell had that number. Shit, they'd shared the box for a couple of years before the wife in Veracruz found out about the one over in Sonora.

"Will they all be there?"

"I don't know." He made whisking motions with his hands. "Look, I got friends coming to meet me, so if you could just clear some space here."

Son scooted away on the bench, then stopped. "Tell me where this reunion is. Please."

Having spent so much time in Mexico, Prairie knew more than the average gringo about pathologically proud people and he knew he was staring at one right now and that begging like this was emptying her out. Even though she did not deserve one, he gave her a break.

"Why? What's the point? Your father's not going to be there. The odds are impossible."

"No, they aren't." She'd suckered him. Gone right from pleading to imperious. "If you want to talk odds, the probability is very high that either you are my father or you know the man who is. I mean, there are only a handful of trick ropers in the world."

"Hey, start off by removing me from your probability chart there. First off, I'm not Indian."

"You wouldn't be the first culturally dislocated indigenous person to 'pass' in the dominant culture."

"You know, I always wondered where all these batty old broads came from. Now I know. They come from batty young broads like you."

"Have you ever been to Germany?"

"I am through being polite. You're one of those polite-proof people."

"Do you know Tinka Getz?"

"Who?"

"My mother, Tinka Getz."

"Listen, you're barking up the wrong tree. I'd help you find old Dad if I could, but I've never known a loop man ever been to Germany. So, okay. *Adios, sayonara, arrivederci.* It's been real."

When Prairie turned his back on Son, she panicked and blurted out, "I'll pay you."

"Pay me?"

"Yes, if you will guide me to this reunion, I will pay you."

"You don't exactly look like the prosperous type."

"I can pay. I am not without resources."

Even Prairie could hear the edge of desperation in her voice. A new set of 7.50–16 LT Dunlops at eighty dollars a pop appeared in his mind. Either that or a new clutch.

"You do know where this reunion is to take place?"

"Yeah, sure, of course I know. Me and the Sailor's *cuates*. We go back forever."

"Well, perfect. Then sketch out a map."

"Just like that, huh? I don't think so. I mean, of course I know roughly where the reunion's gonna be, but I gotta verify the specifics, you see. I have to double-check with some other sources."

"Oh."

"So, as a, you know, show of good faith, you know, I'll need some kind of deposit before I do all this checking."

Son reached into her mess kit purse and pulled out all the money she had left. Eighty-three dollars. It didn't look like very much. She regretted the bumper stickers and lemonade. She handed the money to Prairie, "This is all I have. Now. I can get more. Perhaps I could put you on some sort of retainer basis."

"Perhaps you could."

"When might I hope to have this information?"

Folding the crumpled bills into his pocket buoyed up Prairie's spirits. " 'When might we . . .' I love the way you talk, Duchess. Okay, the earliest we 'might' have this information would be to-morrow. Early afternoon. You want to meet me back at the rodeo grounds at, say, two? Two-thirty?"

"Splendid!" Son threw her arms around Prairie and held him in a hug that could have been filial, comradely, or simple animal exuberance.

At that moment, Jo Lynne came out of the kitchen and beheld Son's orange-paneled rump hoisted in the air as she leaned across the table and engulfed Prairie. Jo Lynne tucked her chin into her corded neck and pressed her lips together into a tight, disgusted, but not surprised smile. Jo Lynne didn't have any illusions about men, especially not ones like Prairie James. She turned and marched back into the kitchen.

"Could you shove off now?" Prairie asked. That look on Jo Lynne's face had not been promising.

Son stood. "Yes. *À demain. À deux heures.*"

Prairie felt more charitable the instant she stopped crowding him. "Hey, listen. Thanks for the support out there tonight. It's not often you run into anyone anymore who savvies the old moves."

"It was my distinct pleasure."

"Yeah, Duchess, me too."

Prairie shook his head and twirled his drink. He had the glass to his lip when the Duchess stopped and turned around, one questioning finger in the air. She put the finger to her mouth for a moment of contemplation, then looked up.

"Why would a person name a pure white horse Domino?"

Prairie laughed with relief. She'd asked his favorite question. "I don't know why anyone *else* would do it, but I do it to get the crowd to pay attention. Get 'em looking for the black."

"But there isn't any."

"Not a speck. He's as white as Queen Elizabeth. One thing's certain, though: it's always better to keep people guessing."

For the first time, Son smiled. Prairie was startled by what a difference it made in her face. All the angles went from nagging and sharp to cockeyed but okay. Really all right. If people could say Barbra Streisand, for example, was beautiful, they could say this babe was all right. And teeth. He always noticed teeth, and hers were world class. The calcium-to-burn, whiter-than-white kind he liked best; they seemed to go straight across the front of her mouth like the grille on an old Buick. It was a hell of a smile. Wasted, actually, on someone like her who never used it.

Son kept grinning at him as if the horse's name was a joke they'd thought up together. "Keep the common herd guessing." She nodded, storing the thought away as if it was the combination to a safe.

"Yeah, well, *auf Wiedersehen.*"

Her teeth were gone in a flash as her jaw gaped open in astonishment.

Two words of German? Prairie thought. It doesn't take much to impress some people. She looked on the verge of returning. He put his head down. No more eye contact. If she came back, he just wouldn't speak to her.

When he looked up, she was gone.

Chapter 7.

When the red, red robin, comes bob, bob, bobbin' along, along,

There'll be no more sobbin' when he starts throbbin' his old, sweet song.

Wake up! Wake up! You sleepy—

Son abruptly stopped singing as she turned off Gunther onto Schwarzwald Street. Her mood swings had been exorbitant since Prairie James rode into her life three hours ago. One second she was scaling the heights of ecstasy; the next, plumbing the slough of despond. One second beaming beneath his crown of rope, the next reeling from his rebuff. Son heaved a massive sigh, and the overtaxed snap at the top of her jeans popped open.

The dark street seemed to sparkle in the moonlight. Moonbeams danced on the miniature mountain chalet mailboxes, the miniature mountain chalet tool sheds, and the miniature mountain chalet bird feeders that lined the block.

Auf Wiedersehen. Son forced herself to consider that millions of Americans used this expression. It wasn't necessary to have been a trick roper in Germany in 1964 to know how to say "see you later" in the language. It meant nothing.

When the red, red robin
Comes bob, bob, bobbin' along, along.
There'll be no more—

Again Son abruptly stopped singing, this time when she saw lights on at Tinka's house and the Skylark parked in the carport. She cut her engine and glided to a silent stop. For the first time ever, the little.house was lighted like an aquarium by the flickering violet glow of a television set. Son stared through the picture window and noted bitterly that Walp had wasted no time in establishing his hegemony.

Besides the addition of the Walp television set, the living room was now dominated by the presence of two massive Barcaloungers, presently occupied by the bridal couple themselves. Between the two chairs was a neat pile of suitcases ready for the honeymoon. The bray of a laugh track floated out into the quiet night. Inside the house, Tinka looked over at her new husband, laughed, and covered his hand with hers.

Son reflected on the future that waited for her as a member of the Walp household. It was sure to include opportunities to be waylaid by the unhinged Mr. Capelli and subjected to the depraved importunings of sadistic Christers. Would it also include a Baby Bear Barcalounger wedged in front of the television next to Papa and Mama Bear's for nightly viewing extravaganzas? Would it all eventually end one day beneath a miniature mountain chalet tombstone? All without her ever having met her father?

Son leaned forward against the steering wheel of her little truck, exhausted by the barren alpine outline of her future.

Inside the house, she saw Walp pull Tinka from her throne and onto his lap. Tinka brushed back his sideburns with her tiny fingers just the way she'd done that first day in Edelweiss Optical when he'd come in to see about a pair of the new invisible bifocals. She beamed at Walp, and Son saw something on her mother's face she rarely saw—happiness. Son started the engine.

Chapter 8.

Prairie couldn't find a liquor store open that sold Ronpope liqueur until he hit San Antonio. There he eventually unearthed a dusty bottle of the creamy liqueur in an ice house stocked with *yerba buena* and *barbacoa de cabeza*.

The Carmelite nun on the label of the now half-empty bottle looked up at him from the passenger's seat. He'd been drinking it mixed with 7-Eleven coffee for the last two hundred miles. El Marinero had started him on the stuff way back—when was it, '72, '73? The Christmas they tore up Veracruz together. Veracruz, the Sailor's home port. Just thinking the name filled Prairie's head with the liquid sound of marimbas playing on the *zócalo* and the whisper of little Indian women in long white World War I nurse outfits begging for donations.

They'd started in on the Ronpope after the show on Christmas Eve, as soon as they'd both secured their ropes in the pizza-sized cans they used to keep the cottons and magueys from stiffening in the tropical humidity. Prairie had been delighted to find something so close to eggnog that far south. It just wasn't Christmas in his book without an eggnog hangover.

He and the Sailor ended up cruising the *zoke* with three different groups of hired mariachis following them around the big plaza. They serenaded every señorita, and more than a few señoras, that they came across. Not that they ever did more than make eyes. Not with one of El Marinero's two wives, the one who had given him his first son, Heriberto, living right outside of town. Not with every crazy father, brother, and uncle dying to blow off a horny gringo's *pelotas*. If a man's honor was stained down there, someone's mother got to weep by a graveside.

Prairie had tried for an hour after the Duchess left to rekindle Jo Lynne's flame, but it was stone-cold out. "Make a fool of me oncet, shame on you. Make a fool of me twicet, shame on me" had been her no-appeals verdict. Prairie hated stiff-necked hick wisdom like that. He couldn't believe Jo Lynne thought the Duchess was an actual contender in the bunk department. But she did, and once the bed, the neck bolster, and the Vitabath were lost causes, he decided he might as well tool on down the road to his next gig. Where had Dakota said it was? Jordan? He checked his map. Ah, yes, there it was southeast of his second least favorite urban experience on earth, Houston, Texas. He couldn't remember what number one was, but amoebic dysentery in a Third World venue did ring a distant bell.

Booking out of Dorfburg was probably for the best. No telling how far the Duchess would have tracked him when he didn't show up for their rendezvous at the rodeo grounds. He felt a twinge of guilt about scamming her eighty-three bucks, but then she'd cost him a room for the night and had humiliated him in front of Dakota. It all evened out.

He'd done her a gigantic favor and she'd never know enough to be grateful. That was the last thing Prairie wanted to think about that evening. He cast about for a distraction tantalizing enough to crowd out any further thoughts and came up with a romantic liaison of a commercial nature with a particularly gifted Malaysian vendor back in Penang.

With another little nudge from the Ronpope nun, Prairie slipped into the most sanctified state a traveling man can achieve on our nation's highways: road coma. Prairie had found that just the right combination of exhaustion, caffeine, alcohol, and priapic memories could be more effective than a six-pack of Romilar cough syrup. Original recipe.

In this quasi-narcoleptic state, he segued effortlessly from Penang to Bangkok. Oh, yes, Bangkok. If only more cities were so providentially named or so willing to take such a christening to heart, the world would be a better place. Did those Thai darlings know how to provide a service! Knew what he wanted before he did. Always started out with a nice long bath, up to his neck in one of those big wooden tubs. Then they'd get him stretched out on his stomach and, without a word, those little tongues'd get busy lapping away. Those Thai monkey girls, they knew what he wanted.

He could have ringed his asshole in Krugerrands and old Jo Lynne wouldn't have gone near it with a toilet brush. The farther he got from those cracked lips, the happier Prairie was that his tryst had been aborted. He was tired of turning on the charm and cranking up the old bone for nothing more than a bed and a shower.

It wasn't until the gearshift popped out of fourth, thumping Domino in the chest, that Prairie was aware the horse was breathing down his neck again.

"Do you mind?" Prairie pushed the nag back enough so that he could wrestle the gearshift into place and pull the loop he'd made with an Ace bandage tighter around the stick to hold it there. He wondered how many more days, hours, the transmission had left. The truck had already had a hard life, and hauling a horse to gigs frequently separated by five states wasn't extending it any. Prairie didn't want to think about what was going to happen when the transmission gave out altogether.

A few more jolts of Ronpope and the road coma returned. He was back with the Thai monkey girls scrambling over him. Prairie unzipped, and out it sprang like an ironing board dropping from a cabinet. Perfect. If he handled himself right, this would be good for another fifty miles.

First stroke, however, Domino exploded a gusty, warm blast of horse breath on his neck. Never failed. Whenever he got started, Domino was right there, crowding in as much as he could. Like he wanted to horn in on the action. It bothered him to have Domino watch, but there wasn't much choice.

With Domino's patient exhalations half-deflating him, Prairie had to work to bring back the Thai monkey girls burrowing away. Then he nursed himself along for the next thirty miles, hanging back, slacking off if he got too close. He stopped entirely when some asshole driving an H.E.B. truck stayed on his tail for ten minutes. A homo, no doubt.

When he couldn't hold back any longer, Prairie shifted from vegetative road coma to the more active road seizure state. Tonight felt like a grand mal coming on. His eyes rolled back in his head and his free arm stiffened against the steering wheel, driving him back against the seat. He gulped air with the loud, strangling, sucking sounds he was always reduced to before he bingoed.

"Could you *please* place both your hands on the wheel at two and ten o'clock?"

"Aw-w-w-k-k-k!" Prairie clamped down on himself with such force that he caused a painful vapor lock–type condition in the hydraulic system that had already started pumping the joy juice out of him. With his nards knotting up like a bowline, he looked over his shoulder.

It was a hallucination. It had to be. That Thai stick he'd smoked in 'sixty-eight that was laced with PCP—he'd been a mad dog—it was coming back on him again. He prayed it was. Please, God, let it be a hallucination. Don't let that head case be right behind him staring at his open fly.

"I wouldn't have interrupted if I hadn't felt my very life was threatened. I have no qualms about an individual's manipulating his body in any manner he sees fit. I myself am not above the occasional bout of self-gratification. I would not have interrupted, but your horse seems to have become abnormally aroused and, as I said . . ."

Prairie stared fixedly out at the highway as he tucked himself back into his jeans. Then, jaw tight, he slammed on the brakes. The truck required a hundred yards to shimmy to a halt on the shoulder. Prairie jumped out and ran around to the back. He yanked the door open. Son was standing there, waiting, her hand extended to him like fugging Marie Antoinette waiting for her footman to help her out of her coach.

"I don't care how or why you got into the back of my truck, but you're getting your fat fanny out right now."

Son withdrew her hand and started to shrink back into the truck, but Prairie, his reflexes sharpened by years of dealing with Domino's reluctance to alight, was quicker. He grabbed her by the wrist and dragged her out.

Far off along the eastern horizon a crack of salmon pink was opening up under the night.

Prairie stalked back to the cab.

"I suppose this means you'll be returning my deposit!"

Prairie, caught swinging himself back up into the truck, paused. He'd forgotten all about the "deposit." Without turning around, he said, "I'll mail it to you at the Broken Spoke." He climbed aboard and shut the door.

She ran up to the window and yelled, "Please, I want to meet my father. I feel spiritually incomplete. An alien adrift in a hostile culture."

"Yeah, well, maybe some looser jeans'd help." Prairie turned over the engine. A gruesome scything sound signaled the rapidly approaching death of both his clutch and career. His colon twitched. He let up on the groaning clutch; with a great gnashing, the gears engaged and the truck hiccupped forward.

"Look, wait!" she screamed, running alongside the truck. "I have money. I can pay you."

With brakes and clutch screeching their tortured lament, Prairie brought the truck to a halt.

"Pay me with what?"

"I sold my truck to Walter Dittlinger. The piccolo player. He cheated me, of course. Then he brought me back to the Broken Spoke. I fell asleep waiting for you in the back of your truck."

"That's a lie."

"Well, you left. You took my money and left."

"Who says I wasn't coming back?"

"You weren't."

Prairie started up the engine again.

"No! Wait! I apologize. I shouldn't have sneaked into your truck. Look, I do have money." She opened the sash tied around her waist and showed him a wad of crumpled tens and twenties. As badly as Prairie needed the money, he needed the aggravation much less. A more unappealing fatherless child than this big-butted babe hadn't come along since Norman Bates. He didn't say anything, just studied her in the rearview mirror mounted on the side of the truck.

Her shoulders slumped and that blurry, squirmy look women get right before they cry came over her face. He hated that look. That look meant he'd suddenly been appointed knight in shining armor when he'd never had the slightest desire to even apply for the position. But the blurring and squirming didn't dissolve into the standard waterworks. He had to give the Duchess that; she was fighting the tears.

A puff of early morning wind blew a plastic Wal-Mart bag against her ankles.

"Please take me with you!" she hollered. It took her a second or two to get her chin under control enough to add, "I don't have anyplace else to go!"

Prairie winced. What the hell? Without some outside assistance, he was going to be stranded with a dead truck in about fifty miles. He leaned out the window, looked back, squinting against both the rising sun and the incredibly stupid thing he was going to do, and waved for Son to come on.

Like a puppet being jerked up on its strings, Son came back to life, shouldered her miss kit, and ran to the truck. She stopped at his window, breathless and panting, and stuck her hand out. Prairie stared at it a moment before twigging to the fact that she wanted him to shake it. He dropped a hand out the window; she clamped a killer grip on him and pumped for all she was worth.

"We'll have the merriest of times rolling along the scenic highways and byways of this vast land of ours in your charmingly dilapidated rattletrap of a vehicle. You'll never regret this decision, Prairie James."

Prairie didn't answer. He knew famous last words when he heard them.

Chapter 9.

As they bumped back onto the highway, Son asked the question Prairie was hoping she would when the truck shrieked into first gear: "What is that horrifying sound?"

"That's the sound of a clutch that's about fifty miles from going out."

"Oh."

Good, that seed was planted. Now he had some other crops to dig in. "Uh, you know, we ain't exactly headed straight for the Sailor's. I've got some professional obligations to meet first."

"Fine, fine. Perfectly fine with me. For years I've cultivated the dream of a motor tour of the West. Oh, yes, sign me on for the whole grand excursion. Gads, the panoramic vistas. The Big Sky country. The majestic sweep of limitless horizons where the wind comes sweeping cross the plain." Nervous tension lifted Son's last words into something approaching song. Prairie shot her a sharp glance that ended her lyric impulse.

Still Son bounced and fidgeted in her seat like a kid on the way to Disneyland. She reached for the radio dial and Prairie smacked her hand away.

"No radio," he grunted. "That's rule number one."

Son held up her hands. "Fine with me."

"Rule number two is, don't ever touch that locker." Prairie

pointed a thumb backward. Son turned and noted the gray metal school locker affixed to the wall.

"I won't," she promised.

They drove in silence until the sun was fully up. If it had stayed dark, Prairie would have been all right, but full sun did him in. He knew he had under five minutes in which to get horizontal before he cratered. He pulled over, got out, and yanked open the passenger door.

"Shove it over. Your turn to drive."

"Drive?" Son sputtered. "This vehicle is clearly on the equivalent of an automotive life support system. I can't drive this."

"Sure you can. Every other hitchhiker I've ever hauled has."

Prairie climbed in and shoved until half of Son's generous behind was hanging off the bucket seat. "Turn off at Columbus and don't wake me up until we're in Jordan and you found me a mechanic can work on transmissions."

Son shifted over to the driver's seat. Prairie took her seat, and four events occurred: Prairie balled up his jacket, stuck it under his head, folded his arms, and lost consciousness.

As soon as they were under way, Son feared that the clattering, gasping, shuddering truck would disintegrate beneath her very hands into a heap of smoldering parts smelling of used hay. Domino shared her apprehension, poking his head over her shoulder and snorting criticism the whole way. She was further unnerved by the gearshift's relentless habit of freeing itself and springing into neutral. She had to deduce for herself the function of the Ace bandage in locking the wayward transmission into fourth gear. Son figured that she was probably occupied with this splinting of the gearshift when they passed unawares through Columbus.

Before she even realized she'd missed her turn, she was swept into the sucking wound that is Houston. Son, whose entire previous highway driving experience had been confined to the geriatric pace of Dorfburg, was completely unstrung by Houston traffic. Dumb, callous luck put them squarely into the jaws of the beast at eight fifty-seven in the morning, precisely the moment when panic hits bleary-eyed wage slaves just realizing that they have three minutes in which to complete a fifteen-minute drive to work.

Son made repeated attempts to edge over to the haven of an exit, but was herded back again and again by streams of adrenalized outriders speeding past on her right. Her life had never been in such peril. It was no use to resist. She yielded to the riptide pulling her out toward the rising sun.

Though he slumbered blissfully through the Armageddon of Houston traffic, Prairie awoke the instant silence and stillness invaded the truck. With several mighty snorts, he arose, looked around, and failed to see anything resembling a mechanic's garage. What he did see was a Dairy Queen with a banner across the front window advertising Blizzards for 99 cents.

"Where we?" he muttered groggily.

"The parking lot of the Winnie Dairy Queen." Son was nothing if not precise.

"Winnie? Winnie, Texas? As in sixty miles the wrong side of Houston? Winnie, Texas?"

"I know of no other."

"Great. Oh, well, might as well find a mechanic here."

"Not before I seek refreshment. I'm accustomed to breakfasting at nine on the dot each morning, shortly after my mother has vacated the premises. I like to enjoy my bowl of Uncle Sam cereal with digestion-enhancing flax seeds in relative peace and quiet. As it is now past ten, I'm over an hour late."

"Hey, knock yourself out." Prairie swept a hand toward the Dairy Queen and left to feed Domino.

Son found the Winnie Dairy Queen to be singularly tawdry, sporting the excessive amounts of Formica that characterize establishments devoted to the efficient defrauding of consumers on a nationally franchised level. Though she had no other choice, patronizing such an outlet was nonetheless philosophically repugnant.

At Son's entrance, the faces of a dozen sun-mottled nesters, gathered for the morning coffee break, which ran approximately from the moment the Dairy Queen door opened in the morning until afternoon nap, froze in slack-jawed wonderment. The appearance of any unescorted woman the nesters hadn't known since Dewey lost to Truman would have occasioned some stares, but a strange, single woman, nearly six feet tall, wearing blue jeans with orange panels, a scarlet sash around her belly, and plastic cowboy boots with the toes turned up like elf shoes, well, now, this was a show.

Even more entertaining was when she spoke to Vonda Kaye, the cute little counter girl in her perky DQ cap with her pencil poised above her order pad.

"What do you have in the way of vegetarian fare? I see your menu leans rather heavily toward the carnivorous."

"Huh?" Vonda Kaye goosed her neck forward and squinted at the wordy stranger.

"I don't imagine it would be possible to purchase something as simple as a bowl of Uncle Sam cereal?"

"No, all's what we got's up on the menu." Vonda Kaye waved a hand in the direction of the bill of fare with its Hunger Busters, Dilly Dips, and Buster Bars.

Son studied the menu and was appalled by the prices. Market rectification was in order.

"I'd like to order"—she searched the board for signs of hoofless life—"a lettuce, tomato, onion, and pickle sandwich with the usual array of accompanying condiments and I am prepared to pay you . . . let's see . . . sixty-five cents. And a complimentary glass of water."

Vonda Kaye turned and looked at the menu to see if someone from Dairy Queen Inc. might have sneaked in during the night and added Lettuce Tomato Onion and Pickle Sandwich to the menu. This situation had not been covered in her training. She'd learned how to dip cones in hot chocolatelike wax and all about portion control, but she hadn't learned a thing about weird people coming in asking for weird things that weren't on the menu.

"You're gonna have to talk to my manager. He'll be in at eleven-thirty and you can tell him what you want."

Son sensed an insecure sentry guarding the gates of the merchandising monolith. With a surprising nimbleness, Son threw up the hinged counter and strode into what is known in the fast food world as the food preparation area.

Not trusting where Vonda Kaye's adolescent hands might have strayed, Son quickly assembled the sandwich herself. The portion control alarm clanged in Vonda Kaye's head as she watched Son stack up a sandwich taller than the Best Buy 32-ounce beverage. When she finished, Son handed over seventy cents, left, then came right back to ask for her complimentary water and extra packets of ketchup, mustard, mayonnaise, relish, coffee creamer, sugar, salt, pepper, and lemon juice. After stuffing what little space remained in the bag with napkins, plastic forks, and coffee stirrers, Son left the Winnie Dairy Queen.

The franchise was silent for several minutes until one of the nesters cleared his throat. "I didn't know you could grow a bunny that big on rabbit food."

Back in the truck, a gnashing shriek met Son's efforts to put the engine into gear.

"Clutch is gone," Prairie announced, cheerily. "I guess that's the end of our little rodeo tour."

"What do you mean?" Son demanded. "I have paid you an advance."

"Hey, no truck, no tour."

"Well, fix the truck."

"No money, no fix truck."

Son glared at Prairie. "I'll pay for the repair."

They found a mechanic who told them they were lucky he had parts, which he pulled off a gutted Blossom milk truck. He gigged Son $350 to replace that clutch. Prairie pretended to be occupied checking the windshield wiper blades while Son extracted a crumpled wad of bills from her money belt sash.

After the bill was settled, Prairie returned from his wiper inspection. "You gonna gas her up?"

"Gas her up? May I remind you that I just outlayed three hundred and fifty dollars? I see no reason why I should bear the entire financial burden of our shared journey."

"Jeezo Pete. I liked you a lot better when you were in the down-and-out mode."

It was nearly three before Son, still in the driver's seat, escaped from I–10 and onto the back country roads winding through fields of sorghum and pastures clumped with gargantuan wheels of hay and lazy clusters of horses and cattle. The air was as hot and muggy as the breath Domino exhaled on Son's neck. Son began to feel a few twitches of fondness for Tinka's polar AC, as the sweat, repelled by the hundred percent synthetic fabric of her shirt, ran down between her breasts and pooled beneath her sash.

Jordan, Texas, sat on the cusp between the old cotton lands farther south and the coastal grazing plains southwest. Nearly everyone who lived in the small town was descended from slaves who had worked on plantations or ranches. A banner fluttering over the main street advertised "Jordan's 43rd Annual Juneteeth Rodeo. Open Entries. Harriet Tubman Arena. 1:00 P.M. June 19."

"Prairie. Prairie!" Her companion maintained the same pose he'd held for the past two hours: head back, mouth open, bottom lip sucking in and out with the tide of his gargled breath.

Son jostled him. "We're in danger of being late for your performance. I believe that punctuality is a cardinal rule in show business unless movies have been made, albums produced, and a pattern of chemical dependency established. As you have not yet arrived at that plateau, Prairie, I suggest you wake up." Prairie did not move.

Son craned around frantically, searching for the arena. Fortunately, the road, crowded with pickup trucks parked on either side, and swarming with black people in boots, jeans, and cowboy hats, deadended at the entrance to the Harriet Tubman Arena.

The instant the truck stopped, Prairie sat bolt upright. "We here?" He looked around at the crowd filing past with coolers and lawn chairs. "Jesus Christ. The jungle bunnies are out in force for the rodeo."

Son pressed her lips together tightly. "I'd appreciate it very much if you'd not use expressions like that in my presence."

"What? Rodeo? You're in a world a trouble, babe, you don't like the word 'rodeo' traveling with me."

"You know perfectly well what I mean. If you can't express respect for this commemoration of the day that Emancipation was proclaimed in Texas, then please don't say anything at all."

"Yeah, right. Okay." Prairie sat in a sleep-dazed silence for several minutes, digesting Son's criticism, before he spoke again. "Hey, I just want you to know that I feel real honored to have a snow-white Kraut from Kraut Town, U.S.A., who's probably spoke to, maximum, two, maybe three individuals of the black persuasion in her whole frapping life, here, in my own vehicle, giving me tips on successfully relating with members of the Negroid race. Especially since my own background of growing up in Detroit and working on merchant vessels from the equatorial regions limited my acquaintanceship entirely to a select circle of creamy white Ivy League graduates. Thank you very much, Coretta Scott King."

"Perhaps you should expend less energy in racially derogatory comments and more toward preparing for your performance, as the rodeo starts in"—she glanced at her watch—"three minutes."

"Hah! Three o'clock! That's three o'clock *Kraut* time. You think a . . . colored rodeo is going to start on time?"

By four o'clock the hot, high sun shone down on a ramshackle old arena of boards weathered to a silvery gray that had yet to be entered by a single contestant. Not that the crowd seemed to mind. The arena was ringed by pickups facing backward so that they formed one giant tailgate party that spilled over into the stands behind them. Above them all a tinny speaker mounted on a power pole squawked out, "Buh-buh-buh, boogie fever! Get on down! Get on down!"

A pack of little boys ran underneath the bleachers whirling lariats, trying to rope each other, and the three-legged dog chasing after them. Up on the bleachers, those not early enough to have gotten a place in the tailgate roundup sat fanning themselves, drinking beer, and sheltering under umbrellas. A chubby girl in glasses and braids went from one gossiping cluster to the next, selling bars of chocolate for the Ebenezer Baptist Church Bible School Fund.

The crowd was far more festive than any Dorfburg rodeo audience Son had ever been part of. She suspected that the Wild Turkey boilermakers the tailgaters were tippling might be the cause. A black woman with one front tooth outlined in gold and her thick neck creased with rings of fat that looked like the necklaces of a tribal bride threw her head back two times. The first time, she upended a bottle of Wild Turkey. The second, she opened her mouth wide to laugh and the pink-painted straw cowboy hat atop her pouf of henna hair rolled off into the dust. At the sight of her hat falling off, the other three women perched on the tailgate of the pickup cackled until they had to slap their chests to stop.

Jackson and Mickey, the concessionaires Son had met in Dorfburg, were setting up business over by the beer booth. All Jackson's signs for corny dogs and Sno-Kones had been replaced with one giant sign proclaiming BAH-BEE-CUE!!! Jackson himself was stationed beside a fifty-gallon drum split into a barbecue pit.

In the shade of a cottonwood, a little way off from the barbecue pit, Son found a broken piece of planking balanced between a chunk of cinder block and an old paint can and took a seat to watch Jackson. He hauled open the silver lid, dived into a hot cloud of smoke fragrant with the pecan wood he favored over mesquite, and basted a mob of briskets. Rivulets of sweat ran from his receding hairline down his dark face. A sputtering, grease-fed flame blazed up.

"Mickey," Jackson called to his helper, wiping a sleeve across his forehead, "would you be so kind as to bring me the squirt bottle of water?"

"The one what the Joy or the Dawn dithwathing thoap wath in?"

"Either one will do nicely, Mickey."

Son waited, hoping Jackson would speak again. He doused the flame with the detergent bottle now filled with water, pulled off a slab of meat, plopped it into a pan, glanced up, and spotted Son. "Miss Lemonade," he hailed her. "My well-spoken friend."

Son, caught completely off-guard by Jackson's greeting, blushed a rare and roasting blush. After a lifetime of having to dragoon people into paying attention to her, she'd come to feel virtually invisible when not speaking in her most commanding fashion. She had not expected Jackson to notice her at all, much less remember who she was. "Hel—" She cleared her voice, unrecognizably reedy thin, and tried again. "Hello."

"You *are* a rodeo fan."

It took Son another second to realize that it might be her turn to contribute to the conversation. "Uh, yes. Yes . . . Actually, no, I don't really like rodeo that much."

Jackson's expression was friendly, waiting.

Son stammered. "I have a long-standing interest in the—"

"Jackson! My man!"

Son winced at the sound of Prairie calling out as he approached from the shady creekbed where he had tethered Domino. Without a word to her, Prairie took a seat on the plank next to Son. "You need someone to test-drive that brisket?"

Jackson brought out two sandwiches, and gave one to Prairie and one to Son. Then he stood directly in front of Son and said, "Prairie, introduce me to your new running buddy."

Prairie looked over at Son as if he'd just noticed her. "Her? Running buddy? Her? No. Her car broke down over there by Flatonia and I stopped. The hood was up, you know. Anyway, she's got an emergency in Houston. An aunt with diabetes. They're afraid they're going to have to take the leg. But, no, no, she's not with me. I'm just giving her a lift into Houston."

"Uh-huh." Jackson nodded. "Uh-huh. Aunt's got the sugar." He caught Son's eye, smiled, and winked before turning to walk back to the concession stand.

"Why did you tell Jackson that my aunt has diabetes?"

Prairie finished the sandwich and screwed a napkin around each of his fingers. "Ah, well, you want the whole world knowing your business?"

"You're embarrassed to be with me."

"What the hell you talking about?" He turned his gaze on the rollicking crowd. "You ever see such a raggedy-ass excuse for a rodeo in your life?"

"You shouldn't impose your cultural expectations," Son advised.

"So, it's like too much to expect there'd be a horse or two, perhaps even a contestant, at a rodeo?" He referred to the total lack of livestock. "Jeez, these Lamumbas couldn't get a fire started in a paint factory on time."

"As a person of color, the daughter of a Native American, I deeply resent—"

"Yeah, yeah, okay, Pocahontas, I got you. Here, have some fire water. Mellow out." Prairie stuck a bottle of Baby Chams in her hand.

"Well, I don't normally drink, but perhaps I might derive some nourishment if nothing else from this"—she examined the label on the bottle of imitation champagne, a fortified concoction that was outselling beer two to one at Jordan's Juneteenth Rodeo— "grain-based beverage."

"Hah!" Prairie snorted goodnaturedly, opened his bottle, guzzled half of it, and continued, "What you might derive is a free drink. You'd chug Windex if someone else was buying."

"Oh, so, I'm to be pilloried because of the inequalities between the earning power of men and women. Need I remind you of who replaced the clutch in your truck? Perhaps such ritualized displays of largesse as buying 'drinks for the house' are—"

"Drink up." Prairie tipped the open bottle into Son's mouth, bringing her screed to an abrupt halt. "Here. Take another." He put a refill in her hand and they both drank.

After a few more refills, supplied by Prairie, Son was so jollied by the pink bubbly, and by the thought that she was in a setting that would send Tinka into cardiac arrest, that she actually did engage in a ritualized display of largesse and buy a round. Prairie clinked bottles with her and they both went back to watching the festivities buzzing around them like an African bazaar. Shouting, catcalling, laughing, eating, drinking, the crowd obeyed the incessant tinny command buzzing from the loudspeaker to "Get on down! Get on down!"

Behind them at the barbecue stand, Mickey was a frazzled mess. This was the one rodeo where he did most of the work, because Jackson considered it a holiday and spent all his time visiting with old friends.

"Mick, you doing all right in there?" Jackson, who was helping pass a bottle of Black Velvet around a circle of old-timers, called in to his helper.

"Yeth!" Mickey called back as he slopped a brisket sandwich with a dollop of sauce that left an orange ring on the white bun. "I gueth," he muttered to himself, looking in his change box and seeing his supply of shiny quarters and sparkling dimes dwindling. He hoped they ran out of brisket before he had to hand back a dirty penny.

Son noted that, with each bottle of Baby Chams, Prairie's criticism of black culture and lack of punctuality softened. With each subsequent bottle, he unwound a bit further, his voice lowered and his Yankee accent slurred. Some time around the fourth bottle, he picked up a rope and began twirling it, spinning little loops that he'd dab over the toe of his boot, Son's knee, a splintered fence post. Prairie did it all without thinking, practically without watching.

With a rope in his hand, Prairie was transformed. He became

a creature with a long tentacle that had a life of its own. After roping the hat off a little boy's head as he passed in front of Son and Prairie, then casually dropping the hat onto the head of the boy's little brother following behind him, Prairie reeled in his loop. Son was to learn that she had just witnessed a rare moment. That Prairie almost never roped unless a spotlight was trained on him and he was being paid. That loops were just not something that he normally did for fun.

While he was coiling his rope back up, Prairie noticed Son watching him, her face gone soft from the heat, the Baby Chams, from admiration. He leaned back to take a long look at her. "You ever use make-up? Fix yourself up? Good pair of jeans, some decent boots?" He touched her hair. "Hair cut in one of those . . ." His hands orbited his head, describing a hairdo he found particularly attractive. Sheila used to have one. Prairie remembered the word "shag" being used.

"You mean, turn myself into a lacquer-haired, mascaraed mantrap?"

"There's not much danger of—"

"I do not choose to make the snaring of a man the central drama in my life. I have set my sights higher than that."

"Oh, yeah? You have? Well, okay, bully for you."

"The desire to be attractive to men enslaves more women than any of the other myths foisted upon us by the merchandising monolith."

"Yeah. Oh, yeah, well, you got that one beat, sister. No problem there."

Son thought for a long time about clarifying her position. It wasn't until she stopped thinking that she realized Prairie had been trying to give her a compliment. "Thank you," she said softly. But Prairie squinted at her as if he had no idea what she was talking about.

Just as Son started to elucidate her position further, Jackson, standing in the middle of a cluster of older black cowboys, called out, "Prairie! Prairie James! Come on over here; these gentlemen want to talk to the man rode with Dusty Sam."

Prairie wobbled to his feet. "Dust? My man Dust? Greatest goddamm trick rider ever drew breath. *Black* or white."

Son gasped at Prairie's insensitivity in calling direct attention to an individual's race. She followed after him as he made his way over to the cluster of men.

"Prairie." Jackson grabbed him by the elbow. "I want you to meet this man." He pulled him over to a cowboy in his mid-sixties, no taller than a robust fifth-grader. "Prairie, this here's Little Man, Elmore Claypool, the Godfather of Black Rodeo."

"Hell, I know Little Man," Prairie said, sticking his hand out for Elmore Claypool to shake. Little Man reciprocated with what was left of his hand, three fingers and a wad of calluses and burn scars. Ropers lost fingers the way lizards lose tails; they just didn't regenerate them nearly as easily.

Prairie pointed at Little Man as he continued shaking his hand. "This man here could have been one of the great trick ropers of all time."

Son was electrified by the words "trick roper." She felt inside her bag until her fingers touched the photo of her father.

"But no!" Prairie exploded. "Has to be a goddamm calf strangler. He could copy every trick I showed him. Every one! Shoulda been a trick roper, Little Man; you'd still have your fingers."

"Yass, but my soul'd be sold to the devil," Little Man answered softly with a shy grin. When the laughter and palm slapping stopped, he continued, "This here's Junior." Little Man's black country accent made the introduction come out "This chere's Joonyah. We cowboyed together at Shanghai Pierce all up through the forties, early fifties." Junior, a tall man with elegant cheekbones wearing a black tie and smoking a cigar, tipped his hat to Son and shook Prairie's hand. Little Man pointed his remaining fingers at the three other men: "Gaylor, Chollie, Homuh."

The old-time cowboy's courtly reticence attained a kind of

majesty in these four men that kept Son from interrupting. All four wore crispy starched white shirts with snap buttons and belts decorated with shiny, saucer-sized buckles celebrating championships from decades gone by. But only Little Man wore one of pure silver with WORLD scrolled across it above the year, 1946.

Prairie pointed to the buckle. "I don't recall there being any colored world champions before what? The sixties at least."

Son winced again.

"That's because there woin't none," Little Man affirmed. "Not officially. By the clock I was, but not by the officials. Back in them days, we rode after the rodeo, you understand. *After*, if we rode at all."

"Uh-huh," a couple of the other men put in. "Thas how it was. Uh-huh. Back them days. It surely was."

"Clem Stephens and me was neck and neck on our times going into the finals," Little Man went on. "He had the best overall, so they gave him the buckle and put his name in the record books. But I beat him later that night after the white folks cleared out. Clem stayed, though. He saw me, saw the times. It was Clem himself give me this buckle."

Little Man looked down and tilted the big buckle up as if he'd forgotten what was written on it. "He was a fair man. Died in *Korea*. Always wanted to send this buckle on back to his folks but never had no address."

All the men stared sorrowfully at the ground as if the unknown address might appear in the dirt at their feet.

"Mr. Claypool." Son's voice, too loud for the slow, hot afternoon, broke the silence. "I am searching for my father. He is a Native American. A trick roper who went by the name—"

"Son," Prairie interrupted, calling her by her real name for the first time, "these fellows don't know any—"

"What was the name?" Little Man asked.

"Gray Wolf," Son answered. "He performed under the name of Gray Wolf."

"Gray? Wolf?" Little Man repeated thoughtfully, pinching his chin between two fingers as he considered. "Indian trick roper name of Gray Wolf? Hmmm."

The other men searched their memories, shaking their heads as they tried to remember.

"Knew a Gray *Elk* once," Little Man offered. "Saddle bronc rider from Idaho, believe it was."

"There's *Cotton* Wolf," Junior reminded the others. "Braids belts and bridles out of El Campo. Course he's only 'bout thirty."

They all agreed that Cotton wouldn't be the one.

"Yeah, okay," Prairie said, voice prickly with irritation as he pushed Son away from the circle of black cowboys. "I told you Little Man's a calf strangler. Ropes the timed events. He's not a trick roper."

"Yes, but he's been on the circuit. He might—"

Little Man held up one of the three fingers on his right hand. "I know exactly who the young lady should talk to. El Marinero! You used to be pretty tight with the Sailor, didn't you, Prairie? He'd know. Anybody on this earth'd know, he would."

Son glared at Prairie. "Apparently they've had a falling out," Son said. "Though maybe you could tell me where the ropers' reunion he has every year is going to be held."

"Now, *that's* trick roping. Bet I know who could tell you, though. Cootie Ramos! Old Coot'd know. He's half-Indian his-self."

Son squeezed back past Prairie. "He is?"

Little Man looked at Prairie and asked, "Apache, isn't it, Prairie? Didn't Cootie have a full-blooded grandmother?"

"Apache," Son whispered, dazzled.

Prairie snorted. "Every other loop hound I ever knew says he's half-Apache. They're worse than cowboys for having full-blood grandmothers tucked away. Let's go." He tried dragging Son away again. But Son was not to be dragged.

"Where can I find—" she started to ask, but her question was drowned out by the loudspeaker over their heads.

"Welcome, welcome, welcome! Ladies and gentlemen! This here's Sedgewick 'Dog' Dawkins, your announcer for this One hundred twenty-fifth Annual Jordan Juneteenth Rodeo!"

Before Son could ask again, the group around her disappeared as the cowboys headed off to ready mounts and tack.

Only Jackson remained. He put a gentle hand on her shoulder. "Good luck." And then he was gone too.

"We comin' to you today with a good show, a fast show."

Son ran after Prairie, who was heading toward the arena where shaggy broncs and bounding calves were being unloaded from a trailer emblazoned with Casey Dakota's Flying D brand.

"Well, hey, the hump finally sent an opposing team. A mere four hours late," Prairie said when Son caught up with him. "Of course, the 'big man' himself would not actually come to a black rodeo. No, he sends the king calf strangler of them all." Just the sight of Dakota's son, Dewey, was enough to scalp the buzz off Prairie's high.

"When do we begin our search for Cootie Ramos?" Son asked.

"*Our* search for Cootie Ramos?" Prairie stopped himself before he gave her an answer that worked within the same approximate time framework as hell freezing over. He still needed a new set of tires and she still had lots more of those crumpled tens and twenties in her sash. "Uh, yeah, yeah, I got a couple of ideas. A couple of people I can talk to. I'll get back with you on it." Prairie tacked off toward the chip truck.

Son looked over the stands. They were packed past capacity. She ducked underneath the bleachers and found herself a seat on an old five-gallon lard can. She was pleased with her perch out of the sun, peeking at the rodeo through a forest of ankles and eavesdropping on conversations. If it had not been for the constant rain of greasy barbecue wrappers, sloshed beer, and dust falling on her, Son would have found her spot ideal. Still, her post did allow her to make several anthropological observations, and she puzzled contentedly over the marked popularity of pickles among her predominantly black rodeo-going sample.

"Bronc riders!" Dog called out. "Be getting your minds on it, now, y'all hear, because those broncs be planning on a late summer and an early fall!"

Out in the arena, up near the chutes, a line of three would-be bronc riders, all teenagers from Houston suburbs, stood pinning contestant numbers to one another's back. One wore a finely woven straw hat close down on his short hair; another had a knitted Rasta cap with a pompom snuggling over a mass of dreadlocks; the last one in line had on a long-sleeved Western shirt with a Heavy Dee decal ironed on the back.

A cloud of dust roiled up as Dewey Dakota, armed with his ever-present cattle prod, drove the bareback broncs into the loading chutes, yelling, "Sixty-five, load up there! Move, sixty-five! Move! Sixty-seven, you move too! Forty-three, quit looking at me that way and do what I say!"

The three young cowboys grew silent as the snorting horses were prodded in. The first boy in line sat down and solemnly strapped a pair of spurs on boots held together by duct tape and fantasy.

"Now, ladies and gentlemen, this is where the pavement ends and the West begins! Fans, fasten your eyes on Chute Number Three. Our first rider today is Kevin Caldwell."

Kevin glanced up. He looked like a man about to be dropped behind enemy lines.

"Kevin comes to us from Houston, Texas. Houston, Texas! His folks's all from Jordan. They been many a fine Caldwell rider; we'll see if Kevin got him any the good genes. He's on the rank horse, Banana Split! Okay, Kevin, let's go, let's go, let's rodeo!"

Kevin lowered his lanky frame down onto Banana Split's back and scrunched up against his hand dug deep under the bareback rigging. The Caldwell family honor hung in the balance. Kevin jammed his hat down until his ears flapped out. He set his face in a determined expression, tensed every muscle in his young body, and gravely nodded, signaling for the gate to be swung open.

Banana Split glanced out at the open arena and did not move. Kevin Caldwell, clamped onto his back, rigid with fear, did not move either. A quick jolt from Dewey Dakota's hotshot, however, inspired Banana Split to make one lunge for freedom. The instant the animal moved, poor Kevin toppled off.

"Ooo-weee! Ole Kevin got his banana split for sure!"

The crowd came alive, hooting and catcalling as Kevin dusted off his hat and ran for the chutes.

"Next outta chute . . . Which chute that? Chute Four! Chute Four! A handsome cowboy from down around Plum way, Hush Aldine!" Kevin's humiliation was already yesterday's news in everyone's mind except his own.

In Chute Four, Hush, a short chubby man, looked like a mushroom in cowboy boots. A woman wearing gold metallic loafers and a halter top stood and yelled, "Hush, I paid two dollar see you ride! I be talkin' 'bout you, you don'!"

Though he appeared not to have a neck, Hush swiveled his head in the woman's direction and yelled back, "Why own't you air out! You loud enough to be *twins!*"

The crowd whooped, and bottles from every direction were passed to the woman. Hush settled back down and nodded. The gate swung open and his mount broke for daylight. Once out of the chute, though, all the spirit drained from the beast and he delivered a ride that would have had a three-year-old at the machine in front of Kmart asking for a refund. But it was enough to dislodge Hush, who was dropped gently into the plowed earth.

"You let that dink fro' you!" the woman in the gold loafers yelled, and the crowd hooted with her.

Hush got slowly to his feet, then dropped back down to his knees, doubled over, clutching his chest as if the crushed cigarettes in his breast pocket were a vital organ.

"Faker!" the woman accused, and the crowd merrily picked up the jeer. "Faker! Faker! Faker!"

Hush, who'd limped about halfway across the arena, stopped supporting his wounded cigarettes long enough to shoot the crowd an angry bird. "Fuck you!" Hush suggested. "Fuck you all!"

The rodeo secretary, an overburdened woman with about half a foot of taffy-colored wig between her scalp and a tiny cowgirl hat trimmed in pink-dyed chicken down, got on the p.a. and timidly asked, "Would all's y'all be so kind's to move your automobiles so's the bulls be unloaded? Thank you."

It did not appear to Son that the woman's soft words had had much effect on the crowd, as no one left the party.

"Hey! Ho!" Dog boomed. "Evvy ennybody who has a car over there, move it or we own turn them bulls loose on 'em!"

The rodeo ground to a halt as most of the men working the chutes left the arena.

"We take a little breather here. I got an announcement. We regret to have to inform y'all that Latasha Mitchell will not be able to perform for us tonight at intermission."

A groan went up from the crowd.

"Instead we have a fine substitute. The roping magic of Mr. Prairie James and his wonder horse, Domino!"

The crowd groaned again, all except for the old-timers led by Little Man, who put their remaining fingers together in enthusiastic applause. Son could not understand the trick roper's singular lack of popularity among today's rodeo-going public. She hoped Prairie, getting ready for his performance back in the chip truck, could not hear the groans. She knew what it was to travel the lonely path of unpopularity.

The secretary's pleading voice came on again. "Now, we still got one automobile out here. A black Impala. Someone said owner's got a wife name Pam. You got a wife name Pam, *poe*-leeze move your automobile!"

The pleas continued through the rest of the bareback riding and well into the calf roping. By that time there were a couple dozen men milling about inside the ring: judges, arena directors, mounted pickup men, most of the bareback riders, and an increasing number of spectators who'd hopped the spindly fence separating watchers from riders.

The calf ropers bolting out of the box ran interference around the group, zigzagging through the clusters of beer drinkers to flush out their calf. Dewey Dakota, the only white roper to enter the competition, burst out of the chute after his calf. Like a programmed machine, he ignored all life in the arena except the fleeing calf, and would have trampled a toddler had the child's mother not grabbed him up by his overall straps at the last second. He strutted back to the chutes with an unbeatable time of 9.3 seconds. Or it would have been unbeatable if Little Man hadn't ridden out and done the deed in 9.1 with his eight fingers.

Son stared hard and still couldn't figure out how a man who lacked a prehensile grip managed to rope and tie down a bawling calf. Not many spectators appreciated the feat and kept right on sucking on pickles or Baby Chams bottles.

Audience interest picked up somewhat when the saddle bronc riding started. As this event required ownership of an approved saddle, there were few contestants. Junior, Little Man's cowboying buddy, was one. He let two drunks borrow his saddle and go ahead of him. They paid their entry fees and each one received a quick flying lesson in return.

Then Junior calmly saddled up the stout roan he'd drawn while Dog announced, "Hot to go in Chute Number Two! Junior Cantrell on Meltdown. This bad bronc don't know the meaning of the word *co*-operation!"

Moving like a priest presiding over a Zen tea ceremony, Junior tucked his black tie into his waistband and set the butt of his cigar in the corner of his mouth. Finally, he lowered himself onto the horse's back and said softly to the gate tenders, "Turn him out, boys."

Junior marked his bronc out like a stop-action photo of perfect saddle bronc form: free hand held high, both his dull spurs planted high in the roan's shoulders, the roan with all four hooves off the ground bowed into a shuddering arc. The horse landed and Junior took the shock with the nonchalance of a man getting comfortable in a rocking chair.

"Style her, baby!" a voice from the suddenly silent crowd rang out. "Style that mothuh!"

Junior rocked casually through the rest of his eight seconds. The worst that Meltdown could do was to pull Junior's tie loose from his waistband. When the horn blared, the old-timer slid off the horse's back before the pickup men could reach him. Taking no notice of the inept riders thundering around him in pursuit of the horse they'd let escape, Junior flicked a few stray horse hairs from his shiny chaps, smoothed his tie back down, and took a deep draw on his cigar.

With each of these manicured movements, Son sensed the crowd in the bleachers forming at last into an actual audience. When Junior took the stogie from his lips and puffed out a perfect ring, the former mob, sanctified by the sheer loveliness of what it had witnessed, became a unified whole.

"Cold! Cold! Cold!" Dog warbled. "Thas Junior Cantrell showin' y'all how the tale is told, how the bronc was rode. Don't never count these old mens out! They'll show you how evvy time! Evvy time!"

Far away from the arena, out in the blackness of the night, the sound of the crowd going wild was a distant mutter to Prairie as he led Domino along the creek. He grabbed the reins and pulled Domino away from the juicy clump of mallow he was cropping. Once he had the animal's attention, though, he couldn't get up the heart to mount up and ride over toward the lights. He'd heard the reaction when Dog revealed that Prairie James and Domino would be replacing Miss Latasha Mitchell. He'd heard the disappointed groans. He was sick and tired of hearing disappointed groans, of being the last-minute fill-in. Most of the time, Dakota never had a star performer to begin with. He just put the bait name up on posters, then switched him in at the last minute.

At the first hint of a groan, Prairie had gone directly to Dewey Dakota and demanded that the calf-roping robot pay what was owed him. Dewey told him that his father had another substitute gig lined up for him—an all-girl rodeo way the hell up in Hereford —and that they'd be holding the "balance of his payment" until he played it. Prairie considered a swift, killer, Kung Fu kick to the side of Dewey's immense head, the kind of kick he'd learned from the Filipino "stealie boys" in Subic Bay, followed by a swift removal of Dewey's wallet, choked with cash as it was from the Juneteenth Rodeo Committee.

Then Prairie considered Dewey Dakota standing there in front of him, six feet, five inches tall, an ox in blue jeans gripping a hotshot. As Casey Dakota made clear to everyone he met, Dewey wasn't his "real" son. The boy had been an eleven-year-old "un-placeable" orphan when Dakota started bringing him out to the ranch on weekends and summers. Dewey considered "vacations" at the Flying D to be immense fun.

From that first summer on, Dakota had Dewey bucking eighty-pound bales of hay off the back of a flatbed for entertainment. It was Dakota's painstaking tutelage that had turned the boy into a livestock-tending android. Dakota had officially adopted the boy two years ago, when he'd turned sixteen and the issue of wages —pay for all the wholesome fun Dewey had been having—reared its ugly head. As his son, Dewey labored tirelessly for the simple privilege of calling Casey Dakota "Dad."

Prairie put away the swift-kick-to-the-head plan. Dewey, in his mindless devotion to "Dad," would happily choke him death. He took the all-girl gig and the hundred Dewey advanced him.

"You should be grateful for the work," Dewey said. "You ain't all that popular no more."

"Thanks. You really know how to get a performer up." Prairie stalked off, his ears ringing with the crowd's groans and the judgment he knew came straight from "Dad."

Prairie let Domino go back to chomping mallow clumps and opened the big tin rope case he kept his magueys in. He spun his favorite, the one he'd gotten on his last visit to the Sailor's. It wouldn't obey him any better than Domino did. Prairie swore that

Domino was worse than a wife for reading his moods and using the secret knowledge against him. Even though Prairie had dutifully taken him out for a good long warm-up stretch earlier, Domino was as balky and high-strung as his rope.

The crowd noise was a distant, anarchic murmur. Solidified for a moment by Junior's ride, the crowd had crumbled again into a rabble. The humid night air was pierced by the blare of the eight-second horn, then a woman's braying cackle as some bronc rider made a fool of himself.

All of a sudden, Prairie felt as if the laughter were for him, and he let the rope that refused to come to life in his hands sag onto the marshy ground.

What was the point?

He looked back at the arena and saw a man in a giant cartoon sombrero, a can of Schlitz Malt Liquor Bull balanced in his free hand, crawl over the fence into the arena, yelling for his turn at a bronc so's he could show "y'all cripples and drunks" how to ride a horse. Half the audience was in the ring by that time.

What was the point?

This crowd was on one giant bender. The last thing in the world they wanted to see was a bunch of rope tricks. They'd be just as happy—shit no, Prairie had to admit it—they'd be *happier* with a goddamm fruit scramble. Just throw some apples in the middle of the arena and let the kids race for them; that'd be plenty of enter-tainment for them. Not that he was racial. He didn't give a good goddamn what Pocahontas said. Hell, nine tenths of the gigs he'd played for the last few years he could've been out-entertained by a fruit scramble. It just wasn't the same anymore.

He looked down at his hands and for the first time wished they hadn't turned out to be so good with a rope that El Marinero had given up trying to think of tricks his gringo student couldn't learn. It was a curse. Here he was, the God all-Friday absolute best in the world, and a bunch of colored drunks didn't want to see him.

Domino heaved a giant dispirited sigh.

The more Prairie thought about where he was, where he'd come from, and where he was probably headed, the farther away the arena seemed. Soon all he could hear was the narcotic buzz of the cicadas. The candy-sweet scent of pink mimosa blossoms came to him and he could have been a thousand miles away. Just like that, he decided he would be a thousand miles away. He had the same detached, final feeling he'd had when he made up his mind to leave the sea. When the story was over, you closed the book.

If he felt any regret, it was about leaving the Duchess behind, and that was minimal. He was sure that she'd make out fine here among people with such a keen appreciation of her kind of heavy-duty mud flaps and flamboyant manner of dress. Without the slightest touch from Prairie, Domino turned back to the truck, plodded toward it, and walked right up the ramp. He knew it was time to go.

Inside the truck, Prairie was taking the bit out of Domino's mouth when his music came crackling over the p.a. The theme to "Bonanza." Prairie remembered the year he'd played the Calgary Stampede, 1971. His first and best year as a civilian entertainer. He'd charged out with that music blasting like Manifest Destiny telling a whole continent to go west. The arena was pitch black and he'd had one pinpoint spot and a crackerjack operator who'd stayed right on him every inch of the way. He'd blasted out to that "Hoss and Joe and Adam know" music and ten thousand audience members had applauded. Before he even started!

Hearing the familiar music, Domino bobbed his big eyes over to give Prairie the kind of glance a drunk's wife would shoot her husband at a wedding reception when they start passing the bottle around.

"Don't gimme that look; we aren't going anywhere."

"Bonanza" stopped and a loud amplified *ska-weeek* told Prairie that the dipshit announcer was rewinding his tape. Sure enough, the music, louder this time, started again. For the first time, nothing charged in him when he heard his entry music. He had no idea what he was going to do with the rest of his life, but it wouldn't be competing with fruit scrambles. He was calm inside and resigned to his decision.

"Your public is becoming restive."

He didn't have to turn around to identify that snooty tone coming at him from the open doors at the back of the truck. Okay, he'd take her as far as the highway. He might even buy her a Greyhound ticket back to Kraut Town. But at that precise moment, he wasn't going to turn around and talk to her.

"Are we playing the prima donna, Prairie? You left me with the impression that you are a seasoned veteran."

Prairie continued unharnessing Domino. The truck tilted under Son's weight as she hefted herself in and came up right behind him.

"Obviously you heard the reaction when it was announced that you would be performing in lieu of the chanteuse."

Something happened to her voice. For the first time ever, she didn't sound like one of the psychopath nuns who'd taught him. It was soft, close to being a woman's.

"I had hoped," she continued, "that you wouldn't hear the crowd voicing its disappointment. The boos, the jeers, the hissing, the catcalls, the—"

Prairie's neck stiffened. "I heard!" Jeez, what was she? Freaking Ro-jay's Thesaurus?

She put her hand on his shoulder. "I know just how you're feeling. Believe it or not, I too have known moments of rejection." She heaved an airy sigh before enumerating them. "The dirty jock straps in my school locker. The empty seat beside me on the crowded bus during band trips. The complete absence of an invitation to the Junior-Senior Prom. Not, mind you, that I would have participated in such a merchandising bacchanalia.

"But I digress. My point being, I too have felt the sting of rejection and simply want you to know that I understand what you're going through. I will tell Mr. Dawkins that you are unwell and cannot perform." She patted his back and whispered, "I understand." The truck rocked as she stepped off and Prairie turned slowly. Son had flabbergasted him to such an extent that it took him a moment to react.

"This isn't about not getting a frapping date for the frapping prom!" he yelled, but she'd already left.

"She 'understands'?" he asked Domino.

It was obvious that Son was taking her time about informing the announcer, because the theme to "Bonanza" was stopped and started two more times. The longer it took to end this fiasco, the more it galled Prairie that she put him on her loser level. He'd been popular in high school before he dropped out. A cut-up. Everyone had loved him. Even the nuns. They told him he was "a caution." He'd been popular. He didn't turn into a loser until much later in life.

The second time his music started up with the rolling overture that never before had failed to gun his motor, his whole face prickled with irritation. He rubbed it hard. Shit. He had only one way of showing her how wrong she was, how far apart they were. He slid the bit back into Domino's mouth and the horse sprayed him with the raspberry of all time.

"Hey! One more like that and it's the glue factory for you, pal."

Then, just when he got the nag back out of the truck and mounted up, his music went dead. On the other side of the arena, he could see Son blabbering away to Dog Dawkins, who had his hand over the microphone. Prairie spurred Domino. Dog's brow creased in puzzlement as she blathered on. Finally he nodded, she backed away, and he took his hand off the microphone.

"Ladies and gentlemen, we regret to inform you that there won't be no intermission entertainment tonight. Mr. Prairie James's doubled over with some elementary canal distress which has incapacitated him. Anyway, he sick. Won't be here."

Just as Dog Dawkins concluded his explanation, Prairie, who'd ridden up in back of them, reached down from the saddle and clicked the tape player back on. The music blared.

"I'm feeling better," Prairie said.

He didn't even consider his usual full-gallop entry; the arena was as crowded as market day in Mombasa. Besides, there was nothing approaching a spotlight. What illumination there was filtered down from a string of bare bulbs hung over the bucking chutes and one outdoor light tacked up on a ten-foot pole. He picked his way in amidst the drunks, the flag men, the pickup men, judges, arena director, and every contestant who'd competed that evening. He even spotted a baby in a stroller sucking on a pickle.

Prairie looked over at Dog. "I could use a little room here!"

Dog got on the microphone. "Clear the arena, please! Could y'all clear the arena?"

Not a soul moved for the exit gate.

"Y'all are going to have to clear the arena, give the man some room to work."

Still no one left.

"Proceed posthaste to the exits!" Son's face was wedged in front of Dog's and her voice sounded like that of every principal, loan officer, telephone company representative, and social agency operative every person in the arena had ever heard. Enough of the crowd obeyed to make a space large enough for Prairie to twirl a rope. Not that it made all that much difference to him. He was there in body, but his spirit had never come out of the truck. Mentally, he was packed up and heading on down the road. He just had to make this one little point to the Duchess about the world of difference between being a high school loser and a professional entertainer. Then he'd be gone. Solid gone.

He set a desultory Tornado spinning above his head, though he might just as well have been adjusting his fly for all the attention anyone paid to him. After it had been whirring over the crowd for a minute, there was a loud "Poom!" as Son wedged herself in in front of the mike again.

"Tornado!" She called out the name of the trick with the same delight she'd shown in Dorfburg when Prairie had half-fallen in love with her. Before the lights hit her.

This time, though, he didn't want any attention directed his way. He wanted to get this over with and get out. Forever. A few of the little boys who'd been chasing after each other practicing heel catches looked up at him and were captivated by the funnel cloud of rope whirling above his head, but the rest of the crowd kept milling about, taking no notice whatsoever of the "entertainment."

Prairie had always believed that the measure of a true performer was in how little he had to do to capture an audience. For the greats, that art went way beyond talent; they could put a crowd in their hip pocket just by breathing. The greats never worked at it. Sinatra, for example, he didn't even have to sing anymore; it was all a magnetism thing. That was what Prairie had always strived for. Projecting so much mojo into a crowd that they half-belonged to him before he did a goddamm thing with the rope. Tonight he was proving his principle in reverse. Tonight he was seeing just how far he could lose an audience when his heart was not in it.

With less flair than a school crossing guard could muster, he dropped his arm and opened a great loop in front of Domino. It turned there, flicking up little puffs of dirt when it chafed the ground, stolid and unspectacular as an old mill wheel. He clucked his tongue and gave the nag a jab, prodding him to step through the spinning rope.

Domino cocked his head back to fix Prairie with an exasperated stare. Domino always required some extra encouragement to participate, but this evening Prairie couldn't find the energy to overcome the horse's reluctance. Neither of their hearts was in it. He was just starting to ease off on the rope so they both could plod out of the arena and out of rodeo forever when POOM! "Look! Look at that!"

Heads craned around, looking in all directions. Eventually they all fixed on the most riveting spectacle in the area: a horsy-faced white woman packed into orange-paneled jeans throttling Dog Dawkins with an elbow to the announcer's windpipe as she grappled for control of the mike.

Dog tried to keep the microphone out of Son's grasp, but she succeeded in screaming into it, "Please, my brothers and sisters in cultural alienation! Direct your attention to the Miracle in Manila being performed in our center ring by none other than Mister Prairie James! Known on five continents as *le roi du rope*, the lord of the lasso, *el jefe de la hemp!*"

No one knew exactly what Son was saying, but they all liked the sound of it: Wah du rope! Hefay day la hemp! The crowd focused on Prairie James. They saw a man with his mouth hanging open, staring dumbfounded at what, for all the world, appeared to be his new announcer.

Dog Dawkins loosed his death grip on the mike, ceding it to the phenomenon at his side. The feel of a microphone in her hand, the sound of her voice amplified for hundreds to hear at once, it all seemed so natural, so astonishingly right to Son. Years of listening to the oiliest announcers in the business at the annual Dorfburg Rodeo had mated blissfully with her high-octane vocabulary and gusty style, creating a strangely mesmerizing hybrid. It was as if the brain of William F. Buckley had been transplanted into Beau Beaulieu's patent-leather head.

Even as she was scrambling to save Prairie's career, an exultant, disembodied thought flew across the top of Son Hozro's mind like an advertising banner flying through a distant sky: *I was born for this.*

"We are indeed graced this evening, for it appears that the Prince of the Prairie is attempting—at this very moment!—to execute a feat that left the crowned heads of Europe gasping in amazement. I speak of course of the ineffable . . . Wheel of Fire!"

Prairie screwed his face up in annoyed bafflement.

"This trick derives its name from the Indian practice of forcing horses through a burning hoop of fire in order to inure them to the flames of battle. The mandates of various animal humane societies and several Byzantine fire codes, unfortunately, prevent Prairie from actually igniting his lasso as he would like to do. But watch, my friends, watch and imagine that the rope spinning before you is a flaming hoop, that Domino is a noble Indian war steed,

that Prairie, a redskinned warrior, is fighting for the very survival of
his race against the dreaded white man!"

Son sat back, pleased with the way she had established audience identification. Her years of study of the despised merchandising monolith had paid off. Though it went against her most deeply
held principles to use enemy tactics, desperate situations demanded
desperate solutions. Had she not intervened to muster some consumer interest in Prairie's product, the performance would have
been a total disaster.

Instead, Prairie now found every eye in the house riveted on
him. In some of the younger eyes, he actually saw the reflection of a
blazing hoop of fire. Less than thrilled with the attention, Prairie
realized that he would now have to perform the *pinche* trick. Whatever the hell it was. He whipped up his loop again and, magically,
the space all around him cleared as people moved out of the way
and scrambled back to the bleachers, where they could get a better
view. Prairie nudged Domino in the ribs. The horse took two steps
backward.

"Quiet, please," Son whispered into the mike. "We are going
to need absolute silence." She turned his music off. "Back in the
days when Prairie was allowed to execute this maneuver with live
fire, Domino was once dangerously singed about the flanks and
hindquarters."

"Oooh!" The crowd gasped in sympathetic understanding.

While Prairie clucked and spurred, Son held forth.

"It now requires an extra measure of bravery on the part of
this estimable steed and an extra measure of mastery on the part of
the rider to perform such a harrowing deed. Were the celebration
of your forefathers' Emancipation not an occasion especially dear
to Prairie's heart, he would not further traumatize his noble mount
by attempting this feat. So, now, in honor of the Jordan, Texas,
Juneteenth celebration, the WHEEL OF FIRE!"

Hands pounded together in anticipatory applause. That sound
goosed Prairie to life in a way that only hands pounding together
could, and he gave Domino a "Ha-YAH!!" that the horse instantly

knew meant serious business. Domino surrendered and plodded wearily through the spinning rope.

"Jordan, Texas, we give you the WHEEL OF FIRE!!"

Wild applause. Whistles. Domino looked out at the crowd with a glance that asked whether they had all lost their minds.

"Thank you, thank you, thank you, noble citizens of Jordan. The next trick you will witness tonight has a history particularly relevant to the occasion. It is a veritable microcosm of the majestic pageant of suffering, endurance, and triumph that the black race as a whole has experienced during its four-hundred-year tenure on this the North American continent!"

Give her this, Prairie thought, amazed as a smattering of applause and "Amens!" broke out: the Duchess could talk. He cranked a loop absentmindedly as he waited to hear where this bit of bombast was going to take him.

"This trick comes down to us as the magnificent legacy of the first great black roper, Eunobia Heath. Eunobia was a slave, back in those dark days before the event we have gathered together today to celebrate. He worked not on a plantation, no, but on a ranch, not so very far from here. In Eunobia's vein flowed the blood of the greatest herdsmen of them all, the majestic Masai with their great herds of cattle. And Eunobia was the best sweat-and-hide cowhand, black or white, anyone had ever seen. His secret? The rope. The steer had not been born that Eunobia could not catch with his humble loop of hemp.

"But, as is so often the case in a society dominated by the overbearing ego of the hypersensitive white male, Eunobia's master did not rejoice in his servant's prowess. No! He was threatened by it. Threatened!"

"That's the troof!" a voice rang out, followed by several more "Amens!"

"And so that pride-blinded master never let slip an opportunity to punish his gifted slave. One tragic night, the master, even more besotted than usual, clamped the shackles around Eunobia's ankles too tightly. When he returned to his brutish senses late the next day, he found that the stoic Eunobia's feet had swollen into two gigantic eggplants and that the deadly red fingers of gangrene were already reaching for the cruelly used slave's knees. Late that night, without so much as a swallow of the master's whiskey to deaden the pain of the saw, Eunobia lost both legs."

The crowd gasped.

"Only Eunobia's body had been conquered. His spirit remained unvanquished. It was this spirit that shot through any piece of rope he touched like an electric current shooting through a wire!"

"Yes! YESS! YESS!!!"

"Where brave Eunobia had once been a good roper, he now became a great—the greatest—roper of his day. Anywhere he once went on his legs, he now sent his rope. That rope caught cattle that men on horseback could not reach. That rope danced in the air and came back with fruit from the trees. That rope snaked into the kitchen and came back out with the drumstick master was saving for his lunch. Eunobia's rope even slithered into other men's cabins late at night and made their women happy."

"I know *that* rope!" the bawd in the gold loafers shouted. But the crowd was too intent upon Son's story to notice the outburst.

"Eunobia was so proficient with that rope that one day Jesus Christ Himself appeared and said to Eunobia, 'Eunobia, you have suffered much and proved yourself a worthy man. Here are your legs, my son. But in return you must give me your rope.' And do you know how Eunobia answered?" Son asked the crowd.

The pint-sized ropers looking up at Prairie shook their heads and answered, "Uh-uh."

"Eunobia just looked at his old legs, then at his rope, then he told Jesus, 'I thank you kindly, Lord, but I believe that I will keep my rope, for I can do more with my one rope than most men can do with their two legs.' "

"Tell it, Eunobia! Tell it!"

"And so, in honor of the indomitable black spirit, I give you Prairie James and his awe-inspiring Eunobia's Rope!"

Prairie knew a cue when he heard one. What he didn't know was any trick ever performed on any continent called Eunobia's Rope. He started thinking with his fingers, playing out rope, flicking in a few Wheels, a couple of Reverses, building up to this mythical trick the Duchess had just laid on him. He thought about throwing a Buzzard, but his loop would just get lost in the darkness. Prairie was arcing a Blowing Bubbles over his head, playing for time, when it came to him, the perfect trick. He and the Sailor had spent hours perfecting it out on the big water, but they'd never played a house small enough for an audience to appreciate it. But with the crowd jammed in around him the way they were, the setting was ideal. If only he could still do it after twenty-five years.

He looked at Little Man, the one person in the crowd who'd given him his total, rapt attention from the moment he'd cranked off the first loop. Another roper like himself, like El Marinero. Right next to Little Man was Junior Cantrell. The big, thick stogie Junior had held clamped between his teeth throughout his bronc ride had been replaced by a fresh one even thicker and longer.

Prairie fed out his rope, sending it to do his bidding just like the legless Eunobia. It shot out and plucked the cigar from Junior's mouth so fast that the man was left feeling a warm spot on his lips and wondering what had happened. By the time he figured it out, the cigar was smoking in Prairie's mouth and the crowd had gone berserk.

Son gave them a few minutes to wear themselves out and then, in a solemn voice, said, "Mark my words well, all ye gathered here: you will speak to your grandchildren in hushed tones of the day you witnessed the last, recorded performance of Eunobia's Rope." She laid the microphone down as exhausted as a Pentecostal after speaking in tongues. She had never done anything so well or so completely in her life. Shining with the pride of it, she smiled at Prairie, who was being mobbed by the crowd surging back into the arena.

Prairie felt like the King of Mardi Gras. He glanced over at his new announcer and was amazed. She was glowing like freaking

Bernadette of Lourdes or something. He couldn't stop looking at her. It made him think that there were a lot worse things in this life than a woman who appreciated what it was a man did best in this world. And he meant *really* appreciate. He took a deep draw on Junior's cigar. It was a damn fine cigar. Possibly the best cigar he'd ever smoked and that included the Havana Tampas from before Fee-del.

As the hands reached up to touch him, to pat Domino, to feel for the magic in his rope, Prairie thought that he just might start smoking cigars again.

Chapter 10.

It was nearly nine o'clock the next morning before the sleepers stirred. Son struggled for an hour to fight her way out of a heat- and Baby Chams–induced stupor. It wasn't until she snuffled a fly up her nose, however, that she attained actual consciousness. In those twilight minutes before sleep fades, she dreamed she was back in her bed and that Tinka was madly spraying Lysol around her room. The dissonance between the dream smell and the stinging ammonia odor that actually struck her fly-tickled nostrils was what finally brought her around.

Son opened her eyes. Yes, it was as she feared: she had slept in the back of the converted chip truck. Though Domino and his droppings were not in evidence, their smell lingered and ripened as the day's heat began to build. She sat up and examined the narrow plank covered by a clearly inadequate piece of foam that had served as her bed. From the other side of the truck issued an unholy assortment of snuffles, mutters, groans, and a strange ratcheting noise from the back of the nose as Prairie came to. The ratcheting ascended the scale as he took in a long continuous breath that crescendoed with a mighty snort. He opened one eye, sat up, peered malevolently around the truck, uttered the question "Eunobia's Rope?" and fell back onto the nest of dirty underwear and old socks.

"Prairie, you can't go back to sleep. Prairie! Prairie!" She shook him with each repetition of his name. "This is the first day of our new association! We must fine-tune certain elements of our act. Matching costumes might not be a bad idea. A logo. I'm rather good at visuals of that sort. Perhaps a stylized medicine bundle within a corona of rope? Prairie? Prairie James!"

She shook him still more forcefully and was rewarded by a counter motion as Prairie hunched up and, without ever opening both eyes, felt around in amongst his clothes. Son assumed he was searching for a shirt to cover himself. What in fact he unearthed was a small pistol, which he pointed directly at her head. He croaked, "One more word and you're a dead woman," and was asleep again before the empty pistol hit the floor.

Discouraged by Prairie's lack of enthusiasm for their newly born partnership, Son stepped out of the truck onto the unpaved parking lot of the Blue Lagoon Club. The Blue Lagoon was an old skating rink that had been converted into a dance hall. Son strained but could not recall how the gas-starved truck had effected the transfer from the rodeo arena. The last thing she did remember clearly was Prairie's bringing the house down by floating a rope halo over the tiaraed head of Miss Jordan Juneteenth. That was when the bottles of Wild Turkey started passing her way. Not wanting to offend local sensibilities, Son accepted all offerings. Prairie was swigging away, too. After that, no power on earth could get the arena cleared, and that was pretty much the end of that year's Jordan's Juneteenth Rodeo.

At some point that Son could not specify, the festivities shifted to the Blue Lagoon, where she felt herself a veritable homecoming queen. She recalled the pleasant sensation of being the belle of the ball. For once in her life, there had been no end of partners. Memories of the compelling African-American beat stirred through her. Son dropped her head, put both her hands up in front of her face, and executed the spine-shimmying waggle she had perfected the night before.

"Pink cadillac, pink cadillac," she sang to herself. The most astonishing moment in a long day filled with astonishing moments had occurred in the middle of one particularly inspired fandango involving a rhythmic thrusting to the side of her elbows accompanied by a spirited bobbing of her head, Son had looked up and seen, coming through the cloud of cigarette smoke and atomized sweat like a knight parting the mist of a fairy tale, a white horse with a black cowboy dressed in white standing, standing! on its back. It was Jackson!

For several long moments, it had seemed that only she could see the handsome concessionaire. Jackson came slowly to life and danced with measured grace, danced right where he stood on the horse's back, danced only for her. Then the crowd had erupted and pushed in around him. Jackson held out his hand to her. Son had looked around for Prairie, wanting him to witness her triumphal moment, but she couldn't find him in the smoky darkness. When she looked back, Jackson had vanished.

She'd searched for him in the parking lot and discovered that a bird-chirping day had dawned. Neither Jackson nor the horse was anywhere in sight. Sagging with disappointment and exhaustion, she'd made her way to the truck. Domino was gone and Prairie had already passed out on the floor. She thought that a moment's rest would be sufficient to refresh her for further terpischorean triumphs, but the second she lay down, she too was out.

Now, Son ducked around to the back of the Blue Lagoon, where she found Domino tethered to a long lead, chomping his way contentedly through a lush pasture. She made for the nearest cluster of trees. While she squatted in the shade, feeling the coolness from the damp earth, she noticed a certain gaminess about the armpit and orange crotch areas.

A stock tank at the far end of the pasture provided the perfect answer. As Son soaked naked in the murky water, lathering up the odd limb with a tiny bar of soap she'd stolen from the Dairy Queen, she already felt closer to her father. She'd penetrated and been accepted by his world, a world of pastoralists of color. Now that they were both inhabiting the same world, all that remained was to find him in it.

"Cootie Ramos." She repeated the name, happily sudsing under her armpits.

Son was so lost in a reverie in which she and her father were reunited that she failed to notice the sound of an approach behind her or to even see the shadow that fell across her naked shoulders. Not until hot breath poured in volcanic streams onto her bare neck did Son scream. Her shriek was answered by a startled whiffle, and Son jerked around to find him there, eyes bulging, ears pinned back, tether line dragging behind him.

"Domino, I'm sorry."

The horse bent down over her shoulder to take a drink. Son stroked his mane as he siphoned water up the great pipe of his neck. She sank back into the water. Far overhead a hawk wheeled. For the first time in longer than she could remember, she was in harmony with nature. *Hozro.*

"Pink cadillac, pink cadillac," she sang, working up a vigorous handful of suds. She waited until Domino was through drinking to rinse off.

Prairie felt like a heat wave wobbling in the sun as he leaned against the truck, attempting to reacquaint himself with verticality. While he rested, surveying the scene, searching for Domino, his mouth swung open on its hinge. Son was rising from her ablutions. Prairie was dumbstruck by the sheer quantity of that much pinky-white female flesh. It put him in mind of a mammoth Hostess cupcake, one of the pink marshmallow ones. On second glance, he realized that, in fact, he had known heftier women, just none that pale. Her radiance was what gave that ultra-jumbo impression. That while there was indeed a healthy abundance of womanflesh there, it was well-proportioned. Sheila and Hope had, if anything, been a bit too meager.

Abruptly, Prairie stopped his musing on Pocahontes' body. It had nothing to do with anything. She could have a rear end like a rhino and tits like a Las Vegas showgirl; neither condition was going to have the slightest effect on their relationship. Especially, Prairie corrected himself, since there was no relationship to affect in the first place. Other than the pigeon plucker-pluckee relationship. Which reminded him: he'd have to turn some attention to getting her to finance a run up to Hereford for that girls' rodeo gig.

She did have nice tits, though, Prairie noticed just before they disappeared beneath the maroon-piped shirt. He looked quickly away. He didn't want his new announcer catching him staring at her. Possible new announcer. He was still going to have to think this whole deal through. In any event, there was no chance that things would ever get personal. None.

As Prairie was dismissing the very possibility of any involvement, last night's triumph came back to him like a tune he'd been trying to place and filled his head with its sweet melody. He'd had the crowd eating out of the palm of his hand. With a little assistance from Son.

"Eunobia's Rope." He snorted, smiling as he saw again the look of amazement on Junior Cantrell's face after he'd snaked that cigar right out of his mouth. He wished the Sailor could have seen it. As Prairie stumbled away from the stock tank to find a place to piss, a tune came to him, and under his breath he sang, "Pink cadillac, pink cadillac."

Chapter 11.

The old cotton lands of east central Texas were already behind them before Son asked, "What is our destination? I
assume we're going to find Cootie Ramos?"

Prairie pulled onto Highway 59 heading north toward Houston. "Oh, yeah, right, Cootie."

"Sounds as if he'd know exactly where the reunion is to be
held."

"Yeah, sounds that way."

"Perfect, then. Where shall we begin searching?"

"I've got some ideas along that line. As I recall, last I heard
Cootie was up north. Herefore, I think it was. As chance would
have it, I'm also working a rodeo up there."

"Perfect," Son said again, settling in for the trip. Her hair,
washed with bar soap and dried in diesel exhaust, flew around her
head in the highway breeze whipping through the truck.

"You, uh, you did a good job last night. The announcing. You
can talk more shit than a Mexican radio."

Son, looking out the window at a stand of pine lumpy with
vines, smiled, and a strand of hair flapped across her lips. She wiped
it away with one finger and Prairie's heart knocked. But then she
held the finger up and started in again.

"What your basic mistake is, you are totally ignorant of the fundamentals of merchandising."

"My 'basic mistake?' What the hell are you—"

"Prairie, Prairie, rein in that male ego. A new day is dawning for us. We need to work together to seize it. Now, clearly, the time I spent being buffeted by the hurly-burly world of commerce has left me much the shrewder judge of human nature."

"Oh, my aching fanny! You? A shrewd judge of human nature?"

"I'll choose to ignore that. As I was saying, in dealing with the public your basic mistake has been to sell the meat rather than the marinade."

"What in Christ's name are you talking about now?"

" 'Sell the marinade, not the meat.' Really, Prairie, it's one of the cornerstones of advertising."

"You mean 'sell the sizzle, not the steak'?"

"The marketing principle remains the same. Create a need; that's your basic mistake."

"Just a warning. That 'basic mistake' back there, that was your last one."

"All right, all right, I bow to the debutante sensitivity of the male ego. I know the havoc that can be wreaked if one does not tread warily. The death threats. The high-speed car chases."

That was the other thing Prairie was getting tired of, hearing these stories about all the men that had done her wrong. Death threats and guys coming after her. She didn't look the type that would excite those kinds of passions. He sneaked a sidelong glance at her.

Good coloring. Her cheeks had flamed up a little when she started talking about ideas for the act, and her hair, loose and blowing in the wind, was shiny as wet seal fur even though she had washed it in a stock tank. Still, she was not the kind to excite passions. Certainly not his. But he knew that there was a world of loser men out there just waiting to make giant fools of themselves over loser women. She must have hooked up with her share.

"The challenge we face, then, is to create a need where none exists. The cruel fact is that no one actually *needs* a middle-aged man with a bit of a paunch performing various gyrations with a length of rope."

"Hey, hey, hey!"

"Please, don't become exercised at what is nothing more than a bald statement of fact. Need is the most unreliable predictor of a product's success. Take toothpaste, for example."

"Would you mind not referring to me as a 'product.' I'm a performer."

"Performer. Product. Talent. Toothpaste. The careers of any number of adolescent screen idols prove the differences to be neglible."

Prairie slid a discreet hand off the wheel and, pretending to adjust his belt, felt the tube of flesh around his middle. Tonight, two hundred sit-ups. And no more sweet bubbly drinks for a while. "You're a hell of a one to be talking about paunches."

"Oh, now I'm to be berated for the metabolic differences between men and women. It's a known physiological fact that women are far more efficient consumers of calories than men are. That is simply an evolutionary given over which I have no control. It was not my idea to be born a walking incubator, capable of sustaining myself and thereby, theoretically, perpetuating the species on the barest of morsels. Dieting for women, especially an amply loined woman such as myself, is an exercise in futility. The less I eat, the less my body requires to keep my Junoesque proportions fully maintained."

For a second, Son convinced Prairie. Then he mustered compelling evidence to the contrary. "So, what accounts for Jackie O?" He named the skinniest woman he could think of.

"Oh, well, certainly, if a woman has a Greek shipping fortune to draw upon in her battle with the imperatives of reproduction . . ."

"Come on, there's lots of skinny babes out there who don't have a Greek shipping fortune."

"I will not sacrifice my dental enamel upon the altar of some male-manufactured ideal of feminine beauty!"

"Jeez, who was asking you to? You mean that bucolia stuff? That eat-upchuck syndrome?" He'd been married to Sheila for two years before he found out that her weight control secret was a finger down the throat after she'd eaten everything in the refrigerator, right down to the Miracle Whip. Come to think of it, her teeth had been going a bit gray there at the end.

For the next forty miles, they listened without speaking to the multitude of grinding creaks and shredding groans of a front-end suspension lethally abused by the demands of a chip route. Just as Prairie had lost himself in the problem of how to get Son to buy him some new shocks, she screamed "Stop!"

Startled into action, Prairie hit the brakes so hard that Domino slid forward until he panted big hot circles on the windshield.

"What!" Prairie yelled, his heart jackhammering in his throat.

"That franchise outlet we just passed back on the right. It had a Salad Bar Special advertised."

Prairie tried to paste Son one right in the freckles, but Domino was wedged between them. "You screamed like that for a freaking Salad Bar Special?" Even Domino, long acquainted with Prairie's temper, shrank away from the blast.

"Well . . ." Son quailed just a bit, enough for Prairie to realize that for once he'd taken the wind out of her sails. "All that talk about dieting excited my hypothalamus and my system is now suffused with hormones madly signaling an impending electrolyte imbalance if I do not receive nourishment immediately."

"PUUUH!" Domino's lips flapped with a mighty expulsion of air.

Prairie massaged the tight wedge of pain between his eyebrows, then rammed the truck into reverse, and backed it up along the shoulder until he could swivel into the parking lot of the Sizzlin' Sirloin Steakhouse. He stepped out of the truck and knew immediately from the rotten-egg smell of natural gas that they were in Luling, Texas. He always avoided eating in that town.

Inside, they were the only patrons pushing their orange trays along a cafeteria serving line set up beneath a chandelier made from an old wagon wheel. Or what looked to Prairie like an old wagon wheel until Son pointed out the seams running along it where the molded plastic had been glued together. The first stop on the line was a self-service case of desserts. Prairie surreptitiously touched his midriff bulge again. When he stood up, it was hardly noticeable. He took a piece of congealed chocolate pie and put it on his tray.

Son, in line behind Prairie, commented, "Diabolical arrangement. Put the discretionary choice items first before the tray fills up with necessities. Clever. Very clever indeed."

At the drinks, Prairie passed over glasses of orange and red punch and took an iced tea. Son snagged a water and seven wedges of lemon.

"Hep you with an entrée today?" asked a sprightly girl with an orange-and-brown-print bandana around her neck. Prairie studied the wood-burned rope letters of the menu and ordered the eight-ounce sirloin, medium well. Fries instead of baked potato. The girl put a plastic triangle embossed with the number 32 on Prairie's tray, and he slid along.

"Hep *you* with an entrée today?" the girl asked Son.

Son ordered a baked potato.

"With fixin's?" the counter girl asked.

"How much extra are they?"

"Depends." She turned around to point to the menu. "The Texas Tater with mesquite-smoked bacon and cheese is two fifty-nine. The Veggie Spud with broccoli and cheese is two thirty-nine. The—"

"No, I'll have the plain baked potato for one twenty-nine."

Prairie turned to her. "I thought that the whole idea behind our emergency stop was for you to get this Salad Bar Special." Son kicked him in the shins. Prairie's brow furrowed. "The fug you kick me for?"

The counter girl stood motionless, waiting for a resolution.

"A plain, completely unadorned baked potato will be sufficient," Son ordered serenely.

The girl pulled a foil-wrapped baker out of the warming oven, slid it onto an oval plate, and delivered it to Son's tray, where it sat next to her glass of water and lemon wedges on an otherwise empty orange expanse.

"Is that all you're eating?" Prairie asked.

Son eyed him icily. "Yes, thank you for your concern. This is all I will be taking in the way of nourishment."

Prairie liked the women he was with to heap their plates high, to order the most expensive thing on the menu along with an appetizer and dessert. Whether they ate the meal or not was immaterial. That was one of the things he liked best about Hope, the way she ordered ten times more than she could ever fit into her birdlike body. She'd just pick at the enormous slabs of meat, the wedges of cheesecake dripping with cherry goo. He enjoyed telling waiters, "I believe the lady is through with that." Of course, Sheila had her own way of dealing with a stacked plate.

The girl hit a few buttons on a computerized register and chirped out, "That'll be eight eighty-four." Prairie grabbed for his wallet. He'd cover the baked potatoes as long as she was shelling out for clutches and gas.

As he reseated his wallet, Son pushed ahead and staked out a table. Prairie followed, holding his tray in one hand and sliding his wallet into his back pocket with the other. He stopped when he saw the table she'd picked. He couldn't understand why, in a nearly empty restaurant, she had to choose the one table that was wedged between two families of the heftiest human beings he had ever set eyes on.

"How about this one here?" Prairie called out to her, stopping at an isolated booth. His tray was fully unloaded before he noticed that Son had gone right ahead and colonized the table crowded in between the two teams of eating machines. Prairie glared at her and jerked his head over to his booth. Son ignored him. He looked around, rolled his eyes, let a long, irritated sigh hiss out between his teeth, loaded his tray back up, and stalked over to her table. He carefully offloaded tea, steak number, and utensils, and placed the empty tray on a nearby table.

"Why did you pick this table?" he asked, sitting down.

Son was engrossed in sliding her baked potato off its plate onto the tray she had not bothered to clear and remove, and didn't answer. Prairie considered it a sign of very low breeding not to unload and remove the tray.

Son methodically squeezed all seven lemon wedges into her water, then emptied a quarter of the sugar container into it for a free glass of lemonade. Prairie scowled. Already, the greasy-chinned families staked out on either side of him were cutting into his appetite. The noise was like two sump pumps in full sucking operation as both groups—elbows on the table, heads way down low—sluiced up gargantuan quantities of food.

Son took the potato plate and trotted off to the salad bar. Prairie watched as she wedged her way in between two intent diners bellying up for their umpteenth refill at the potato salad trough.

Watching Son break for the victuals, Prairie noted the sort of elbow action that earns penalties in the NBA. It paid off, though, and Son edged up to the salad bar. More jockeying ensued when all three of them went for the last gherkin in the crock. Son lunged for it, overshot, and crashed into the sneeze guard. It swayed and rattled over the action. The collision upset Son's timing. She would have lost the tiny pickle entirely had she not eschewed the plastic tongs placed in each tub and simply snatched up the prize with her hand.

Once the brine settled and the sneeze guard stopped swaying, the two belly-gods backed off and gave Son some room. They knew they were in the presence of a serious all-you-can-eat competitor. As for Prairie, he too came to a new understanding: Son had picked this table to be closer to the action.

She returned with her plate mounded triumphantly with

crudités, macaroni salad, corn relish, black olives, garbanzo beans, shaved bell peppers, sliced cucumbers, croutons, and Thousand Island dressing. Everything was stained bright pink from the pickled beets and topped with one warty green gherkin.

Son's long experience with overstuffed plates became immediately apparent when she artfully imploded the hillock of food in front of her by removing several carrot stanchions to create strategic cave-ins. Prairie was so fascinated by the machinelike disposal of food taking place at his own and the surrounding tables that he was surprised when the bandanaed counter girl slid his steak in front of him.

The girl started to leave, stopped, and turned back. Without breaking stride, Son discreetly nabbed the receipt for their meals that Prairie had laid down beside his glass of tea and casually dragged it through her three-bean salad.

"Uh, excuse me?" The counter girl touched her lips with a tentative finger, then pointed at Son's potato. "Uh, did you have the salad bar? I don't remember you ordering the—"

"What sort of accusation are you making?" Son asked.

Prairie glanced around. He'd never before been with a woman who could hit the decibel levels this babe could.

"You just had the plain potato," the counter girl answered.

"Please, simply check the receipt you yourself rang up before you accuse my companion of fleecing you on the bill."

"Me?" Prairie hit himself in the chest.

Son fished out the receipt. The girl took the transparent scrap in her pincered fingers. "I can't read this; it's all oily." The girl, evidence dissolving in her hand, backed down. Prairie stood to leave.

"Don't you want a doggie bag for that?" Son asked, pointing a fork at the untouched steak.

"I might. If I was a doggie." Prairie's barb was lost on Son, who was already appropriating his Texas toast and making a cottage cheese–and–bacon bit sandwich to eat later. Prairie left.

He went to the truck and spent the next twenty-five minutes debating why he shouldn't leave this loony tune with the other manatees at the salad bar. He told himself that it was because of her scarlet money belt sash. When Son finally came out, she was carrying his steak in a piece of foil and had two large plastic cups full of soft ice cream that came to a whirling point on top. She handed him one.

"It comes with your meal for a nickel. A most ingenious serve-yourself, honor-system arrangement."

Prairie took the cup. "So what did you pay? Four cents?"

"No, I consider a nickel to be more than reasonable."

"A nickel? You're sure about that? You sure that isn't too steep? You sure the merchandising monolith isn't gyping you?"

"Your sarcasm is not lost on me," Son said grandly, climbing into the truck.

Prairie got in. Son was slurping away at the ice cream. Her shirt was spotted with clots of cottage cheese and dribbles of mayonnaise. Prairie wondered how he ever could have found her the least bit attractive. Back on the highway, he asked testily, "Are you planning to wear that terrific outfit the whole trip?"

"When I require the services of a fashion coordinator, you will be the first to know," Son answered. She finished the rest of the ice cream without a sound.

The next two hundred miles passed in a silence broken only by Domino's eloquent array of snorts, huffs, and other unclassifiable equine exhalations. By the time they hit Brownwood, Prairie had just about decided that he'd been a little too harsh and was considering breaking the silence. They were stuck behind an old lady, frozen at a four-way stop, when Son beat him to it.

"I'm not making the most of this opportunity for spiritual growth," she said.

Thinking that Son had been brooding for the last four hours about what he'd said to her in the Sizzlin' Sirloin Steakhouse parking lot, Prairie was caught off-guard by her remark. "Hey, you going to move any time soon!" he yelled out the window at the hesitant old lady.

"Yes, I think that in order to be fully prepared to meet my father, I must first know myself. For that reason, I will be embarking upon a vision quest."

Fifty miles later he asked, "What's a fricking vision quest?"

"It was central to indigenous North American populations, particularly the buffalo-hunting Plains Indian. Practically every young brave went on such a quest in the hope of having a spiritual vision to guide his life. Typically, the young man would go off by himself for several days to a high hill to fast and search for that one essential link between himself and nature."

"Huh."

"We have the account of a young Sioux brave, Chewing Black Bones, who, when he was only twelve years old, left his camp and journeyed to a high bluff. There he fasted and put sharp stones between his toes and sand in his eyes to make himself stay awake. For three days he waited for a spirit or a message. His eyes burned and his stomach growled. He became sick and dizzy and felt prickles in his hands and feet." Son added a couple of her own symptoms. "He tried to return to the spot where he had hobbled his pony, but fell, delirious, under a large cottonwood tree.

"A man came riding, light and airy, on a wide-rumped Appaloosa. The arrows and lead balls of the Long Knives floated harmlessly past this warrior. His cheeks were painted with a zigzag of lightning. His body was polka-dotted with the marks of hailstones. Over his head flew a small red-backed hawk. The man's own people came around him, reaching out their arms toward him.

"When Chewing Black Bones awoke, he knew that the red-backed hawk was his supernatural helper and his marks of personal power were a zigzag lightning and dotted-hailstone design. That boy went on to become a great warrior and a great chief."

Prairie loved stories about boys from humble backgrounds who rose to greatness on their own hook. He hid his interest in Chewing Black Bones with a blasé "You don't say. So that's what you're going to do, huh? Fast and put pebbles between your toes? You want me to drop you off at the next high bluff?"

"Hah. Very amusing. No, of course my quest will have to be modified somewhat in deference to the changing circumstances wrought by our modern age. Though I would, naturally, prefer a remote setting of harsh natural beauty, I believe that the spirits will understand why I must seek for my personal vision here on the interstate."

"Yeah, the spirits are probably real flexible guys. House calls and everything."

Son ignored the remark. Already she could feel her spirit rising to a higher plain. "I shall begin fasting immediately."

"Shit, what you put away at lunch, you could not only fast, you could go into hibernation."

"I have a rather elevated metabolism. Given the efficiency of my system, I predict I shall be on the verge of hallucination within a day."

"Well, just so's you're okay for announcing."

"Unless actually in the throes of a vision, I can promise you that I will be fully capable of narrating your performance."

"*Perfecto*. Knock yourself out."

Son didn't hear Prairie's last comment. She was staring, unfocused, into the middle distance, testing how long she could go without blinking before the pain became so intense that it brought on visions. She wondered if any of the great chiefs of the past had ever stood up to the autonomic nervous system.

As they passed through Abilene, Prairie sung tunelessly about the "prettiest town that I ever seen. Abilene, my Abilene." He had to wonder if the composer had actually ever visited the desolate burg or if he'd just never been anywhere else to make a comparison.

"STOP!"

Son's scream jolted Prairie out of the very comfy road coma he had settled into, involving a couple of double-jointed Brazilian sisters he'd met in São Paulo back in 'sixty-two. With a great scraping of hoof against metal, Domino skidded forward, coming to rest once again with his panting nostrils fogging hot circles on the windshield.

"Could you please back up?" Prairie heard Son request, though he couldn't see her for Domino's bulk.

"What! What! I hit someone?"

"No. I want to make certain that the sign on that clothing store says 'Going Out *of* Business' and not 'Going Out *for* Business.' I've been victimized by the merchandiser's preposition ploy before."

All the adrenaline molecules stampeding through Prairie's body halted abruptly. In less time than it takes to say "Fight or Flight," they switched their compass headings from Panic to Anger, and Prairie barked out, "You're talking about a goddamm sale! For the second time in a row, you almost put my horse's head through the windshield because of a goddamm sale! Because you want a deal on a pair of pantyhose, you put my horse's head through the windshield! You are one for the books, sister, you really are."

"I only noticed because of what you said about my attire."

The adrenaline molecules stopped and looked at one another in confusion. "You mean because I asked if you had another outfit?"

"Normally I care very little for sales, discounts, cost-cutter specials, bargain bonanzas, and the like, but as my means are limited and your comment wounded my pride . . ."

Not wanting to hear any more, Prairie backed up the truck and stopped in front of Karla's Kasuals. Satisfied that Karla was indeed going belly-up, Son hopped out to pick the bones of the beached merchandiser. Prairie elected to wait in the truck.

He studied the map, plotting out the rest of their trip. Right where the handle would have screwed onto the pan was his destination, Hereford. He was not cheered by the desiccated sound of the names in between: Chalk, Needmore, Sand. The map flapped in his hand when Domino blew a mighty gust over his shoulder.

"So what's *your* complaint? You need a new pair pantyhose too?" Domino snorted again, and Prairie put the map aside and straightened up in the seat. "All right, all right, walksies." The last word excited Domino unutterably. His flanks shivered as if he were flicking off a swarm of black flies. He shook his head and blew slobbery raspberries. When Prairie got out of the truck, he glanced in at Son through the store window. She was standing beside a bin filled with clearance items, checking seams and searching for make-up smears.

After exercising and watering Domino, Prairie returned. Son was still grubbing through the bin. There was something cozily domestic about waiting for a woman while she shopped; it lulled Prairie. He awoke to the loud crinkling of plastic bags, large as beanbag chairs, being stuffed into the rack he'd built in the back of the truck. Like a cowbird seizing another's nest for her own young, Son knocked his things out of the way to make room for her purchases. Prairie was too mesmerized to protest.

"That is quite some outfit," he said, still trying to take it all in. Son, decked out in a starchy new square-dance ensemble with the scarlet sash knotted around her waist, looked now like a Hostess Sno-ball with a waist. Many rows of silver rickrack circled the enormous pouf of the skirt floating atop a stiff cloud of petticoats.

"Yes, well." Son smoothed down the skirt, which bounced right back up. "I thought that a bit of flamboyance might not be amiss in my capacity as announcer. That it would contribute to the . . . the act."

Prairie didn't know what to think. On the one hand, he was touched that anyone gave that much thought to his performance. On the other, he didn't know how much of a contribution a big, fluffy, hot pink square-dance get-up would be.

Son dug around through a hefty pile of merchandise in one of the bags and pulled out a package. She held it out to Prairie. Before he could take it, she jerked it back, tore off the many-times-re-duced price tag, and handed it back.

Prairie read the label. "Tube socks." And, indeed, the package contained three pairs, two with red and blue stripes at the top, one with green and yellow stripes. He looked up, baffled. "Thanks. I needed some new ones." He tried and failed to recall the last time someone had bought him a present.

"They're all cotton. Exclusive of decoration," Son explained.

"Well, that's . . . that's good. That's the best kind."

Prairie looked at Son. Her legs seemed more naked beneath the puffy skirt than they had in the stock tank. In spite of her being a brunette, the hair on them was blond. Her plastic boots with their turned-up toes looked worse than ever. Prairie absentmindedly squashed the puffy bag of socks.

"Does Karla have boots?" he asked.

"In fact, she has quite an attractive selection. However, she appears to be holding an unrealistically firm line in the shoe department that—"

Son's last statement ended when Prairie came around to her side of the truck, opened the door, and escorted her out. Inside Karla's, he found a pair of fancy boots that came all the way up to Son's dimpled knees. On the front of each boot bloomed a yellow rose with thorny branches wrapping down around the ankles. As soon as he'd ascertained that the boots fit, and seen the longing way Son looked back over her shoulder at the thorns on her ankles, he bought them over her loud protests. She maintained stoutly that a truly hideous pair with lime-green butterflies splayed across them was a much better buy at half the price.

"You're my announcer; you need to look good," Prairie said, dragging crumpled ones and fives out of every pocket he had. Then he threw the plastic boots away.

Son never thanked him, but she stared at the yellow roses all the way to Hereford.

Chapter 12.

After driving from one corner of the largest state in the contiguous United States all the way to a corner at its opposite side, Prairie and Son managed to pull into Hereford at the exact moment that the big Friday evening parade, signaling the start of Hereford's Frontier Days, got under way. Because the street ahead was blocked off and several pickups had crowded in behind him, Prairie switched off the ignition, and they sat with one half of Hereford, Texas, and watched the other half marched past.

The Deaf Smith County Home Demonstration Clubs sponsored a flatbed truck crowded with grandmotherly types in over-sized bifocals, their names written in rhinestones along the bottom corner, wearing sunbonnets, churning butter, and holding off Indian attack.

"Scary," Prairie commented, shuddering. Son didn't know if he referred to the Indians or the clubwomen.

A Frontier Days princess, wearing a big smile and a tiara, rode by straddling the T-top of a Pontiac Firebird. Her red velvet train trimmed in softball-sized white pompoms trailed behind her, flowing over the trunk and brushing the tops of the tire wells. "Bet you could fry an egg in that babe's armpit. Little hot for capes, wouldn't you say?"

•   "The beauty pageant sort will endure any torture for the privilege of displaying her dental arch to an adoring throng," Son informed him. "Where," she asked, "do you intend to begin your search for Cootie Ramos?"

"Cootie? He here in Hereford? Oh, yeah, no, right. Sure, I'll get a line on old Coot. Ask around. But I have to be discreet, understand?"

"I do."

"Hey, look." Prairie pointed up the street, ending the conversation. "You could hop right on board that float. Blend right in."

The Hereford Charros float slowly ground up the street. On board were a dozen men in heavily embroidered short jackets and wide sombreros, hands clasped behind their backs, facing a dozen lovely señoritas done up in billowing fiesta dresses not unlike Son's square-dancing ensemble.

"There are similarities." Son patted the rickrack-encrusted V-neck of her hot pink top.

The Antique Car Club putted by next, followed by the Hereford High Marching Band and Twirlers.

"Oh, look at those lines, will you?" Son, the old veteran, wailed. "Tighten up the ranks, you clodhoppers!" she yelled out the window. A row of gangly teenage boys, attempting to render Lionel Richie's "Dancing on the Ceiling" on slide trombones and march at the same time, turned to stare, barely missing guillotining one another with their instruments.

Prairie's attention, on the other hand, had been riveted by the panties of the Hereford High Twirlers as they swept spinning silver batons between their luscious pubescent thighs.

"What sort of formation is that?" Son continued to fume as the band wobbled down the street. "Mr. Kugelhoff would have marched us until our feet bled, had we ever performed so poorly."

"Yeah, it's shocking," Prairie commented, his voice throbbing with heartfelt emotion as he watched a twirler bend over to retrieve an errant baton. "A real crying shame."

Following the Rotary Club's grand prize Chevy Biscayne, the

Lazy R Riding Club, and the Sheriff's Posse came the contestants for the women's rodeo. They were a no-nonsense crew who looked as if they could get the job done, whatever it might be. Without exception they wore long-sleeved Western shirts, hats and girdle-tight jeans accordioning over the insteps of their boots. Everyone from the minute barrel racers with their sixteen-inch waists to the brawny rough stock riders with their weight-lifters' torsos sat tall in the saddle.

"I'd hate to meet any of those babes in a dark alley," Prairie said as a bullrider passed by. He looked over at Son; her normally peckish expression was replaced by open wonder.

"What a thrilling victory over the male pastoralist tradition," she whispered.

Prairie squinted. "Come again?"

"Women in rodeo. It confounds all of the most sacred symbols of masculine domination inherent in the pastoralist tradition as portrayed in America via cowboy mythology, wherein cattle and women both belong to a natural world that must be conquered."

"Oh, yeah. Right. My thoughts exactly. Sheesh."

The stiff-backed horsewomen seemed aware of a continuing obligation to prove themselves to the many inheritors of the cowboy myth standing in the crowd, arms folded belligerently across their chests, sides of their mouths goitered with wads of chewing tobacco. Their mounts were freshly washed and clipped, hooves blacked. They all held the flags staked on their saddles up straight and stared ahead like choir members looking off to glory.

All, that is, except for one red-haired prankster who was turned completely around in her saddle, staring at her horse's tail at the exact moment it arched up to allow several bonus-sized plops of used grass to fall. With her hands behind her holding the reins, the jokester goofing on the artificial solemnity of the event looked like a handcuffed police suspect. But her posture wasn't the only un-usual quality about the rider. She had one red-haired child mounted in front of her and another one wedged in behind.

"Tuffie Branch!" Son yelled.

"You know Tuffie?" Prairie asked, incredulous.

"Yes. We met at Deutscher Downs. We became exceptionally close in a short span of time."

"Sounds like Tuffie."

"She's the one who first told me about you and El Marinero's reunion."

"Gee, I'll have to thank Tuff soon as I can."

Prairie stared at the mother of five turned around in the saddle like a monkey on a donkey's back at the circus, smiled, shook his head, and said, under his breath, "Tuffie Branch."

With no warning, Son jumped out of the truck, stepped over the barrier, and strode through the tangle of riders. Horses were pulled up short and reined in sharply to avoid her.

"Tuffie. Tuffie Branch! It's me, Son Hozro!"

Tuffie grinned her Huck Finn grin. "Son! I *love* your outfit! Where did you get them boots? I'd give my eyeteeth for a pair of boots like them!"

"I took your advice!" Son had to break into a light jog to keep up with Tuffie. "I hooked up with Prairie James! He's helping me find my father!"

Tuffie's smile faded and she searched the crowd. "Prairie's here?"

Son pointed back over her shoulder to the chip truck, where Prairie was slumped behind the wheel. Tuffie followed her finger straight to Prairie's face. "I'm the narrator now for Prairie James's History in Hemp pageant."

With a crinkly-eyed stare trained on Prairie, who raised a slow finger to his hat in salute, Tuffie smiled again, shook her head, and said, under her breath, "Prairie James."

"We're looking for Cootie Ramos!"

Tuffie's horse trotted ahead to fill a small break in the line, and Son ran after her.

"You heard anything about where he might be? Where El Marinero's reunion is?" Tuffie shrugged, and Son stopped and let the riders eddy around her. "See you at the rodeo!" she yelled to her friend.

Tuffie waved, seemingly unaware that the child behind her, Lasso, the eight-year-old girl twin, was sprawled across her horse's neck, and the small-sized child in front, Jonathan, four, was putting a tiny boot in her eye as he attempted to scale her head. Other horsewomen passed Son, and the ranks closed around Tuffie.

Son climbed back into the truck. "Tuffie doesn't know where Cootie Ramos is, but this is still going to be a great rodeo. All women. Can you believe it?"

"Just barely," Prairie answered, still staring after Tuffie. He looked away when the riders turned a corner. "Let's grab something to eat."

This time Prairie insisted on choosing their dining spot, and led the way to Dagoberto's Café. Dagoberto's was long on black wrought iron, serapes in poisonously vivid colors, and straw sombreros tacked to the walls.

"The chiles rellenos are great here," Prairie advised after he was installed at a table behind a Jumborita the size of a small wash basin with, as he had requested, sugar on the rim instead of salt.

"I will not be taking any nourishment," Son declared, closing her laminated menu decisively. "I must continue mortifying the flesh in preparation for my vision quest. I will consume neither food nor drink until the spirits have communicated their higher plan to me."

"It's your funeral, babe." Prairie slurped up his Jumborita, using the tiny stirrer as a straw.

"If my thirst becomes more than I can bear, I might suck on a pebble. But that is all I shall allow myself."

"Well, I didn't see pebbles on the menu, but I'm sure Dagoberto can fix you up with some road gravel or something. Listen, can you advance me a few bucks until I get paid? The boots kind of cleaned me out."

The request dismayed Son. Reflexively, she reached for a tortilla chip and took a handful. "I doubt that even the great chiefs of the past would count a bit of ground maize as food," she explained through a fine spray of chip particles. She swallowed. "Why did you order that birdbath of a drink when you knew you couldn't pay for it? Alcoholic concoctions are the restaurateurs' highest mark-up items. It would have been much more cost-effective to have purchased a bottle of tequila and downed several snorts on the way over here. The effect would have been the same."

"Hey, why don't I just go out right now and find a big rock and hit myself over the head with it? The effect would be the same, and think of the savings. You gonna front me the dough or what?"

After dinner, Son went reluctantly into the ladies' room, where she secreted herself in a stall and removed the scarlet sash. The stack of bills Walter had given her for her truck was dwindling fast. Since she was already half undressed, Son decided to take full advantage of Dagoberto's ladies' lounge. She locked the door, filled up the basin, and had herself a little sponge bath to clear away the road grime. When she stepped out, fresh and perky again, she saw that Prairie had used her long absence to cultivate the friendship of their waitress, Frenchie, a middle-aged Latina, still pretty in spite of a bad bleach job and too much eye make-up.

Frenchie was leaning far over, affording Prairie an unobstructed view of her thorax as she cleared away the four chip baskets Son had emptied in her struggle not to eat anything. Prairie crooked his finger at her and Frenchie leaned in closer so that he could whisper in her ear. She stood back up, gave him a shocked look, then broke into flirtatious titters.

Son looked down at the money in her hand and removed the overly generous ten percent tip she had included. Prairie could just worry about the gratuity all on his own.

Out in the truck, Prairie drove them through the darkness to a neighborhood on the outskirts of Hereford made up of old Quonset huts shipped in when a temporary flight school had shut down after the Korean War. The odd, humpbacked dwellings stood on piers like giant, jacked-up pillbugs abandoned on the flat scrubland.

Prairie pulled up in front of one that had a tire painted white and filled with daisies in the otherwise barren front yard.

Prairie said, "Frenchie? Our waitress? Anyway, she's a big animal lover. Said we could park here tonight. Put Domino out in the back."

A car's headlights came up the road and turned into the driveway beside the hut on stilts. Frenchie got out and waited on the porch.

"Uh, look," Prairie said, checking his hair in the rearview mirror and raking his fingers through the dusty strands. "That's her now. Listen, I'm just going to go in. Thank her. You know, for her hospitality. Like that. You want to set Domino up in the back?"

He started to get out, but paused. "So you'll be okay?"

"I shall take full advantage of your absence to concentrate on my vision quest."

"Good, babe. Great. That's the attitude." He hurried away.

Son watched him trot up the waitress's front steps. The porch light shone briefly on the thinning spot at the top of his head as he held the door open for Frenchie, then followed her inside. Son wasn't aware of how long she stared at the porch light until she noticed Domino craning his neck, staring too. He looked at her, puzzled.

"In answer to your question," Son informed him, "he won't be coming back."

The porch light clicked off.

Chapter 13.

The Hereford Rodeo Arena on the outskirts of town didn't look as if it could serve for a B-team scrimmage. It was little more than a dusty field, recently disked, five miles from the nearest tree, where spectators could sit on wooden bleachers and bake in an inhuman heat. A banner welcomed the National Women's Finals Rodeo.

Dozens of cowgirl contestants stood around in clusters on the unpaved parking lot, talking or warming up their horses. The lot was littered with horse trailers, pickup trucks, and, here and there, tucked onto the shaded side of trucks and trailers, a playpen. In one of those playpens, a toddler with sunburned cheeks, wearing a T-shirt that read, "My Momma Is a Roping Lady," held his arms up to his mother, a cowgirl in a dark hat with a number safety-pinned to the back of her long-sleeved Western shirt.

"I gotta go find the secretary, find out what the program is here," Prairie said, sliding out of the truck. He backed Domino out and took him along to give the horse a stretch.

Son was still feeling like an indentured servant after her night alone in the chip truck. Although Prairie had brought her out a piece of toast spread with Sioux Bee honey that morning, she had not been invited into the Quonset hut. She refused the toast, saying

that she had to continue mortifying her flesh. Prairie hadn't tried
to argue with her.

All during the ride over to the arena grounds she wondered
what the piney scent pouring off him might be. Only as they were
parking did she identify the fragrance as one Tinka was much given
to marinating herself in before "special" dates with the Count. She
recognized it as an especially noxious green bath slurry called
Vitabath.

As she walked through the parked trucks, Son noticed that
most of the fancier ones had bumper stickers identifying their own-
ers as barrel racers. Searching for a bathroom, she found her way
over to a large metal building with *Show Barn* written on the side.

Inside, contestants bustled back and forth. Son stepped in and
experienced a feeling she had never known before. Dressed in her
fluffy pink outfit, with her knee-high yellow rose boots, surrounded
by women dragging spurs, occasionally sporting the faded outline
of a Skoal tin in the back pocket of their Wranglers, Son felt not
only feminine, but too feminine.

To hide her consternation, she retreated to a nearby bulletin
board and joined a woman studying it. Son pretended to do like-
wise and found two long lists, one of female names, the other of
numbers, letters, and animal names.

"You get a good draw?" asked the woman? Son faced her. She
stood six feet tall, had the shoulders of a hammer thrower, the
broad-brimmed, high-crowned cowboy hat of a thirties cowgirl,
and the smile of a homecoming queen. Two meager squirts of
brown pigtail popped out behind her ears. "Look who I got." The
woman put a cracked thumbnail under her name, Bucko Bukowski,
then ran a crease over to the name beside it, Terminator. "Just my
luck, huh? I can't never draw me no cruncher when I need 'em."
Son glanced up to the top of the column. It was headed by the word
Bulls.

"You're not rough stock, are you?" Bucko spoke with the
growly kind of west Texas accent that caused her jaw to sling forward a bit and sound as if there were a pool of saliva under her

tongue she was trying not to disturb as it washed her speech with an odd sibilance.

"Me?" Son asked.

"Naw, you got them roper's eyes. Where you from?"

Son liked the idea of having roper's eyes and she narrowed them in a keen-sighted sort of way. "San Antonio," Son lied.

"San An*tone!*" Bucko whooped. "You go the finals they had there back in, when was it, 'seventy-eight, 'seventy-nine?"

Son lied and said she had. That the experience had been most exhilarating.

"You think so?" Bucko asked. "I thought they's the most fucked-up finals we ever had. You see who Boots drew?" She turned back to the roster and pointed to the name of Tuffie's adorable seventeen-year-old daughter, Boots Branch, then read aloud the name of the bull she'd drawn, Leatherface.

"And look at this." Bucko pointed her cracked thumbnail to "Tuffie Branch" and "Rambo." "Oh, well, good-by Champion Bulls. They might just as well rename it the Branch Buckle, with all them girls she's got coming up. Not to mention she rides best when she's pregnant anyway."

"Do you mean that Tuffie and her daughter both ride bulls?" Son asked.

"Well, don't sound so danged astonished." The voice behind Son had the reedy, cracking tones of an incomplete recovery from a case of laryngitis.

"Tuffie!" Son turned around to look down on the short redhead.

"I see you met the third best female bullrider in the world," Tuffie said, taking a playful poke at Bucko.

"You better watch who you're calling third best. I'm comin' after you, girl! You look in your rearview, that'll be me on your tail!" She returned Tuffie's poke and the two women danced around, taking good-natured swats at each other. It was like watching a bear spar with a fox.

Suddenly, Tuffie got hold of herself. "Whoa! What am I do-

ing, carrying on like a crazy woman? I'm the designated representative for the rough stock riders." She grabbed Son and pulled her
away from the bulletin board. "Come on, you're the one's good
with words. I got to go speak to the board. You can help me get out
what it is I want to say." With Son in tow, Tuffie pushed through
the crowd. The people she knocked aside whirled around to face
her with angry scowls that melted away the instant they saw it was
Tuffie Branch. She was greeted from all sides.

"All *right!* The Tuffwoman is among us!"

"Tuffie, come over say hello when you get through!"

"Tuffie, ain't you given up this crazy life yet?"

"You see me in a pine box!" Tuffie shouted back as she kept
forging ahead. Odd as it had been for Son to feel feminine, the
overwhelming sensation of being liked that poured off Tuffie like
wake from a boat was even stranger. Just bathing in the propwash
of popularity was a revelation to Son.

Midway through the crowd, Tuffie took a sharp detour toward
the only group of males in the building. There were half a dozen of
them, late teens, early twenties, slouching in a circle, pant legs
purposely tucked half in, half out of their boots, hips cocked,
thumbs hooked over their belts. From the center of their cluster
came a crystalline, soprano laugh that danced on the air, bewitch-
ing the cowboys, then suddenly seized up and cracked into the
trademark Branch tones.

"Boots!" Tuffie yelled. "Come on out here!"

The male huddle stiffened and fell silent.

"Boots! Get your fanny out here this minute!"

Boots Branch stepped tentatively out of the forest of muscle.
Her color was high and her eyes danced with the lively sparkle of a
girl who loves nothing more in the world than to be in the middle
of a circle of boys competing with one another to make her laugh.
She opened her mouth to join in the laughter, and Son saw the one
thing that marred her prettiness: teeth mottled brown from well
water. The color and sparkle left Boots's face as soon as she saw her
mother.

"Mo-o-om," she whined, exasperated.

Tuffie grabbed her and pulled her along. "I told you we was gonna speak to the board today. You got a comb on you?"

Boots dived into her shoulder bag and pulled out a styling brush with a perforated handle and black plastic bristles. Tuffie ran it through her shoulder-length hair without slowing her brisk, choppy stride at all. Bits of sawdust flew into the air as she brushed. She handed her daughter back her brush. "How 'bout a lipstick?" Boots pulled out a tube and Tuffie ran it around in the general vicinity of her lips and lower nose.

"Gimme a couple quarters," Tuffie demanded, stopping in front of a drink machine and holding her hand out to her daughter. "I'm dry as Ferdinand's tit."

"Mo-o-o-m. You already owe me eight dollars and ninety cents."

"Well, ain't you the little banker. Who bought gas all the way up to Red Bluff after you went out and spent your paycheck on a pink leather jacket?"

Boots slapped the quarters into her mother's hand. Tuffie got a Dr Pepper and they slipped into a room with a penciled sign reading *Board Meeting* taped to the door.

Inside, the National Association of Women's Rodeo board meeting was under way. The six board members sat behind a metal folding table. All six looked as if they had been plucked straight out of a Tupperware party, then staked out in the Mojave Desert for a few decades. They had the leathery look that comes to all cowgirls if they live much past twenty-five. In front of them sat the fifty general members interested enough to attend. One of the board members glanced up and motioned for Tuffie to take a seat. Son listened for a second to whatever by-law it was they were debating, but Tuffie caught her attention with a hoarse whisper.

"You and Prairie an item?"

"No! Nothing of the kind. He's just sort of a guide that I've hired." Son strove to put distance between herself and a man that Tuffie, no doubt, considered to be the worst sort of macho reactionary. And with good reason. In her mind, Son saw again the waitress's porch light blink off.

"It's just a pure business deal thing between you two?"

"Absolutely. Prairie James suffers too acutely from *Koyaanis-qatsi* to ever interest me on any deeper level."

Tuffie nodded. "Yeah, you name it, that man's probably had it and is in the process of passing it on." Son gave her a knowing smile, pleased that they were of one mind on the matter of Prairie James. "Well, good luck on finding your daddy. Like I said, takes a trick roper to find a trick roper."

Son was buoyed by Tuffie's confidence. Again they were agreed: the devil had his flaws, but he could be useful.

Crack! The gavel slammed down, and the room, including Tuffie, fell silent.

"Motion passed!" called out the executive director, Shirley Dockery. Shirley, fifty-three, was the godmother of barrel racing and dressed her small, whipcord body accordingly in powder-blue pants and matching ruffled shirt accessorized with kelly green boots, belt, and hat. The hat was the classic barrel racer model with none of the cowboy's manly brim span. No, Shirley's brim was creased nearly straight up so that it ascended in much the same manner as her upswept hairdo. Son mentally dubbed the hat style Prissy Brim. She contrasted it with the Swooping Brim of rough stock riders like Tuffie. Prissy Brims predominated in the room.

"Tuffie," Shirley said. "You're gonna be telling us one more time why we oughta be using men's rules for the rough stock riders."

Tuffie jumped up without waiting to be recognized. "And why the hell not? Ever one of you in here know that girls' rules just make a dangerous sport a little more dangerous. That letting the girls use two hands when they ride bulls doesn't do a thing in the world except guarantee that every woman bullrider has false front teeth from leaning in too close to the horns. And making the rides six seconds instead of eight, all that does is just say we're not as good as the men. Any of you in here who've ever ridden rough stock know that if you can put a six-second ride on a bull, eight ain't gonna be no chore."

"Is there any further debate?"

A slender cowgirl in her mid-twenties put up her hand. In her Prissy Brim hat and all-black outfit highlighted by more Indian jewelry than you see on the average Santa Fe opera patron, she was obviously a barrel racer.

"Tracy Daines." Shirley recognized her.

"Come on, y'all," Tracy pleaded in the nasal tones of distress indigenous to Texas sorority houses, cheerleader squads, and aerobic dance studios. "You know what some of the guys say about rough stock riders already."

"No," Tuffie challenged her. "What do they say?"

"You know."

"No, Tracy, you tell us."

"Well, you know, they're lesbo-dykes on steroids."

The Prissy Brim crowd chuckled with what Son instantly recognized as an in-crowd's comfortable, excluding scorn. The familiar sound of it made her pulse pound and her face flush with anger.

"But not you, Tuffie," Tracy added.

"If there is no further—" Shirley was bringing down her gavel to dismiss the discussion when Son stood up.

"If I might be permitted to make a few observations of a socioanthropological nature."

Chairs scraped as every hat, both Prissy and Swooping Brim, turned toward the rolling academic tones, then stopped dead as they beheld the hot pink square-dance dress enlivened with silver rickrack and scarlet money sash. A sound like a great wind sweeping through the top branches of tall trees radiated through the crowd as everyone turned to her neighbor and whispered, "Who is *that?*"

"As a trained anthropologist, I feel competent to offer several insights. They concern hat-brim size. I detect among you two varieties, the upright and the outstretched. You of the upright-brim

camp clearly predominate here. Just as your interest in barrel racing dominates the larger group. This interest obviously under-
mines that of the opposing camp, the outstretched-brim rough
stock riders.

"I would further suggest," Son went on, "a correlation between your relative brim expansions and the sheer amount of physical space each of you is willing to occupy in what many would like
to keep the man's world of rodeo."

Tracy Daines took the floor.

"I had hoped," Tracy started off, "that we were pretty much
through with all that women's lib stuff. I mean, we're just getting to
the point where the guys don't resent us as much now that they
know we're not out to try and compete with them. I mean, I accept
that I'm not physically able to do that. I accept that women just
don't have that kind of strength. So let's not get back into that
whole mess."

"Who is that woman?" Son asked Tuffie.

Tuffie widened her eyes in amazement, then answered, with
mock awe, "You mean, you don't know the one and only Tracy
Daines? She's been all-round world champion cowgirl for the last
three years. Beat Bucko a couple times in bulls to do it."

"Ah-hah!" Son said, jumping up for a rebuttal. "I find it most
intriguing that you would bow to the superiority of masculine
strength when, *in fact*"—Son took on the punchy cadences of a
prosecuting attorney—"you yourself, a rather dwarfish specimen of
humanity, have bested the likes of the far bulkier Bucko Bukowski.
Through dint of skill, one presumes."

"Hey, that's right," Tuffie burst out.

"Just exactly who sent you?" Tracy asked, tilting her head to
the side to level a one-eyed squinty gaze on Son.

"I am Son Hozro, emcee for Prairie James's Twirling Down
Through the Ages Roping Extravaganza. I represent only the voice
of a more enlightened universe beyond these narrow walls."

"You mean, you're not even a member of the National Association of Women's Rodeo?" Shirley asked.

"No, though I would not be averse to accepting any emeritus position you might care to offer."

"You are out of order," the chairwoman declared, before turning to the woman on her right. "Sergeant-at-arms, please remove that individual." Shirley pointed a wrathful finger at Son.

Son was committed to a physical struggle of the sort that would be certain to attract the attention of national media representatives. She stopped flailing, however, when she realized that the sergeant-at-arms was anywhere from nine to ten months pregnant.

The Swooping Brims followed Son outside en masse. Tuffie clapped her on the back. "I ain't sure what you said, but I'm all for anything that gets both Shirley Dockery and Tracy Daines torked off. Let me buy you a beer."

As Son stood at the bar of the Conquistador Lounge in the Hereford Days Rest Inn, surrounded by Swooping Brim cowgirls buying her beer, she had to believe that the ingestion of a few mild intoxicants and an unprecedented euphoria would not interfere in any significant way with her vision quest.

Chapter 14.

"You are blotto!" Prairie exploded when Son's new friends delivered her to the truck following their long afternoon at the Conquistador Lounge.

"M-m-m-m," Son muttered. "I am feeling a bit bilious."

"Small wonder, putting away a junior brewery on top of enough chip grease to lubricate an ox cart. You know, it's kind of strange, the way you booze it up every chance you get, but you're so concerned with fiber and nutrition and whatnot."

"Consistency is the hobgoblin of little minds." Son closed her eyes and was overwhelmed by the intriguing impression that her head was simultaneously swelling and shrinking. "Could it be that my discomfort is precisely the catalyst required to trigger a vision?" she wondered aloud. She jerked her eyes open as Prairie grabbed her arm to prevent her from falling face forward.

"You're stewed, Pocahontas. The only vision you're going to trigger is the DTs. Tuffie do this to you?"

"Nothing was done to me. I merely joined my new friends in a liquid tribute to the cowgirl." Son tittered at the memory. "They were actually competing with one another for the honor of buying me a drink. Me. Can you imagine? I think Tuffie is my friend."

"Hey, don't sound so blown away. You got your qualities.

Besides, Tuffie specializes in taking home strays. Hey, listen, you gonna be okay to do the show?"

"I have never been known to disappoint an audience yet."

"Well, don't tell Guinness Book of Records yet. You've only had one. Why don't you just go find a shady spot and I'll hunt up some coffee?"

Son was in the middle of informing Prairie that coffee was, in fact, a very poor remedy for drunkenness when she realized that she was sitting all alone in the shade behind a tall row of bleachers. When the Flying D Rodeo Production Company trucks pulled up, she was lost in a dazed stupor. She smelled the green diarrhea smell of frightened livestock long before she turned to the cattle cars filled with skittish roping calves, woolly broncs, slobbering bulls. The sound of metal grates clanking filled the hot, still air as gates were flung open and animals herded into holding pens. Most of the helpers were short Mexican men wearing the official headgear of *los indocumentados*, flat-crowned straw hats with a strap that tied them on at the back of the neck and a little pompom dangling off the back brim.

Directing the operation was the roping robot, Dewey Dakota. He worked at a furious pace and expected even greater speed from his helpers. The only word in Spanish he seemed to know was *"Andale!"* which he screamed every time one of the Mexicans took a few seconds out to keep from being trampled by a bull or for another such act of blatant malingering.

It made Son's head spin even worse than it already was doing to watch so many green-streaked animal backsides moving so swiftly down ramps and into the maze of chutes behind the arena. The chorus of *"Andales,"* animal bellows, and clanking metal rose with the dust being kicked up by the furious activity. It all mixed together with the gagging smell of manure.

She closed her eyes against the haze of dust, and the screams of men and animals and the choking dust of a sun-baked rodeo arena receded far into the distance. Suddenly, Son found herself walking down a long, broad aisle covered in beige linoleum of the sort on nearly every floor of every discount outlet she'd ever trod. The only sound was the reassuring buzz of the fluorescent lights overhead.

Gradually Son realized that she had to go to the bathroom. Using her intimate knowledge of discount outlet layouts, she headed toward the back but was distracted by bargains greater than any she had ever known.

She wandered through an Eden of Markdowns, Discontinueds, Clearances, Red-tagged Merchandise, and Take Another 50% Off. She picked up a pair of lederhosen and found that the crotch seam was ripped. Good, she knew, for even further reductions. Jubilant, Son tucked the leather shorts under her arm. She kept walking and found a man's pinky ring with a horseshoe of diamonds reduced from eighty-nine thousand dollars to fifty-nine cents. Ecstatic, she put the ring in her pocket.

Suddenly, though, the beige linoleum swirled with a multitude of colors that abruptly settled into a clear pattern of green polka dots on a white background. Son was struck by the beauty of the design, but it shrank away as soon as she bent over to study it.

In its place was, of all things, a family of miniature dachshunds —father, mother, and baby—just like the one sitting on Tinka's étagère. Though she had run from them in her former life in Dorfburg, she now felt a strong and benign tug coming from the stubby creatures and a compulsion to follow where they led. They scampered off and she ran behind, barely able to keep up.

When she looked around, she was inside a grand coach, a railroad car perhaps, that was moving at a frightening rate of speed. Swaying with the moving coach, she made her way to the front to inform the driver of the greater statistical probability of their becoming involved in a collision at such an unsafe speed. She stopped at a restroom and attempted to use it. But when she was already seated, she noticed that it was in the middle of a ballroom. Too inhibited to relieve herself, she pressed on.

At the front of the coach, she saw that they were traveling through a land of vast and empty spaces. Suddenly, she realized that they were on a ship sailing on an endless ocean. A highbacked captain's chair was placed in front of a complicated control panel. Son knew immediately that whoever sat in that chair was her father.

Her heart hammered with nervousness as she reached out a shaky hand. The instant she touched the chair, it whirled around and around, blurring the face of the man who sat in it.

Far over her head, in a dream sky that opened above the ship's roof, a turkey vulture wheeled through the air. The sun blinked on and off as the giant bird, swooping down lower and lower, passed back and forth between Son and the light. She knew that if the bird could reach her in time, she would know everything. But it was descending too slowly.

Her pulse hammered. For several minutes, she sat up in a strange bed in a pitch dark room and tried to figure out if she should run for her life. The notion that she'd been dreaming occurred to her. Except that this was unlike any dream Son had ever had. Even after she was fully awake, none of the images receded. They grew more vivid. A field of green polka dots remained imprinted on her inner eye and she felt a strange, new affinity for dachshunds, pinky rings, and turkey vultures.

In a flash, Son knew: she had had her vision. The fasting had paid off. She couldn't wait to tell Prairie that it had happened; she'd received her guiding vision. Her whole life would now have to be reinterpreted. Everything was different. Only the pressure in her bladder remained the same.

She felt around on the bed. It was a bare mattress that smelled of mildew. Her head throbbed and her throat was dry. She remembered first the Conquistador Lounge and then the rodeo grounds. As the memory of the heat, noise, and manure odor of the rodeo grounds faded, Son became aware of another smell. It filled her nostrils with an ether-sweet astringency. She swung her arms around in the dark until they collided with a lamp. When she turned it on, she saw that she was in the bedroom-workshop of a prefab house so flimsy it bordered on being a mobile home.

The machinery and products of the bumper sticker business, a hand-cranked printing press, cans of toner and ink, piles of bumper stickers both printed and blank, spread across a long folding table told Son that she must be in Tuffie's house. The floor of the bedroom was hidden beneath a layer of crumpled stickers and empty boxes that overlapped with a thick covering of jeans, Western shirts, grimy ropes, spurs, fliers for car-wash openings, and unopened bills.

Son found that she was wearing a pink sleeveless nightie of a type she vaguely attached the label "baby doll" to. It was scratchy, too tight, and when Son stood up, she discovered it was also too short. A pink ruffle on the lower hem barely skimmed her bottom. Son rummaged through a pile of Tuffie's dirty jeans, shirts, and underwear, but none of the doll-sized garments would fit. Son gave up; she had to find a bathroom.

The sleeping house creaked and swayed like the coach in her dream with every step she took. In the darkness outside the bedroom, she banged into a chrome dinette set.

"No, I ain't!" she heard a young sleeper mutter and thought she recognized Jonathan's voice.

The thin light of a Coors sign, with an electric clock implanted beneath a glittering mountain stream, helped her make out the shapes of Boots, Tuffie's pretty seventeen-year-old girl, asleep on the couch. Curled up with his feet in Boots's face was the youngest, Jonathan. Son felt bad that she'd probably put them both out of their bed.

"You can't make me!" Jonathan yelled out in his sleep, paused for the challenger in his dream to respond, and added, "Can not!"

Son crept through the living room and opened the first door she came to. It wasn't a bathroom. Enough streetlight filtered in for her to see that she was in the kitchen. A waist-high trashcan sat in the middle of the room. It was filled with greasy chicken boxes, sticky Coke cups, and hamburger wrappers. Flies buzzed over it.

The next room contained a set of bunk beds. Spur, the fourteen-year-old, and Lasso, the eight-year-old twin girl, shared the bottom bunk. Latigo, the boy twin, was sprawled across the top bunk. Son pressed her hand between her legs to staunch the flow pressing down and tiptoed on. There were only two doors left. She made what she was sure was a logical blueprint of the small house and figured out that the door on the right had to be a bathroom.

She silently turned the knob, opened the door, and beheld Tuffie and Prairie, naked in the silver moonlight streaming in through an open window. Tuffie, facing down, rested her head on the low bed. Prairie stood holding her legs around his waist like a farmer holding a plow as he gently pushed himself into her wiry body.

Son closed the door as soundlessly as she'd opened it. Without risking the bathroom, she crept back past the Coors sign and into her bedroom, where she waited with her legs crossed until the sun came up. Then she waited several more hours before the Branch household roused itself and she could finally go to the toilet.

During that long period, she tried to focus on her vision and what it meant. But she kept getting derailed by the memory of Prairie, Tuffie's legs around his waist, naked in the moonlight.

Chapter 15.

"I hate the ones with gooey stuff in the middle," wailed Jonathan. He held a doughnut in his hand with one disappointed bite taken out of it. A blob of raspberry-colored filling oozed out and plopped onto the kitchen floor.

From her room earlier that morning, Son had heard Prairie make a big show of appearing at the front door with the box of doughnuts for breakfast, pretending that he'd spent the night in the truck. She had waited until he announced that he was going to shave and shower before she came out.

Tuffie greeted her with "Well, look what the cat drug in!" She seemed even bouncier than usual.

Since she still hadn't located her clothes, Son had the cheap spread from the bed wrapped around her.

"You know you talk in your sleep?"

Son, suddenly shy, shook her head.

"Talk? Yell's more like it. You was telling us to get away and let you go. Took me and Prairie and Boots and her new boyfriend to get you in the house and into bed."

Son pulled the spread tighter around her.

"Don't worry. Prairie didn't see nothing. Me and Boots got you undressed."

Feeling strangely hollow and fragile, Son picked up a cake doughnut with Dutch crumbles, normally her favorite sort. But the odd wistfulness that had overtaken her had conquered her appetite.

The tribe of tiny Branch children stampeded around her as if she were a wooden Indian in a flowing robe. The kitchen was even worse in daylight than it had been the night before. The only dishes visible were printed with fast food logos. None of the open windows had a screen. Armadas of flies buzzed in and hovered around the open trashcan set in the middle of the kitchen.

Tuffie sat on a chair at the edge of the kitchen, a doughnut stuffed in her mouth, while she brushed Lasso's hair into a ponytail and listened to the breathless explanation of the boy twin, Latigo, about why his mother should buy him a moto-cross bike like the one his friend, Ronnie Earl, had. Boots came into the kitchen, took one look at Spur, and announced that she hadn't told her sister she could wear her top and to take it off right now or she'd take it off for her. Spur asked, "You and whose army?" At which point Tuffie began pulling off her own blouse to shame Boots into a more generous outlook.

With his mother's attention lost to refereeing the girls' dispute, Jonathan, dressed in a straw hat and a pair of Batman underpants, opened the refrigerator and took out a can of Coke.

Tuffie stopped shouting at the two girls long enough to yell at her son, "Jonathan Eugene Branch! If you drink you a Coke for breakfast, I will thump your gourd but good! Put it back and get you a juice."

The boy's shoulders sagged and he whined, "Mo-o-om." But a sharp look from Tuffie convinced him to trade in the red-and-white can for a Nehi grape. His mother nodded her approval before Latigo overwhelmed her again with his lobbying effort for a moto-cross bike.

Soda pop for breakfast. For the first time, Son truly missed Tinka. The life she'd had with her mother on Schwarzwald Street may have been cramped, boring, and hopelessly *Koyaanisqatsi*, but at least she belonged there. She was Tinka's daughter. Though her mother may not have always been delighted with that fact, she never tried to deny it. There was no place for her here. She was not really Tuffie's friend, and who could say what she was to Prairie? She'd bullied and bought her way into his life.

"Are you going to eat that?" A reedy Branch voice addressed Son from a point below her waist. She looked down, and Jonathan held up a doughnut that was oozing raspberry filling over his hand and onto the floor.

"Trade me, okay?"

Though Son abhorred the glaring artificiality of filled dough-nuts, she didn't hesitate, and gave the boy the one in her hand. It was an automatic response. Only after she'd made it did Son realize that she had unconsciously imitated Tinka, who'd always let her daughter have the cherry kolaches in the assorted packs, taking the scorned prune-filleds herself. Jonathan chomped happily, sprin-kling himself and the surrounding linoleum with crumbles. Son looked over at Tuffie to tell her what a mess her youngest child had made, but Tuffie was still absorbed in arbitrating the dispute be-tween Boots and Spur over the borrowed blouse.

"Bet you can't guess how much I weigh," Jonathan said.

Son was caught off-guard by the odd challenge. What was Tuffie raising? A miniature carnival sharpie? Didn't he realize that she was no good with children? That she had no idea of what to say to them? Even as a child she hadn't been good with other children. Weren't children supposed to be able to sense that in adults? To know which ones had no stories to tell them, no comfort to offer?

"Bet you can't guess how much I weigh," the little boy said again.

Son glanced around, but no one was paying any attention. "No, I don't suppose I can."

"Ain't you even gonna try?" An odd, pleading note tinged the little boy's question, and he held his arms up to Son.

Son was forced to the puzzling conclusion that the child

wanted to be picked up. By her. She couldn't recall ever having picked up a child. Tuffie was now gripping the squirming twin boy, Latigo, with one sinewy hand while she attempted to comb his cowlick-swirled hair with the other. The boy ducked away from the comb, and Tuffie jerked him back. "Latigo Cody Branch, you better hold still, son, or I will snatch you bald-headed, boy."

When Son looked back down, Jonathan still held his arms out to her, so she picked him up. She had held larger dogs. It astonished her that a creature as small as Jonathan was an actual human being. Had she ever been this small? Had Tinka held her? She must have, though Son could not remember such a thing ever happening.

Jonathan twisted in her arms to look up at her. "What do you guess?"

He seemed to weigh far less than one of the forty-pound sacks of sheep manure that Tinka had insisted Son spread about her yard each spring. "Thirty pounds," she estimated.

"Thirty-three!" Jonathan crowed, delighted.

Assuming the interaction was over, Son started to lower him to the floor, but Jonathan scrambled higher into her arms and asked, "Why do you got a bedspread on you?"

"Because I couldn't find my clothes."

"Oh, them. My mom took 'em off you when you was passed out dead drunk last night."

"I've never been passed out dead drunk in my life," Son corrected the tyke.

"Well, you was last night."

"Were. You *were* last night. Subject-verb agreement. Very important."

"You talk funny." He tilted his head and gave her a sly, exasperated smile. Son started to tell him about the vital role of adverbs, but knew that the puzzle in his mind was already too scrambled for that one piece to make any sense.

A few whole grains, some actual juice in the morning, together with a firm grounding in grammar, and the boy would have a different life. A better life. She thought briefly about a quiet kitchen where she'd serve oatmeal to Jonathan and teach him about personal pronouns. Jonathan wriggled out of her arms when Prairie appeared in the doorway of the kitchen and ran up to the roper with his arms outstretched.

"Pocahontas," he hailed Son, simultaneously scooping the boy into his arms, "you're up!"

Son couldn't tell if it was the shave or the night before that gave Prairie such a self-satisfied glow. Either one, she detested it.

"Hey, you crumbgrinders!" he boomed out jovially, addressing the junior Branches. "You ate all the doughnuts. What's the deal? A man could starve around here." He play-boxed Jonathan in the tummy. "Was it you? Huh? Huh? It was, wasn't it? You ate all the doughnuts and didn't leave even one for old Prairie."

Son thought she would be sick at Prairie's farcical rendition of the paterfamilias.

"You missed a performance last night," he told Son. "I just might have to dock your pay."

"My pay?" Son asked in a tone she considered ripe with ironic emphasis.

"Yeah, Snake Oil Beaulieu announced the act last night and he was as sorry as ever. Just didn't capture the art of the whole deal, the way you did there at that colored rodeo."

"Oh, yes, well." Son straightened up and took in her first full breath since last night. "The man just has no concept of marketing principles. I'm sure he didn't target his presentation for a women's audience."

"Snake Oil couldn't target an audience of baboons if he had a crate of barianas. You going to be doing the show tonight?"

Son tightened the bedspread up around her armpits. "Yes, I'm feeling much better now."

"Well, we're glad to hear it," Tuffie said, letting Latigo slip out of her grip, his hair still sticking up in odd cowlicked horns and dust devils. "Prairie's been braggin' on you. Telling me what a dandy announcing job you done for him in Jordan."

Son hid her pleasure at the statement. "Oh."

Tuffie turned to Prairie. "Go on back to the Krispy-Kreme. These little piggies ate up all them doughnuts before Son had a chance to get her one. You're hungry, aren't you, Son? I know I could eat me a couple more."

"Well, yes, actually, my appetite is picking up a bit," Son admitted, surprised to find that she was hungry.

"And don't bother with them jelly-filleds," Tuffie yelled to Prairie as he stepped out the door. "We all hate them jelly-filleds." She turned quickly to Son. "You like them jelly-filleds?"

"No. They're awful," she assured Tuffie, putting down the one Jonathan had given her. Then, to Prairie's retreating back, she yelled, "Cake! Cake doughnuts with Dutch crumbles!"

"Same for me!" Jonathan yelled, coming to Son's side and pulling on her hand until she looked down at him. "Do you know what I'd do," he asked when he finally had her attention, "if a big, big, big storm came and this whole house was under water and we didn't have no air to breathe or nothing?"

Son was just about to illuminate the boy on the matter of double negatives when he took her hand in his and tugged her out of the kitchen.

"Come on. I'll show you. I got all the stuff in my room where my mom prints her stickers."

Son followed Jonathan into the back bedroom. Perhaps she would teach by example instead.

Beaulieu called for the first rider of the day. "Jonni Caulkins out of Sand Springs, Arkansas, riding the bad horse Basher Boy!"

Like the riders who had preceded her, Jonni looked crouched and tentative, gripping forward with both hands instead of arching backward and letting one hand fly free as the men did. The audience's response had the same crouched, tentative quality.

"No score for Jonni Caulkins!" Beaulieu called out when Basher Boy dumped the cowgirl onto the seat of her jeans. To Son it seemed that the audience nodded its collective head in satisfaction at having had its expectations satisfied. After the black rodeo, where audience and performers had thrown a party together, this crowd seemed distant and unresponsive.

A few of the old ranchers and their wives were the only ones watching and clapping for the next event, calf roping. The women's version of steer wrestling, steer undecorating, followed. Instead of leaping from a running horse onto the horns of a steer and muscling it to the ground, the riders whipped by a running steer and plucked a ribbon off its back. The potential for a good goring perked up the logy crowd a bit. But when all the horses and steers had thundered past with no bloodshed, the crowd slumped back into a heat-dazed stupor. ·

"And now for a special presentation," Beaulieu said by way of introducing that year's inductees into the Cowgirl Hall of Fame. Five wizened old women in Western-cut pantsuits with ruffled blouses hiding the crepy skin at their necks and cowboy hats perched atop bouffant hairdos tottered into the arena, gripping the arms of five escorts. Each of the women relaxed her grip long enough to give a game wave when Beaulieu introduced her. Cowgirl of the Year, Tracy Daines, bustled out and pinned corsages on women who had ridden galloping horses standing on their heads in the saddle before sell-out crowds in Madison Square Garden and finished off the evening with a midnight supper at the Astors'.

Son stared hard at the old women. They were as wrinkled and weathered as mummies. As Beaulieu alluded to a time in the twenties and thirties when cowgirls were as famous as movie stars and "these here" were the most famous of them all, the crowd warmed and awarded the cowdowagers the first big hand of the day. The audience immediately slumped back into lethargy when the team ropers came out to stretch steers.

"Ladies and gentlemen," Beaulieu said as the last team trotted off, "I know that a lot of you were expecting the Tish Sisters to be performing for us tonight, but they've had to cancel."

The crowd groaned with disappointment.

Son held out her hand for the microphone. They'd agreed that she would make the introduction. She had one all ready. She'd decided to concentrate on creating the most valued of market conditions—scarcity. But Beaulieu, mesmerized by the sound of his voice, would not relinquish the microphone.

"Yes, we're real sorry that those dee-licious Tishes couldn't be with us today, but all three them have took sick with mononucleosis and they're feeling just puny. However, since Dakota Productions promised you entertainment, that's what we're going to deliver. So, before we get the barrel racing started, here are Prairie James and his horse, Domino, to do a few rope tricks for you."

The disdainful introduction appalled Son. She reached out to snatch the microphone from Beaulieu, but he pivoted away from her.

"Prairie?" he called out over the mike. "You there or did your rope get broke?"

"He's not going to come out until I announce him," Son informed Beaulieu, but he wasn't listening. Son felt she had no choice then but to stand and grab the microphone out of his hand. Beaulieu attempted to snatch it back. It hit the floor with a POOM that had the entire crowd putting their hands over their ears. Son retrieved the fumble and started speaking before Beaulieu could make another grab.

"Hello, I'm Son Hozro," she blurted out. The microphone squawked and tweeted. Son looked to Beaulieu for help. The announcer leaned back in his chair and held his hand out to her in an all-yours gesture.

"Ladies and gentlemen." Son moved the microphone away from her until it stopped squawking. "I have, tonight, the great honor of narrating the fabled performance of the legendary Prairie James and his myth-making equine companion, Domino. Prairie

may be delayed for just a moment or two, as he is probably overcome with paralyzing jet lag. We had to cut short the Oriental leg
of our world tour and fly in from Singapore to be here today.
Prairie never reneges on his commitments, but he made an exception to be with all of you."

There was a confused silence in the stands. Her attempt to
create scarcity was falling flat, since Beaulieu had already made the
act seem about as rare as a pothole in the road. Son's mouth dried
as panic fluttered up through her. She struggled for words to introduce Prairie, but the instant she thought of him, her mind went
blank. All she could think of was moonlight on a man's bare buttocks and a family of dachshunds. She tried to speak, but the only
sound that came from her dry mouth was a mousy squeak.

Beaulieu lowered his head to hide a smile. This was making his
day. He'd heard all day from James how his new announcer was
really going show him how to chew his cabbage. Mike fright; he'd
seen it a hundred times. When he figured the humiliation had gone
on about long enough, Beaulieu lifted his head and held out his
hand for the microphone.

Never before had words failed Son so completely. She was
about to surrender when she caught sight of Beaulieu's smirk.
She'd seen that smirk all her life and had always battled it with
words. She would not give in to a smirk. She snatched the mike
back.

Dammit, after decades of studying every rodeo announcer
who'd passed through Dorfburg, she could "do" Beau Beaulieu
better than he could do himself. She seized on his most offensive
performance, the sniveling Timmy's Prayer, and dived in.

"Being here with y'all today at this wonderful cowgirls' rodeo," Son said, adopting the hick inflections she'd heard Beaulieu
use to win over the crowd, "brings to mind another cowgirl I once
knew. Sandy was what we called that little gal on account of her
golden blond hair. And you've never seen a little girl loved horses
the way Sandy did. Seems like she was just born a'rodeoin'. Warn't
no other little cowgirl or *cowboy*, for that matter, could beat her."

Once again, Son was a woman speaking in tongues as the foreign language of bad grammar possessed her.

"Well, Sandy grew up and she was a joy to her daddy. She didn't have no time to get into the kind of trouble that so many kids in this here *modren* day get into because she was too busy a-ropin' and a-ridin'. But then the day came when Sandy just got too big for them Little Britches' Rodeos.

"That left a mighty big hole in little Sandy's life. A hole that bad companions was only too eager to fill. Well, Sandy got herself trapped in that downward spiral of drugs and rock 'n' roll. And, ladies and gentlemen, I'm sorry to say it, Sandy went to the bad. Today would have been Sandy's birthday. If she'd lived . . . But we buried Sandy, her hair still golden, seven years ago."

Son paused for dramatic emphasis, then added in a hushed voice, "Oh, there's just one other thing I forgot to mention, folks. Little Sandy was Prairie James's daughter."

She paused again.

"So, folks, I guess you can understand now why Prairie insisted that, no matter how much money we'd lose canceling out in Singapore, we just had to fly in to be here with y'all today. Like Prairie says, maybe if Women's Rodeo had been there for Sandy, she'd still be here for him today."

Finding Beaulieu's look of amazement most edifying, Son roused herself to belt out, "Ladies and gentlemen! It is my great honor to present to you the greatest living trick roper in the world today, *Mister* Prairie James! Riding the Horse With a Human Brain, Domino!"

Son tucked the microphone under her armpit and led the crowd in applause as she switched on the battered cassette recorder and played Prairie's music. When the strains of "Bonanza" reached their thundering apex, Prairie barreled into the arena. He wore Tuffie's favorite shirt, the cavalry-style red satin with the two-foot fringe hanging off the sleeves. Then, just to show old Snake Oil who he was dealing with, Prairie reined Domino into a full-dress

sliding stop. The horse went from an all-out charge into a squat, sat
way, way back, *charreada*-style, on his haunches, and slid seventy-
five feet. Prairie looked back at the furrow they'd plowed and
thought that El Marinero himself couldn't have done any better.

Son was thrilled.

Domino sat still as a stone temple dog while Prairie stepped
off the horse's back, an emperor stepping out of his palanquin.
Prairie then reached up over the crown of his hat, gripped the brim
on the opposite side, and swept off his hat so that it ended upside-
down in his hand. He pointed his free hand to the still-squatting
Domino, and the crowd went wild.

Son went to work, snapping out of the groveling yokel pose.
"Thank you! Thank you! That was the amazing Standing Hare
Stop, a feat of equestrianism that only one horse in the world,
outside of the legendary Lippizaner stallions, is capable of performing, and that one horse is before you tonight: Domino!"

Prairie glanced into the stands hoping none of the *charros* from
the parade was in the crowd. Considering that every decent Mexican cowboy who'd ever put spur to horsehide did the slider, he
doubted they'd buy the Lippizaner line. From the happy clapping,
though, it didn't look as if there was enough ethnic give-and-take
in Hereford to blow his cover. With the instincts of a Vegas lounge
singer, Prairie sensed the exact moment when the applause had
been milked dry. He plopped his hat back on his head, remounted
Domino, and brought a big loop to life eagerly anticipating Son's
puffery.

Looking out at the crowd of tobacco chewers and hair spray
abusers, Son suddenly realized that the bold, feminist narrative she
had planned just wasn't going to play. But her mental gears seemed
to have ground out, and she couldn't come up with another way of
selling the act.

Prairie looked up at the announcer's booth, wondering what
had happened to the patter. An audience was like a hooked fish; you
had to keep up the tension if you wanted to keep it on the line. In

the silence, he felt that line begin to sag. He spun a tight, buzzing Tornado up over his head, held it there, then opened it like a giant parasol that cast a wobbling shadow of circle on the ground all around him until he closed it up tight again.

He finished the trick to dead silence. Prairie glared at the announcer's booth. He sure the hell hoped Son wasn't conked out having another vision. He was dying with no one to cue the rubes in to when a trick was over, much less what an awe-inspiring achievement it had been.

Tuffie, who had been hurtling around behind the bucking chutes helping new girls to locate spurs and keeping them convinced that riding horses and bulls that wanted to stomp you to death was the act of a sane individual, stopped long enough to notice that Prairie had gone on. "Hoo-eee!" She let out a piercing yell followed by some sharp clapping. This nudged a few audience members into scattered applause.

Prairie tipped his hat in the shiteatingly humble way he'd learned rodeo crowds required. *This is worse than frigging Dorfburg.* He took his time coiling his rope, hoping he'd get some signs of life from the announcer's booth.

With a creak of his swivel chair, Beaulieu leaned slowly forward to reclaim the microphone. Son snatched it away, and as she did so, her gaze fell on the row of ruffle-necked blouses and Supremes hairdos perched in a line on the bleachers. Of course. The cowdowagers.

"Excuse me, folks, I was momentarily overcome by the technical perfection of that last trick. Next up on today's program is Prairie's homage in hemp to our foremothers. He'll be kicking off his tribute to the brave women of the Western frontier with a trick he learned from his mother, Montana Belle James, the most famous female roper to ever perform with the great Cowboys' Carnival.

"I'm sure you all recall the Montana Belle's oft-quoted rejoinder to the Prince of Wales when he asked her if there were any cowboy tricks she wouldn't attempt. 'Prince,' Prairie's plucky mother piped right up with our characteristic American disdain for fancy titles, good breeding, and education, 'I can do any trick a cowboy can do. The only difference is, I got to keep my lipstick from smearin' while I'm a-doin' it!"

Satisfaction washed over Son as the audience laughed appreciatively. As she'd intuited, it was all right for a cowgirl to be as good as a man once she'd been mummified.

"Now, with the greatest of pleasure, I give you a page out of Western history. The son of the Montana Belle performing the Prince of Wales's favorite rope trick, the Spinning Wheel!"

Prairie spurred Domino through the twirling loop. Personally, he liked the Wheel of Fire rap better, with the Indian war steeds and fighting the white man, but this new version was playing well. Montana Belle? Where did she get this stuff? Wherever, an endless flow of it followed.

Son took Prairie's usual line-up, pulled it apart, and stitched it back together into a history of the contribution of the pioneer woman to American history. He did a Butterfly, floating a big figure 8 on its side, and Son talked about the birth of a new land as midwived by that gallant heroine of the Old West, the cowgirl. Prairie went through his act with extra panache, snapping his loops into the air with a crisp flair, trying to make his performance live up to Son's homespun rhetoric.

In a break between his good tricks, Prairie did the Texas Skip. He dismounted, stood on the hundred-degree earth, and built a loop seven feet tall. Then he pulled it back and forth over his head, skipping over the bottom of the loop on the ground. It was, far and away, the most ordinary trick in his repertoire, which is why Prairie jerked his head around, searching the arena for some grotesque accident when Son let out an amplified gasp.

"Oh, my heavens!" she exclaimed as he skipped. "I can't believe he's doing that!"

Prairie craned his neck searching for a catastrophe. Perhaps Casey Dakota was motivating his adopted son with a radiator hose or inspiring his Mexican workers with a cattle prod. What had happened, however, was that Son had decided it was time to fully unloose the unctuous spirit of Beau Beaulieu.

"Something very special is happening here today, ladies and gentlemen. Prairie James is doing Sandy's Trick. We always called it that because when his golden-haired daughter was growing up, she liked nothing better than to come out and do this trick with her daddy. And, oh, how the crowds loved seeing that little mite of a girl in her little hat and little fringed chaps, her golden curls just a-bouncin' in the sun, jump rope with her daddy."

Prairie, mesmerized by Son's mawkish recitation, was startled when a sudden honk interrupted. He glanced up for signs of early Canadian goose migration, but quickly realized that Son herself was the source of the sound. It was followed by several sniffles; then Son gasped out, "Forgive me, folks. I just got a little overcome there for a moment. You see, Prairie hasn't done Sandy's Trick for seven long years."

"Oh, for cry——" Prairie whispered to himself, still bouncing up and down over the rope. He clearly heard Domino, beside him, blow a fat, disgusted raspberry through flapping horse lips. Prairie looked at him sternly, and Domino rolled his eyes. Prairie was certain the nag couldn't actually understand what Son was saying, but maybe he had some kind of equine bullshit detector. In any event, Prairie was starting to feel embarrassed in ways he hadn't experienced since his voice cracked. And it only got worse.

"I just can't believe what we're seeing down there," Son went on. "This is just how much women's rodeo means to Prairie James to bring out a display of pure, moral courage like what y'all are witnessing."

Prairie could no longer look up. He was terrified that he'd find Casey Dakota or, worse, Tuffie sneering down at him. He watched his boots pop up and down in the dust as the rope passed under them. Minutes, hours, days seemed to pass. He prayed that Son would show mercy and wrap this one up so that he could move on to the next trick. He heard a snort of laughter come from the stands, and his face, already flushed, heated to an intolerable level.

"That this man, who has had so much taken from him, should still have so much to give, I think is—"

That was it. Prairie was not going to hang around and listen to what Pocahontas thought. He would incinerate if he heard another word. Still without raising his head, Prairie let the loop drop and stomped off to the exit, letting Domino saunter casually after him. He waited for hoots and catcalls and tried to figure out how he could arrange the rest of his life without ever again stepping onto the Panhandle of Texas. He heard an unfamiliar roar as he left the arena, but, from the way his blood pressure was jacked up by anger and humiliation, assumed it was just the sound of blood pounding in his ears.

A car with an expensive-sounding engine purred up behind him and a voice sneered, "Sandy's Trick?"

Prairie had always thought that if a big, fat black crow could talk, it would have Dakota's high-pitched, sneering voice. Prairie whirled around to tell him to get screwed, but Dakota was already accelerating away into the setting sun, off to some other rodeo. The last rays of the day slanting into his eyes and Son's next words made Prairie wince.

"I guess we all know what the pain of losing what you most love feels like." Son imbued the words with a full measure of C and W sentimentality. "Sometimes it gets to be more than even the strongest man can handle. So let's try to take a little of the hurt away."

Prairie turned back to the arena and saw Tuffie. She wasn't hard to spot in her standard rodeo outfit of red pants, red boots, red hat, and red shirt with giant white hearts on it. As soon as he spotted her, she dipped her head. Intense mortification shriveled him at the thought that even Tuffie couldn't face him. He went to her.

"Listen, I had nothing to do with that bullshit she's—" It took

Prairie a while to realize that tears were running down Tuffie's face. "Tuff, you know I never had a daughter named Sandy."

"Of course I know that, you fool. It was just a real pretty story. Is there a law somewhere says a person can't enjoy a pretty story?" Tuffie wiped her face angrily. "Go on. Get out of here. Go take a bow."

It wasn't until that moment that Prairie identified the sound he'd dedicated his life to hearing: a standing ovation.

Prairie looked at Tuffie, not believing his eyes or his ears: Pocahontas had gotten the citizens up off their keisters. For him. He hadn't gotten a standing O up in Calgary. He hadn't gotten one back when he and El Marinero played together. He hadn't even gotten one out of those kids from the state school. And now, to get a standing O here, in Hereford, Texas. Tuffie pushed him.

"Go on. Your fans is callin' you."

Prairie stumbled back into the arena, and the tidal wave of applause crested again. For once he didn't have to fake modesty. He was genuinely overwhelmed and, after his bow, retreated to the chip truck for the rest of the rodeo.

Up in the announcer's booth, Beaulieu finally succeeded in grappling the microphone away from Son.

"That was mighty kind of you, folks," Beaulieu said, trying to turn the applause into a charitable gesture.

Son rushed downstairs intending to follow Prairie, but was waylaid by a tall cowgirl with white-blond hair chopped off into a Dutch boy cut. "You the one doing the announcing for that roper?"

Son admitted she was.

"Outstanding," the young woman said, sounding like a naval cadet or an honor scout, the way so many of the cowgirls did. "An outstanding effort."

Son thanked her. The blonde went off and informed some of the other contestants who she was, and Son was swept up in a mini-wave of celebrity as several other cowgirls came over. Among them was Bucko.

"Hell of a job!" she said. "Sure beats this sorry sack of shit." She pointed up to the announcer's booth. "Sounds like he can't decide what kind of freaks of nature we are." They listened for a moment to Beaulieu.

"And don't forget, folks, soon's the goat-roping's over, some of these cowgirls'll be getting up on some bulls for us. So stick around. That's actual human women on actual bulls. Now let's go to the barrel racing!" Beaulieu put on a frenetic version of "Turkey in the Straw" and called for the first rider. A dinky cowgirl bobbing atop a charging horse burst past the electric eye at the starting gate.

"Come on." Bucko motioned to Son. "You can watch some 'actual human women' get ready to ride some actual bulls instead of these stick-figure girls on their four-legged bankrolls."

Behind the bucking chutes, an air of grim concentration hung over the bullriders preparing for their event. The manic strains of "Turkey in the Straw" repeated a couple of dozen times grated on raw nerves and pushed up already high pulses. Only Tuffie was unaffected. She buzzed about playing her usual role, mothering everyone around her. She was kneeling in front of a chubby young woman, wrapping an Ace bandage around the outside of her jeans, when she saw Son and waved her over.

"Best announcin' I've heard in years," she congratulated Son. "Son Hozro, this here's Jonni's little sister Carla Caulkins out of Sand Springs, Arkansas. Carla's fixing to ride her first bull tonight, Terminator." Carla gave Son a sick smile. "I was just tellin' Carla I drawed Terminator yesterday and he turned real snaky on me." Tuffie looked back up at the tense newcomer. "You think you're settin' back in granny's rocker, peaceful as can be; then that booger heaves up and blows you out the back end."

Carla's face, pale beneath her wide-brimmed hat, went a shade paler. Tuffie pinned the wrap in place and laughed. "Don't worry. You know all his tricks. Bulls are like men; long as you know their tricks, they can't surprise you. You might still *let* 'em fool you, but at least it ain't no surprise. Right?"

Carla gamely attempted a nod.

Tuffie glanced around and spotted Boots rubbing rosin into her riding glove. "Boots!" she yelled. "Do like I showed you and stretch them legs out. You pull a muscle, don't come to me for no Ben-Gay!" Tuffie turned to Son. "Go on and make that girl stretch out."

Son went over to Tuffie's oldest and suggested a stretch "for the anterior cruciate ligaments." Each stood on one foot, holding the toes of the other foot behind.

"You and Prairie going together?" Boots asked, out of what seemed to Son the clear blue.

"Going together? You mean is there a romantic attachment? No. Nothing of the sort. We're partners of circumstance and now there is a professional affiliation. Nothing more."

"So you ain't screwing him?"

Son blinked twice. Before she could answer, Boots said, "Don't worry. My mom wouldn't care anyhow. You'd be amazed at the trash he's trailed through here with. Yeah," she drawled, pulling her other leg up behind her, "I don't guess any of 'em were actual hookers. They just looked that way. You're the first decent one. Where you from, anyway?"

"San Antonio." Son could see no reason to claim a hometown she despised.

"There much a market for models there? Catalogue work? Local TV? Anything like that?"

"San Antonio is certainly a major media market. I'm sure there's a demand for women willing to"—Son decided not to say *prostitute themselves for the merchandising monolith*—"do that." She had the same feeling talking to Boots that she'd had with Jonathan. Not only wouldn't the club of her vocabulary work on Tuffie's offspring. She didn't need it with them.

She studied Boots and realized that Tuffie's children weren't all stamped out with a cookie cutter. The girl had thick, deep copper hair, a wide mouth, small nose, and, surprising for a red-head who was out in the sun as much as she was, unfreckled golden apricot skin. Her only flaw was her teeth. For possibly the first time in her life, Son looked at a pretty girl and saw beauty rather than one of the high school prisspots who had tormented her.

"A petite line, perhaps," Son suggested.

"Oh, don't worry. Runway work is out for me. I know that. I'd stick mostly to studio work. That would be the perfect thing to combine with my rodeoing. Western stuff, probably. Panhandle slim jeans. Justin shirts. Someday I'd like to get me my own line."

Boots looked out at the arena. A grim-faced pixie flogged her mount around a padded barrel. She gave an exasperated cluck. "They're still chasin' them cans." She looked back at Son. "Would you pull my flank strap for me? When I get down on my bull? You know, jerk the flank strap right before I turn out."

"Yes. Well, certainly." Son felt honored.

"My mom usually does it, but she's up first. I told her to keep away from me today anyway. She's too danged jumpy. She gets like that whenever Prairie's around for too long."

"She does?" Son wanted to know all about this jumpiness, about everything between Tuffie and Prairie. Before she could ask anything more, though, the frenzied strains of "Turkey in the Straw" fell silent and Beaulieu called out for a "big hand for these little ole gals and their little ole cowponies!"

Then he announced solemnly, "Bullriders, be gettin' your minds on it! Our first rider today will be Tuffie Branch on the bad bull, Equalizer! I'd like to put my mother-in-law on that bull. Aw, I'm just kiddin'. Actually, she's a very nice lady. She's down in San Diego right now teachin' the Marines how to fight dirty. Okay! We got Tuffie in the box, Bucko Bukowski on deck, and Boots Branch, you're in the hold."

While the crowd laughed, Boots scooped up her flat, braided manila bull rope with a bell attached to the end. She motioned for Son to follow and swung up on the catwalk behind the chutes. Son hauled herself up, but almost fell off when a bull in the chute next to her bellowed. Boots's spurs clanked and jangled as she walked down the wooden planks to chute Three, where the bull she'd drawn was waiting.

Dewey Dakota, Bucko Bukowski, and several more cowgirls were clustered around Tuffie's chute. Tuffie was already planted atop Equalizer. Boots walked past her without a glance. Tuffie broke her concentration long enough to watch her daughter. Son thought that she was going to say something, but she didn't.

Beaulieu spoke. "Tuffie herself told me that that feather in her hat is a toucan feather cost three-hunnert-fifty dollar." A long red feather sticking out from Tuffie's red hat bobbed in the still air with each movement she made. "She had to have that feather 'cause, as Tuffie says, she likes any color long as it's red."

Tuffie smiled automatically, showing unnaturally white front teeth but not breaking her concentration.

"We about ready to ride a bull, Tuffie? Hey, did I mention we got a mother-daughter challenge going today? Tuffie's going to be riding against her own daughter, Boots. Boots beat her mom yesterday riding Leatherface. So Tuffie's going to have to ride herself a bull today less she wants her young 'un to snatch the title away from her. Okay! Tuffie says she's ready! Here's the nod!"

Tuffie jerked her head down, the red feather whipped the air, the chute gate was thrown open, and the cream-colored bull beneath her erupted into the arena. It didn't break for freedom, though, but concentrated instead on trying to rid itself of the pesky human on its back, twisting and spinning. Tuffie's hat sailed off with the first buck, but she kept in perfect rhythm with the rampaging quadruped. She used a one-hand hold like male riders, swinging her free arm in back of her for balance.

Son froze, watching Tuffie's face. To Son, it seemed that the mammoth slab of beef was trying to dive deep into the earth. When he plunged down, Tuffie's face looked like a picture Son had once seen in a science book of a test pilot in an acceleration study, his face stretched backward by G-force. Across the arena, Son saw Prairie watching too. He stood outside the arena, his fingers clawed around the chain link fence.

The buzzer honked. Tuffie smiled and let go, toppling to the ground as easily as a young girl somersaulting down a hill. Now

that the bull was no longer a threat, the untried high school boy
Dakota had hired at minimum wage to be the rodeo clown, to be
the person who was supposed to save riders from enraged bulls,
danced in front of the animal. The bull ignored the beginner clown
and plodded off to the holding pen as peacefully as Elsie the Cow,
his long-lobed parts swinging behind him.

Tuffie rolled twice in the dirt, then sprang to her feet, grabbed
her hat, and waved it triumphantly in the air as the crowd applauded.

Son continued on to where Boots was getting ready. Tuffie's
daughter stood above her bull, straddling his bulk with a foot on
either side of the chute. Two of the cowboys she'd been flirting
with the day before were helping her get her bull rigged. The one
that was making Boots laugh the most had *Chance* tooled on the
back of his belt. He wore a tight T-shirt that showed off the muscles in his arms. Licks of dark brown hair stuck out from under his
straw hat.

"Yessir! Mama's making it tough for her baby today!" Beaulieu
yelled. "The judges have given Tuffie Branch an eighty-four!"

Boots stopped laughing at whatever Chance was saying long
enough to watch her mother caper jubilantly across the arena, stirring the crowd to thunderous applause. "She's such a show-off,"
the daughter muttered, before pulling on her glove and holding it
tight with her mottled brown teeth while she wrapped a rawhide
cord around her wrist to keep it from getting torn off. Son tried to
edge forward to help Boots with her glove, but Chance and his
friend blocked her way.

A cluster of cowgirls welcomed a grinning Tuffie. "Boy-
howdy!" Tuffie said, heaving a happy sigh. "That son of a bitch
does try to alley-oop you. He about jerked me out my own asshole."

Beaulieu went on. "That was some ride! And that bull was no
dink! These gals have the option of using both hands and most of
'em just don't have the strength to do it any other way . . ."

"Less'n they're diesel dykes," Chance said. Immediately, he

looked at Boots. "I didn't mean your ma. I meant some of these other hunkers out here. Like Tinker Bell over there." He jerked his head back toward Bucko Bukowski rigging up in the next chute.

Boots glanced over her shoulder at Bucko, who was scooting down, almost sitting on top of her right hand, which was wrapped in the bull rope. Bucko pounded the rope down on top of her riding hand, grimacing in a way that showed her false front teeth as she closed her riding hand over the rope. The muscles in her arm jumped into strong relief. Chance rolled his eyes at Boots in a way that said, "See what I mean?"

Chance climbed on the gate and dropped the rope, weighted by a cowbell, down beside the bull. Boots lowered herself onto the bull's back. His ribs were hard against the chute and she had to jam her leg between the bull's heaving side and the metal grating. She slipped her gloved hand into the grip, paused, and looked over at Chance. Then she stuck her other hand, the hand she usually left free, down next to it. Chance wrapped the free end of the rope around both her hands with the palms facing up as if she were scooping up water.

Son attempted again to muscle past the cowboys clustered around Boots. "You really shouldn't," she tried to yell past the impassible barrier of their backs. "Your mother doesn't want you to ride with both hands, you know!"

Boots caught Son's eye and ordered Chance, "Tighter. There's no way I'm going to be able to hold on to this bull unless I'm practically tied on." Thrilled by her admission of feminine fraility, Chance leaned over close to Boots and applied the full force of his manly power to strapping both her hands in.

"My chaps is hung up," Bucko called to Son from the next chute. Son gave up on warning Boots and went to Bucko. She pulled the chap free from where it was trapped, twisted, beneath the cowgirl's leg. With the speed of a snake striking, the bull flicked his head back and split the Son's lip. The salty, metallic taste of her own blood filled Son's mouth. She had been initiated. She was a blood cowgirl now.

"Next up we have a local cowgirl, Bucko Bukowski, on the bad bull A-Team!"

Bucko nodded and barked, "Outside!"

Dewey Dakota threw open the gate; Bucko tensed every muscle in her toned body in anticipation of the whiplashing to come. A-Team didn't budge. He was the picture of suspended animation until Dewey swung up on the catwalk and delivered a few volts to the reluctant warrior's backside with the hotshot. Even then, the bull did little more than amble into the arena. Bucko tried spurring the beast. A-Team responded with a shudder that rippled his flanks as if he were trying to shoo away a deerfly.

The cowboys in Boots's chute looked at each other and shook their heads at the comic predictability of it all. Girls riding bulls.

After six seconds, the buzzer sounded. Bucko unwrapped her rope, and the cowbell underneath the bull pulled it free. She put both her hands on his enormous skull and vaulted over his head, landing on her feet in front of him. A-Team stepped politely around her and trotted to the holding pen.

"That ole bull just didn't come to play today, folks," Beaulieu told the crowd. "That's all there is to it. Judges have given Bucko a score of fifty. That's the most they can award a rider. But they had to give ole A-Team a zero. Bucko can take a reride if she wants it. Next up, we'll see how the younger generation does it. Tuffie's little gal, Boots Branch, on the bad bull Freddy!"

Son finally managed to crowd forward between the cowboys.

"Squash my hat down," Boots asked Son. "Chance's going to pull my strap," she said when Son leaned close to push the Resistol down on Boots's head until her ears stuck out. "You don't mind, do you?"

Son shrugged as Chance pushed her out of the way and grabbed the strap hanging loose around Freddie's flanks. He looked to Boots for the nod that would be his signal to yank the sheepskin-lined strap tight and, he hoped, start the animal bucking.

"Ged oudda way." Dewey Dakota muscled Chance aside and grabbed the flank strap. The young giant was seething with humiliation at the embarrassing performance put on by the last member of his father's team. He was certain that the flank strap on Bucko's bull hadn't been pulled tight enough, and he was there to see it didn't happen again.

"You ready," he told rather than asked Boots. Dewey was eager to see one of his boys take a cowgirl apart.

"No, she ain't ready!" Tuffie shoved Dewey aside and wedged into the circle hovering around her daughter. Boots looked up, gave one exquisitely exasperated hiss, and turned away grimly.

"Girl! What in hallelujah's name do you think you're doin' with both your hands wrapped?" Tuffie asked. Boots continued to stare ahead grimly, sinking into a state of teenage Zen in which she mentally erased her mother's presence. Tuffie, however, especially a mad Tuffie, was simply not a presence to be erased. She slugged her daughter on the forearm. "You answer me now, you hear?"

Boots looked out into the arena and said, "I ain't strong enough to ride one-handed."

"Ain't strong enough! You was strong enough last night when you got you an eighty-three with one hand. It's these boys. You can't get your mind right with these boys sniffing around."

"Mo-o-om," Boots said shrilly, "I know what I'm doing."

"You haven't known what you was doin' since you got into panty liners. You want to end up like me? Like Bucko?" Tuffie stuck her thumb behind her front teeth and tugged. She pulled out the front five and waved them in her daughter's face. "Thith what you want?" she asked.

"You ride one-handed," Tuffie promised, replacing her teeth, "you'll end up without your grinners. And look the way you got your hands wrapped. Ain't no way you can bail out if you get in a storm. You're gonna hang up sure as anything."

"You just don't want me to beat you," Boots said. "That's it, isn't it? The great Tuffie Branch, queen of girls' rodeo, can't stand to get beat by her daughter. Why don't you just go away and let me ride my bull?"

Tuffie, wounded, backed off. "All right. But don't come to me for no partial plate."

Son, feeling useless, backed away too.

Tuffie turned to her. "Stubborn." Tuffie shook her head and the toucan feather cut through the air. "Stubborn. Just like her daddy. Course he was a bulldogger and got that way from landing on his head one too many times. Lord! She's a stubborn child." She searched the arena. "Where the hell's that sorry kid's pretending to be a clown?" She located the scared boy and screamed down to him, "Move in closer! Get ready, son! There's a cruncher coming!" The boy held his arms out and bounced from foot to foot. He looked a lot more like the high school basketball player he was than a bullfighter.

Dewey held up an okay sign to the announcer and Beaulieu went back to work. "All right! The girls are done with their little powwow. We're ready to ride a bull. Outta Chute Number Three your hometown cowgirl, Boots Branch, riding the good bull FAH-RED-DEE!"

Dewey hauled up on the flank strap until the muscles in his right arm bulged with the strain. With his left hand he jabbed the hotshot at the bull. Freddie bellowed in rage. When the chute gate was thrown open, the beast erupted into the arena.

Son watched in frozen horror. Freddie was a force of nature. He made the bulls who had preceded him look like Shetland ponies.

The first buck jerked Boots's hat off. The second unseated her. The third jerked her forward so that her front teeth collided with the back of the bull's skull. Freddie didn't notice the impact, but Boots was knocked out cold. The next buck tossed her off his back. But she was still not free. The rope Chance had wrapped around her hands held tight. Boots dangled lifelessly from Freddie's great neck. Her small body flopped against his side like a streamer in the wind as he kicked his hind legs out, trying to shake loose of the strap tourniqueted around his flanks. Then he dived to the earth, his hooves barely missing Boots.

"Oh, God! She's hung up!" Tuffie screamed and jumped down off the catwalk.

The first-time clown danced about on his tiptoes, flapping his arms and pretending to jockey for position without ever actually advancing one inch closer to the bull.

When Tuffie saw that no one was helping her daughter, she broke into the arena, running as fast as her red boots would carry her through the plowed earth. Prairie had already scaled the chain link fence. He hopped to the ground and intercepted Tuffie, pushing her back to the chutes.

Prairie maneuvered himself in front of the cycloning bull, stopped dead, and held out both arms. The fringe on his shirt made them look like giant, glittering wings. For a moment, the bull thought a huge strange bird had dropped to earth. Freddie stopped trying to crash through the earth's crust and studied the creature flapping its arm-wings at him. Prairie took advantage of the animal's brief distraction to dart in and yank the flank strap loose. Freddie calmed down the instant his nether regions were set free.

Taking courage from Prairie, the clown actually moved forward and diverted the bull long enough for Prairie to work loose the rope handcuffing Boots. The girl dropped into his arms and he ran with her to the sidelines. Tuffie went wobbly when she saw her daughter's face pale as death everywhere that it wasn't sheeted with blood.

The public address system crackled back to life after a long, stunned silence. "Boys, you better throw the gate," Beaulieu said, as a station wagon converted into an ambulance backed into the arena. Paramedics pulled a stretcher from the back and opened out its long wheeled legs. Prairie laid Boots's inert body on it, and the paramedics closed in around her.

"These gals come out of their own free will," Beaulieu reminded the audience. "Nobody makes 'em get up on these big ole bulls."

Tuffie crowded in next to her daughter as a paramedic leaned in to listen to her heart.

"Praise the Lord," Tuffie whispered as Boots's eyes fluttered open.

Feeling wetness on her cheeks, Boots touched her face. She touched the hole behind her lips where her front teeth had been. "Mama, I'll never be a model."

"Don't talk that way," Tuffie said sharply, forcing her fear into a place where she could fight with it. "You told me all about that one model in New York got all sliced up with razors now every make-up company in the country's after her."

Tears mingled with the blood on Boots's battered face as she touched her empty mouth. "But, Mama, my teeth."

"Them old spotty things? We'll buy you some lots better than them."

The paramedics strapped Boots onto the stretcher and slid it into the back of the ambulance. Tuffie climbed in, pushing away the paramedic who made the mistake of trying to keep her out.

Son was on the ground by the gate when the ambulance pulled out. Tuffie screamed and the ambulance stopped. She pushed the back door open. "Son," she yelled, "look after my kids, will you?"

Before Son could agree, Tuffie tossed her the keys to her truck. The driver closed the doors and the ambulance pulled away. In the greenish light illuminating the back of the station wagon, Son could see Tuffie brushing the hair out of Boots's face while a paramedic attached an IV to the girl's arm and another pressed gauze pads into her mouth stop the bleeding. When the paramedic held up Boots's arm to start the IV, Son saw her hand dangle from her wrist like a broken lily.

Prairie came up and stood beside her.

Beaulieu sounded far away as he announced, "I just heard that that cowgirl's gonna be okay. They tell me that the main thing she's worried about is if her boyfriend saw her with her make-up smeared."

Son bent over and picked up Tuffie's red hat. The toucan

feather was broken. "Someone should take a gun to that man," Son said, surprised that she couldn't control her voice. She stroked the crumpled feather, trying futilely to straighten it out.

Prairie put his arm around her and they watched the ambulance's spinning red dome until it was lost in the sunset.

Chapter 16.

Once he and Son had collected all the young Branches, Prairie loaded Domino into the trailer hitched to the back of Tuffie's truck and took the chip truck to the hospital. Tuffie's children were unsettlingly quiet as Son gathered them into the truck. Usually they fought over who would ride in the camper; tonight all four crowded into the cab with Son. As she drove, Son noted that none of the children had said a word since they'd left the rodeo grounds.

Spur, the fourteen-year-old girl, stared intently out the window, paying no attention to Jonathan squirming on her lap or to the twins clumped dolorously beside her. Suddenly she burst into tears and wailed, "I told Boots I hoped she got on some kind of cruncher turned her lights out for her."

All the other children began sobbing, and Son decided that they needed some cheering up. Already slowing down to turn off the highway onto the half-mile road that led to Tuffie's, she braked to a stop, turned around, and went back to town.

Unused to putting the starch back into children, Son was forced to rely on the wisdom of the merchandising monolith and pulled into McDonald's. As soon as they were inside, the air conditioning started perking everyone up, and she instructed the four petite redheads to order anything they wanted. Then she went into the ladies' room and pulled some bills from the rapidly shrinking bulge still tied around her waist. Feeling low, she succumbed to a hamburger herself.

The three youngest bolted their food and dashed outside to play in a net-enclosed structure filled with colored balls. Son began to appreciate the appeal of the Golden Arches.

Spur, sitting across from Son, put down the McRib sandwich she was nibbling wanly. "Boots used to be a real good whistler."

"She'll still be able to whistle," Son answered, not knowing or caring whether it was true.

"No, Mama used to be a real good whistler. After she got her teeth all knocked out, she never whistled no more."

Jonathan, who'd come back in to report that Latigo was beaning him with the colored balls, agreed sadly—"Yeah, she don't whistle no more"—even though he hadn't yet been born back in Tuffie's whistling days.

Son stood and herded the two Branches outside, where she pointedly ignored the sign at the entrance to the ball cage that no one over four feet tall was allowed inside the enclosure. She pushed Spur and Jonathan in, then dove into the pool of colored balls herself and began winging them wildly at the children.

Jonathan recovered first from the shock of seeing an adult woman wallowing in the McDonald's ball room and yelled out, "Dogpile on Son!"

All four Branches responded, jumping on Son until she felt as if she were being smothered beneath an octopus with small bony arms and legs. Jonathan managed to end up near her head, where he decided that it was his duty to trap Son by wrapping his arms around her neck. He held her captive, pressing his soft cheek tight against hers. The smell of his little-boy breath, sweet and milky as caramel candy, filled Son's nostrils while the other Branches rained a bright hail of balls down on them both.

Son figured she had done a fair job of brightening diminutive outlooks.

Back at Tuffie's house, the twins showed her how to take care of Domino. They insisted that Domino's dinner must start off with a flake of hay. "It's like a salad. Horses need their greens just like we do," the Branches explained, even though none of them ever personally made contact with a fresh vegetable that didn't sit atop a hamburger patty.

The twins measured out the rest of the formula. "Then two quarts uh sweet feed, two uh oats, and the vitamins." Domino nibbled at the mixture, nostrils distended like a gourmet reduced to canned hash. Jonathan stood at Son's feet, stretching up as far as he could to whisk the hairs on Domino's belly with a body brush.

When it was nearly one o'clock, Son suggested that they might want to go to bed, but the children assured her that Tuffie let them stay up as long as they liked. Then Spur, who still hadn't said much, asked whether Sandy ever rode bulls.

"Sandy?" Son repeated blankly. Suddenly she remembered the heroine of her maudlin tale. "Bulls, broncs, anything with hair," she answered, borrowing another Beaulieu line. The instant she started talking about Sandy, the children fell silent. Son looked at the small faces fastened on her and began embroidering a charmed life for the doomed Sandy, a life that involved living among the Indians, wing walking, and standing on her head in the saddle of a galloping horse.

Son didn't fully believe in the power of her recently discovered gift for narrative until she saw all four Branch mouths hanging open as the children absorbed Sandy's exploits in slack-jawed wonder, then wandered off to bed without another word. Son carried the youngest, Jonathan, already fast asleep, back to Tuffie's room and tucked him in. When she started to leave, planning to sleep in the printing room, Jonathan woke up and informed her in a level voice, "There are monsters in here who will put June bugs in my hair if you leave." So Son lay down next to the little boy. He snuggled against her and, snoring loudly, re-entered sleep at precisely the extreme depth he'd momentarily left it.

The feel of the small, warm body next to hers was one Son had trouble categorizing. Though she was far from comfortable, shoved nearly off the edge of the bed, with a surprisingly sharp elbow poking into her, she would not have moved the little boy for anything. She watched him in the moonlight. He seemed to concentrate much harder on sleep than on anything she'd seen him attempt in his waking moments.

The more she studied the little sleeper, the more Son realized that, like Boots, he was no carbon copy of Tuffie. Like all her children, he had her red hair and slight build, but there was something else in his face—an awareness, a detachment. Son decided that he had the bearing of a scholar.

Unbidden, an image floated across Son's mind of Jonathan on the playground of one of the ramshackle hick schools he would have to attend, surrounded by smirking bullies. They taunted the little boy, calling him names until he cried. Then, when the tears they'd worked for finally came, they gathered closer and jeered into his face, "Crybaby, crybaby! Run home and cry to your mommy 'cause you ain't got no daddy!"

The blood throbbed in Son's temples as she imagined herself, big as the Colossus of Rhodes come to life, stepping into the circle of tiny tormentors. All the bullies would see of her would be a pair of legs like stone pillars and hands big as the shovel on a backhoe coming down out of the sky to scoop up their prey. When they were frozen in place, paralyzed by terror, a voice would boom down at them from a head lost in the glare of a sun she nearly covered, "If you ever bother Jonathan Branch again, I will step on your house!" When the screaming and shrieks of terror had died down, she would add, "However, if you are kind to this wonderful child, he will be the best friend you have ever had and I will protect you all your days."

Son wrapped her arms around Jonathan and thought about reading him *Treasure Island*, then making a treasure map for him to follow to the chest of chocolate doubloons wrapped in gold that she would have buried earlier. It could be an important lesson in compass headings. Son was still awake, planning a treasure hunt, when

Spur came into the room near dawn with tears running down her face. "Is she gonna be okay?" Boots's sister sniffled in a small voice.

Son, who'd always cried alone, didn't know quite how to comfort the teenager. Without a word, Spur got into bed with Son and Jonathan. Son's hands twitched above the girl's red hair a few times before they settled down and stroked it. This seemed to slow Spur's sobbing, and even after she fell into a fitful sleep, Son continued stroking her shiny copper hair.

Son heard Prairie come in a little later. She untangled herself from a cocoon of thin arms and legs and slipped out of bed.

"How is she?" Son asked, surprised to see how old and tired Prairie looked in the thin gray light of early morning.

"Good; she's good." Prairie heaved an exhausted sigh and slumped into Tuffie's armchair with vinyl-cushioned wagon wheels on the sides. "They wheeled Boots out of the operating room. And she looked like the mummy's bride or something. No teeth in front yet or anything, but she's going to be okay. Doc said it wasn't really as bad as it looked.

"But here's the incredible part. Tuffie's got insurance. Can you believe it? Her and Boots just started working split shifts at this convenience store and they actually have insurance. Typical Tuffie. Just when you're sure the wheels are going to fall off, she pulls it out. Un-fragsping-believable. God, I'm hammered."

Prairie sprawled his legs out in front of him, folded his arms across his chest, and was instantly asleep. Son fished the truck keys out of his pocket and drove into town to find the hospital.

It was nearly eight in the morning by the time Son reached Hereford General Hospital. On the third floor, surgical wing, Son found Boots's room and hesitantly pushed back the swinging door. She'd stopped in the gift shop downstairs and paid the exorbitant price demanded for a stuffed polar bear simply because that particular animal had the softest white fur imaginable. At times it helped to have small, exceptionally soft things to cuddle.

Tuffie was not in the room, and Boots seemed to be asleep.

Her copper hair fanning across the pillow blazed even more vividly than usual. Son was about to let the door swing shut again when Boots flagged a wave with her good hand and croaked out, "Hey."

Son went into the room. Most of Boots's face was covered with white gauze. The parts left exposed, the left cheek, her eyes, nose, mouth, were blotched with purple bruises going eggplant black. When she smiled, though, the bandages and bruises seemed like cartoon props, as if cartoon stars should be the only emblems of pain. Her smile, more gum now than tooth, was the silly sweet smile of a baby.

Son couldn't figure out what to say and thrust the stuffed animal into the girl's left hand.

Boots stroked the toy for several moments. "He's so soft." She could no longer pronounce *s*. It came out *th*, just like Mickey's Jackson's helper.

"Is Tuffie around?" Son asked, simply because it was the first thing she could think of to say. She had never visited anyone in a hospital.

"She went down to the coffee shop." Boots looked back down at the polar bear and continued stroking it.

Behind Son's head the wall-mounted television set played softly. Son ignored Regis and Kathie Lee interviewing Donny Osmond as she struggled for something to say. "Do you need anything?"

"Yeah, you could hand me that cord there." Boots flapped her left hand behind her awkwardly, trying not to disturb her splinted and bandaged right hand, which rested on her chest.

"This?" Son held up a button on a cord and handed it to Boots, who pushed the button. A tiny *ding* sounded.

"Are you calling a nurse?" Son guessed.

"No, I'm getting high. This is hooked up to that." She nodded to a machine mounted on the far side of the bed that had a tube running into a vein in Boots's right arm. "It's a morphine machine. I'm supposed to give myself a ding whenever my cheek or something starts hurting. I guess I must be 'bout half dope fiend. I like feeling all floaty and off in the clouds somewhere."

"Actually, studies have shown that patients who are allowed to administer their own pain medication tend to use less than . . ." Son caught herself lecturing and trailed off.

"You know tons of shit, don't you?" Boots's voice was dreamy as an opium smoker's.

" 'Tons of shit,' " Son repeated. "Precisely." The thought depressed her so much that she sank into the chair Tuffie had pulled up right next to her daughter's bed and stared at Kathie Lee's orthodontic perfection until Boots asked, in her floaty, dreamy voice, "You ever curl your hair?"

"Um, well, yes, I have. Whenever the marching band performed."

"It'd look good in a kind of a page boy." Boots shifted herself up a bit higher on the pillows. "Let's see, okay? I got my styling wand in my bag. Go on, get it out."

Eager to provide any distraction she could, Son dug the cordless curling iron out of Boots's purse. Turning to the mirror over the corner sink, she dutifully began rolling her hair on the implement. Boots watched with complete absorption as Son, who quickly learned to keep the hot iron away from her neck, attacked the task.

One half of her hair was resting on her shoulder in a gleaming roll, fat as a sausage, with the other half still hanging down straight, when Boots asked, "When you were growing up, did you think much about your daddy?"

Son stopped, her hair clenched in the jaws of the curling iron. A long moment, filled first with forced television brightness, then with the smell of burning hair, passed before Son answered, "Every day of my life. Every day of my life."

Boots looked down and stroked the polar bear. "Yeah, me too."

Son opened the curling iron, and the charred strand dropped free. Cursing the merchandising monolith under her breath and the sadistic Sodomites who used fashion's dictates to enslave women to such instruments of torture, Son turned the implement off and started to return it to Boots's purse.

"You should keep it," Boots said, reaching for the morphine button again. "I got another one at home. The cordless kind's good for travel. You don't have to plug it in."

"No, I really—"

"No, take it. You look good with your hair curled. The top part falls over the place you burned off. I don't hardly never use that one anyway."

"Actually, I—"

"It'll be good on the road. That way, when you find your father, you can fix up before you go to meet him. Maybe it'll be at an airport and you can get one of them computer banners made up to meet him with. Or, no, no, it'd probably be better just to have a bouquet. Don't get roses, though. People always get roses. Roses are sad. Roses are a very sad flower. Especially them red ones that are almost black. Even carnations are better than roses. No, no, I know, when you go to meet your father, you should get tulips. Tulips are the best. Yellow. Yellow tulips are the cheerfullest flower there is."

Son held the curling iron for a second. "Thanks," she finally said. "I have a picture of my father."

"You do?" For a second Boots came out of her dreamy haze.

Son pulled the publicity still from her mess kit purse and handed it to Boots, who studied it for a very long time. "He's handsome." Reluctantly, the girl handed the photo back and Son put it and the cordless curling iron next to the antique photo-gray sunglasses in her bag. "Do you . . ." she began, feeling around for the right words. "Do any of your brothers or sisters . . . Has Tuffie ever told you—"

"Who our daddies are?"

"Yeah."

"No, she's just said they're all real sorry. That if any of them cared enough, they'd make it their business to find out about us.

None of them ever did, but Mom says if we really want to know, she'll tell us when we turn eighteen."

"What about Jonathan? Do you remember who Tuffie was . . . dating about that time?"

"Well, now, dating's one thing. There's a whole list I could give you there. Screwing, that's another thing. I couldn't say exactly who she was screwing back then."

"Didn't any of them ever want to marry Tuffie?"

"Lots of 'em. They still do. Mom's been married, even though she says she never was. She was married to my father when I was born and even for a few months after. I'm legitimate. But that was enough for her. She says marriage is like a hot bath. Once you get used to it, it ain't so hot anymore."

Boots fell silent again and they both stared at the television for several minutes. When Son glanced up, the girl was asleep. Son tiptoed to the door, pushed it open, and stepped into Tuffie, who collapsed into her arms as if she'd been waiting on the other side of the door to do just that.

"She's asleep," Son whispered.

Tuffie reached out for Son's hand. "Don't never be a mother. There is no pain on this earth like seeing one of your own hurting. How's my kids?"

Son told her all about the previous night. Tuffie listened for several minutes, then pushed against Boots's door. "I got to get back to her." Before she went in, though, Tuffie stopped. "Listen, I was thinking, if you can't find Cootie, ask Casey Dakota about this reunion deal."

Tuffie had the door half-opened when Son stopped her with a hand on her shoulder. "Casey Dakota was a roper?"

"He's thrown a fancy loop or two."

"How old is he? Dakota?"

"Forty-nine in human years, which makes that son of a bitch what? Eight?"

"He's forty-nine and he was a roper? Does he have any Native American blood?"

"Whoa. Whoa. Whoa. I know what you're thinking, but you can forget it. Casey Dakota shoots blanks."

"He what?"

"Shoots blanks. He can't be your father. He's sterile."

"Are you sure?"

"Well, we didn't do any lab tests, but I took a couple of turns around the dance floor with him before my taste was fully developed and *I'm* not raising any living memento of his. So, yeah, I'd have to say he's no threat in the population explosion department. Look, I gotta get back in there. Could you get Prairie to bring me a toothbrush?"

By the time Son agreed, Tuffie had already gone in to her daughter.

Son had to concentrate, as she drove up the road to Tuffie's house, to avoid ruts that would have eaten up a truck tire. Finally the house came into view, and she gave it the careful once-over she'd had no time for in the morning. It was covered in cracked asbestos shingles the color of cement. A rusty stain dribbled from beneath the leaky outside water faucet. The front yard was a plot of hard-packed dirt decorated by an occasional clump of Johnson grass. Son parked the truck and heard noise in the back.

She wandered around to the back yard, and there was Prairie, surrounded by all four remaining Branch children, rehanging the window screens that rested against the house at odd angles. The crew was so absorbed in their work, they didn't notice her.

"This one here came out when He-man flew through it," Jonathan explained to Prairie as he seated the rusty screen.

"Yeah, well, He-man ever comes through this one again, he's going to get his skinny butt blistered. Hand me the needle-nosed pliers."

"No, stupid." Latigo grabbed a wrench out of Jonathan's hands and picked up the correct tool. "This's the one he wants." He held the pliers reverently in both hands as he offered them up to Prairie.

"Thanks, knucklehead." Prairie took the pliers and twisted a paint-encrusted hook so that the screen would hang from it. "Hey, Spur, Lasso, why don't you girls turn to and muscle some of the crud off that windowsill." He tossed each one a piece of sandpaper. They snapped them up like seagulls grabbing bread crusts out of the air and started in on the next window.

Still twisting the hook, Prairie asked Jonathan and Latigo, "Doesn't it bother you boys having the house full of flies? You should fix some of this shit up for your mother."

He handed Latigo the pliers. "You're not the boss of me!" Latigo croaked out. "I don't have to do nothing you say!"

"That's right, knucklehead, you don't. Me and Jonathan can finish up just fine without you. Can't we, Big J?"

"Yeah, we don't need knucklehead. Give them noodle-nose pliers to me."

Jonathan tried to wrest the pliers from Latigo's grip. When Latigo wouldn't relinquish them, Jonathan turned loose a Conelrad alert scream.

"Belay that!" Prairie's bellowed order surprised Jonathan into silence. "One more eardrum buster like that and you're in the brig, buddy!"

Jonathan turned to his big brother. "Whud he say?"

"Time out, stupid."

"Oh."

"You bet your sweet Aunt Fanny 'oh.'" Prairie sized up the last fallen screen and moved to the window the girls were scrubbing away at. "Outstanding job, troops," he pronounced, pushing a dirty curtain back inside the house and brushing paint chips out of the way.

As he was jamming the crooked screen back into place, Prairie noticed that Jonathan seemed to have taken his correction hard. The little boy's shoulders and head were slumped forward in a four-year-old's finest dramatic interpretation of dejection. Son was on the verge of stepping out to comfort the boy when Prairie turned to him. "Hey, squirt, you're just the man I need. Come here and let me hike you up so you can get this son of a buck hooked."

Jonathan looked like a time-lapse film of a wilted daisy perking up in the rain; he raised his head and ran to help. Prairie swung him onto his shoulders and the boy latched the top hook of the screen. As they worked on the rest of the screens, Prairie sang:

Jimmie crack corn and I don't care
Jimmie crack corn and I don't care
Jimmie crack corn and I don't care
My master's gone away.

Which, for reasons Son could not fathom, absolutely convulsed Jonathan.

When they were finished, Prairie looked at his bare wrist and called out, "Whoa! Beer-thirty! Break time! Union rules! We're entitled. Who knows how to make brown cows?"

"We ain't got no root beer," Latigo piped up, "but we got Coke. We can make black cows."

"Excellent!" With Jonathan still riding on his shoulders, Prairie marched into the house, the young Branches all crowding after him. Son met them in the kitchen. The room had been transformed.

"Hey, Duchess, what do you think?" Prairie asked, taking in with one expansive gesture the mopped floors, clean countertops, and dishes drying in the rack.

"We all did KP," Lasso explained.

"And you did it spectacularly well," Son said.

By the second day of Boots's hospital stay, her doctor allowed the brothers and sisters to visit. Jonathan took along a drawing of a tyrannosaurus rex eating a backhoe, which the little boy felt would cheer up his sister. Son asked to stay behind, and Prairie drove them in. Son intended to use the time to think, to sort out her thoughts about Prairie and Tuffie and Tuffie's tribe.

Instead, she found herself scrubbing the fuzzy green ring from Tuffie's toilet. When she realized she was re-creating the antiseptic *Koyaanisqatsi* atmosphere Tinka had raised her in, Son threw down the toilet brush in horror. But she couldn't bear thinking of Jonathan being so close to that fuzzy green ring when he went to the potty. Obviously, the stringent code she herself followed in seeking to bring her life more into harmony with nature as her Native American ancestors had done would have to be modified when dealing with humans under four feet tall. She picked up the brush again, and finished the job.

When she was through there, she fixed the front screen door, reattaching the spring so that it would close behind the little Branches as they thundered in and out. Then Son went on to clean out Tuffie's refrigerator; she tossed away curled-up pucks of bologna, three completely bare blue tubs of margarine, and a desicated head of lettuce dried down to the size of an onion.

"I was gonna eat that bologna," Jonathan wailed when he beheld the gleaming appliance.

"Looks empty" was Lasso's comment.

Son rectified that condition with a shopping trip during which she pared down her disappearing stack of bills even farther. She returned with sacks full of Uncle Sam cereal, bell peppers, Minute Maid orange juice, whole wheat bread, strawberries, various dried legumes, muenster cheese, dried apricots, and peanut butter.

By the end of the week, at about the time they received word that Boots was going to be discharged, the Branch children had stopped regarding whole wheat bread as a highly threatening foreign food. When Boots was discharged, Son waited at home while everyone else crowded into the chip truck to pick the patient up. She'd soaked a selection of beans the night before, and now she put them on to cook. She had decided to make nine-bean soup from a *Woman's Day* recipe she'd managed to memorize while standing in the checkout line at Albertson's. Son had thought that a soft food like soup would be easiest on Boots's tender mouth, but as sweat started running down her face, she doubted the wisdom of her decision.

When she heard the truck pull up outside, she wanted to rush out and be part of Boots's welcome home. But the odd diffidence that had overtaken her ever since having her personal vision and then glimpsing Prairie and Tuffie making love held her back. She stayed in the kitchen, her face flushing red as she stirred her soup and listened for a sign that her presence might be desired.

"I can't believe this is the same nasty old house I left a week ago," Boots said as she walked in, her gait wobbly after a week spent mostly in bed. Prairie followed, holding her bag and several bunches of Mylar balloons. "Smells like pine trees and lemons."

"Well, thank my good fairy, Son," Tuffie said.

"I helped too!" Jonathan squawked.

Tuffie picked him up and smooched his neck. "I know you did, you little snuggle bug. You were the best helper of all."

"Actually," Spur corrected her, "Latigo and I were the ones responsible for most of the helping."

"You 'actually' was?" Tuffie said, laughing. "Prairie, we'd better get your announcer to move in permanent. She's educatin' my kids."

Son wanted to rush out and tell Tuffie how remarkably intelligent all her children were. She wanted to say something that would keep Tuffie glowing with happiness the way she was now that she had her brood all back together.

"Son got us li-berry cards!" Jonathan yelled in his mother's ear. "And you know what? You know what? You know what?"

"No. What? What? What?"

"I got me a book what shows all the dinosaurs. But we putted back the screens so now tyrannosaurus rex cannot come in my window and eat me."

"I know. I saw."

Prairie put Boots's bag down and tethered the balloons to the arm of a chair. "Well, as Jesus said, 'My work here is done.' "

"What do you know about Jesus?" Tuffie swatted him with her free hand.

"I know I'd think a damn sight better of him if he'd have delivered unto *me* a rich woman with a heart condition who was going to die and leave *me* her first husband's rodeo company instead of the pigporker."

"Don't blaspheme," Tuffie scolded. "Why do you keep working for Casey, you hate him so much? Where is Son anyway? Son!"

Son almost put her spoon down and came out, but a sharp edge in Prairie's voice held her back.

"Tuff? Tuff! I can't believe you're even asking that. You come up with the name of one, just one, other contractor still hiring a rope act and Casey Dakota can kiss my ass good-by."

"I don't know why you let him get to you so bad. Casey Dakota's just some old Okie worried about the size of his pecker."

"That's exactly the kind goes out, buys a rifle and a Zebra scope, and gets up on top of a tall building. You shouldn't talk like that in front of the kids."

"Don't tell me how to raise my kids!" The sudden flash of Tuffie's anger carried straight to Son in the kitchen. "The day you start paying my rent and making my truck payments and putting boots on little feet is the *first* day you get the right to tell me shit like that!"

"Look, you want me gone, I'm gone!" Prairie blasted back. "Son! Son, where are you? Where's my announcer?" Son hung back and Prairie turned to Tuffie. "For your information, I talked to your friend yesterday and he has a gig for me. I was thinking about turning him down so I could hang around here some more, but I see that my presence is no longer required or desired. Son! Where the hell are you!"

Son stepped out of the kitchen. "Oh, hello. I didn't hear you come in."

"When the hell you turn into frigging Donna Reed?" Prairie growled. Son pulled off the apron she'd forgotten she had on. "We're leaving. Get your stuff. Be on board in ten minutes or we sail without you. I'll wait in the truck." Dust billowed from the screen door when Prairie slammed it.

The Branch children stood watching his retreat in silence.

Jonathan slid down from his mother's neck and went to press his nose against the screen. "Why's he mad for?"

Tuffie shrugged.

"He's not mad at you." Son knelt down beside the boy. The screen smelled of old rust. They watched Prairie's angry, jerky movements as he loaded Domino.

"I got to lay down," Boots said. Spur followed her. A moment later, the twins, then Jonathan, trailed after them.

Son and Tuffie were alone. Son stood up. "I don't think that he intended to criticize you."

"Probably not." Tuffie had crossed her arms across her chest. "I was just giving him an exit line if he wanted to grab for it and he sure enough snapped it, didn't he? He was ready to move on. I don't ever intend to hang on to a man doesn't want to stay. Spent my whole life growing up with a father didn't want to be there and I will *never* do that to my kids." Tuffie uncrossed her arms and they drooped to her sides. "You're more than welcome to stay as long as you want. I appreciate everything what all you've done."

"I wish I could." Son was starting to question what difference it would make if she found her father. Being around Tuffie and her children made the whole question seem highly optional.

"Well, you can." Tuffie stared out the screen door at Prairie's jerky, angry movements. "There's plenty of room."

Son was almost ready to accept that lie when Tuffie continued, "I wasn't supposed to tell you this, but you got the right to know. Prairie James doesn't tell me what to do." Tuffie paused. "I found out where Cootie Ramos is."

"You did? Where?"

"Some kind of strange deal over in New Mexico. Place called Rancho Encantada north of Santa Fe. Why didn't Prairie want me to tell you?"

"That's a very good question." Son stared out at Prairie, trying to imagine a good answer. She was too confused to come up with one.

"Like I said, you can stay here's long as you want."

In an instant, Son's confusion cleared and she felt one thing and one thing alone: pissed-off. "No, dammit all to perdition! Prairie James contracted to help me find my father and that, by thunder, is what he is going to do! He owes it to me to at least take me to Cootie Ramos. And he should take me all the way to the ropers' reunion."

"Amen to that!" Tuffie looked at Son and nodded fierce affirmation.

Son nodded back. "Also, he's depending on me to announce for him. I realize it's not much, but being a rodeo announcer has come to mean a great deal to me."

"Don't talk to me about 'not much.' I been making it on not much all my life. Besides, as far as rodeo goes, not much is about the most anyone gets. Well, if you're planning on going, you'd better go. That man will leave you."

It was only when Tuffie hugged her that Son became aware of how very much larger she was than the little bullriding mother of five.

"Oh, there's bean soup on the stove," Son said as she pulled out of Tuffie's embrace. Tuffie didn't answer, just flapped a wave in front of her down-turned face as walked out of the room. Tuffie was crying. Son didn't know if the tears were for Prairie or for her, but they were there. Not knowing what else to do, Son stepped awkwardly out the screen door. The spring she had fixed snapped the door shut smartly behind her. As she walked away, she could hear Jonathan tunelessly singing,

Ginny crap corn and I don care!
Ginny crap corn and I don care!
Ginny crap corn and I don care!
Ginny crap corn and I don care!

Chapter 17.

The chip truck banged over the gullies in Tuffie's road, Prairie cursing every one, Son biting her tongue and waiting until they reached the highway. The instant they hit smooth road she demanded, "Why didn't you tell me you knew where Cootie Ramos was?"

"God*damn*, Tuffie's got a big mouth. I wanted to tell you that myself. I was always planning to take you to Cootie's. I just had to arrange it all special with Dakota so that we'd play a rodeo over that way and we could coordinate our two schedules and—"

Son, who'd started untying her money sash halfway through Prairie's explanation, slapped her remaining bills down on the dashboard. "Here is every cent I have left. It's yours. I'm happy to finance your rodeo tour. Just stop lying to me. You do not have to invent ways to tie in my search for my father with your engagements."

"Oh, hey, listen."

"No, you listen. I'm not the person I was when I left Dorfburg. I'm not little Tinka's oddball daughter. For the first time in my life, I'm not the photo negative of someone else. I've seen that there are worlds where no one cares that I was always the last one picked for field hockey. I am taken or left on my own terms."

"That's what they invented the West for. Be whoever the frap you want to be. Then be someone else tomorrow. You want to be a bullrider? Climb aboard; we got people lined up to buy tickets. Rodeo." Prairie shook his head.

"And now I'm an announcer."

"Yes, you are, and you know what? I was planning on putting you on salary."

"You were?"

"Yeah." Prairie pushed the stack of bills back. "Hey, you're good. No denying it. You're as good as I've ever heard. Although, actually . . ." Prairie peeled a few bills off the stack before pushing the rest decisively back. He folded the bills into his front shirt pocket. "Ran kind of low at the hospital. Tuffie had some trouble with the deductible. Few other little odds and ends. I'll pay you back."

"You don't have to. I want to help Tuffie too. Is Casey Dakota sterile?"

"As a mule."

Son eyed him warily.

"Don't take my word for it. Ask him. He'll tell you. Ask anyone. It's usually the second thing he tells you, right after, 'My bull T-thirty-eight went to the National Finals in 'sixty-seven and knocked *everyone's* dick in the dirt!' Then it's 'Dewey's not my real son. He's adopted. I shoot blanks.' "

"I find it very difficult to believe that anyone with the pathological levels of testosterone that Casey Dakota exhibits would ever willingly reveal that he is sterile."

"Are you kidding? He'd a lot rather have people know he's a gelding than think he threw Dewey. And he makes a real point of telling the babes. Thinks once the pregnancy thing is out of the way, there's no reason on earth any woman wouldn't want to bunk him. According to Dakota, shooting blanks gets him more ass than a toilet seat."

"So you're taking me to Rancho Encantada?"

"Planned to all along."

Son stared out the window and wished she could call Tinka.

But her mother was incommunicado, bobbing on a houseboat in the middle of Lake Powell, sitting on Earl Walp's lap, whisking back his sideburns. Son imagined herself asking Tinka about Casey Dakota. Tinka would look up, her face an impenetrable mask of incomprehension, and ask in her patented Deutscher-cutie accent, "Cazey Dakota?" And that is absolutely as far as the conversation would ever get.

Son fell asleep wondering what Jonathan Branch had eaten for breakfast that morning.

She jerked awake as the truck shifted into a lower gear, and looked out at a world that was cool and green. It was as if they had driven out of a heat-mad summer into a lovely, crisp fall. She took her time waking up, taking in the piney scenery rolling past the high window and feeling cool air against her cheek. Where there had been nothing but dusty plains when she'd gone to sleep, there were now sizeable hills building into cobalt blue mountains ahead. "Where are we?"

"Speeding-merrily-along-the-fabled-Route-Sixty-six-coming-up-on-Cline's-Corner-New-Mexico-you-have-a-good-nap?" Prairie didn't wait for or want her answer. "What-I-wouldn't-have-given-for-a-good-nap-on-some-of-the-blows-I-lived-through-Christ-you-don't-sleep-for-three-four-days-a-time-and-it-isn't-just-that-you're-down-there-in-those-goddamn-holds-securing-cargo-you-ever-been-caught-in-a-Force-Eight-gale-off-the-coast-of-South-Africa-with-a-loose-tractor-trailor-rolling-around?"

The white water rush of Prairie's manic words began to alarm Son. "Would you like me to drive for a while so you can sleep?" she asked.

"Sleep?" Prairie snorted a friendly laugh. "Not with that RJS I took."

"I didn't know you were on medication."

"Naw. I pulled over at a truck stop back there outside of Santa Rosa and scored an RJS off this trucker, a real lowlife fathead with a roll of blubber around the back of his neck and a hairline that

blended in with his eyebrows and those little-bitty shrunk-up fingernails. You notice how often big fat guys have those disgusting
little fingernails? You know, the kind that look like a button sewed
on a big pillow of fat where the finger puffs up all around it and—"

Prairie's stream of consciousness ramble might have gone on
forever if Son hadn't interrupted. "I presume that an RJS is a
stimulant of some sort."

"Correction. An RJS is a stimulant of the *best* sort. A Road-
Jumping Son of a bitch. Methamphetamine! Black Molly, the
trucker's friend. Get your two-day haul done in one, get your one-
day done in none. Anything shorter and you're there before you
leave." Prairie gave a laugh that sounded like a winded dog panting, and stretched his neck from side to side. "From the way my
heart's going, it ought to be about Christmas before I sleep again.
But you go ahead. Catch a few z's."

"I'm not going to sleep with a drug-throttled maniac at the
wheel."

Prairie looked over and give his panting-dog laugh again.
"Good policy, Poke. The best. Okay, you keep your eyes peeled for
the Grim Reaper and I'll steer the death wagon."

Son turned her head to look out the window. She didn't really
believe that she was going to die that day. She thought about Jonathan curling into her as he slept and wished she'd left Tuffie more
money than she had. No amount of money could make up for not
having a father, but it might help if Jonathan could occasionally
buy a Mattel Action Man Missile Launcher or one of the other toys
he'd expressed such fervent, brand-specific longing for. As a girl,
Son had often comforted herself with small purchases, golden kitty
brooches with eyes of red cut glass; small black cubes that oozed
smoking black snakes of foam when lighted; Pixie Sticks.

"You sure haven't talked much last week or so," Prairie said.
"Not since you conked yourself out. You knock a screw loose?"

Son had to shake herself out of the dreaminess she'd fallen
into to reply, with her former starchiness, "You may rest assured
that all my mental faculties are intact."

"Hey, no slight to your faculties intended, I know from personal experience how ringy a hit to the head can make you. Goddamn! You shoulda seen me this one time. El Mare and me played this pissant rodeo in Houston back in, Christ, 'sixty-seven, 'sixty-eight, somewhere in there. It was me and El Marinero trying to tear the town apart. You know how you get when you got just the right load on? Okay, maybe too much of a load?"

Son would have offered her experience on a band trip when a jug of Thunderbird made its way around the bus, but Prairie was talking too fast for her to wedge in a comment.

"It gets like the world is this great happy, safe place. Everyone's buddy-buddy. You're surrounded by a glow that tells the world that you're a good guy and everyone should be your friend. Anyway, that's how both me and the Sailor got. Another reason that we was so tight. He wasn't like a lot of Mexes I knew. One drink and they think the whole world's laughing at their mothers. All they want to do is fight.

"Not us. We're staggering around the Houston ship channel. Which I guarantee you, back then was not the family picnic area it is today. It was rough as any waterfront from Miami to Murmansk. But we have no fear. We got the good-guy glow on, you see? We waltz into the Shanghai like it was grandma's parlor. Okay, you don't know the Shanghai. It got closed down in 'sixty-nine. They couldn't build up a repeat business since so many of the regulars ended up dead." Prairie chuckled to himself and fell into a reverie.

Son waited for him to continue; when he didn't, she prodded him. "And how does this story relate to my condition?"

"I don't know. You tell me. Oh, oh, right. The hit to the head. Uh, right." Prairie then tied up the loose ends with a monologue about Cootie Ramos saving him and the Sailor from a savage beating at the hands of a 280-pound Hawaiian seaman.

"Guy looked like that Samoan sumo wrestler, you know? The ones the Nips won't make grand champion on account of his racial impurity. Anyway, that's why I went ahead and played that homo rodeo last year," Prairie continued in a segue that Son had trouble following.

"Strange kind of a deal. You ever been to a homo rodeo? They're like one of those puzzles, you know, where you see this picture. Perfect family sitting around in the living room and reading or something. Everything looks perfect except the goldfish in the bowl's wearing a monocle, you know, something way out in left field. So that's what this was like.

"I get there, a little edgy. Shit, I don't know what to expect. Maybe some queer steer wrestler's gonna get a crush on me, something. I don't know. But everything looks real kosher. Like, there's all the guys back behind the chutes limbering up, getting ready for the bareback. They got on jeans, boots, Western shirts. They're putting on spurs, taping their elbows, knees, what have you. They're rosining their riding gloves.

"It all looks perfectly normal, then, whammo! You see a judge in his official red judge vest go back and plant a giant wet kiss on some big bronc rider buckling on his chaps. Whoa! What is wrong with this picture? Two guys Frenching behind the bucking chutes. Different. But I don't pass any judgments. Not since the night Cootie kept my head from getting bust open like a watermelon."

"So the Hawaiian never hit you on the head?"

"Shit! You kidding? He was packing enough pipe to open a plumbing store. I wouldn't be here to tell you about it."

"What does all this have to do with gay rodeo?"

"Oh, didn't I tell you? Cootie's queer."

"Cootie Ramos is homosexual? How do you know?"

"Hey, it's not like I made him prove it to me personally or anything. Everyone knew. Not that he was one of your swishy faggots. I mean, he was an okay guy. Only gay roper I ever knew. It wasn't a big deal."

"It does become a rather bigger one when one is searching for one's biological father."

"Oh, yeah, right. Sorry. Guess there's another one you can

scratch off the list. So, you want to skip this Rancho Encantada? No real reason now."

"We will *not* skip it. If Cootie Ramos is, in fact, an invert, the chances that he is my father are, admittedly, somewhat decreased, but they are not entirely eliminated. Besides, whatever his sexual predilections may be, he might be able to tell us where El Marinero's ropers' reunion is to be held."

"Yeah, but this Rancho Encantada, it's way out of the—"

"Who has been paying for gas since we left Hereford?"

Before Prairie could mount a defense, Son hit him with another question that had just occurred to her. "Wasn't this whole bar-fight story supposed to be about how 'ringy' a hit to the head once made you?"

Her question tumbled through the churning current of Prairie's speeded-up stream of consciousness. "You know, you're making me sound like a goddamn cowboy. Among the many things I hate about those calf stranglers is the way they're always bragging about their injuries. I mean, the way they talk, you'd think every time they got a horn through the groin or a hoof to the head, it was a freaking Congressional Medal of Honor. They love to tell you about how a horse kicked them in the head and they stumbled around with a concussion for three days and can't remember a thing, but they never went to the doctor.

"That's like the one ultimate cowboy thing: never go to the doctor. You get a cowboy going on his injury stories—which isn't too hard, since that's their favorite topic in the world next to how many miles they put on their pickups that season. Buncha real raconteurs. Anyway, you get a cowboy going on his injury stories, and no matter what happened to him, broken leg, ruptured spleen, decapitation, you name it, none them will ever voluntarily take themselves to a goddamn doctor. That's being a pussy, right? That's breaking the sacred cowboy code. No, the way you got to do it is *pass out* and then one of your buddies takes you.

"Then, the next part of the code is the doctor tells you you're never going to ride again and whacks a big cast on you and puts you in intensive care. So what's the cowboy thing to do? Stay in bed, get your three squares brought to you on a tray, try to talk the nurse into giving you a sponge bath? No, of course not!"

Son was startled when Prairie started yelling.

"Your cowboy hero *cuts* the cast off with a *penknife! Sneaks* out of the hospital! And rides another frigging bull or bronc *that* night! *That's* the cowboy way. You'd think they'd notice that all the cowboy heroes who manage to stay alive are gnarled up like bonsai trees by the time they're thirty. But no, hey! These are real mental giants. You know that any sport which includes dropping onto the head of a charging steer, then wrestling it to the ground, is going to pull in the *real* geniuses." Prairie tapped his head as he glared at the road. "The *real* brainiacs."

His heavy breathing was audible for several minutes over the grind of the motor before Son spoke. "It's part of the cowboy tradition of domination over nature. Just as he forced the land, cattle, and native inhabitants to submit to his will, he now typically has only himself and perhaps his mate to submit to his will." It took more of an effort than Son could ever remember having to make to come up with an analysis that would have been as easy as drawing breath only a few days before.

Prairie held up a finger, opened his mouth to speak, then stopped. He looked over at her for so long that he lost track of the road and bumped off onto the shoulder. He got the truck back on course and fell into a contemplative silence, staring straight ahead, occasionally nodding, and quirking his eyebrows when he agreed with whatever he was thinking. Finally, he shook his finger in the air, touched it to his lips, held his finger out again. At last, he spoke. "You're right" was all he said, but it flabbergasted Son.

As they approached Albuquerque, Son forced herself to concentrate on the fact that she was entering the sacred land of the Navajo. She clung to the knowledge that the one authentic item in Gray Wolf's costume was a Navajo blanket. In spite of her excitement, Son found herself thinking about Jonathan, worrying about what the lack of whole grains was doing to the development of his nervous system.

But all the mental chatter fell silent as they reached the Sandias, the first mountains Son had ever crossed. As they began the ascent, she had the odd feeling of going deeper and deeper under water. The truck strained and slowed to a crawl. The abused engine protested loudly.

Prairie's brow furrowed. "This is going to be fun. Piece of shit . . ." His curses were lost in a tortured symphony of clanks and squeals. Son rolled down the window and breathed the cool air until Domino stuck his head out and nearly crushed her as he tried to get his twitching nostrils in line with a good breeze.

When they finally labored to the crest and started down, Son thought that if nothing else happened on this trip, it would be worth it for the view of Albuquerque spread out before them. Back on flat land, they sped through the city. Midway through, they turned off Route 66 and headed north toward Santa Fe. Traveling along beside them was the broad green snake of the Rio Grande Valley. It changed to a charred black lightning bolt as it cut through the basalt left from ancient lava flows.

Son studied the dark zigzag. "The Navajos believe that certain lava fields are the dried blood of monsters."

"That so."

"At first the Holy People lived beneath the surface of the earth," Son continued. "But because of a great flood underground, they ascended to the present world, where Changing Woman, who brought the gift of maize to the Earth Surface People, was born. She was impregnated by the rays of the Sun and by water from a waterfall and gave birth to the Hero Twins, who went to find their father."

Son looked over at Prairie, who appeared to be calming down. "Yeah? And then?"

"The Hero Twins had many adventures on their search. They slew many monsters, and their dried blood became black lava fields. But the Hero Twins could not kill all of the eternal enemies of the

Earth Surface People. So the monsters Old Age, Hunger, Poverty, and Dirt survived."

"Hey, they didn't get Alimony either. That monster survived. Sheila wouldn't let them take that one down." Prairie fell into a silence punctuated by grumbled outbursts along the lines of "Bloodsucker!" "Parasite lawyer!" "Tapeworm in a tie!" His curses switched back to the chip truck, however, as they ground up a high mesa and finally pulled into Santa Fe.

Though he tried to bypass it, Prairie was sucked into the snarl around the plaza. Tourists wandered across the town square, dazed and straggling as aimlessly as sheep. While Prairie idled in the stalled traffic, his dyspeptic gaze fell on an affluent young couple kneeling in front of a blanket thrown on the ground and covered with jewelry. Both members of the couple wore houndstooth jackets with patches at the elbow, Frye boots, and were stoop-shouldered under the load of Indian jewelry they already wore.

Prairie snorted in derision. "Trust fund buckaroos. I love it when those Ivy League assholes go native. Annie Hall meets Annie Oakley."

His comment was lost on Son. She studied the Hopi Indian seated on a kitchen stool behind the blanket. Heavy black bangs covered his eyebrows. Below them was a face that belonged above a shrine. The couple knelt before him fondling bracelets, watchbands, bolo ties, pendants, earrings, and one magnificent squash blossom necklace.

Prairie snorted. "You think Mr. Red Man doesn't enjoy that? Having the white man kneeling at his feet?"

Son refused to dignify his comment with a response. Traffic finally started moving again. She craned her neck and watched her first live Indian for as long as she could.

Back on the highway, Prairie handed her a tattered map. "Give me a mileage estimate to Rancho Encantada."

Son unfolded the floppy map, supporting the sections that hung limp, and studied their route.

" 'Jesus Is My Co-Pilot.' " Prairie read aloud a bumper sticker affixed to the back of an old Dodge van. "Whoa! I guess so," he called out as they drew abreast of the van and he caught a glimpse of the driver, a bucktoothed woman with a severely receding chin and heavy eyebrows. "Jesus is the only date that babe's ever gonna get."

"Not every man is a mindless dupe brainwashed into accepting the idiotic standards of beauty imposed by a cosmetics industry bent on transforming women into powdered puppets."

"Wo-ho! Hit a nerve, eh? What? Not too many *escorts* back there in Kraut Town?"

"I had an amplitude of suitors, if that is your question."

"An amplitude, huh? Sounds like some heavy action. You go glandular at an early age or something?"

"I choose not to have this discussion with a chronic self-abuser and victim of satyriasis." Son turned away primly.

"Hey, that cleared up years ago. Look." He held one scarred and hairy paw out to her. "The scaliness, the itching, it's gone."

Son glanced over to see if he could really be so dense, but his kinetic attention had already been snared by a bumper sticker on the back of an old Ford pickup. " 'I'd Rather Be Bass Fishing,' " he read aloud. " 'I'd Rather Be Square Dancing,' " he called out when a Winnebago passed them.

A flurry of cars passed the truck as they labored up another high mesa. " 'I'd Rather Be Windsurfing.' 'I'd Rather Be Tole Painting.' 'I'd Rather Be War Gaming.' 'I'd Rather Be Drag Boat Racing.' 'I'd Rather Be Power Lifting'?" Prairie finished on a note of amused outrage. As they sped past Pojoaque, the late afternoon sky began turning a golden rose color to the west and polar blue to the east. Prairie watched the pastels darken as the sun set.

About five miles into the sunset, he spoke again. "You know, in a lot of ways, you could say I'm a pretty sorry son of a bitch. I'm nearly fifty years old and I don't own a thing in this world that I'm not hauling down the road at this very moment. Never finished high school. Couldn't make a marriage work. Don't have a relative I'm on speaking terms with. But I'll tell you what, there isn't another *goddamn thing* on this earth I'd rather be doing. Not bass fishing. Not tole painting. I sure as hell wouldn't want to be power lifting. No, when it comes right down to it, there's nothing I'd rather be doing than driving into a sunset to go spin a rope someplace. Even if there ain't a lug nut in the house appreciates what I do and goddamn Casey Dakota's making out the paychecks."

Son considered Prairie's comments long enough for the polar blue to go to a deep violet and the rose to begin fading into night. "All told," she finally said, "I'd deem that one of the finest statements of purpose a person could make in this vale of tears. Perhaps I've misjudged you. Perhaps you're not as *Koyaanisqatsi* as I'd first thought."

"That a compliment? 'Cause if it is, I'd like it in English."

"Your life is not as hopelessly out of balance as it first seemed."

"So there's hope for me, huh?"

"Some."

Chapter 18.

Night came, bringing a sudden, startling end to Prairie's locquaciousness. The instant darkness fell, his expansive responses to Son's comments and questions shrank to a narrow spectrum of grunts. Soon even those disappeared. In their place came the sound of deep, meditative breathing, which Son took to be the melody of a man at peace with himself. She glanced over and saw that he was staring intently at the tunnel of light the truck cut in the darkness ahead. Son was comforted that Prairie could lose himself in thought so completely in her presence. That showed just how much in harmony they were. She had never expected to be so in tune with a man that they could sit side by side, pondering their own deepest thoughts, yet sharing a silent communion.

She exulted in that mysterious closeness right up to the moment a ratcheting snore tore through the truck and Son realized that her soulmate and the driver of their vehicle going sixty-five m.p.h. was fast asleep with his eyes wide open.

"Prairie!" she shrieked as the truck drifted across the center line into the path of an oncoming eighteen-wheeler. It wasn't until the truck driver gave Prairie a blast of the air horn, though, that he came to and jerked the chip truck back into its proper venue.

Prairie threw back his head and snorted several times, holding his eyebrows high so as to ventilate his eyeballs. "Jeezo Pete, those Road Jumpers go, they gone!"

"First your onanism, now your drug abuse. Prairie, are you bent on making me the innocent victim of your vices?"

"Only in your dreams, sister." He swung the truck onto the shoulder and pulled into the sole spot of illumination for miles along the deserted highway, the King's Rest Motel.

"We're stopping? But Rancho Encantada is so close."

"I have got to get some mattress springs under this old body. Period. Nonnegotiable."

The King's Rest had seen better days and had seen them roughly thirty years before. While all hint of regal elegance was long departed, the monarchy theme remained. The office was in the shape of a crown, the roof rising to eight tall peaks. The stucco had been worn away on most of the peaks, exposing the lath work beneath. A twin cab pickup fishtailed to a stop in front of Room 7. A hail of Coors cans from the truck's cab preceded the exit of three men in gimme caps and quilted vests.

The door to Room 7 opened and a woman with a black rose tattooed on her shoulder emerged. She slouched provocatively against the door frame. A black leather miniskirt hugged the top ten inches of her chunky thighs. A slinky black top revealed most of the woman's minuscule breasts. Her eyebrows had been plucked to a thin thread arching high above steely eyes. The men's high spirits wilted under the shrewd gaze and they filed past her into the room like naughty third-graders called in from recess.

"I can't stay here," Son protested. "That woman is a harlot! A trollop!"

Prairie studied the woman. "Looks like a common, garden-variety whore to me," he said, stumbling out of the truck.

"Imagine the opportunistic infections one would be prey to. The sheets are sure to be virtual petri dishes."

"So stay out here. A horse trailer, that's a *real* sterile environment." Prairie slammed the door. The back doors opened and Prairie led Domino out and tied him up before entering the office.

An overweight, bald man wearing rundown house slippers and a gray sweatsuit shuffled to the front desk and checked Prairie in.

From her stubborn seat in the truck, Son watched Prairie feed, water, and walk Domino, then go to the back of the motel to stake him out in a field. Prairie waved jauntily at the truck when he came back, then went into Room 8 and shut the door.

Son studied the black stretch of highway ahead and behind. A semi roared by. When the chip truck had stopped shaking in the semi's wake, Son could not hear another sound or see another speck of light beyond that cast by the crested office of the King's Rest Motel. A few minutes later even that was switched off. Son became acutely aware of her bladder. Then of how sore her behind was. Still, she had her principles. Though she and Prairie had now spent close to two weeks together, none of that time had been in a bedroom.

By the time two more semis had hurtled past, a chill was creeping into Son's bones and her bladder felt like a dairy cow's udder at daybreak. She had no choice. She would have to go in.

She opened the door to Room 8. It was dark as a mine shaft inside. "Do not misinterpret my presence," she began before the hinges had stopped swinging. "Were it not for the agonizing distension of my bladder, I would never have entered this crowned hut of ill-repute. Though I am sure that you are only too used to the easy gratification of your every carnal desire, I look upon myself as something more than the cloaca for the release of male concupiscence."

Son's bold declaration was answered by one of Prairie's Kodiak bear snores. She tiptoed inside. In the dim porch light, she made out the shape of one bed with Prairie sprawled across it, arms and legs flung out in a wide X.

After visiting the rust-stained bathroom with a woodburned sign over the commode reading *The Throne*, Son slipped, fully clothed, onto the far corner of the bed. Prairie was gargling air loudly, but not loudly enough to block the negotiations coming from the room next door.

"I don't give a shit if he DID get it shot off in Operation Desert Storm!" the woman yelled. "If your buddy stays, he pays. This ain't television. Now you boys ready to go or not? It'll be one at a time. Full rate. You other two wait outside."

Son was riveted by this transaction. As fascinated as she was, the long day on the road and the longer night before it caught up with her and she slept through customers two and three, as well as all of the next morning and a good part of the afternoon.

"Hey, Pocahontas!" was the greeting she awoke to. "You couldn't keep away from me!" Fourteen hours of sleep in a real bed had energized Prairie to a degree that exceeded even the level achieved by amphetamines. He plucked up the sheet, held it in front of himself, and shrieked, in a falsetto, "If you took advantage of me in my sleep, I'll die, I'll simply perish!" In his normal voice, he added, "Why have you got your feet up here?"

Son raised her head from its position at the foot of the bed. "I find this a much more suitable arrangement. Besides, your snoring was making my teeth vibrate."

"*Your* teeth. I been listening to you for the last half hour and you put out some sound effects raised the romantic interest of several bull mooses in the area."

"I have never snored in my life."

"First time for everything." Prairie laughed like a pirate on grog and jumped out of bed. He had on nothing except a pair of Jockey shorts. "Pardon me, Pocahontas, I wasn't expecting company." He laughed again and went into the bathroom.

Outside, Son was astonished to find the motel perched at the base of a towering cliff that caught the afternoon sun in a way both majestic and too obviously theatrical. Across the highway was a broad valley. Prairie kept lifting his head, sucking in giant lungfuls of air, and blowing them out with a satisfied "Ah-h-h!" · ·

They drove into Espanola and Son spent the rest of the afternoon trying to track down the exact location of Rancho Encantada. The first person Son asked, the clerk at the Kwik Pik Gas 'Em Up, a skinny Chicana with the name *Lourdes* sewn on her red-striped work smock, eyed them suspiciously and answered, "You don't look like you're from California."

Son answered tartly that they were not from California and asked again about Rancho Encantada.

"I don't know nothing about that place," the clerk answered, turning away.

When Son started to ask again, Prairie said, "She don't know, she don't know," and walked back to the truck. Son was not going to be deterred so easily. She asked two customers in the store. The first claimed never to have heard of Rancho Encantada. The second said, "They's supposed to send you directions," and walked away.

"Well, you ready to pack it in, get on down the road?" Prairie asked when Son got back into the truck.

"You're awfully eager to abandon the search."

Prairie started up the truck and they pulled away. "What's Cootie going to be able to tell you? No telling what shit he's into. Doesn't sound like he's the most popular guy in town. Hey, look, I got a rodeo to go to. We got a rodeo to go to. I wanted to save this for a surprise, but what the hell. Our next gig's in Gallup. An Indian rodeo. You're probably not interested. Probably rather stay here and—"

"An Indian rodeo! You didn't tell me were going to AN INDIAN RODEO!"

It was a long time since Prairie had made someone so happy, and he liked the feeling.

"What are we waiting for? Proceed to Gallup!"

And that is exactly what they would have done had they not become mired in the three-mile-long beauty contest that passes for Espanola traffic on Sunday afternoon, when all the area lowriders turn out to parade their machines. They stalled out behind a particularly lustrous sapphire-blue El Camino with a thorn-crowned head of Jesus floating across the fathomless cosmos of the hood.

"Perfect!" Prairie exploded, turning off the engine. "Leave it to a Mexican to turn his car into the goddamm Sistine Chapel."

Son opened the door and hopped out.

"Where the hell you going?" Prairie yelled out the window as she made her way up the line of cars.

"As long as we're stuck here, I might as well make inquiries!" Son yelled back.

" 'Inquiries,' " Prairie muttered.

The driver of the El Camino, a proud *abuelo* with his eight-month-old grandson strapped into a car seat next to him, faced straight ahead with a stony stare when Son asked about Rancho Encantada.

She got similiar receptions at the windows of a gumdrop-green Impala and a Biscayne with chrome mudflaps. But the driver of a swimming pool–blue 'fifty-three Packard, with a miniature chandelier hanging from the dome light, was more forthcoming.

He was young, not yet twenty; his impeccably razored hair was covered with a hair net. His girlfriend, barely a teenager, had one teardrop tattooed under her right eye. The driver glanced over his shoulder and leaned in close after Son said the words "Rancho Encantada."

The boy seemed to be speaking to the door lock when he answered, "I got weed, downers. I can get *chiva*, rock. Tell me what you want."

Though it took a few tries, Son convinced him that all she wanted to know was where to find this enchanted ranch. The young man finally drew her a map, but he whispered as she walked back to the truck, "I can get bottles."

It was dark by the time they finally emerged from Espanola's lowrider gridlock.

"Take the Chubasco turnoff," Son directed him.

"I thought you wanted to go to an Indian rodeo."

"We're here. Look for the Chubasco turnoff."

"The guy's a nethead. I'm not chasing off through the boonies on the say-so of a nethead."

The headlights hit a road sign. "Here it is! The Chubasco turnoff! Take a right! Take a right!"

"All right! Nerve down! I'm turning."

They drove through a couple of miles of black nothing, where the only light that shone back at them was the haunted flare of a jackrabbit's eyes hit by the high beams.

"Okay, we had enough fun?" Prairie hit the brakes. When the truck had come to a stop, Son opened her door and started to get out. Exasperated, Prairie asked, "What are you doing now?"

"For whatever reasons, you are clearly not committed to my finding Cootie Ramos. I shall continue on my own."

"Don't be stupid. Get back in here! Son! The coyotes'll eat your ass!"

Son set off down the dirt road. The night smelled delicious, cool and astringent with the scent of piñon, juniper, and yellow chamisa.

"Son! You coming?"

Son did not turn around. The headlights slashed across her as Prairie K-turned the truck on the narrow road guttered by ditches.

Just as he was about to leave her in the darkness, Son shouted, "Prairie! Stop! Look! Over there!"

A flicker of light that was clearly a fire blazed from a nearby ridge.

"They're over there!" Son ran to the truck and jumped back in.

"How do you know it's them?"

"It's on the map! Come on! Come on!"

"Maybe it's Nethead and a bunch of his buddies waiting for some big, fat *gabacho* assholes like us to stroll up."

"That's ridiculous. If you don't want to take me, just say so. Come on! Let's go!"

With great reluctance, Prairie angled the truck back onto the road and they headed toward the flicker of light. Long before they reached it, Prairie switched off the engine.

"Listen, if we're going ahead with this idiot plan, I'm going first to check it out. You got it?"

Son was touched that Prairie wanted to ensure her safety and did not protest.

Prairie slipped out of the truck, making a big show of silently pressing the door closed behind him. The bonfire was the equivalent of two or three blocks away. He crossed the distance quickly and saw that the fire licked flames of light across a couple of dozen faces. An old man with the huge potbelly, long arms, and stumpy legs of an orangutan was the only one standing. On the old man's head was a flat straw hat bristling with feathers. Long silvery-white hair streamed out from beneath the feathered hat nearly down to his elbows. An embroidered red capelet was tied under his chin and over a plain white shirt and white drawstring pants, also richly embroidered.

"Well, shit me out and call me a brownie! If it ain't Cootie Ramos!" The night air was closing in on chilly when Prairie stepped into the circle of light. "Cootie Ramos! What the hell you doing out here dressed up like a rooster in pajamas?"

Cootie, who came about to Prairie's nipples, clapped his old buddy on the arms with hands that were shy one complete index finger, several joints of both middle fingers, most of the right little finger, and a significant slice of thumb.

"Don't call me Cootie," he whispered to his old *compadre.* "I'm Don Ramos here."

Prairie, long a respecter of a man's right to vary his identity as the circumstances demanded, nodded and looked around at the congregation. They were all male. All Anglo. Most had feathers stuck haphazardly in their hair. Drums sat neglected between many knees. About half were bare-chested. There was evidence of weight lifting. Several complexions glowed from what had to be recent facials. The labels on cast-aside fleece jackets read Patagonia and L. L. Bean. They all stared, glassy-eyed, into the fire. Prairie leaned down to his old buddy. "They all stoned?"

"Sit, sit," Don Ramos said grandly, ignoring Prairie's question as he swept the ends of his short cape toward a blanket in what appeared to the place of honor.

."Here's the deal," Prairie said, leaning close and whispering, even though he knew none of the zombies around him was exactly taking notes. "I've got someone with me. A woman."

Cootie tipped his head back, mouth open in an O of understanding.

"No, it's not like that. She wants to know about the ropers' reunion. About the tour. Germany. Who was there. Bunch of questions. Be best if you'd dummy up, know what I mean?"

Coot laid a finger alongside his nose and patted it in the Mexican gesture that meant no further discussion was required, all was understood. "What about you? You going to the Sailor's deal?"

Prairie shrugged. He wasn't going to make a thing out of it. Not if El Mare wasn't going to officially invite him.

Cootie read the ambivalence in his old *compadre's* face. Without another word, he pulled out a neon lime-green car-wash coupon and sketched a map on the back, showing the way to the Sailor's place. "You wanna go, here's how to get there." Prairie liked that about Mexicans: you didn't have to draw diagrams for them to get the picture.

When Cootie finished marking the Sailor's place with a big X, Prairie leaned in close and whispered, so that only Don Ramos could hear, "Cootie, man, what gives? You running a shooting gallery here? I seen more pep in an opium den. Who are these tourists? He slipped the map into his pocket.

Don Ramos shook back his flowing silver locks and stuck his chin up in the air and said loudly, "These men are seekers."

"Seekers?" Prairie glanced around the crew of stoned men and shrugged. "Yeah. Whatever." He turned back to Cootie. "How long's it been, Coot? Eight? Nine years? Remember that time down in Oaxaca, during that big, what was it? Some radish festival?"

Cootie shifted his eyes from side to side before supplying, under his breath, "The Guelagetza."

"That's it! That's right. The Gala Ginzu. Remember? You ended up with that bucktooth woman had the tattoo right here—"

As Prairie craned around to indicate a spot on his left buttock, Cootie cut him off. "The past is a pit of quicksand that will suck us under if we let it."

Prairie glanced around at the immobilized men staring at the fire and announced, for their benefit, "Now that I think about it, Don, that wasn't you at all." He lowered his voice and asked, "Where are these tourists from?"

"The City of Lost Angels, *amigo*. My booker flies them in for either the three-day Ceremonial Weekend or the five-day Shaman Package."

"These lubbers are paying to come out here and sit on the dirt? They're fried, Coots. Tell me these people are not flatlined."

"They are communing with the great deity Pioniyo."

Prairie stared into the blasted faces, then snorted derisively. "Ee-yeah. So how much do they have to commune with their Visa cards to get out here?"

"They make them free-will donations, what have you."

Prairie's eyes sparkled with admiration. "Coots, Coots, you son of a buck. What a scam."

Cootie's bright onyx eyes shifted quickly from side to side. He made sure that his clientele was thoroughly occupied before he shot a sly glance at Prairie and winked largely. Prairie laid *his* finger alongside his nose and tapped. All was understood. It felt great to be in the know with an *hermano* again, and Prairie trotted back happily for Son.

Son stepped out ahead of Prairie on their return and rushed up to Cootie, her hand stuck out. "Señor Ramos, I'm honored to meet you. I care not about your sexual orientation. We Native Americans honor the *berdache* tradition that celebrates the homosexual as a spiritually gifted member of the community."

Cootie shot Prairie a puzzled look. Prairie shrugged as if he had no idea what Son was talking about, and Cootie shook the hand she held out.

As Son stood there, she realized that the question of his sexual orientation was beside the point. He was simply too minuscule to

possibly be her father. There was no way such a dwarfish fellow
could have teamed up with the doll-like Tinka Getz and produced
her own highly substantial self. All she could hope for from Don
Ramos were other leads.

Son related to the shaman the saga of her search for her father,
concluding, "I believe that he, my father, Gray Wolf, would have
been in Germany in 1963 through 1964. Have you ever heard of
him?"

"Can't help you," Cootie answered.

Son sagged with disappointment. "Are you *certain?* Have you
ever known any ropers who were in Germany?"

Cootie scratched his chin. "Germany? Germany, the country?"

Son clarified the geographical point, but it didn't help. Cootie
maintained he'd never heard of any trick roper who had ever performed in Germany.

"Well, have you *ever* known any Native American, any Indian
ropers?"

"Hmmm. Can't say that I have. Course there was . . . What
was that fellow's name, Prairie? Tall skinny guy? Stuttered real bad,
but could throw a triple catch'd make Will Rogers look sick. He
might have been Indian."

Son leaned forward anxiously.

"Black Irish," Prairie corrected him. "Name was Mohoric."

"Oh. Right. Well, what about, you know, Pepper Pot? Had
them long, long arms like—"

"Jamaican," Prairie supplied.

"Right. *West* Indian." Cootie turned back to Son and shook his
head sorrowfully. "I'm sorry."

"Well, perhaps you can tell me where the annual ropers' reunion is to be held this year."

"Ropers' reunion?" Cootie's face went blank.

Prairie hadn't expected Cootie to be such a good liar. He went
back over his memories, trying to figure out if there'd ever been a
time Cootie could have pulled one over on him.

"I believe," Son explained, "it is held every year at El Marinero's ranch. If you just could tell me where his ranch is . . ."

"Prairie's the one's big buddies with the Sailor. I never knew the guy that much."

"You didn't?" Son tried to blink back a sudden gush of tears; they sparkled in the firelight.

Prairie looked away at the sight of her tears and stared up at the mist of stars banding the dark sky. "Shit," he whispered, wishing he'd driven straight on through Dorfburg. "Hey, come on, have a seat." He motioned toward the blanket on the ground. Son wiped away the tears of disappointment as they settled themselves on the blanket next to a couple of gourd bowls. One contained some shriveled fruit. In the other was stacked what Son took at first to be a pile of dusty dried figs. Farther back, out of the firelight, was a six-pack of Budweiser.

Don Ramos tossed a handful of powder on the fire. It burst into flame, releasing the fragrance of juniper. He picked up a toy-sized guitar and strummed frenetically as he wailed a chant. Coyotes in the distance yipped back a mournful reply. Without averting their zombie gaze from the fire, several men patted accompaniment on their drums.

Abruptly, Don Ramos stopped and sat down. He picked up the basket and held it out to Prairie. "You want to raise your sights. Look heavenward. Look inward. Find the god within us all."

"Peyote!" Son burst out, having finally placed those dried figs. She had read extensively about the rituals of the Native American Church of North America and supported the members' fight to incorporate this ritual into the mongrelized shreds left to them by the Christers.

She reached around Prairie, took a large button, and put it in her mouth. It was surprisingly rubbery and foul-tasting. She accepted that the sacred cactus could propel the user into higher realms of consciousness, realms that she herself would like to achieve. What Son was having trouble getting past, however, was that the sacred cactus in her mouth tasted and felt like a huge vulcanized caterpillar. She was wondering if she could spit it out without giving offense.

"Perhaps this will help you to wash it down." Don Ramos handed Son a plastic cup.

She gulped down the lukewarm beverage. The peyote was so bitter that it took her a second to realize that the liquid she'd washed it down with was even worse.

"Sometimes the tea's not much better than the buttons," Don Ramos observed as Son got her gagging under control. "But that's a good sign. That heaving and all, that's just Pioniyo's saying he recognizes that you are a powerful being."

"You gave her tea *and* buttons?" Prairie asked. "Whoa, doggies, you're going to regret doing that, Cootie. Once that mescaline kicks in, you're going to hear motor mouth like you never heard before." Prairie glanced around at the stony-faced men memorizing every flame in the fire. "Hey, what's the deal with these yobs? They're not doing buttons. There's no way they're doing buttons. I've heard more chatter on a coma ward."

"They have chosen the inward path of contemplation."

"What? You cut their tea with 'ludes or something?"

Cootie answered, loud enough for the paying customers to hear, "We natives have never needed sunglasses to shield us from the brightness of our Father Sun. But sometimes those who are not used to his healing rays need to be shielded. A simple native herb provides that shield."

Son stood suddenly and bolted for the darkness to throw up.

"Hey, Cootie, I'd be the last person to criticize a little chemical management, but what'd you put in that tea?"

Cootie leaned close and answered, "A little this, a little that. I never get no complaints. Lots of repeat business."

"Hey, yeah, well don't give her any more. You read me?"

Son strode back into the firelight and plopped down. "Well, I'm pleased to say that *Lophophora williamsii's* characteristic stom-

ach-unsettling effect has passed. I expect to be moving on swiftly to
the sense of exhilaration that usually results when any one of peyote's twenty-five alkaloid compounds takes effect."

"Prairie, won't you join us?" Don Ramos held out the basket
of peyote buttons. "Won't you see what message Pioniyo has for
you?"

"Uh, naw. I don't think so." He reached back and snapped one
of the beers out of its plastic ring. "I believe I'll just sit here and
find out what message Anheuser-Busch has for me."

"Please excuse Prairie." Son's voice was loud in the silent
circle where the sound of the fire crackling was the dominant noise.
"He has very little experience of the divine."

"Oh, well, screw me. Just because I don't want to eat a goober
the size of my hand, I'm a heathen." Prairie drained most of the
can in one long gulp.

Son looked away. "What tribe are you from, Don Ramos?"
she asked. "From your dress, I would guess Huichol of the Sierra
Madre Occidental of northern Jalisco."

"You are right. And what, might I ask, is your name?"

Prairie belched. "Oh, excuse me. I have very little experience
of the polite. This is my announcer, Son."

"*Mucho gusto.*" Don Ramos took Son's hand in what remained
of his and kissed it. "*El sol,* that is a beautiful name. Among us
Huicholes—"

"You Huicholes?" Prairie interrupted. "Oh, my aching—"

Son threw Prairie a sharp glance.

Don Ramos continued. "Yes, we Huicholes give our children
two names. One name that the world uses and another name that is
secret, private. Their Indian name."

"The child's paternal grandmother," Son interjected, "sup-
plies the secret name and it is usually indicative of some attribute of
the child's character that the grandmother has noticed or it reflects
a natural phenomenon, some remarkable event that transpired in
conjunction with the child's birth."

As Son rattled on, elucidating the assembled about the particulars of Huichol naming rituals, the men hunkered around the fire began, almost imperceptibly, turning their faces and attention toward her. Finally, they all were watching her mouth move with the same blank, mesmerized expression with which they had watched the flames of the fire flicker. Even Don Ramos' alert face had begun to go a little slack by the time Son wrapped up her colloquy on tribal-naming practices. He stared, gape-jawed.

"I warned you," Prairie told him.

Son touched her cheek. "Oh, dear, my face is starting to flush, salivation is increasing, and I imagine my pupils are dilated. Any moment now I should enter a period of withdrawal accompanied by intense color awareness and a succession of hallucinations. Don Ramos, tell me something. You are a shaman—"

" 'A shaman?' " Prairie snorted loudly.

"I am a guide," Don Ramos corrected gently. "My humble task is but to show the path. Everyone must walk their own journey themselves."

"Yes, but as a man devoted to the life of the spirit—"

"I am that."

"Oh, for the love of—"

"And as a person of native origin—"

"I am that as well."

"If this isn't the biggest load of—"

Son persevered. "I was wondering . . . I mean, I've always felt like an outsider in my own culture. I am opposed on moral and ethical grounds to the futile cycle of consumerism that pits each of us against the natural world and against our fellow man."

"You have chosen your path wisely."

Oh, my aching butt. Prairie kept this comment to himself. As he glanced around at the numbnuts staring into the fire and drooling on themselves, it occurred to Prairie that curare was a "simple native herb." Whatever Cootie had cut the buttons with, though, it hadn't kicked in on Son yet.

"Don Ramos, I have always sought a guide like yourself and

wisdom that would lead me back to the native legacy that should be mine by birth."

"We all seek those things. How may I help you, my daughter?"

" 'My daughter?' " They continued to ignore Prairie. "Don Ramos, tell me, what do you think my real name, my Indian name, would have been?"

While Prairie rolled his eyes derisively behind her, Don Ramos examined Son's face before he spoke. "Yes, I think I know what my people would have called you. I feel it in my bones. I see in my mind the day you were born. There was great turbulation in the atmosphere on that day. Was it a tornado? Cyclone? One them hurkins? I do not know. I do know this: on the day that you were born, a great wind was blowing. Yes, I think my people would have called you *Nikta Hey Lo*. Big Wind Woman."

"Big Wind Woman."

These were the last three words Son was to utter that evening. Though she wanted, badly, to speak many, many more, she had been poleaxed by Pioniyo.

Bits and pieces of her personal vision flashed in and out of Son's mind. She watched one of Tinka's dachshunds change from a ceramic knickknack to a real animal, which leaped up into the iridescent green polka dots that danced across the sky like a phosphorescent tide. A sky that the beneficent turkey vulture soared through. A captain's chair swiveled around and around, but never slowed down enough for her to catch a glimpse of her father's face. Colors exploded inside her head and the campfire turned into a time-lapse movie of the creation of the universe. Though the hallucinatory spectacle swept all conscious thought before it, Son kept returning to her mission: find the ropers' reunion. As the campfire that held her mesmerized heaved and squirmed into a full-scale recreation of the eruption of Krakatoa, Son attempted simultaneously to devise another line of questioning for Cootie Ramos.

After enormous effort, she decided to interrogate Cootie about the last time he saw El Marinero. As Son formed the questions, however, she discovered that she could not speak. She could not speak even when a summer storm cracked the dark cave of a still-starry night with stalactites of lightning and flat plops of rain.

The rain woke Prairie. He gently helped Son to her feet and guided her to the truck. The men who were gathered around the fire silently pulled on rain ponchos and continued gazing at the flames as they were reduced to hissing plumes of steam. Son could not even make her mouth work when she turned back for one more look and saw that Cootie Ramos had put on a pair of sunglasses to protect his eyes from the sooty steam. In the last flickers of firelight, Son saw that he was wearing flat-ground, photo-gray. sunglasses.

"We have to go back!" Though this was Son's immediate reaction to seeing Cootie in the vintage German sunglasses, it took her three hours to force the words out.

Prairie had a New Mexico map draped over the steering wheel, studying it in the gathering light of dawn. Outside was the country little Tinka Getz had dreamed of traversing on the back of an Appaloosa pony behind a broad-shouldered brave in a breechclout. More oceanic in its vastness than any sea Prairie had ever crossed, this world dominated by sky awed him.

"So Coot didn't turn you into a permanent zombie."

"I must return and question Don Ramos about the sunglasses he was wearing."

"What about his sunglasses?"

"They're like the ones Tinka made for my father. Like these." Son rooted through her mess kit purse and pulled out the vintage, flat-lensed photochromatics. "Cootie must have been in Germany sometime after the introduction of photochromatic lenses and sometime before convex grinding became standard."

" 'Must have?' Did I happen to mention that Cootie Ramos has been known to place a wager a time or two? Maybe he won them in a poker game. Or found them at the track. Who knows? Maybe he stole them from some poor GI at the bus station."

"Maybe, maybe, maybe. He's a roper. Or he was. And he has a pair of sunglasses like my father's."

"What are you saying? You think Cootie Ramos is your father? You think your mother would sleep with Cootie Ramos?"

Son had difficulty putting together her microphobic mother and a potbellied shaman with feathers in his hat and a little red cape over his shoulders. Particularly a gay potbellied shaman. "I don't know. No. Whatever, I should have followed up on the lead."

"Yeah, well, you got a few episodes to go before you're Magnum, P.I., there, Pocahontas."

Son collected herself. "Please turn back. I know that Don Ramos knows more than he told me. Please."

"Look, in case you forgot, I got an itinerary. I play Gallup tonight and that doesn't leave a lot of time for any more detective work."

"Oh."

Son's meek acceptance of his dictate unnerved Prairie as much as her tears had. "Listen, we'll go back after the show." She didn't answer. "Whattaya say? Son?"

"All right." For several minutes she said nothing further, then, "I would like to be called by my Indian name. Big Wind Woman."

"Big Wind Woman? You gonna let that old fraud name you?"

"The line between shaman and sham is often a very thin one."

"Hell, in Cootie's case it's downright wavy. Last time I caught his autobiography, he come up in a trailer park outside of Plaster City, California."

"In any event, I would like to be called Big Wind Woman. I find it very apt."

"You got it, Big."

"Big Wind Woman."

"Take your choice. It's going to be either Big or Wind or Woman. It's not going to be all three. Though I might be persuaded to go for Windy."

"Never mind. I shall reserve my native name for special occasions."

"Deal." He flapped the map into Son's lap. "Could you please find out where the hell we are?"

"Are we lost?"

"No, we're taking the scenic route."

Son caught a road sign advising them that the town of Nageezi and the turn-off for Chaco Canyon National park were just ahead. Her heart fluttered. She was in the land of her father's people. "We are skirting the southern boundary of the Jicarilla Apache Indian Reservation. To the south are the Jemez, the Acoma, the Zuñi, the Zia, and the Santa Ana Indian reservations. We are headed for the Navajo reservation."

Prairie brightened. "Did I come through or what? You wanted Indians, I deliver Indians."

"May I drive?" Son asked. She sounded strangely reverent to Prairie. He was only too happy to turn this pleasure cruise over to someone else. He stared out the passenger window, his sailor's eye at home in a place where the only thing that stopped the view was the earth curving back on itself.

The sun came up and light traveled flat across the boundless land, creeping up the pillars and peaks of rock formations that jutted into the far horizon in fantastic shapes. Son made out a power plant, a battleship, and a praying robot in the wind-blasted sandstone.

The sun was fully up by the time they passed a herd of goats cropping the sparse grass that had crisped up to a golden brown under the relentless sun. Oil pump jacks ducked their metal beaks in and out of the dry earth. A colt stood motionless in a field, seeming to enjoy the feel of the dry, hot wind blowing his ears. Outside Lake Valley, a hand-painted sign offered COLORADO GRASS HAY, $2.75. MUTTON 89 CENTS A LB. And FAT SHEEP FOR SALE. All the s's were printed backward.

They finally ran into Route 666, the main artery threading through the Navajo Nation. Son read the names off the highway sign like a pilgrim reciting a chant: Tohatchi, Naschitti, Teec Nos Pos. Heading south on 666, they passed mobile homes dwarfed by satellite dishes and monster bales of hay. They passed towns that consisted of one church, one convenience store, a liquor and pawn shop, and two video stores. A dust devil sent up a seventy-five-foot plume into the still air that spun across the road in front of the truck.

Son turned on the radio and a C and W singer proclaimed, "Woman, your love keeps my love off the street!"

"No calf-strangler music!" Prairie decreed from his stronghold, slouched in the corner of his seat, his arms barricading his chest.

Son twisted the dial until she homed in on a sound that reminded Prairie that great buzzing swarms of killer bees were invading from the south. After a moment, the music began to sound more like a convention of Jewish cantors whose dentures were slipping. Abruptly, the chanting stopped and a smoothly homogenized voice announced that they were listening to the Navajo Nation Radio Network, the Voice of the Reservation. Son beamed with happiness and bounced her head enthusiastically along with the next "number," as if extracting actual rhythm.

Prairie, unable to stay grumpy in the face of so much grinning delight, didn't click the radio off as he would have in nearly any other circumstance. The drone of the chanting fuzzed out, then disappeared altogether when they passed underneath a high-power line.

"Can I bring you anything?" Son asked, parking the truck in front of a convenience store in Naschitti.

"No, I'd better walk Domino."

At the mention of his name, the horse began to snort excitedly and stomp on the bed of the truck.

Inside the store a short round Navajo woman, wearing a T-shirt that warned the world that "Looking is free, touching will cost you," greeted Son. Even though she could no longer hear the radio, the chanting of the Navajos still filled her head. Son took this as a sign that she had tapped into a deep ancestral well.

At last, she was where she belonged on this earth, in harmony with nature, vibrating with the life forces all around her. Before she had time to consider what she was doing, Son grabbed the phone book dangling by a dirty cord from the bottom of a pay phone and opened it to the Gs. She found a Graham and a Grayson, but no Gray Wolf.

Still, she was close. Very, very close. Son could feel it humming through her. She was at one with this land, this people. She picked up a package of Little Gems powdered doughnuts. As she paid, she smiled beatifically at her indigenous sister across the counter and offered a traditional Navajo blessing, "Walk in beauty, my sister."

"What did you say?" the woman answered. "I can't hear anything with those power lines buzzing all the time."

Son walked back out to the truck. So the power lines were buzzing. So what? The hum resonating through her very being was a private matter. A thing to be shared only with someone like her father, someone who would truly understand.

As they drove past a rest area outside of Tohatchi, they saw a family of three women, a tribe of towheaded kids, and one man set up like a potentate in the shade eating a picnic lunch.

"Mormons." Prairie twisted around in his seat to watch one of the women bring the patriarch a paper plate loaded down with fried chicken. He felt a deep pang in his heart and ached to have a sweet-smelling woman bring him a plate of food while he watched his well-mannered children eat. Then to sleep with her sister that night. And the new recruit the next. There was something so profoundly right with that system. He knew better than to share his feelings with Son, who was, at that moment, trying to make out the bumper sticker on the van they were rapidly overtaking.

"I Brake for Bingo," Son read in the moment before they passed the van. They followed a Peugeot with Colorado license plates which had bikes standing in a rack on the roof, like the sails on a ship, all the way into Gallup, New Mexico. Purple asters waved in the wind.

The main street of Gallup glittered like Solomon's mine with the emerald sparkle of broken Thunderbird and Boone's Farm bottles. A banner fluttering above the street welcomed visitors to the 72nd Gallup Intertribal Fair and Rodeo.

"You know Gallup's got the biggest drunk tank in the country," Prairie said.

They stopped at a red light behind a brand-new Ford pickup. Three Indian boys sat in the bed of the pickup, all with burr haircuts. They kept the chip truck under constant surveillance. Every other corner seemed to be occupied by either an Indian jewelry store or a pawn shop. Except for the corner where Chainsaw City sat.

"Where did you hear that?" Son asked suspiciously.

"Hear nothing. It's a fact. I read it. Four thousand, eight hundred square feet."

"Where did you read this 'fact,' then?"

"I don't know. Somewhere. The paper."

"Which paper? The *New York Times* or the *National Enquirer?*"

"How do I know which paper! I'm just making a little light conversation. You ever heard of that? Conversation? One person throws out some little tidbit they skim off the top of their brain, the other person grunts, goes 'Oh, really? That reminds me of the time my Uncle Louie got stewed on applejack and climbed the phone pole."

"I don't have an Uncle Louie and I don't perpetuate cruel stereotypes under the guise of 'light conversation.'"

"Well pardon me."

Had Son offered any further comment, it would have been lost in the rattling of a freight train clanking slowly down the tracks that ran through town.

"You missed the turn," Prairie growled a bit later when Son sailed past the entrance to Red Rock State Park.

"Why didn't you tell me earlier?" Son said, turning the truck around.

"Hey, you know everything."

The rodeo arena, exhibitors' booths, and fairgrounds were all spread out in front of the high red sandstone bluffs that gave the park its name. They found the area for competitors' livestock and left Domino crunching contentedly on some of the young Branches' grain mixture as they searched out the rodeo office.

The fairgrounds were packed. As Son walked through the crowd, passing barrel-chested men with skinny braids reaching their armpits and high-cheeked old women in full flowered skirts nearly down to the Keds tennis shoes and little children with shining, tea-colored faces straight out of Mongolia, an odd sensation come over her. She began to feel more and more Caucasian. In point of fact, she began to feel downright pink. She imagined a giant pair of lederhosen sprouting on her dimpled legs and her hair twining into thick braids with a fluff of bangs at the front.

Her body fat simply wasn't lumped in the right places. She wasn't packing it through the middle like the broad-chested, thick-waisted Indian women with their spindly legs and narrow butts. Son had an hourglass waist, a capacious can, and jodhpur thighs. She felt, in short, just as much an outsider here, among her father's people, as she had back in Dorfburg. It wasn't at all what she had dreamed of her whole life.

Chapter 19.

"I'm double-billed with an alligator wrestler?" The news deflated Prairie's ebullient morning mood. They received it in the office of the Gallup Intertribal Ceremonial and Rodeo from the rodeo secretary, Miss Ellie Yazzie, a recent graduate of Gallup High School. Miss Yazzie wore a velveteen blouse the color of arterial blood. A squash blossom necklace rested on her deep chest. Prairie too was looking the part. He had his best maguey rope slung bandolier-fashion across his chest. He'd taken it out of its tin can to "give it an airing." The air was so dry that the dehydrated rope was as limp as a shoelace.

Son was too busy looking through the Gallup phone book under Gray Wolf to pay much attention to Prairie's outburst.

"Who's headlining?" Prairie demanded, grabbing a rolled-up poster off Miss Yazzie's desk. He unrolled it and burst out, "That shreds it! That's it! I'm second-billed behind Creek Pete, the American Glad-i-gator? Who set this deal up? Dakota, right? It was Casey Dakota!"

No emotion showed on what was visible of Miss Yazzie's round brown face behind a pair of glasses that started above her eyebrows and ended midway down her plump cheeks and the two curtains of straight black hair that hid the sides of her large head.

"He's putting it to me again. Really sticking it in. 'Glad-i-Gator.' You think he's not pissing his pants over this?"

Miss Yazzie had no opinion on the matter.

"Let me use your phone."

Miss Yazzie turned around the phone on her desk to face Prairie, who punched buttons furiously. "Yeah, operator, make this collect from Prairie James to Casey Dakota." A moment passed before he exploded, "What do you mean, you won't accept the charges! Listen, Dakota, I know you can hear me on your goddamm cellular phone! You either accept the charges or you'll accept my fist down your—" The line went dead. Prairie attempted to atomize the receiver by clenching it in his fist until it vaporized. The effort required him to squint until his eyes were slits of rage and to bare both rows of teeth as he snarled "Pigporker!" while the carotid artery in his neck swelled wildly.

His lips twitching into a spastic smile over his bared teeth, Prairie replaced the receiver with a trembling hand and backed out of Miss Yazzie's office.

"I am going to kill him." Son was alarmed by the matter-of-fact tone Prairie had adopted. "He has humiliated me for the last time. He's driving up right now in his fat-ass RV. He'll be here tonight and I will kill him."

"Do you want something to eat?" Prairie didn't answer, but she led him away.

Son thought that the Navajo tacos, ground meat on a skillet-sized puff of fry bread, looked good. She lobbied strongly for the mutton stew as well. She put in an impassioned plea for some particularly well-crisped corn dogs, but Prairie continued to stride through the maze of vendors converged on the ceremonial grounds. He stormed past booths selling funnel cake, turkey drumsticks, and Navajo hamburgers. Past a merry-go-round with solemn-faced Navajo children on the backs of horses gliding through their eternal circle to the tune of "The Marines' Hymn." Son had to run to catch up. Then, abruptly, Prairie stopped and ripped a poster off the side of a booth selling water purifiers.

"Second banana to a reptile wrestler! Never thought I'd see the day. Look at this, will you?" Prairie called Son's attention to a picture of a bare-chested man, wearing a headband, loincloth, and sandals that laced up to his knees, who appeared to be performing the Heimlich maneuver on an alligator. " 'Featuring Creek Pete, the American Glad-i-gator. Also appearing Prairie James *comma* roper.' "

Prairie balled up the poster and stuffed it in the nearest trashcan. " 'Also appearing.' I've never been an 'Also Appearing' in my entire career. I've played engagements of dubious caliber, granted. But I have always headlined. Who the hell is this Creek Pete? This 'American Glad-i-gator'?" Prairie dug the poster back out of the trashcan, smoothed it out, and studied Creek Pete's picture. After several minutes, Prairie passed the crumpled poster to Son. "This guy Indian or what?"

The photo of Creek Pete was even more overexposed than the one Son carried of her father, so that it was impossible to make out anything as specific as race. Still, Son tried. "Yes, he does have the look of an Arawakan-speaking sub-Taino of either the Gulf or Mississippian tradition."

Prairie grabbed the poster back. "The hell. You're looking at the goddamn alligator. Casey Dakota is a dead man." Prairie ripped the poster in half and marched off.

As Son was struggling to keep up, she caught sight of a familiar booth and called ahead to Prairie. "He's here! Jackson's here!"

Prairie stopped. "Jackson's here? In Gallup, New Mexico? He told me he was going home to Florida."

Son shielded her eyes and peeked into the screened window at the front of the booth. Prairie, excited to see his old friend, stepped up behind her as she called, "Jackson! Jackson, are you in there? It's me, Son Hozro, and Prairie!"

Jackson stepped out from behind the booth. He was wearing the same white shirt and white jeans he'd worn that night at the Blue Lagoon when he'd appeared like a vision from a dream, dancing on the back of a horse. He also had on black rubber boots caked with mud, and he carried a hose streaming water. Jackson let water pour onto the dusty ground as he stared, stupefied, at his visitors.

"Prairie James, what are you doing here?"

"Just what I wanted to ask you. I thought you went home."

"I did, but I came back out for the show. What are you doing here?"

"I'm working. Don't you read the posters?"

"No, no, we just got in. *You're* working this show?" he asked.

Son thought Jackson was taking an awfully long time sorting out his confusion, but Prairie didn't seem to notice.

"Jackson, damn, I'm glad to see you. I've had your barbecue on my mind ever since Juneteenth. Any chance I could get some?"

"Uh, yeah, yeah, sure. Just a sec; let me cut off this water." When Jackson reappeared, he seemed more the gracious, dignified man Son remembered. He leaned in the window and yelled at his helper, "Micky, get some of that barbecue I put back in the freezer there, you know, my own personal stock, and give it thirty seconds in the microwave. You do that for our friends?"

"Be happy to for Mithter Jamth and the announther lady." Mickey grinned, showing the empty space where his front teeth had once been. Son like the sound of "announther lady."

Son stared at Jackson and wondered if he remembered the night at the Blue Lagoon. Remembered dancing for her. Mickey handed out the sandwich to Prairie.

"Um-m-m, um-m-m-m, um-m-m-m." Prairie closed his eyes and rolled his head ecstatically from side to side when he was halfway through his barbecue sandwich. He was about to embark on further rhapsodies when a resounding bellow rattled the metal booth at their backs.

Prairie jumped up and whirled around, poised to take on an attacker. "What the holy hell is that?"

Jackson looked away guiltily. The bellow, somewhere between a lion's roar and walrus's bark, shook the booth again.

"Goddamn! That sounds a lot like . . ." Prairie didn't finish his sentence. There was another bellow. He put his sandwich down on the plate and asked angrily, "Is that an alligator?"

"Um, well. Yes. Her name's Beulah."

Prairie jumped up and raced around to the back of the booth. Jackson followed. An alligator lounged in the shallow mud-wallow Jackson had dug out and enclosed with some portable steel fencing. Another bellow had cleared a crowd of mostly children from the fence. They huddled several feet away. Beulah opened one yellow eye, lifted her long log of a body up on dwarfishly small legs, bellowed again, then settled more deeply into the muck, closed her eye, and slumbered on.

Prairie turned to Jackson. "And you, I take it, would be Creek Pete, the American Glad-i-gator?"

"Um, well, yes, I would."

Prairie smashed his fist into the plate he held. What remained of his sandwich adhered to his right hand by means of Jackson's special slow-cooked sauce. "Goddamn pigporker, Dakota. He did this to me. He did this on purpose to humiliate me. Second-billed me to a lizard!"

"Prairie, a man could take offense here."

"Dammit it all, Jackson, it's not you. It's the principle."

"Dakota never said a thing about you playing the show. If I'd known, I never would have come."

Prairie noticed the sandwich sticking to his hand and shook it loose. Beulah's serrated jaws flashed open, and the sandwich was gone before it landed in her pen. "I didn't know you had an act. When'd you get an act?"

"Oh, Beulah and me's been together forever. I keep her back home in Lake Charles. We don't get many requests to go on the road, but we've been playing Gallup fairly regular for the last ten, fifteen years. An alligator's a real draw out here."

"Shit, little water as they see, a fish stick could probably pack the house. What's the split? Dakota say anything about a split?"

"He didn't say anything about anything."

"Well, you're the headliner. You're the featured act. You're the draw, you set the split."

"Naw, listen, Prairie, it's not that way. We come out for the excitement. Long's I got enough to get on down the road. You know, whatever's right."

"You *are* Indian." It wasn't until Son spoke that Prairie noticed the dazzled look that had come into his announcer's eyes at roughly the time Jackson had identified himself as Creek Pete.

"Part, yeah. I didn't grow up in a tepee or anything, but my grandmother was full-blooded Creek."

Prairie rolled his eyes. "Another full-blood grandmother heard from."

"She raised me in the Indian way. Take only what you need. Leave some behind for old Mother Earth."

Looking at Jackson, Son suddenly recalled a lithograph of a group of Seminole Indians rounded up from the Everglades and cleaned up for the mission school. The children's skin was like Jackson's, as smoothly dark and oiled as a banister. Their collarless shirts and tuck-fronted dresses were brilliantly white against their mahogany skin; their hair, parted in the middle, was stacked over their wide-eyed faces like thatched roofs. "How could I have failed to recognize you as one of my own?"

"I'm one of everyone's. You name it: black, Indian, Dutch, Portuguese, Cuban. I have some of everybody's genes swimming around."

"But your outlook, your perspective on life. Isn't it Native American?"

Prairie was again rolling his eyes in exasperated disbelief. "Yeah, Hiawatha, tell us about it."

"I guess you could say that my grandmother taught us the Indian way. Never was any of this that's my ball, or my fork, or my toothbrush. Everything went into a big pot and we all shared out. If I got a cap gun, everyone had a cap gun. I didn't know until I came out of the swamp that the world's not like that. That everyone out here has their own toothbrush and their own fork and they all live alone and die alone."

Son nodded solemnly. "That is a majestic commentary."

"Oh, right, better alert Hallmark that you're available." Prairie had uncoiled the maguey rope from around his chest and was popping off little loops to drop on the alligator's snout. "So what's the trick, Jackson? You cork her?"

"Cork her?"

"You know, put something between those back molars so she can't chomp down on you." Prairie shook some action into a loop and roped Beulah's snout. Without opening her eyes, Beulah unloosed a low, grumbling warning that echoed around in her chest.

"There's no trick, Prairie. Just being in harmony with her. Knowing what she's liable to do and what she'll balk at."

"In harmony with an alligator. That's appealing." The instant that Prairie shook off the noose on Beulah's nose, the big jaws opened and Beulah slurped up Prairie's rope like a piece of cooked spaghetti. With a twist of her mighty neck, she jerked the rope through Prairie's hands so fast, he pulled them back with burn marks; then the jaws snapped shut.

"That was my best maguey! Your alligator ate my rope!"

"You've still got hold of it," Jackson pointed out. And, indeed, the rope hung slack in Prairie's hands. The rest of it drooped from Beulah's mouth as if she were taking a break before finishing up her flossing. "Just reel it on in."

Prairie did just that, winding the rope back in until it grew taut. Prairie pulled on it and the jaws clamped down tighter. He pulled harder and raised the prehistoric head a few inches out of the mire. One yellow eye blinked open and fixed on the source of this annoyance with a hungry menace.

"Whoa, how you planning to land her, Prairie?" Son laughed along with Jackson.

Prairie looked one more time into the yellow eye, then over at Son, pink with merriment, standing there chortling in the boots he'd bought her, and he threw the rope down and walked away from the whole mess.

"I should have told him that Beulah wouldn't keep his rope," Jackson said, watching Prairie stomp away. "She'll urp it up in an hour or two. He can just take it over to the laundrymat. I'm sure it won't be the first rope Prairie James has washed." Son and Jackson suddenly realized that they were alone. They both stared at Beulah as if she were a fire in the hearth for several long moments before Jackson asked, "You announcing for him tonight?"

"Yes." Son couldn't say what it was about Jackson that reached behind her wall of words. Standing next to him was like standing next to a calm, deep pool of water.

"You know, you should be announcing the whole rodeo."

A thrill as undeniable as it was unexpected ran through Son at the prospect. She imagined herself in the announcer's booth calling up the bronc riders, giving a calf roper the bad news that he'd broken the barrier, telling the bullriders who was up and who was in the hole. "Do you think so?"

"No question about it. You have got the gift."

Son took the judgment and her excessive pleasure in it and hid them away like a beggar sewing a jewel into the hem of a tattered coat. She pointed at Beulah, who had slipped back into a state of deep reptilian bliss. "Is there much danger? Wrestling with her?"

"Danger? Hell, yes, there's danger. Danger of me ending up in a truss. I'm liable to herniate myself at any moment. Bust a gut, hauling that animal around, maneuvering her into threatening poses, shaking her bumpy ass at the crowd, making like this *suitcase* is about to kill me!"

Son barely recognized the sound of her own laughter. It was the way she had laughed when she was a girl. The sound brought the children who'd been scared away back to the fence. They crowded around, planting their miniature Tony Lamas on the fence and clambering up for a better look. An Indian girl in a peach-colored sweatsuit, streaked with blue dribbles from the Sno-cone she clutched in her hand, poked her head up next to Son. Without thinking, Son smoothed the shiny wisps of black hair out of the little girl's mouth, which had also been dyed a cyanic blue. The girl's hair felt so warm and sleek beneath Son's hand that she couldn't keep from stroking it.

Silence built up around them before Jackson spoke. "You having any luck finding your father?"

"There have been leads. Who knows who might turn up here at the largest intertribal rodeo?"

"A person never does know. Stick with Prairie. If your father's still around, Prairie'll take you to him."

They stood side by side for several more minutes, pretending to be engrossed by the sight of an alligator imitating a stump. Jackson was a wide, open plain, unfenced, unbounded in any way, that stretched farther than Son could travel in a lifetime. Since her new life began, Son had never felt less like Sonja K. Getz than she did at that moment. Certainly Sonja K. Getz would never have asked, "Is there going to be a dance this evening similar to the one that was held in Jordan following the rodeo?"

"Should we find out?"

"Would you dance on the back of a horse?"

"Can't promise I won't." Jackson smiled his startling smile and the little girl's hair grew even warmer beneath Son's palm.

Prairie barely spoke to Son as they prepared for the evening's performance. He communicated at length, however, with the "sorry piece of nylon shit" rope he was forced to use in place of his treasured maguey. After trying a couple of reverses, butterflies, and the Texas skip, he lashed the rope against the side of the chip truck, whipping it for misbehaving. "Rather try and rope with a freaking garden hose. Yeah, big freaking green garden hose. With an oscillating sprinkler attached! Will Rogers himself couldn't rope the front porch with this rag!"

Prairie roped Son's left foot as she walked past him. "Real cagey of your friend to let his *alligator* eat my rope. Sort of cuts the competition down a little, doesn't it?"

"Jackson did not 'let' his alligator eat your rope. You 'let' his alligator eat your rope. Such cutthroat treachery is not the Indian way."

"Oh, Poke, give me a break. Jackson's a great guy, but he's about as Indian as Cootie Ramos."

"One might be fooled into saying the same about me, if one were to judge solely by appearances. Shouldn't we be concentrating on tonight's performance instead of the gnawing canker of your jealousy?"

"Jealousy? Hey! Where'd you get jealousy? I'm jealous of Jackson? Dream on."

"Then perhaps you're jealous of Jackson's attention to me."

"Oh, for Christ's . . . Who promoted you to belle of the ball, huh? Who snuck in and put a tiara on your head when I wasn't looking? Jealous? Me? You?" Prairie rewound his rope, placing one perfect loop on top of the other so that it looked like a Slinky, perfect from the factory. When he was done, he put the coiled rope inside a can, grabbed a halter and a currying brush, and walked away without a word.

Son watched him storm off. With the big silver can tucked under his arm, he looked like an old-time projectionist late for work. He zigzagged through the midway ducking clouds of cotton candy and a stuffed Pink Panther big as a bathtub. Then he was lost in the crowd, and Son turned away.

Almost at the foot of the red bluffs was a pen for contestants' horses. Domino picked his head up when the wind brought him the first whiff of his master. His ears cocked forward in happiness, and he trotted over to meet Prairie as happy as a child in nursery school when Mama comes to take him home. Prairie slipped on the halter and led Domino out of the pen to a spot of evening shade beneath a tall cottonwood.

He put his head close to Domino's neck and swept the brush over the animal's hide from throttle to thigh, muttering with each stroke. "That blowhole! . . . Second-bill me! . . . Who's he think . . . Looking for a job when I found . . ."

Domino's ears twitched forward and back, picking up in speed as the brush hit harder and the muttered curses grew louder. Finally, the horse flinched and danced away when the brush hit his hide and Prairie exploded, "JEALOUS!"

The horse looked back at him with injured outrage, eyes rolled as far as they could go in their sockets.

"Sorry, boy, sorry. Don't look at me like that. I told you I was sorry. Christ! I whack you accidentally once in fourteen years and you act like Mary Pickford."

But Domino kept strafing him with that wild-eyed look of terror until Prairie stopped long enough to feel the anger pulsing out of him. "Goddamn Dakota," he muttered one last time, then let the brush slip from his hand. He threw his arm around Domino's neck and hung on to the horse until the veins at his temples had stopped throbbing. "You got a date for the prom yet?" he asked.

Domino swished his head around. He was his old self again, bored and irritated. "PUHHHH!" He snorted wetly in Prairie's direction.

"Oh, and you're a real prize catch? A dream date?" Prairie stood, picked up the brush, and started in again.

Chapter 20.

"Kick him in the icehole?"

The setting sun reflecting off the red sandstone bluffs that rose behind the arena turned the light a shimmering copper. It shone on the faces of the mostly Navajo, mostly unamused spectators packing the concrete seats as Beau Beaulieu yelled out the punchline of a joke fed to him high in the announcer's booth by Freckles, a clown in denim cutoffs big enough for a hippo.

Son bounced up the last step of the stairs to the crow's nest where Beau was announcing the seventieth running of the Gallup Intertribal Rodeo. She'd managed a shower in the communal bathhouse. Her freshly washed hair was slicked back into two neat braids and she'd washed and air-dried all the pertinent areas of her ruffly, pink square-dancing outfit. She'd even polished her new boots with a couple of smears of judiciously buffed Chapstick and felt fresh and ready for anything.

Beaulieu sat in a high-backed office chair and swiveled from the microphone to Miss Ellie Yazzie, whom he was chatting up during slack moments. A fan blew the sweat away when it trickled down from his patent leather hairline. This was Beaulieu's idea of a decent announcer's booth. Not like that toaster–broiler oven they'd put him in at Hereford.

Son closed the door behind her.

Beaulieu swiveled around. "Well, who do we have here? The little perfesser herself. You gonna give the crowd another vocabulary lesson tonight?"

"If you're asking whether I will be announcing for Prairie, the answer is yes."

"Well, let me give you a little tip. Save the ten-dollar words tonight."

"You mean because the crowd is predominantly Native American?"

"Hey, you said it; I didn't."

"I would like to announce an entire rodeo," Son said.

Beaulieu made a face that betrayed what a preposterously impossible wish that was. "Well, okay. You just do like you're doing. Sit up here, listen in for a few years. Maybe someday you just might." Down in the arena Freckles the clown was finishing up his act of pumping a donkey's tail. "Oops. Showtime." Beaulieu swiveled back around to the microphone as Freckles raised a bucket to the announcer's booth and shouted something.

"You say you found water!" Beaulieu relayed to the crowd. "Aw, get outta here, Freckles." Beaulieu's chuckle was a velvet spill of homespun unctuousness. He winked at Miss Yazzie, who was sitting beside him with contestant lists spread out in front of her. When she ignored him, he turned back to Son. "You watching this? You got to play an Indian crowd a certain way. Been a while for me. Not since that Red Power stuff started up. But that's all pretty much died down now. I'll do the Indian bits. Not many announcers even remember most of the old bits. I do. You watch. This crowd'll eat 'em up."

Beaulieu turned back to the arena, where Freckles was sweeping a floppy hat off his fright wig. The clown got his first big hand of the evening when he bent over to take a bow and a large plastic daisy sprouted out of his bottom.

"Aw, Freckles, you heard me. Go on, get out of here! Or you'll be pushing up day-shees the hard way!" Beaulieu's riposte was unscripted, right down to the denture whistle. He looked over at Son and gave her a wink, the old pro encouraging the wannabe.

"Hey!" he asked Freckles over the microphone, glancing at Son to alert her to pay attention. "I've got a question for you. Tell me this, Freckles. Tell me why Indians wear headbands. Could you tell me? Why do Indians wear headbands?"

Beaulieu allowed Freckles to scratch his head and shrug his shoulders several times before he popped the punchline. "To keep their wigs warm!" Feeling expansive, Beaulieu covered the mike with his hand and turned to Son. "Don't milk the laughs. Keep the pace going."

Son started to tell him how thoroughly offensive she, a Native American, found his racist joke, but Beaulieu was already spinning back around. "You'll learn. You'll learn." He uncovered the microphone. "Okay, we're gonna go now to the most popular event at any Indian rodeo, team roping."

Down in the arena a couple of ropers backed their horses into the boxes on either side of the calf chute. The sun began to set, and the arena lights seemed to grow brighter, as the day slipped away, and turned the rodeo into a bright globe glowing in the night. Son noticed that down in the crowd a knot of Indian men in their early twenties, wearing T-shirts emblazoned with the insignia of the American Indian Movement, were glaring up at the announcer's booth, then back at one another. She could just barely make out Prairie, in the warm-up area outside the arena, astride Domino. He hadn't spoken to her since she laughed when Beulah ate his rope. And now he was waiting to follow an alligator-wrestling act while he listened to the racist gibes of a third-rate announcer. Son determined that she would do an exceptional job of announcing for him tonight.

"First up we got the team of . . ." Beaulieu pawed heavily through the papers in front of him before noticing that Miss Yazzie was silently holding out the list he needed. He grabbed it, and, as he did, another one of the old bits came back. A guaranteed killer.

"Hey, Freckles, did you hear about my old buddy, Chief Two Ponies? Big chief over there in Kiowa, yeah, Kiowa country. Well, old Chief Two Ponies, now, he liked his tea. Liked it hot, liked it iced with lots of sugar and a squeeze of lemon. Any old way, Chief Two Ponies loved his tea. Well, one day, he just couldn't get enough of it. Just kept drinking glass after glass after glass of the stuff. No one could believe it. Old Chief Two Ponies drank fifty glasses of tea! Fifty! You know where they found him the next day? Drowned in his own tepee!"

"That was egregious," Son informed him.

Beaulieu, wiping tears from his eyes, held his hand over the microphone. "I know. The old ones are the best. But just keep working at it, little sister. You'll get there." He took his hand off of the mike. "All right, let's rope a cow!"

He looked at the neatly typed list of team ropers Miss Yazzie had given him. "Next up we've got the good ropers Ed Tallsalt and Calvin Footracer." Beaulieu covered his first snicker with a cough. "On deck we've got J. R. Elk—" Beaulieu had to stop to collect himself again. "J. R. Elkriver."

Two of the A.I.M. men Son had noticed earlier, strapping Navajos, over six feet in their boots and round-topped, retro black Stetsons, were standing up.

"J. R. Elkriver and Gene Black Sheep? The team of Elkriver and Black Sheep . . ." Beaulieu sputtered with incredulity that he tried to get under control, but it was too late by the time he did. Son could hear heavy footsteps rattling up the back stairs.

"And in the hole, Art Interpreter and Eloy Manygoats." In all fairness, Beaulieu did manage to pronounce the last names with appropriate dignity. But by that time it no longer mattered; the door had already burst open. The two A.I.M. members muscled in. Without a word, they lifted Beau Beaulieu from his swivel chair and removed him from the booth.

"Those Tuba City guys," Miss Yazzie told Son softly as the announcer was carried out and down the steps, "they don't take shit off nobody." She stood up. "Well, no announcer, I guess the rodeo's over."

The moment had a dreamlike quality to it, when everything changes in a fraction of a second yet time seems to move in slow motion. Son answered like a bad actor responding to an overly theatrical cue line.

"I've had some . . . I've had a bit of announcing experience." That was all Miss Yazzie needed to hear. She handed Son the lists of contestants, seated her in the swivel chair, and shoved the microphone into her hand. It felt like a royal scepter. "Start here," Miss Yazzie instructed, pointing to the names of the first roping team.

"Ed Tallsalt and Calvin Footracer, you're up. Elkriver and Black Sheep on deck. Interpreter and Manygoats in the hole." Son read the names off with fluid dignity. The entire rodeo was under her control. She wished that her mother could be out there in the crowd. That all her Dorfburg nemeses—Earl Walp, Miss Delfel, Rema Kleine, Walter Dittlinger, her band instructor Mr. Capelli—she wished they could all be there. But it was enough that Jackson was there. Jackson and Prairie.

Son did not need to spend years listening to some blowhard like Beaulieu to discover the secret of rodeo announcing. She knew what it was; she knew what everyone in the crowd was waiting for. They were waiting to hear the name of someone they knew or the name of someone they didn't know and to hear that that contestant was from their town or their tribe. All of them were waiting for someone to care about. Son knew it was her job to give each person sitting in the fading sunset on those concrete benches someone to care about. With each new roper, Son would cover the microphone and confer with Miss Yazzie so that she could then turn back to the crowd and say something like "Eloy and Art have been roping together since they were seniors at Window Rock Junior High." Or "Good going, Calvin. You'd never know that Calvin just got the cast taken off his right hand where his good horse, Chief, stepped on it."

Son felt like an air traffic controller, guiding the emotions of the crowd, helping them to land in the right places. And she *could* do it! Was doing it!

As she moved down the long list of team ropers, Son was far too busy wrapping the crowd in a charmed web of rapport to notice the great plume of dust rising in the last golden rays of daylight and drawing closer and closer at an alarming rate of speed. It came to rest directly outside the arena. At its center was a thirty-seven-foot-long recreational vehicle of the Holiday Rambler type. Dewey Dakota ran up to the motor home and opened the door. His father stepped out and surveyed the grounds as if they belonged to him. Dewey gave an excited report, pointing to where the Navajo men were holding Beaulieu, then put up his arms to shield his face. Dakota swatted at the boy several times before abandoning the effort to stride over and parley with the outraged Navajos. After a few seconds of hostage negotiation, Casey Dakota swept his arm out in front of him and let the men drag Beaulieu off to a Dumpster. They tossed the natty announcer in and walked away.

"No score! No score!" Son announced as the team in the arena stopped chasing a scrawny steer and reeled in their ropes. When she called for the next team, Jackson stepped into the booth. Oiled and girded in full gladiator regalia, he was an Aztec vision straight off a Mexican restaurant calendar. His costume consisted mostly of leather straps: leather straps crisscrossing his ebony chest; a skirt of leather straps flapping over some sort of diaper-loincloth combination; leather straps winding up his sturdy calves to hold his sandals in place; a single leather strap tied around his forehead to keep his wig wam.

Son felt Jackson beside her before he put his hand on her shoulder, making her voice warble slightly as she called out a time of seventeen point twenty-two seconds for the team of Choneska and Kie up from the White River area.

While the crowd cheered their Apache visitors, Jackson leaned forward and covered the mike. "I told you you had the gift."

The kind of uncensored joy Son never allowed herself to feel radiated through her.

"So," Jackson asked, gesturing toward his S and M–looking outfit, "how big a fool am I?"

Son did not hesitate an instant before answering, "Spartacus himself never marched with a finer gladiator."

Jackson shrugged in modest demurral and held out a cassette. "This is my music. Just cue it up when you want me to come on. Uh, if you're still interested, I checked. There is a dance after the show."

Back in Dorfburg, Son had believed that the concept of wishes coming true was mostly a function of the merchandising monolith bent on duping the common herd into escalating binges of consumption. But now, within the space of minutes, two wishes had come true for her. "I am. I am interested."

Jackson nodded. "Good. Okay. Good."

They both stared out the window and watched Harrison Begay double-hock a speedy Corriente steer, then stretch the rangy beast out between himself and his header.

"Good catch," Jackson said.

"The price of team roping just went up!" Son shouted, more enthusiastic about team roping than she had ever been. Jackson stepped away, but the spot on her shoulder where his hand had rested remained warm.

"I'd better get back down to Beulah before she dozes off again." Jackson picked up his shield and sword and left.

A date. She had been invited out on an actual date by an actual man. It had been so easy, really, to leave Dorfburg. She had closed up the endlessly boring years of her past like the pages of a book she had tired of reading. She was a rodeo announcer and she had a date.

"Eleven-five!" Son called out the team's time, but her attention followed Jackson as he descended the stairs. Beulah waited where Jackson had left her, just inside the arena gates, stretched out on a long gurney-like wagon set six inches off the ground. The alligator's bumpy, gray-green tail hung off the back end of the wagon, dragging heavily back and forth in the dry dirt, making swishy designs.

When Jackson reached her, Beulah slammed her tail down like a bull at mating season and let out a bellow that resonated throughout the arena. Up in the stands, kids scrambled into their mamas' arms and the men stood up to see if anything live and unscripted was about to happen. Anything that might involve the spilling of real human blood. The look of unrehearsed alarm on Jackson's face was promising. So was the sight of Beulah flipping herself off the wagon and whirling around to take a wild snap at a passing barrel racer. The horse whinnied, lodging an indignant protest against the very idea of being attacked by a log with teeth.

Once the horse passed, Beulah paused long enough to heave up sixty feet of top-quality Mexican maguey rope, now slimy with the mostly green contents of an alligator's stomach. Son wondered then about Prairie. She searched the area on both sides of the arena fence but could see no sign of him.

Though the last team's score had not yet appeared on the computer sign board, Son knew an entrance when she spotted one. While the crowd was still gripped by gatormania, she quickly popped Jackson's cassette into the player. The aerobic trumpet overture from "Rocky" blared out and Son exclaimed over it, "Let's put those palms together, ladies and gentlemen, for our RAINBOW-HUED BROTHER from the great Creek tribe, the AMERICAN GLAD-I-GATOR, Creek Pete! And DIRECTLY FROM THE FLORIDA EVERGLADES, where a man can hide and never be found, the MAN-EATING BELLOWING BEULAH!"

Leaving her judgment of Prairie seeping wetly into the dust, Beulah waddled with a marked swamp majesty back to her cart, lumbered aboard, and suffered herself to be pulled out to a crescendo of thunderous applause. Jackson charged out, shield and sword held over his head, pulling the gurney behind him. Beulah was splayed out on it, disdain pouring from every bump on her body. A mud pit had been set up down by the calf pens, and Jackson jogged over.

"Let's welcome both of our Native American visitors from the swamp!" Son milked another couple of rounds of applause while the team ropers cleared the arena.

The wrestling was pretty much as Jackson had described, more weight lifting than death struggle. He lugged Beulah around, shifting her from one menacing pose to another. At one point he draped her across his chest so that they were dancing cheek to cheek, and this seemed to cheer Beulah considerably. The giant jaws opened and swung about with a jubilance that was cut short when Jackson heaved the beast off and threw her to the ground. This wounded Beulah's dignity and she participated no further.

Fortunately the Glad-i-gator competition was over by then and all that remained was for Jackson to load his co-star onto her wagon. The crowd was pleased enough with the show. It had not detracted in any serious way from the initial thrill they'd gotten at the idea of a man putting his body next to that of a nine-foot, 250-pound reptile.

Son, on the other hand, had been as mesmerized by the sight of Jackson's perfectly scooped-out buttocks flashing from under the leather straps of his breechclout skirt as little Tinka Getz had been watching the loincloths of Hollywood braves flap across the silver screen. "Ladies and gentlemen, I give you CREEK PETE!" Holding his sword and shield triumphantly aloft, Jackson pulled his co-star out of the arena.

Son let the applause ride until every palm had given all that it would. "We've got a double treat for you tonight, Prairie James's Salute to the Navajo Nation!" Son replaced Jackson's "Rocky" tape with "Bonanza" and turned the volume up to give Prairie the morale boost he appeared to need. She waited for him gallop out and for Domino to furrow the arena with his great, sliding, *charro*-style stop, but Prairie did not appear. Then she remembered the Juneteenth rodeo in Jordan and how many attempts were required to coax him out.

More morale boosting would be required. "We are indeed honored to have with us tonight MR. PRAIRIE JAMES, THE WORLD'S

GREATEST LIVING TRICK ROPER, AND DOMINO, THE HORSE WITH THE BRAIN OF A MAN! "Greatest living" and "brain of a man" goosed the crowd into a healthy burst of clapping that Son was certain would provide suitable inspiration. It did not. The applause died away, the "Bonanza" overture faded, and not one snowy hair of Domino's hide appeared. Son rewound the tape and was about to start it over when Miss Yazzie tapped her on the shoulder and pointed down into the arena. There was Dewey Dakota, drawing his finger across his throat, then waving his hands in front of his face. Behind him stood his father, Casey Dakota, a glower on what little of his face was not hidden in the shadows cast by his black hat.

The sight of a distinctly unhappy Casey Dakota convinced Son that her responsibility as sole announcer for the the success or failure of the seventieth running of the Gallup Intertribal Rodeo had to take precedence over her obligations to Prairie. Miss Yazzie put the list of the saddle bronc riders in her hands, and Son read the line-up without another mention of Prairie. The second the show was over, though, she bolted down the stairs and out into the crowd. The lights from the midway—the green stripes running up the long arms of the Hammer, the wildly pivoting red stars of the Tilt-A-Whirl, the blue spokes of the Ferris wheel—shone on the faces that crowded around her. Everyone was neon. In the darkness sprinkled with confetti-colored light, she hurried toward the chip truck, followed by the amplified scream of the song "96 Tears" coming from the Zipper. Domino, still saddled, was tied outside.

She opened the back door, and the truck's dark interior filled with screams from the Zipper and lurid slashes of colored light. "Prairie? What happened? Where were—" Her question died when she saw Prairie, wrapped in a sheet, lumped on the plank in the back. "Prairie?"

Only the song's refrain answered: "You're gonna cry! Cry! Cry! Cry! Ninety-six tears!"

"He'th hurt. Bad." It was Mickey, Jackson's helper. He switched on a flashlight and Son saw that he stood inside, next to Prairie's metal school locker mounted on the wall of the truck. He chewed on his lower lip as he fitted a key into the lock and turned. The lock dropped open. "I did it! I opened it!"

"Good, Mickey. That's real good. Now get me the bottle of medicine in there."

The hollow, hanging-on tone of Prairie's voice scared Son.

Mickey brought the bottle to Prairie, who groaned once when he reached out and took it and again when he shook the bottle and discovered that it was empty. He rolled back toward the wall.

Son grabbed Mickey. "What happened?"

Mickey gave a breathless account. "Prairie went over to Mr. Dakota'th RV when Jackthon was wrethling and I went too, 'cuth I wuth all out of change and had to get thome more. But when Prairie athked for hith money, Mr. Dakota thaid he wuth fired and Prairie thaid he wuth a thkunkfuck and couldn't fire him becuth he quit. Then Mr. Dakota thaid he wuth a hath-been who never wuth."

Son climbed into the back of the truck and put her hand on Prairie's shoulder, trying to ease him over so that she could look at his wounds. All the while, Micked rattled on.

"Then Mr. Dakota thucker-punthed him and kicked him in the nutth. Then Prairie come back up and rammed hith head into Mr. Dakota'th jaw until he likely bit hith tongue clean off and blood wuth going everywhere. Then Prairie jack up hith arm real good and tell Mr. Dakota to give him hith fucking money or he wuth going to break the cockthucker off at the armpit."

"Shut up, Mickey." Prairie's voice echoed hollowly in his broken, swollen nose.

"Don't talk," Son whispered. "I'm going to get you help. I'm going to fix it. Everything will be all right."

Still without rolling over to face her, Prairie clutched her hand on his shoulder. "Man, I'm fucked up this time."

"That wuth when Dewey come over and grab up Prairie tho Mr. Dakota can work him over real good." Mickey prattled on with his recitation. "Had hith ring on and everything. Then Prairie rear up and kick Mr. Dakota in the head. I thought they wuth going to kill him then, but they had to go back to the rodeo 'cuth Jackthon wuth done wrethling, tho they jutht left him out there and I brung him back here."

Prairie kept a tight grip on Son's hand.

Mickey turned to Prairie. "I wuthn't gonna tell the part about how Mr. Dakota thaid you couldn't even get no deethent poothy to ride with you no more and you told him not to run hith mouth on Thon jutht becuth *he* wouldn't know what to do with a woman had a good brain in her head."

Prairie laughed low in his throat. "You think I've harmed my chances for career advancement?" When Prairie rolled over and glanced at Son, she caught a glimpse of his ruined face.

"Mickey," she said, struggling to keep her voice even, "get out and untie Domino." When the helper had obeyed, she directed him to find a good chunk of pasture for the horse; she was taking Prairie to the doctor.

At the Gallup emergency room, Son dragged Prairie inside, where they joined the other casualties from the Intertribal Ceremonial. Prairie didn't look as bad under the greenish fluorescent lights as Son had feared he would, but his wan, unfocused face alarmed her even more than the blood now drying there in dark, crusty patches. Every time anyone in a white coat walked by, she jumped up and demanded "immediate attention by your most competent staff member." Unfortunately, in a battlefield of knife wounds, gasoline-sniffing poisoning, rape, and one goring, Prairie's pulped face failed to electrify anyone.

After the fifth time Son was ignored in her demand for immediate attention, Prairie struggled to his feet. "Let's shitcan this deal." He was shuffling painfully out the door when a young doctor in a dirty lab coat and spongy running shoes told them to follow him. He sat Prairie down on a metal stool and whisked the curtains closed around them.

The doctor peered up Prairie's nose, said, "This may hurt," and snapped the cartilage back into place. Prairie slumped against Son when the doctor turned his back and wrote out a prescription.

Prairie was sitting upright when the doctor turned back around. "Doc, tell me something. Why bother saying this *may* hurt? I mean, is there ever a time when moving someone's nose from one side of their face to the other *doesn't* hurt?"

The doctor smiled thinly and handed Son the prescription. "This is for pain—"

"Now, *now*, I get something for pain."

"Keep his head elevated for the next couple of days. Plenty of fluids. Let me know if the bleeding starts again."

Son examined the slip of paper. "Did you specify that a generic equivalent would be acceptable?"

Crimping his lips in annoyance, the doctor grabbed back the prescription slip from Son, scribbled on it, handed it to her, and was out of the examining room before Son could open her mouth again.

Prairie snatched the slip out of Son's hand and read, "Percodan! Yes! The night is young, Duchess; let's get fucked-up."

"You seem to be bouncing back rather nicely."

He waved the prescription slip as if it were a winning lottery ticket. "Oh, yes, Mama! Couple hundred cc's of this and manhole covers start bouncing!"

"Apparently the emergency has passed."

"You got that right."

They stopped at Gallup's twenty-four-hour Walgreen's Pharmacy and Package Store. Son waited in the truck while Prairie went inside to get the prescription filled. Armed security guards patrolled the parking lot, breaking up clots of men passing bottles.

Prairie came out of the store washing down a handful of Percodans with a Seagram peach wine cooler. Opening the door, he announced, "Help is on the way," hopped in, pulled a cooler from the plastic ring, and tossed it to Son.

Son twisted the top off the bottle, and a chemical peach smell filled the truck. "You certainly have rebounded rather rapidly."

Prairie shook out another couple of pills. "Places I've been, it doesn't pay to slow down for too long just because someone puts a fist into your sinuses." He pulled the door closed. "But, uh, thanks. You came through for me. You really did."

"Oh." For the first time in all their long hours together in the chip truck, Son became aware of being alone in it with a man. "I believe that you would have done the same for me."

"You bet your braids I would." He held out his upturned palm to her and, after first thinking that Prairie was asking for a handout, she lightly slapped his palm with her own in a gesture of solidarity. Prairie grinned, closed his eyes, and rested his head against the seat, the better to allow the wine and painkillers to seep into his brain. "Yeah, that's better."

The husky intimacy in Prairie's voice panicked Son. In matters of love and the loins, she was the equivalent of a preteen convent schoolgirl. To be so entirely out of her league here with a former merchant marine who'd sampled the pleasures of every fleshpot on the globe thoroughly unnerved her.

"Since you're feeling better," she said stiffly, "perhaps we could head back to the rodeo. I have a date with Jackson for the big dance."

Without lifting his head from the seat or opening his eyes, Prairie snorted a laugh, and a grin spread across his abraded face. " 'The big dance'? Hey, I hope you didn't get that tiara out of storage or anything for the event."

Prairie's shift back to his familiar causticity reassured Son. She quickly reclaimed the safety of her imperious tone. "What's that supposed to mean?"

" 'The big dance'? Yeah, dance of the bearded clam."

"That is vile and reprehensible."

"What do you think this big dance is going to be? Punch in a bowl and a wrist corsage? Hey, think again. You might, if you're real lucky, have three metal-heads for a band making sounds that would drive a Portland logger out of his gourd. More likely, some-one'll just pull the speakers out of their car and plug in a Black

Sabbath tape. For refreshments, okay? For refreshments, all the guys might pool their cans of Aqua Net."

"You're jealous."

"Jealous? Me? Jealous? Of an alligator wrestler?" He started up the engine. "That does it. That's it. You want the big dance. You got the big dance."

The crowds had thinned by the time they got back to Red Rock State Park. They found the secluded patch of pasture enclosed on three sides by sandstone bluffs that blocked out the light and noise of the midway where Mickey had staked Domino. Prairie turned the engine off.

Son knew that she should bolt the instant the wheels stopped turning. That she had made a commitment to Jackson, a commitment that she wanted to meet. But she stayed. Even though she knew it was a bad idea, that one way or another it would confuse and sabotage her search for her father, she sat in the truck's cab and listened in the darkness to the metal pings and creaks as the engine cooled.

Prairie offered Son the Percodan again.

She refused and reached for the door handle. "I should go find Jackson. So. If you're really okay . . ."

"Me? Oh, hell, yes. I'm fine. Knock yourself out." Prairie tossed back a couple more of the pills. "Know why I did that?"

"To escape the demoralizing reality of your life?"

"Ah! Good guess. Good guess. No, I took them to give me enough courage to do this." Prairie turned to Son, leaned over the gearshift, and brought his face toward hers. Unfortunately, the wine, the Percodan, and the beating had distorted Prairie's depth perception so thoroughly that he crash-landed his abused nose into Son's teeth.

"Jesus! Motherfucking son of a bitch! Shit! That hurts!" Prairie leaned back, tilted up his head, and lightly pressed his middle finger to the base of his nose.

It took Son a minute to put the evidence together. "You were going to kiss me."

"Yeah, that was the general idea. Execution left a little to be desired."

"Why?"

"Why was I going to kiss you? I don't know. You want to kiss someone, you make a run at it."

"But me? Why did you want to kiss me?"

"Don't sound so bumfuzzled. You're a . . . You're an . . . I don't know, Poke; you've grown on me."

"You make me sound like some sort of fungus."

"Naw, listen. The drugs. That peach shit. This whole flubbed-up day. My rhythm's way off. Go on. Go to the dance. It'll be fun. Jackson's a great guy. Sincerely. He's as good as they get in this scumpit world."

"You're staring into the abyss. That's it, isn't it?"

"Come again?"

"You have no future and Casey Dakota's comments have effectively negated your past."

"Oh, that? That I'm a has-been? No, that wasn't any giant news flash. I know I'm a historical artifact."

"So why *did* you try to kiss me? Jealousy?"

"Do me a favor, will you? Drop that jealousy shit. Okay, listen, you want the straight stroke? I was curious. I been curious for a long time. What would happen if I kissed you? What would you do? Paste me one? Melt into my arms?"

"Let's try again."

"You're sure you want to? You sure we're not getting too out of control here, leaping in like this?"

"No, I think the situation can be contained."

"Whoa. Are we talking about a kiss or a toxic spill?"

"Go ahead."

Prairie angled into position and leaned forward. Just as he was about to make contact, Son pulled away. "Stop."

"What now?"

"Before we go any farther, I must know one thing. Are you my father?"

"What did I tell you?"

"I know what you've told me. It's just that there are so few trick ropers. The pool is so limited."

"You want me to kiss you or not?"

Son waited. How could she kiss a man who she believed in the bottom of her heart could be her father? A man who was a chauvinist, a racist, an enemy of the environment? A man who epitomized *koyaanisqasti?* Then she smelled him. Prairie smelled the way she'd dreamed all her life that the ocean smelled, of salt and wind and faraway places. How could she *not* kiss him?

She eased forward and met his lips. The result was somewhere between the two outcomes Prairie had forecast. "You smell like ginger snap cookies." He put his abused nose near Son's neck and breathed, then licked. "I didn't expect that." He stroked her cheek, his hand tough as a dog's toenails from a lifetime of cargo cables and maguey ropes. "You've got great skin there, Big Wind Woman." He stroked some more. "Great skin."

Careful to avoid contact with his nose, Son put her lips against Prairie's. Stripped down to the molecular level, Son and Prairie met and found themselves to be a cozily compatible pair. Each was charmed by the other's basal body temperature. That unexpected rapport, however, alarmed Son as much as it mesmerized her. The link between them was too strong, too much in the blood.

The Percodan float contributed greatly to Prairie's enjoyment of having a hundred and fifty pounds of warm protoplasm snuggling against him. In fact, all this cuddling was proving to be such a thoroughly satisfactory experience that Prairie planned to add a few more items to the agenda. His hand was snaking up Son's back to the traditional bra-fastening point when Son spoke.

"I'm a virgin, you know."

"I was kind of afraid of that."

"Would you like to perform the defloration?"

"You want me to?"

"Do you want to?"

Prairie exhaled heavily out of his abused nostrils and leaned back. "That's not the right question here. The only time in my life I truly was *not* interested was for about half an hour after I caught a line drive in the crotch. No, your first time should be, you know. No choice. Can't help yourself. You shouldn't be collecting consent forms. I'm not saying I want to totally take myself out of the running. But, jeez, wasted on Percodan? Just got fired? The only thing worse than a grudge screw is a consolation screw. You deserve better. You know, your first time."

"It's because you're my father, isn't it?"

"Jeez Louise, if you were one-tenth as smart as you are intelligent . . . Forget it. I ain't getting into that shit. Go. Go meet Jackson."

For several minutes, Son stared straight ahead without moving, watching as Domino, washed alabaster in a pool of moonlight you could read a newspaper by, swung his neck and cropped off clumps of salt grass. Suddenly, he pricked up his ears, sniffed the air, and whinnied. A distant nicker answered and, like a night watchman satisfied that all the doors are tight, he went back to his snack.

Exasperated, Prairie asked, "What do you want? What would you like?"

None of Son's doubts had disappeared. A deep instinct told her she should leave and leave now. Still, she heard herself answer, "I'd like . . . I'd like for you to hold me."

Prairie opened his arms. Son hesitated before dropping her head onto his chest. Since she accomplished this while keeping her bottom glued to her own seat, it involved a considerable degree of spinal flexibility and left her neck painfully hyperextended. In spite of these contortions, Son found something approaching bliss in listening to Prairie's heartbeat.

"Come here, you're making my neck hurt just looking at you twisted around like that." Without grunting once, Prairie managed to heft Son out of her seat and onto his lap, where she settled like a kitten. Prairie was amazed for a second or two by his announcer's purring pliancy. Then the various chemical amendments he'd made that night overwhelmed him, and all he was aware of was warmth and softness. All the edges were gone. A porcupine that talked like a college professor had waddled into his life and become *his* porcupine. When he finally learned to pat her the right way, all the quills lay down.

Son listened for a long time to the rasp of air rattling in and out of Prairie's chest. When he was sleeping soundly enough that his jaw hung slack and his eyes twitched with dreams, Son laid her head in the crook of his neck. Snuggling up against him made Son feel as if she had had boyfriends all her life. Boyfriends or maybe a father.

In the pasture, Domino pricked up his ears again, his dreams disturbed by the growls of ancestral enemies. The tender flesh around his belly flinched away from the threat of long claws as he swung his head around, homing in on the shuddersome racket. He found it. There were no bears invading. His head dropped and his belly went slack. It was only the humans making their sleep sounds.

Chapter 21.

A spoke of midday sunlight slivered through a wobbly rivet hole in the back of the chip truck and needled Son right in the eye. She blinked awake.

"Prairie?"

The last hours had hummed away in a state of excitement too keen to pass for sound sleep. She awoke expecting to find herself clumped up against Prairie. But he was gone and she was lying in the back of the truck. Obviously, at some time in the night he had carried her to the plank bunk. Carried. Her.

"Prairie?" She climbed back into the front seat and looked out the window. The contestants' area was deserted. The afternoon rodeo was about to start. Domino was still staked out in the pasture. The old trouper, sensing that an unwanted showtime approached, glanced cautiously over at Son, then looked back down quickly like a bad student who didn't want to be called on.

A family passed the truck and stared in at Son. They all—mother, father, two boys—looked like Secret Service agents in reflector sunglasses, short haircuts, and dark baseball caps. The mother, looking at Son, pulled her boys closer to her. Son checked herself in the rearview mirror. Scary, indeed. Wild wisps of hair had escaped her braids; her face was as pale and puffy as a marshmallow. She unplaited the braids and brushed out her hair.

"It looks good all crimped and fluffed out like that." Prairie's face suddenly appeared in the mirror behind her. Aside from a slight darkening around the eyes, which made him look more like a consumptive nineteenth-century poet than the loser of a punchout, Prairie showed few signs of the beating he'd received. His own hair was wet and slicked back, furrowed by comb tracks, from a visit to the state park's communal showers. He banged his hand on the truck door and stuck his head in the window. "Good morning, Duchess."

Son felt shy. But Prairie, a pot and a half of coffee ahead of her, didn't notice. Far from the broken man Son might have expected, Prairie was bubbling over with a strange excitement. "Get packed up, Pocahontas. We're hitting the road as soon as I finish up one little chore." The back doors flew open, and Prairie jumped in and rummaged through the litter.

He paused and glanced up. "You speak Spanish?"

"*Por seguro, señor. Porque preguntas?*"

"Great, great. I knew I could count on you." He dived back into the junk without answering Son's question and fished out a crowbar. "I knew it was back here!" He hopped out of the truck. "Be ready to leave."

"For where?"

Prairie walked away.

"Where are you going with the crowbar?" Son called after him.

Smiling strangely, he stopped and hefted the tool in his hand. "To make some repairs."

Son watched Prairie walk away. There was a cocky hitch in his stride that gave his butt a syncopated twitch. She could imagine him strutting down the gangplank with a duffel bag thrown over his shoulder and a woman with flowers in her hair waiting for him on the dock.

It was impossible, Son finally concluded. There was absolutely no way on earth that this man could be her father. Prairie disappeared from sight. Humming the lushly romantic *Liebestod* from

Tristan und Isolde, Son ran her hand over the driver's seat, where Prairie had cradled her last night. Then she went to the back of the truck and gathered her things together.

From the distant arena came the first blat of the judge's horn, signifying that the rodeo's opening ride had ended.

Prairie heard the first horn go off as he strode through the other camping area. The good one. This was where all the VIPs stayed, members of the tribal council, visiting bigwigs, celebrity contestants, and performers. By all rights, he should have been bivouacked in this area. Casey Dakota had his RV here. Dakota could have arranged it for him with one word. His grip tightened on the crowbar.

"Repairs," he muttered to himself, grinning uncontrollably. "Got a few repairs to make."

Getting into Dakota's motor home was as easy as slipping the claw of the crowbar between the door and the jamb and popping it open. All Prairie was looking for was what was owed him. Maybe a little severance pay. There was no cash, but Prairie already knew exactly where Dakota kept the big notebook filled with pages of checks for payroll and prizes. He'd stood waiting often enough while Dakota made out a check that was invariably short. He pulled out the book of checks and carefully made one out to Mr. Prairie James. Even wrote his name in on the check stub and the amount of back wages he'd paid to himself.

Then he went out the front door and left it hanging open.

The manager of the Cash 'n' Dash—"All Checks Cashed. No ID Required. Large Coke 69¢"—was pleased to cash the payroll check Prairie presented in return for the usual two percent transaction fee plus three dollars for the verification call to Casey Dakota's bank in Oklahoma.

"What's your event?" asked the manager, a fiftyish man wearing a brown vinyl jacket in spite of the heat, counting out Prairie's money.

Prairie looked up blankly from the stack of bills piling on the counter in front of him. The man pointed a grimy finger to the "Contestant" pass sticking out of his shirt pocket. "Oh. Roping. I'm a, uh, a roper."

The manager grinned. There was a gap between his front teeth he could have spit a watermelon seed through. "That's my favorite part. The roping."

Prairie took the pass out of his pocket and handed it to him. "Here, this'll get you free to all the performances. You should go. Guy wrestles an alligator at half-time."

Son had been waiting nearly an hour when she heard Beulah grunt out a great swamp bellow. A wave of shame swept over her. She had stood Jackson up. It was exactly the sort of thing Gussie Patton or Rema Kleine, her mother even, would have done. Son could not believe that she had betrayed her own moral code. She would have to beg Jackson's forgiveness before leaving.

She wondered where Prairie had gone. She really knew little about him aside from a *Decameron* of bawdy tales. Almost involuntarily, she turned to the gray metal school locker bolted to the wall of the truck that Prairie had warned her away from the very first night. It hung open just as Mickey had left it last night. Son had spent a lifetime holding herself aloof. The one lesson she had learned early and well was that descending to mix and meddle in human affairs was to bring down pain upon herself. But a new life was beginning for her.

She pushed open the louvered metal door. Taped inside the door was a disappointingly predictable centerfold of Miss April, a hydroponic lass who seemed to be attempting to douche with a pink feather boa. Still, Son asked herself, would she want a man who wasn't mad for the female form?

Hastily tossed inside the locker was a neon lime-green coupon offering half off on a car wash. On the other side was a map with a large X at the bottom labeled "El Marinero's Place." The mystery was solved. Prairie had found out where the reunion was to take place. That was the secret destination he wanted her to be ready to leave for when he returned. She studied the map. El Marinero's ranch was right on the border. That was why he'd asked if she knew Spanish. She touched the map to her lips, then tucked it into her mess kit purse. Prairie was taking her to meet her father. He couldn't *be* her father. Her heart sang with happiness.

She unearthed a small woven basket and pulled off the lid. Coins from around the world were heaped inside: silver yen with square holes at the center light as fallen aspen leaves; massive old silver pesos; centimes the size of baby fingernails. Son smiled as she touched each coin. Imagined she could still feel the heat from Prairie's body trapped in them. Wished she could have ridden in his pocket as he sailed around the world.

At the bottom of the basket, amid hard, fuzzy, pilled remnants of the ticket stubs and receipts that had gone through the laundry in his pockets, were several St. Christopher medals and a tattered scapular with a faded image of the Infant of Prague printed on one of the squares of cloth backed with brown felt. From the grimy look of the cords linking the squares, the scapular had obviously been worn. Prairie was a Catholic. Son was moved that he was a man of devotion. She would convert if that became an issue, which she understood it frequently did for Catholics.

She hesitated a moment before pulling out a large scrapbook. Then she opened the album in the middle, right to the glory years of Prairie's career, the late sixties. Pages of old newspaper clippings hung, brittle and crumbling, from darkening pieces of tape. Most were feature stories. One, dated July 28, 1968, had a half-page photo of Prairie humming a Sombrero over his head. A smile of the purest joy spilled across his upturned face, as if the heavens were raining gold coins down on him. His belly was flat as a cross-country runner's and the hair that curled out from under his hat was pure black.

Son calculated that he would have been twenty-four years old when the photographer caught a happy man doing what he did better than almost anyone else in the world. She was four and just starting to discover the unbridgeable chasm that lay between her and everyone she would meet for the next two dozen years.

If Will Rogers had anointed a successor [the story read] it is pretty certain he would have passed on his best rope to the nimble-fingered Prairie James. James will be appearing at the entire run of the Frontier Days Rodeo, Aug. 12 through 18, at the the Chappell-Long County Arena.

"I am mighty honored to be mentioned in the same breath with Will Rogers. I don't reckon old Will would be too danged excited about it, though," said James with a ready laugh.

"Danged?" Son smiled at Prairie's calculated manipulation of the cowboy image.

James got his start roping the family dog on his daddy's ranch [the article continued].

"Yeah, I about wore out old Pooter. Got to where he wouldn't come nowheres near me if I was swinging hemp. Them days, I would rope anything that didn't have fangs or a badge. I got into the fancy stuff gradual like. Had me a great-uncle who rode with the original Wild West shows way back when. He was stove up pretty bad, but he got me hooked. Preacher used to joke, 'Don't go to the Jameses' house for dinner. Prairie will rope the biscuits clean out of your mouth, and if he misses, he'll take your tonsils out for you!' "

"Had me a great-uncle!" Son recited out loud, delighted by Prairie's mastery of Western folkspeak. It rivaled Beau Beaulieu's.

She checked the front window before leafing through more of the crumbling pages of Prairie's scrapbook. Domino made his first recorded appearance at the Oklahoma State Fair in 1976. A color photo showed Prairie wearing a peacock-blue satin shirt with more silver studs than Vegas Elvis. Domino was fitted out with a matching blue and silver-studded headstall, noseband, and throatlatch. They both looked magnificent. Prairie's grin, however, seemed to be pinching him like a pair of tight shoes. It was his first appearance at a Flying D Rodeo. Owner, Casey Dakota.

From that point forward, Son charted a steady downward career trajectory as first photos, then stories, disappeared. Some time in the early eighties, Prairie was reduced to a mention as the "evening's entertainment" at progressively smaller towns. The date of the last entry was 1983. Son thought that was probably about the time when he was demoted to Casey Dakota's serf and sacrificial last-minute "fill-in" for name acts that were either never booked or never expected to show up.

The empty pages at the end of the book bothered Son, so she turned back to the front to experience the thrill of seeing Prairie's career as it was just beginning to bud. The first few items taped into the scrapbook were pages from a ship's bulletin. The ship was the U.S.S. *President Wilson*, and the day's activities started with a shuffleboard tournament on Deck E and concluded that evening with "a demonstration of trick roping performed by Bosun Innocente Rincon and A.B. James Wojciehowski.

James Wojciehowski. Prairie's real name. He was Polish. Son determined that she would share her true name with Prairie at the earliest opportunity.

From a blip in the day's activities aboard a passenger liner, Prairie and El Marinero were elevated to a featured attraction in promotional brochures:

> Back in the days when crews were shanghaied, the most sought-after kidnap victim was the cowboy. What were the lifelines of those old-time sailing vessels? Ropes. And who could work a rope better than those heroes of the Wild West? The cowboy.
>
> Continuing that glorious tradition, we've shanghaied a couple of our very own crewmen to entertain guests on the

San Francisco-to-Yokohama crossing. Join us and marvel as
the Roping Seaboys, El Marinero and Prairie James, perform their feats of aerial magic.

From on-board headliners, Prairie and the Sailor progressed
to ever-more impressive gigs on the beach. But their stock publicity
photo remained the same. Prairie and the Sailor wore matching
charro outfits, sombreros with silver-tipped headbands and tight
bolero-style jackets with intricate scrollwork flaring across the
chest that matched the embroidery running down the sides of the
fitted pants.

It wasn't the identical outfits, though, that caused Son to stop
dead and linger long over the photo. It was the look that Prairie
was giving El Marinero. Son didn't expect that look. Not after the
stories of drinking bouts and whore chasing. First of all, she didn't
expect Prairie to be so young. Young and spindly. A boy who
needed feeding. But the look he was giving El Marinero, that was
what she couldn't get over. He was gazing at his *charro*-sailor mentor with the kind of open admiration a son bestows upon a very rare
and fortunate father.

Son gave a hurried glance out the front window and quickly
turned to the next page. It was a patchwork of clippings, largely
from foreign papers. She made out the letters USO in most of the
headlines. An especially small item might have escaped her attention altogether except that it was in English; it had been clipped
from the *Stars and Stripes*. The date was February 11, 1964.

The place was Frankfurt, Germany.

A sound like rushing water filled her head. It was the sound of
thirty years catching up with her. A horsefly landed on Son's cheek.
She didn't feel it. She read:

Get your tickets for a special appearance of the Joint
Services Tour of the Roping Legends. Through special arrangements, the four greatest trick ropers of our time will
perform together tonight at 2000 hours at the Pershing

Parade Grounds. Bring the family and experience the thrill of this great American tradition.

February 11, 1964.
Prairie had been in Germany.
Prairie.
He had lied to her.

The back of the truck swung open. In one hand Prairie held the crowbar, in the other, Domino's reins. The horse hovered behind.

"You're snooping through my stuff. What are you doing, snooping through my stuff? You got my scrapbook. I told you to keep out of my stuff. Put that down and come on out of there."

Solemnly, Son replaced the scrapbook, pulled her mess kit bag onto her shoulder, and stepped down from the truck. She composed herself and looked at Prairie Jones straight in the eye. "You were on that tour. What didn't you tell me you were on that tour?"

"Look, the years El Mare and I were together we did nothing *but* tour. How am I supposed to remember one docking at some—"

"It was a whole tour. A Joint Services tour. Who was Gray Wolf?"

"Son, come on, you don't want to get into this. That's all ancient history."

"You see me here in front of you? Right now. I'm not history. My history is not history. History is what you know about the past. When you know it, then you can put it in books and put it away on the shelf. My history is *right now*. It will always be *right now* until I find out."

"You need a handkerchief?"

"As if you carry one."

Prairie grabbed an empty white take-out bag and fished out a wad of napkins. Son pushed them away and squeegeed her tears off with the back of her hand. Domino took the opportunity to edge forward and chomp down the stray french fries that had fallen from the bag. Prairie jerked him back.

"Did you know my mother? Did you know Tinka Getz?"

"You have got to be kidding. I'm supposed to remember one little cutie pie from nearly thirty years ago?"

"Why did you say 'cutie pie'?"

"I don't know. It's just a figure of speech. What am I supposed to say, 'one hound from hell'? She's your mother."

"If someone who'd never met my mother, who only knew me, were to guess, I doubt very seriously that they would have assumed that my mother was a cutie pie. If, on the other hand, they had known Tinka, that is exactly how they would have characterized her."

"What? You saying you're such a dog, your mother'd have to be Lassie? Poke, you don't give yourself enough credit. Soon as you got away from Dorfburg, your looks improved one hundred percent."

"You're trying to divert me."

"Yeah, as a matter of fact I am." Son stared for several moments at the roses spiraling up the side of the boots Prairie had given her. Domino pressed forward and exhaled a great sympathetic breath that lofted Son's bangs off her face. She looked up.

"You slept with Tuffie."

"Damn straight. I sleep with Tuffie Branch every chance I get. Just wish the opportunity came around more often. You gonna rag on me about that?"

"No, it's obviously irrelevant to you. Probably almost as irrelevant as what happened between us last night. Though, at the time, it held great import for me, I can see that the moment was predicated on deception and bad faith and is, ergo, meaningless."

"So you're giving me the word screen again. Great."

"Tell me! Tell me!" Son screamed. "I want the truth and I want it now! No more lies! Tell me everything you know immediately!"

"Don't take that tone with me, sister. Day I stepped off my last freighter was the *last* day on this earth anyone allowed to use *that* tone with me."

"Okay. Okay. Just tell me . . . Just tell me . . . Who is Gray Wolf? Okay? That's all."

"Son, come on. We got a deal worked out here."

"You never intended to help me, did you? You just strung me along so that I'd buy you gas and keep your truck repaired and work for free as your announcer. You never had any intention of helping me find my father, did you?"

"This is a special case. I had my reasons."

"You were there. You were in Germany. You knew my mother. Tell me!"

Prairie rolled his head and flapped out a long hiss of exasperation. "Look, Poke, we don't have too many ways to go on this deal. You either drop your line of questioning or—"

"Who were the other three ropers in that photograph with you?"

Prairie rolled his shoulders like a fighter staying loose. "Son, listen to me, you're picking a hard way to go here. You're not leaving me much room to maneuver."

"Who were they? Tell me. I have the right to know."

" 'Right to know. Right to know.' There's such a thing as *wrong to know* and that's what we're getting into here. The wrong-to know category. Listen, Son, don't box me in on this. Just don't do it."

"I have to know."

Prairie set his jaw. "Then I have to go." He led Domino into the truck, jumped out, and slammed the doors shut. "Are you coming?"

"I can't."

There was a sadness that even Son could feel when he answered, "Yeah, well, I can't either." Prairie walked to the cab and swung up into it. A minute later, he was gone.

Son stood in the rectangle left in the dust by the departed chip truck, its margins marked by dribbles of horse piss and the grease from a fine rain of fried foods. She stood for a long time.

Chapter 22.

If Prairie had been much in the mood for scenery, he'd have noticed that he was driving through a world-class pile of it as he barreled down Highway 666. But he wasn't. Nature could throw out all the yellow pines and orange-and-purple-striate gorges with little rainbows dancing above them that she wanted to, but Prairie James would not have cared. He was not even moved by the sight of a stand of saguaro cactus, arms held up to the sky, like a bunch of scrubbed surgeons. No, Prairie was touring the internal landscape and finding it fairly bleak at the moment. His only thought for the road he was thundering down was that it had taken a life full of wrong turns for him to end up on it.

He mentally checked Cootie's directions, even though he'd had the map memorized before the old fake had finished drawing it. Don Ramos. Shaman. Dope pusher to a bunch of California suckers. It was a sad end. Prairie had seen too many sad ends. At one time Cootie Ramos was the only man in the world who could throw a Nap Time at full gallop. Prairie reflected on the weeks it had taken him to steal that trick and leave Cootie without a move that was his alone. He wished now that he had not done that. El Marinero had cautioned him against it. He said it was bad luck to steal a man's boots or his pride. Prairie had one hope left in the world. He prayed with all his heart that the Sailor had not met some equally pathetic end.

Midway through his supplication for all old ropers, Prairie was jolted into full alertness. He sat bolt upright and strained forward, searching for some sign of civilization. For a phone. He couldn't believe he hadn't thought of this earlier. He had to warn Son.

Chapter 23.

Son held on to the slender hope that, once Prairie had made his point, he would return. The wind picked up late in the afternoon and blew fried bread wrappers translucent with grease against her ankles. Just as the first spectators trickled out of the rodeo arena, Mickey, white apron tied over his clothes, paper cap advertising Rainbo Bread stuck on his head, ran up to Son and grabbed her arm. Out of breath and wild-eyed, he tugged at her, picking up her bags as he tried to drag her away.

"Mickey! What are you doing?"

He grew frantic when Son jerked her arm from him. Glancing around nervously, he grabbed it back. "Hurry! You got to hurry! Mithter Prairie theth tho!"

"Prairie? Mickey, where is he?"

"Come now! Talk later!"

Son allowed herself to be pulled away. When they reached the concession stand, Mickey pushed her inside, locked the door, and made her squat down out of sight on the floor.

"Mickey, what's going on?"

"I'm doing like Mithter Prairie thaid. He thent Mith Yathee over to tell me that I wuth thuppothed to go and get you and hide you and not let Mithter Dakota thee you or thomething bad wuth going to happen. And I done it."

"Why isn't Mister Dakota supposed to see me?" Son asked, using the soft voice she'd learned with Tuffie's children.

"He jutht ithn't cuth thomething bad will happen. Tho you thtay down. Jackthon will know. He jutht went to get more wienerth. He will be right back. He will tell you."

A few minutes later Jackson pounded on the door. "Mickey! Mick! Why have you got the door locked? I told you you did not have to lock the door if you wanted to read my special magazines!"

Son winced at the sound of Jackson's voice, his honorable, decent voice speaking with his inevitable patience to his slow-witted helper.

Mickey threw the door open, wilting with relief. "I done what Mithter Prairie thaid and I only left the thtand for three minute and bethides there wuthn't nobody coming to buy nothing anyway and Mith Yathee thaid thomething really bad wuth going to happen if I didn't go and get Thon and—"

Jackson put his hands on Mickey's shoulders to calm the excited man. "You did the right thing, Mick. You did just fine."

Mickey gulped several times, calmed himself down, and noted, "We're out of red thno-cone thyrup."

"Good. Thank you, Mickey, I'll add it to the list." He turned to Son. "I imagine this all has something to do with Prairie's breaking into Dakota's motor home."

"He what?" Son momentarily forgot about begging for Jackson's forgiveness.

"They haven't found anything missing yet."

"Prairie broke into Casey Dakota's motor home?"

"Seems a reasonable assumption, don't you think? After last night?"

Son didn't answer but thought of Prairie walking off with the crowbar in his hand. "Dakota will kill him."

"They both been looking for an excuse for years. At least Prairie made sure you were safe."

"Has he gone to El Marinero's?"

"I have no idea."

"Yeth you do!" Mickey turned to Jackson, who was already screwing his face up in anticipation of the bomb his helper was about to drop. "You know. He thaid he wuth going to thee his friend with that ranth down there on the border—"

"Don't you remember," Jackson interrupted softly, "we were not supposed to talk about that friend."

"You mean the one with the ranth on the border right out-thide of Treth Caballoth?"

Jackson heaved a sigh. "Yes, Mickey, that would be the one we were not supposed to talk about."

"I already knew anyway," Son said, not trying to hide her disappointment that Jackson too had been part of the deception.

"I . . . We . . . Prairie has his reasons."

"Can you take me there?"

"Son, why bother?"

"Can you take me? If you can't, I will hitchhike."

"No, don't hitchhike. I can drop you off at the bus stop in Sanders. You can catch something heading south on Six sixty-six. I'd take you all the way, but I've got that evening show to do. Now that Prairie's gone, it's just me and Beulah."

"I was at the emergency room with Prairie last night."

"I figured that might be the case."

"I'm sorry I missed our date."

"I am too."

Jackson turned away, and Son felt the Dorfburg curse reclaim her once again.

The Greyhound station in Sanders, Arizona, was deserted except for a pair of Mexican nationals asleep in their plastic chairs. The ticket booth was empty, but a black felt sign with white letters posted on the wall showed that a bus would be leaving for St. John, Alpine, and Douglas at six thirty-five, less than an hour away. One of the Mexican men slumped back in his chair. The white material of his tight shirt pulled out of the waistband of his jeans, exposing half a foot of belly.

Jackson insisted on carrying Son's bag inside for her. "I hate to leave you here like this."

"Even after last night?"

"Hey, emergency rooms are always excused absences." Jackson put down Son's bag. "Son, listen, why don't you just come on back with me? They pulled Beaulieu out of that truck, but he's still talking trash. I could use a good announcer."

"As soon as I finish my business, I'd like to take you up on that offer."

"I understand. I sincerely do. Good luck."

"*Vaya con dios.*" The words came out more as a statement than as a blessing. If Son had ever known anyone who went with God, it was Jackson.

Half an hour later, a weatherbeaten woman, her hair skinned back tight by a plastic headband, sat down behind the ticket window. Son asked for a ticket to whatever was closest to Tres Caballos.

"That would be Douglas," the clerk informed her.

Son dug through her purse for her remaining bills. "I'll take one, please."

The clerk punched out the ticket. "Forty-three fifty."

Son pushed the money over to her. The clerk handed her the ticket. "Be back here by six Monday evening."

Son's hand fell heavily on the bills the clerk was raking in. "Monday evening?"

"That's the next scheduled departure. Everyone knows that the Douglas bus doesn't run on weekends."

Son lifted the woman's hand off her money, yanked it back, and returned the ticket. "I didn't."

She considered her options. They were depressingly limited. She shouldered her mess kit, strode out to Highway 666, and stuck her thumb out.

A man in his mid-fifties wearing a short-sleeved plaid shirt and driving a Chrysler New Yorker with maroon velvet upholstery immediately picked her up. The car smelled of Vitalis hair oil and sweat. Son got in, buckled her seat belt, and announced, "I have had no special training in the martial arts, but if you make the slightest improper advance, I shall attempt to kill you by thrusting the palm of my hand against the base of your nose, thereby unhinging the cartilage and driving it into your brain."

The man answered that he taught shop at St. John's High and had no interest in improper advances.

Those were the last words the teacher spoke until he dropped her off. "Have a good one," he called out to her from behind closed windows. His farewell was punctuated by the sound of all four power locks dropping simultaneously.

Son was not as lucky with the next half-dozen cars. They blasted past, drivers' eyes glued to the stripe as if they didn't see her. She felt again that the long claw of Dorfburg was reaching to pull her down. She beat it back just the way she had beaten it back every day she had spent in the town that wanted nothing more than to change everything about her. "Don't pretend you don't see me!" Son yelled after the seventh driver, a woman in a Geo Prizm. "You soulless android pawn of the merchandising monolith in your death gas–spewing wagon!" Son felt a bit more cheerful after the yelling, but her mood ebbed again as the shadows cast by the gnarled juniper tree bushes lengthened until they crept completely across the road.

The situation did not look good. The long shadows on the road started to meld into a uniform darkness and the air turned cool. When she looked back up, night had fallen. A minute or two later, Son could no longer see her feet at the ends of her legs. She strained to make out any pinprick of light in the distance, but there was none.

She had set off hiking down the highway, determinedly following the center stripe, when the road began to hum beneath her feet. Then she heard the powerful motor. Topping a rise, she beheld two blinding headlights. The twin lights bore down on her. As they came closer and closer, they joined into one bar of light that shimmered in front of Son like Judgment Day as she held her ground. The vehicle stopped and Son was not squashed into the pavement. Headlights blazed over her head brighter than a Broadway marquee. She shielded her eyes from the glare, which prevented her from discerning anything about the vehicle other than its immensity. With lights dazzling all around, it was more spacecraft than car.

"Hello?" Son tried. There was no answer. The driver was hidden behind a glare of illumination.

"Hello!"

A door at the rear creaked open. Son strode back, ready to get this matter cleared up. As she stepped aboard a thirty-seven-foot recreational vehicle of the Holiday Rambler type, she noticed that the frame of the door was bent dramatically out of shape. Almost as if someone had taken a crowbar to it. A hasp and staple bolted onto the frame kept the disabled door closed. As soon as she was inside, the RV started to move.

"Stop!" Son demanded. "We have not established my intinerary!"

In answer, the RV picked up speed, more speed than Son would have thought such a behemoth could attain.

"Stop immediately! I order you!"

The RV rocketing along now at a frightening speed seemed as long as a railroad coach. Son held her arms out at her sides to buffer her swaying body and moved toward the front. Next to her head buzzed a row of fluorescent lights as they cast their dim drizzle of illumination.

She staggered past a bed filled with a lump of something vaguely human covered with a dingy sheet printed with green polka dots.

The words *déjà vu* barely had time to fly across Son's consciousness before she became aware of a captain's chair at the front of the coach. It was just like the one she had seen in her vision. She struggled forward. A miniature dachshund bit her ankle. Another visitor from the vision. Fortunately, the dog had the bite power of a salamander, and her skin was not broken. The captain's chair turned. Son's heart pounded. The chair creaked as it swiveled around.

"Well, who do we have here?" Casey Dakota asked.

Chapter 24.

Prairie reached Tres Caballos near three that morning. A full moon was still washing the whiptailed ocotillo bushes and spiky agaves with silver light. They were less than a mile north of the border. Listening to an overheated engine cool beneath a Mexican moon made Prairie deeply nostalgic. A wrought-iron archway hung with old horseshoes rainbowed across the entrance to the Sailor's place. Prairie eased off the accelerator and studied the letters that spelled out Rancho del Marinero. Every loop spinner Prairie had ever known had talked about saving some money, getting a piece of land, having their own place. The Sailor had done it.

Domino shuffled forward to investigate. He flapped a long, contemplative sigh against the windshield as he too studied the archway. Prairie rubbed a hand down the long column of his neck.

"We're buddies again, buddy. Just you and me. Just you and me and the road."

Domino snatched his head from side to side. It was as close as he could get to enthusiastic agreement.

"Yeah, you like it better without her, don't you, boy? Don't you?" He scratched the horse under his throatlatch, and Domino closed his eyes and ratcheted his head up several notches so that

Prairie could reach all the good places. The hand suddenly stopped scratching.

"Weird deal, isn't it?" Prairie looked out at the summer night for a long time before starting up the truck again. The horseshoes dangling from the archway clattered against the metal roof as they drove under it. Prairie cut the engine when he came in sight of the *hacienda*. Last time he'd seen the Sailor, his partner had sworn to slit Prairie's throat if they ever met again. That wasn't what had kept Prairie away. They'd taken turns threatening to slit each other's throat for most of the thirty years they'd been together. No, it was the part about Heriberto that bothered him.

As he coasted in closer, Prairie noticed the flickering of a dozen banked campfires. Here and there, pickups with camper shells were pulled off into the brush. The event had grown in the five years since he'd last attended. He wondered how many of the old-timers had shown up. Hat Trick Nelson, no doubt. He'd drive across Antarctica in a dog sled for the chance to booze it up with the boys for a few days. Y.O. Wyoming was sure to be here. No doubt that showboat would be driving a flashy new car that would get repossessed the minute he parked it again on pavement. Dooley Hempstead? If Dooley came, then Cash Vautigan would turn out. Prairie snorted to himself remembering the way those two assholes cut up.

Prairie nosed the truck off the dirt road. It rolled to a stop in the sand. He walked around back and led Domino out. The smell of so much wildness around them caused the horse to twitch and nicker.

"That's Mexico," Prairie explained. "You're just smelling Mexico. It makes everyone go a little loco." From a distant camp-fire came the sound of a guitar and the Mexican singing that always made Prairie want to weep and then slug someone. El Mare must have gotten some of the local *vaqueros* to fall by.

He led the horse up the road for a better look at the house. It was a sprawling affair covered in swirling pink stucco. Leggy antique roses in rusting coffee cans lined the walk to the front door.

The door was every old swabbie's dream door. A massive affair of oak planks with an arched top held together by black studs and staves, it could have come off either Nottingham Castle or Ye Olde Cork 'n' Barrel Taverne. This wasn't the kind of house an old rope tramp ended up in. Not unless he married lucky. Prairie made a note to himself to start hanging out with a higher class of women. There were lots of changes going to get made.

As he led Domino around to the back in search of a water trough and some decent grass, Prairie heard a creaking sound like a rusty nail being pulled out of a board, followed by a gaudy stream of bilingual curses. Even Domino recognized the trademark mastery of profanity and pivoted his ears in a happy forward tilt.

"The Sailor," Prairie whispered, torn between conflicting desires to rush to the old man's side and to seek cover and heavy armament. In the end, Prairie decided that if El Marinero was going to shoot him because of a rope trick, he'd just as soon get his life over with. He finished walking to the back of the house and found his old *compadre* sitting in the moonlight on a stack of tires, hauling on the pair of channel locks he had wedged into his mouth. The creaking sound stopped abruptly and the Sailor pulled out an abscessed eyetooth. Cursing the provenance of the whore-begotten tooth, he pulled some gauze out of his shirt pocket. Just as he was packing it into the socket, he caught sight of Prairie and whirled around, looking for the gun he'd left back in the house.

El Marinero faced Prairie unarmed save for the channel locks still gripping his bad tooth. "Santiago! If you're going to kill me, do it now while I'm medicated and already bleeding."

The Sailor sitting there, big thick head of silver hair shining in silver moonlight, looked ageless as a hero on a coin. Prairie felt he could stand there and stare at the son of a bitch all night, it was that good to see him. "Sailor, I wouldn't waste a bullet on your wrinkled ass. Looks to me like you're trying to commit suicide anyway."

"*Chingadera* motherfucking tooth keeping me awake. Had to pull the motherfucker."

"Whyn't you go to a dentist? Looks like you got the money."

"Ain't my money, *cuate*. It all belongs to Leticia."

"That the Veracruz wife?"

"No, that's Blanca, Heriberto's mother. She's up here too. Her and Leti, best friends. They spend all day talking about what a son of a bitch I am and who I treated worst. They gang up on me now. Both them, getting back at me for all them years. Can't blame them. I got it coming. I told them I had this toothache make a mule howl, they bought me a little *cajita* of aspirin like they sell at the Seven-Eleven. That's it, nothing else. They treat me bad, these women." The Sailor touched his jaw. "You got a handkerchief on you? All this talking's making me bleed."

Inside the house, they found a clean dish towel in the kitchen, and Prairie wrapped it around some crushed ice to keep the swelling down. As the Sailor pressed the ice pack against his cheek, Prairie noted that the old man had aged after all. But in his own way. It was as if, early in life, the Sailor had attained the age he was meant to be, somewhere in the vicinity of lean, grizzled mid-fifties, then just stopped getting any older. Instead of aging, he seemed to be concentrating, distilling himself down to his essence. It wasn't that he looked shrunken. No, like a slab of steak that had been reduced to a strip of jerky, El Marinero appeared ready for the long haul.

The Sailor put the ice pack down. "You ever get Domino shod right?"

"Yeah, I found a farrier works out of Ozona. Does a good job for me."

"We got us a good shoe man. Comes up from Agua Prieta. Does all the riding stock on the place. You ought to try him."

"Naw, I've tried Mexican shoes. They don't last."

The new hole in the side of the Sailor's mouth showed when he smiled. He'd been there twenty-five years before, when Prairie bought that pair of boots out of a stall in the market in Tampico. He'd warned Prairie to stay away from merchants who catered to sailors on shore leave, but Prairie had already fallen in love with a pointy-toed pair that had sharp-angled riding heels and a striking rattler's head tooled into each vamp. Prairie might have made it back to the ship in his new rattler boots had it not been the rainy season. As it was, they started to dissolve shortly after the first puddle.

"Where you been for the last five years? How come you ain't come down?"

"How's I supposed to know which of your many *esposas* you were living with?"

"A roper can always find a roper, he wants to."

"That's true," Prairie agreed. That was what he'd told Son and it was the truth. But he'd told it to her as a lie.

"*Una copita?*" the Sailor asked, already pouring the golden Herradura tequila from the bottle with the trademark horseshoe on the front. Prairie, wishing for some 7-Up and grenadine to cut the tequila with, threw his back in one shot. The Sailor held his drink in his mouth, rolling it over the empty socket in his jaw, trying to deaden the pain.

"What have you got in there? An aquarium?" Prairie, drawn by a dim, purplish fluorescent light, walked toward the living room which opened off the kitchen. Instead of an aquarium, there was a row of half a dozen dressmaker's dummies wearing *charro* costumes in five shades of brown, from fawn to chocolate, and one in black. El Marinero always insisted on having an outfit to match the color of the horse he was riding. It wouldn't matter if he didn't have money to buy a pack of butts; he'd put the order in to his tailor in Veracruz as soon as he started training a new horse. The bolero jackets were heavy with rows of real silver buttons and filigreed with scrollwork. Sombreros of the finest felt banded with gold braid rested on the shoulders of the dummies. Prairie touched the sleeve of a jacket, the fawn one that El Marinero used to wear when he was riding that gorgeous palomino, and he was sucked back in time. Back to the last warm day of summer high in the Andes.

They were standing in the middle of a dusty arena in Lima, Peru. The sky in that high, dry land was as blue as window cleaner over their heads. They were doing a benefit show for an orphanage, so it wasn't exactly as if the pressure was on. Out of nowhere, the Sailor popped a big loop in front of him and he jumped through, then back, and sent one of his own to follow the Sailor's home. The Sailor jumped it coming and going and brought his own back. For five, ten minutes easy, they kept it up, jumping through this tunnel of loops they kept throwing each other, the kids putting their hands over their mouths and laughing more every time they did it. Prairie didn't even remember who missed first, who broke the chain. Prairie let the sleeve of El Marinero's fawn *charro* jacket drop.

"Funny how you never know when you're happy. You know it when you're looking back, but you never really know it at the time. You'd think something would light up. That there'd be some kind of sign to tell you, 'This is the happiest moment of your life.' "

The Sailor hocked some bloody spit into his empty tequila cup. "Ah, who'd want to know that? You might as well have you a sign says, 'It's downhill from here.' "

"*Tienes razon.*"

"I heard you was carrying a woman with you. What happened? She get tired of looking at your ugly face?"

"It's a long story, Innocente."

"They always are when a woman gets mixed up in them."

"No, it's not like that." Prairie let El Mare pour him another.

"What? Two wives and you ready to stop? Where's your *huevos?*" The Sailor cackled.

"No, this is a *real* long story. Goes way back."

"I ain't going nowhere."

"Okay. Remember that Joint Services Tour we did after Kennedy was assassinated?"

"Yeah, all through Germany. Couple bases in Spain. England."

"Right. Well, this story goes all the way back there." Prairie paused.

The Sailor got a fresh glass. Then sat down. "*Digame.* I sure ain't gonna sleep with this tooth hole in my head feel like I got a jackhammer going up there. Pour me another one."

As Prairie tipped the bottle, he looked carefully at El Marinero. Five years since he'd seen the old man and it seemed like five minutes. Time never put walls between them. Even when they were pissed off at each other. If that wasn't a good definition of family, he didn't know what was.

"What you staring at, *guero?*"

"Nothing, *viejo.* It's just good to see you."

"Yeah, okay, only you call me old man again, I'll have to cut you, gringo."

"You got it, Innocente."

"Call me Innocente and I'll cut you twice, Santiago!"

Prairie drank. He didn't even miss the 7-Up and grenadine anymore.

Chapter 25.

The instant Casey Dakota turned around, Son wanted to run for the back door. But the green polka dot lump had risen off the bed and materialized into a sheet-draped Dewey Dakota. He blocked any thought of escape as effectively as a concrete wall.

"Dewey, get away from her! This little lady's a guest in our RV and we oh make her stay with us pleasant as we can. Come on up here, sugaree; sit down next to me."

As Dewey herded Son forward, the dachshund harried her ankles, nipping and squeaking until reaching Dakota's chair. The dog then jumped into her master's lap. Dakota reached down and pulled out a box of Livasnaps Dog Treats. "Be sweet! Be sweet!" Dakota urged the dog when she nipped at his fingers trying to get at the treat.

Son studied Casey Dakota as he poked the liver-flavored pellets into his pet. It surprised her that she could actually feel power coming off him like excess current humming from a high-tension line. He was a massive man; his hands draped over the steering wheel were huge as the paws of a beast. A beast who wore too much Old Spice aftershave. His shoulders, bulling up around his neck, were even wider than the ultra-deluxe captain's chair he sat in. On the floor next to his seat lay his ever-present companion, the electric cattle prod.

"Stop immediately and let me out."

Casey Dakota turned and smiled a shy, country smile at her as if she were flirting with him. "Now, sugaree, we're just getting to know each other here. Come on, now, have a seat. I'm oh tell you a little about myself, about how I come up, then we oh find out a little about you. There's some'd say I'm a hard man. Most'll say I'm fair."

Son sat down. "I wouldn't count Prairie James among them."

"Now, Prairie and I go way back and we kid each other. But it was all fun until now. Now he's gone way over the line. Man steals from me, I have to drop the hammer. Set a real bad precedent if I was to let a man steal from me. Be real bad personnel policy."

"What exactly did Prairie steal from you."

"As if you don't know."

"As if she don't know."

"Butt out, lug nut!" Dakota snapped at his son, who had crept forward until he had his head wedged between the two front seats in just the way that Domino so favored.

"Yessir, Dad, sir."

His father continued his interrogation. "So James dumped you, huh?"

"We came to a mutual parting of the ways."

"Why're you tracking him then? Didn't figure you to be one'd go wiener happy. Course, the drier the wood, the hotter the flame. He's hiding from you, ain't he?"

"Don't attempt to goad me into revealing his whereabouts with your barnyard allusions."

"Don't matter. I got a pretty good idea where he's holed up anyhow."

"I doubt that."

"Then why am I on this road?"

"I would imagine that one of your underlings followed Jackson and called you when he left me at the bus stop."

"Wow, Dad, she's smart!"

"Clam up, feedbucket!"

"Yessir, Dad, sir."

"Okay. You're right. I don't know precisely where Prairie is. But all's what I want to do is settle up with him."

"All you want to do is inflict physical mayhem upon him."

"Now, that may have been my first-off reaction. But I have freed my heart of anger's evil grip. All's what I want to do now is clear the books. We put in too many years together to let it end like this."

"Why should I believe you when you have never let an opportunity pass to degrade and humiliate Prairie?"

"Aw, that? That's just my way. Prairie knows I don't mean none of that stuff. We kid around; that's all it is."

"Not paying a man wages owed is more than kidding around."

"Well, that's why I want to find him and make it all square and legal. Actually, the other reason I been looking for him is that I wanted to talk to you."

"Why?"

"You don't need to sound so excited."

Dewey echoed his father's hollow laugh.

"Slam it, dough boy! No, really. I'm fixing to put Beaulieu out to pasture and I was wondering if you'd be interested in the position."

"As announcer?"

"Sole and exclusive announcer for all of Flying D's productions."

"I shouldn't think that my style would be to your liking."

"Oh, I like it fine. You'd bring up the tone of the whole deal."

"There is some truth in what you say."

"Oh, yes, a gospel's worth. We'd be flying you around the country at company expense. Putting you up at the Best Western of your choice."

"How can I believe in such largesse when you treat all your employees in so niggardly a fashion?"

"Man, them slave days is over! I have seen the error of my ways. Got me a whole new personnel policy I'm oh put into effect."

"Yes, well, it could hardly be cost-effective to keep losing your most valued employees."

"Hardly ain't the word for it; it's killing me, what it is. So you in?"

"I'm considering it."

"Great! We'll draw up the contract documents soon's we get down to this roper's fandango. You want to make it a joint deal with Prairie, or is you two really split?"

"That is none of your business."

"You're right, you're right, and thank you for reminding me of my manners. Do you require your own dressing room?"

Son tightened the grip she had on her mess kit purse and Casey Dakota glanced down at it. The neon lime-green car-wash coupon with Cootie's map drawn on the back was stuck at the top of the bag. She covered it with her hand.

"Casey Dakota, I'll admit I am tempted by your blandishments and swayed by the deferential manner you have adopted, but I see them for the ruses they are and I will not reveal where Prairie James is and expose him to possible harm even though he has disappointed and betrayed me."

"She talks so cute, don't she, Dad?"

Instead of barking at his adopted son to shut up, Casey Dakota slid a boot over onto the brake. As he bumped off onto the shoulder, Son turned to him in surprise. She had expected Dakota to continue trying to wheedle information out of her for several more hours. Instead, he brought his recreational behemoth to a slow stop, flicked off the engine, and turned to her.

"You're right, princess. You don't have a reason in the world to trust me and I'm sure not able to come up with one that an intelligent woman like yourself would accept. So it would probably be best if we was to go our own ways." He leaned across Son and pushed open her door. Outside was nothing but several hundred miles of darkness populated by snakes, scorpions, gila monsters, and serial killers.

"You can't be planning to dump me beside the road in the middle of the night."

"What's the point in you staying with me? I don't know where you're headed, and you won't tell me. We got us a Mexican stand-off. So, *adios, muchacha*. I got to go find your boyfriend."

Son turned away sharply toward the darkness, the snakes, scorpions, and serial killers, and started to ease herself off the seat.

"Before you go, I think we'd better just verify that location." Dakota reached out a long arm and yanked Son's bag from her hands. "I thought that might be a map," he said, plucking out the car-wash coupon. "Tres Caballos, huh? Good for you, baby doll, you didn't roll over. Don't think I don't admire loyalty in a woman. I do. I do very much." And he closed the door.

While Dakota lumbered back onto the road and quickly built up speed, Son's spirit plummeted. She had failed after all; she knew punishment was certain. She had no idea, however, it would be so swift. Casey banished her to the back of the RV to watch videos with his son.

Dewey Dakota turned out to be a devotee of the adventures of Tom and Jerry, and she was subjected to a feature-length cartoon on the VCR. As the big boy chuckled happily at the antics of the two clever mice and far-less clever cat, disappointment crushed Son. No matter how inadvertently, she had betrayed Prairie. Her one thought was to break free and warn him. When convulsions of laughter overtook the boy at the sight of Tom's face assuming the shape of the frying pan Jerry had held in front of it, Son jumped up and grabbed the cattle prod leaning against Casey Dakota's chair.

Her finger found the trigger, and the familiar crackling buzz alerted both Dakotas.

"Shitfar, Dad! She's got the hotshot!"

"Tell me something I don't know, dumb ass," Dakota answered, his tone casual, not even bothering to take his eyes off of the highway.

"Casey Dakota, stop this vehicle immediately!"

"Purely for your own health and well-being, baby doll," Dakota remarked conversationally, "you ought to know that the last person use that tone with me is still taking all his meals through a straw."

"Your threats and intimidation won't work with me, Casey Dakota, for I have spent a lifetime standing up to bullies and blowhards."

"You think you got the *cojones*, peanut, step right on out there. Come on, shoot me the juice."

The sliver of time that then elapsed carried within it every moment of freeze, choke, and panic Son had ever experienced in her wide array of P.E. class humiliations. She stared at the spot cleanly shaven by the barber at the back of Casey Dakota's neck and it was as if she were staring up at all the balls that had ever hurtled down toward her out of a blue Dorfburg sky. The result was the same: paralysis. Only now, instead of getting beaned in the head by a pop fly or a vicious spike, she felt Dewey jerk the cattle prod from her hands. Her chance to rescue Prairie James was lost forever.

Chapter 26.

"What you been doing to your ropes, Santiago? This one feels like someone threw up on it."

"Naw! Naw! Put that one down!" Prairie knocked the maguey that had resided briefly in Beulah's digestive system out of El Mare's hands. Sometime after they'd drunk the tequila down below the horseshoe on the bottle label, the two old friends had gravitated without a word to the chip truck to do what they'd always done: spin ropes.

"Hey, you still got that piece of cotton shit Hat Trick stuck you with." El Mare scrambled up into the back of the truck, pulled down a dingy coil, brought it back outside, and tried stirring some life into it. It had all the vibrancy of a length of clothesline. "Piece of shit," he grumbled.

"I guess Hat Trick's camped out here somewhere." Prairie looked around at a desert night that was ending fast. It was almost light enough to see the smoke rising from half a dozen burned-out campfires.

El Mare stopped spinning. "You didn't hear?"

"Hear what?" Prairie asked, already knowing that the answer couldn't be good.

"Hat Trick. He had a stroke two, three years ago. Whole left side of his body's paralyzed."

"Jesus."

"At least he retained his bladder control. That's more than I can say for Dooley Hempstead."

"Shit, Dooley too?"

"Some kind of nerve deal."

"Well, someone's got to be here. Who's here? How many of the boys turned out?"

"Not that many."

"Cash! Cash Vautigan! Remember him from Monty Montana's show? Remember his wife? Bitsy? Could do a handstand in the saddle of a horse at full gallop. Man, Cash! What a sorry roper he was. And a gasbag! If that son of a bitch is drawing breath, *he's* here. Right?" Prairie asked hopefully. "Right?"

El Mare answered by casting down his eyes and shaking his head solemnly.

"Y.O? Y.O. Wyoming?"

El Mare shook his head again.

"Naw, I didn't think so. That guy was about a hundred and five the day I met him."

"Hey, they was *all* old time you met them."

"Damn."

"If you'd come around more than every five years, it wouldn't be such a shock."

"Hey, it was you told me to stay away!"

"I never!"

"Yeah, you did! You did! Because of El Zopilote."

"A rope trick? I sent you away because of a rope trick?"

"Yeah, you said you was saving it."

"I did? What was I drinking?"

"Pulque."

"You took me serious and I was drinking pulque?"

"Yeah, you said you was saving it for Heriberto. Your *real* son."

"I said that? That's crazy. Heriberto? I love him with all my heart, but the boy's got hands like a bear. I had trouble teaching him to tie his shoes."

"Yeah, well, that's what you said."

"And you stayed away for five years?"

Prairie glanced around at the smoldering campfires and, not knowing what else to say, asked, "Well, who the hell *is* here then?"

"Just some of the local boys, *vaqueros, campesinos. Hombres del pais.* I'll tell you what, though; most of these old boys with their braided straw bridles and a piece of cardboard for a saddle are still twice the cowboy of any *gringo* who ever jerked leather."

"What? So now I'm supposed to defend the great American cowboy? Biggest bunch of dopes and jugheads ever born. No, I'll tell you who the real cowboys are. You want to know who the real cowboys are? I'll tell you. The Mongolians. They're the real cowboys."

"Them guys with the little bitty eyes, tongue too big for their mouths?"

"No, no, not Mongoloids. Mongolians. Now, them boys, they live in the saddle. You got three-year-olds in Mongolia who can ride two hundred miles a day, turn around, and head straight back home."

"I'll put my *vaqueros* up against them any day."

"They live on dried yogurt balls. That's all. Dried yogurt balls. Ten, twelve days in the saddle and nothing but dried yogurt balls."

"Don't talk about dried yogurt balls; you're making my tooth hole hurt. Give me that bottle." El Marinero took the bottle and held it over his head. "Here's to Y.O. Wyoming." He took a slug and passed the bottle to Prairie.

"I'll drink to Y.O."

"What you planning to do?" the Sailor asked.

"Shouldn't we drink to Hat Trick first?"

"He ain't dead yet."

"Well, doesn't sound like he's too far from it. Okay"—Prairie held the bottle aloft—"to the *vaqueros.*"

El Mare drank, then proposed a toast of his own. "To the Mongoloids."

"Mongolians."

"To the Mongolians."

It was in the middle of a liquid tribute to Genghis Khan that the two old roping buddies ran out of tequila and went into the house for a nap.

"Whoever thought we'd see the day when we'd *nap?*" Prairie asked as they passed the antique roses in rusty coffee cans that Blanca, the wife from Veracruz, had planted.

"Man lives long enough, he turns back into a baby," said El Mare, poking his tongue into the empty socket where his tooth had been. "Sleeps all day and no teeth in his head."

"So, that why you did it? That why you settled down? Tired?"

"Hell, no. I come back because I want somebody crying for me when I die. I want my wives to miss having me next to them. I don't want them already used to warming up the whole bed by themselves."

Prairie was too tired to comment. He followed El Mare into a small room off the kitchen, designed for the maid the two wives planned to hire someday, and fell into a narrow bed. He hoped he'd be asleep before he finished the inventory of his life. But he wasn't and had to conclude that, though it had had its moments, they just had not added up to much. Not a house. Not a family. Friends dead or dying. Now, not even a job. It was not enough. Not nearly enough. In the moments before he blacked out, Prairie decided that it was time to start claiming what life *had* brought his way. Tomorrow he'd sneak back into Gallup and get Son.

"What do you mean, you forgot the gun?" Casey Dakota's hand itched for the radiator hose he usually carried to emphasize the points he made to Dewey, and he reached down and grabbed the first thing his big hand fell on, which turned out to be his dachshund's rhinestone-studded leash. "We go on a revenge mission and you forget to bring the gun?"

"I didn't know I was the one supposed to bring it." Dewey cringed beneath the green polka dot sheet. "You told me I wasn't never supposed to touch your guns."

Being reminded that, in fact, he was the one who had forgotten the gun enraged Dakota even further, and he commenced to thrash the boy with the wiener dog's leash. "How are we supposed to smoke James out now? The plan was to hold Domino hostage and threaten to shoot him if James didn't come out!"

This plan had been concocted several minutes earlier when Dakota had coasted the RV to a silent stop next to the corral where Domino was penned, and had seen the dangers of trying to go into El Marinero's thick-walled ranchhouse after Prairie. Dewey had been the one to point out that Domino was standing, unguarded, only a few yards away.

"Now what are we going to threaten him with?" Dakota fought to keep from bellowing. He didn't want to waken any of the sleeping forms clumped near the ashes of dead campfires. He glanced around. In impotent fury, he held up the leash. "*This?* We going to threaten to spank his horse? That'll really bring him running." Dakota flung the leash away in disgust. It landed on Son's foot; she had been listening with immense satisfaction to these two thugs talk of their bungled terrorist tactics.

"I see you want to add criminal endangerment to the kidnapping charges I shall be préssing at the earliest opportunity," she informed them evenly.

"You've about pressed me to my limit, sister." The misfire of recent events had quickly worn through Dakota's thin veneer of patience and manners.

Dewey, cringing beneath the sheet, whimpered, "You could use the hotshot. Good jolt to the heart'd kill a horse."

Dakota's color settled back down to something outside of the volcanic lava family. "That's a hell of an idea." He picked up the hotshot and fired off a jolt into the air before turning back to Son. "I don't suppose you'd stay put here while we get this matter cleared up?"

"No."

"I didn't think so. That doesn't leave me any choice but to lock you in." Dakota grabbed a padlock off a knickknack shelf that held nothing else except a bullhorn, which he grabbed with the other hand. "Come on, son, guard my rear."

Dewey Dakota jumped from the bed and bounded after his father as he stepped out of the RV into the stillness of a day that was dawning for him now with a bright, new promise.

Dad had called him "son."

Domino glowed as brightly as a unicorn in an enchanted forest in the misty half-light of night's end. He was not an easy horse to catch when he did not care to be caught, and the sight of two hulking cowboys, one carrying a hotshot, was enough to put him in just such a mood. At the first sniff of the two Dakotas, Domino slicked back his ears against his head, meaner than a teased pit bull, and shied away. It turned out to be so easy to elude the two lumbering humans, however, that Domino soon took to sporting about El Marinero's pole corral, allowing his stalkers to almost reach him, then breaking away with a quick, taunting feint.

The sound of hoofbeats coming in fast, broken bursts drummed through the earth and slithered into the dreams of the horsemen sleeping on it. The local *vaqueros* camped out on El Mare's land decoded the message Domino was sending and dreamed of swift gallops from one hiding place to another. Of laughing at their clumsy pursuers. When the running stopped, they awoke and saw a beefy *gringo* of the *jefe* type pull a Zagnut candy bar from his pocket and unwrap it. At the first crinkling of the paper, the *caballo bravo* trotted up to the man.

Back in the RV, Son was sore on both sides of her body from throwing herself against the door Dakota had padlocked from the outside. She pushed back the curtains on one of the RV's four mail slot–sized windows just in time to see Domino gobble down the Zagnut, then wait passively, hoping for another, while Dakota slipped a bridle over his head. The instant the bridle was buckled into place, Son began screaming, *"Ayudame! Ayudame! Ladrón! Ladrón!"*

As Dakota led Prairie's horse from the corral, he noticed that a silent contingent of four or five *vaqueros* had gathered to watch. The rodeo producer thought he knew these men; he thought they were like the *mojados* in cheap straw hats with the one dingleberry hanging from the back who came north, bought Goodwill polyester jeans and T-shirts advertising Camel cigarettes, then lived on tortillas and Alpo while they mended his fences and tended his stock. Dakota was used to men like these. What Dakota was not used to was having these descendants of the men who had taught the cowboys their trade stand in his way and silently demand an explanation.

Leading Domino with his right hand, Dakota came close to reflexively jabbing their leader, Javier, with the hotshot. But the hard look on Javier's face, which was decorated by a handlebar mustache, sideburns below his ear lobes, and a breakfast cigarette that hung by a dot of spit from the downturned corner of his mouth, stopped Dakota colder than the rifle Javier cradled in his folded arms. Dakota knew a man who could give tractor tires lessons in toughness when he saw one. Javier quirked an eyebrow in the direction of the woman screaming from the window of the RV.

"Uh, uh. Wife." Dakota searched for Spanish words. *"Esposa. Loco."* He pointed to his ring finger, then whirled his index finger around his ear.

Javier looked over at his *compadres*. They too were men who had ridden in from ranches along the border and, like Javier, were not eager to relinquish the opportunity to hold a gun on a large-gutted white man wearing a diamond pinky ring. In fact, the experience was so gratifying that they were willing to break with tradition and take a woman's part in order to prolong it. They all walked together to the Holiday Rambler.

Javier pointed to the door and Dakota unlocked it. Before it was fully opened, Son was delivering her closing argument to the jury in fluent Spanish. "This man is attempting to steal that horse and must be stopped." She didn't know the Spanish for "cattle prod" and "fibrillations of the horse heart," so she went with the more attention-getting crime of horse theft.

Javier's eyes narrowed into a smile that never reached below his mustache. Horse theft. Horse theft! Now this, this was an injustice that a *vaquero* could honorably sink his teeth into.

Casey Dakota tried to tell the men that whatever Son was saying, she was lying. Unfortunately, he had the disadvantage of possessing a Spanish vocabulary composed almost entirely of the imperative and had to settle for yelling in English and waving his arms around in the air to erase Son's words.

"I am speaking the truth," Son continued in her grandiloquent Spanish. "This horse belongs to the famous *charro* Prairie James, a very good friend of our host, El Marinero, and this man is trying to steal him."

The words "*charro*," "host," and "man" exercise a powerful hold on the soul of the Mexican male, and combined with the name El Marinero, they worked magic. Guns were pointed at the *gabacho* with the pinky ring.

"Jesus Christ, look what you done!" Dakota told Son frantically. "They're going to shoot me."

"Shoot you? No, they can't." She switched to Spanish. "*Señores, señores,* please don't be hasty. Flog him, yes. But shooting? That is too much."

The sound of a hammer being cocked back inspired Dakota to attempt new heights of communication. With what Spanish he had, he put together, "Horse of bad man. I cost much money. We go to my duck's foot." To underscore his plea, Dakota pulled his bankroll out of a hip pocket and began peeling off twenties. By the time every man in the crowd had one, popular sentiment started to shift ever so slightly. By the time each had a couple of twenties, Dakota had established himself as the aggrieved party and Prairie as the villain.

"Other *gringo* bad. He come out of *casa pronto.* You help me fight bad man. You back me up. I pay one hundred dollars. *Cien dolares. Cien.*" Dakota dropped the prod and bullhorn and flashed all ten of his fingers ten times.

"He is lying!" Son countered in the elegant Spanish that the men were starting to think sounded stuck-up. "The other man is not bad. He is a good, kind, and wise man. He is my friend. He is the best friend I have ever had." Though saying *el mejor amigo* affected Son so greatly that tears began to roll down her cheeks, the *vaqueros* simply found the declaration of friendship part of a pattern of increasing irregularity.

Son gathered herself together and tried to go on, but the men had already huddled, their backs turned on her. Tired of character analysis, they segued effortlessly into collective bargaining. Javier stepped forward and rattled off a demand in Spanish to Dakota.

"You want twenty dollars a day expense money!" Outraged, Son supplied an unwitting translation.

Dakota jumped forward. "*No problema. Bueno. Bueno. Veinte mas. Por hombre.*"

Objective achieved, the men turned their attention to loading and calibrating their weapons. Those without guns went in search of knives, garrotes, and slingshots with which to qualify for the one-twenty a day.

"This is monstrous," Son informed Dakota. "I can't believe what is happening. For less than the price of a contract killer, a mob hit, you have purchased yourself an actual mob!"

"And they say you can't make things happen down here. Damn!" An amplified crackle cut the air when Dakota activated a bullhorn with one hand and, with the other, brought the business end of the cattle prod up to Domino's heart.

Chapter 27.

"I can't believe you told that *pendejo* where I was." El Marinero peeked over Prairie's shoulder and they both took in the disaster unfolding in the front yard.

"I didn't tell him. I wouldn't tell that hyena where the water fountain was in hell."

"That your woman with him?" El Mare's jaw was puffed out on the side where he'd yanked out his tooth, and the skin under his eyes was gray.

"She's not my woman."

"I guess she told him where you were."

"I guess."

"COME ON OUT, JAMES! IF YOU AIN'T OUT IN THIRTY SECONDS, I'M OH SHOOT THE JUICE TO DOMINO! ONE, MISSISSIPPI. TWO, MISSISSIPPI . . ."

"You going out?"

"He's got gunmen. Hell, no, I'm not going out."

"That's just Javier and that bunch."

"So they wouldn't shoot me?"

"Never can tell with those hotblooded Sonorans. Compliment a Sonoran on his new boots, he just might take it as an insult against his old ones and shoot you dead. I better go get dressed."

Prairie looked at El Mare. His old mentor was already dressed, but Prairie didn't say anything. You reach a certain age and there's no shame in backing off from trouble. The Sailor paused for a moment. "I'd call the law, but everyone on the place's illegal. Starting with the wives."

"Yeah, it's okay. I'll work it out."

"Domino's a good horse, but he's only a horse. I wouldn't die for a horse."

Prairie nodded and El Marinero left.

"TWENTY-THREE, MISSISSIPPI. TWENTY-FOUR, MISSISSIPPI. TWENTY-FIVE . . . Fuck this shit, he ain't coming out."

Prairie pulled on his boots. Before he'd finished, a familiar voice drowned out Dakota's. "Do not come out, Prairie James!" Even without a bullhorn, Son still had enough volume to tell a tanker captain where to go. "He has employed *pistoleros!*"

"YOU BETTER COME OUT, JAMES. AND YOU BETTER HAVE FIFTY-THREE HUNDRED DOLLARS OF MY MONEY ON YOU. YOU GOT FIVE SECONDS. TWENTY-SIX, MISSISSIPPI. TWENTY-SEVEN, MISSISSIPPI. TWENTY-EIGHT—"

"Prairie, don't come out! Your very life is in jeopardy! You owe me nothing! Whatever else you may be to me, you have been a friend! You have fulfilled your obligation to me!"

Prairie experienced a tremendous desire to lie down for a very long nap. Why, he wondered, did a person always end up feeling most responsible for the ones he helped. "Goddammit," he whispered to himself. A second later, he heaved himself up, pushed open El Marinero's Olde English plank door, and walked out. Immediately, half a dozen guns were trained on him.

"Don't shoot him until I get my money!"

"You're not going to shoot anyone," Prairie said in a voice only fractions of a decibel above conversational. "Dakota, your complaint is with me. Let my horse and my announcer go."

Dakota twitched his head back arrogantly toward his hired gang. "I don't think you're in any position to be giving orders, Prairie James."

Prairie glanced at Javier and his boys, hard-looking characters all of them, and wished he'd gotten in on the bidding in time to buy himself some reinforcement.

When El Marinero's heavy door opened, Son knew one thing and knew it more clearly than she had ever known anything before: she owed her life to Prairie James. She ran to him, her mess kit purse bumping her side, and placed her body squarely between his and the *pistoleros'*. "You must not harm this man," she ordered.

Son saw the power of true moral authority when Javier and his men all lowered their guns. "Well, now, we're making some progress," she commended them. It was then that she noticed that none of them was actually looking at her. All eyes had twitched to something behind her. She turned.

There was El Marinero, riding up astride an Appaloosa that stood at least sixteen hands high. The Sailor was outfitted like a Spanish grandee in full *charro* costume, from silver spurs that chinked in time to the Appaloosa's smooth, loose gait right up to a $400 gray felt sombrero. Big as the brim of his hat was, it seemed somehow to gather light into El Marinero's face rather than shield it. It nearly blinded a man like Javier to behold that visage. Mounted on a horse he had trained himself, risen from a poor family, sailor of all seven seas, lover to two wives, turned out now like a *hacendado*, El Marinero was the embodiment of all that Javier dreamed of.

With the slightest flick on the reins, El Marinero brought the big Appy to a halt. His voice, when he spoke in Spanish, had the ominous rumble of distant thunder. "*Señores*, should we not allow these two men settle their differences without our interference?"

Javier nodded agreement and let his rifle dangle from his hand. The men behind him dropped their eyes and stared into the dirt as if they might have lost some coins there.

Son gazed upward into the *charro's* noble face. So this was the Sailor. The old roping seadog was proud and powerful in his snug jacket. Here was a man anyone would be proud to claim as father. And, not incidentally, the kind of man Son knew Tinka would have swooned over.

She saw in El Marinero's face the same strong lines that distinguished her own. The proud nose, the noble brow, the indomitable native blood meeting that of the conqueror's. El Marinero's face held all the answers to the mysteries that had plagued her life in Dorfburg. She was El Marinero's daughter, and that explained everything. She had the blood of an aristocrat in her veins and had been condemned to life as a scullery maid. It all made sense now.

While this worshipful regard was going on, Dakota decided on a pre-emptive strike. Knocking Son out of his way, he charged Prairie.

"Give me my money!" BIZZZ! Dakota plugged the cattle prod into Prairie, who flew backward from the jolt, then flopped to the ground. Son ran to him and cradled his head in her lap.

Prairie was gone to a beautiful world of bathhouses and B-girls. The dream seemed to last for hours, but he was actually out only for a few minutes. He opened his eyes to see who was holding him in her beautifully upholstered lap and whose lips were pressing against his face. "Pocahontas, when did you start working at Short-Timer's Massage Parlor?"

"Prairie, thank the Great Spirit, you're alive."

"Son, old buddy, when do we go on?"

Before she could remind him of where they were, Prairie regained his senses and jerked up, ready to defend himself against Casey Dakota's next attack. He sagged back into Son's lap when he saw that El Marinero had roped the pigporker and had him trussed up, standing next to the big Appy.

"He's my father, isn't he?" Son nodded in the direction of both El Marinero and Casey Dakota.

Without looking around, Prairie made an assumption about which man Son had nodded toward. "I should have known you'd figure it out. I guess you can see why I tried to keep you from finding out. Hell, it never was any of my business."

"It's all right."

Something about the reverent way Son was blinking at the two men behind him made Prairie realize that a terrible mistake had

been made. Before he could embark on the unpleasant task of cor-
recting it, Dewey's giant head rose up behind Son like a bad moon.
One of the flagstones wrenched from between the antique roses in
El Marinero's walkway eclipsed Dewey's face as he hoisted the big
flat rock up above his head and ran forward on a kamikaze mission
to squash his father's foe.

Prairie grabbed Son and rolled them both away, vacating a
spot that Dewey Dakota then filled with a slab of slate.

"You stump." Casey Dakota was demoralized by the sight of
the big boy standing over the creosote bush he had succeeded in
flattening and all his "gunmen" with their weapons dangling by
their sides.

El Marinero offered a timely suggestion. "Prairie, get the hell
out of here! I don't have any more wives down south to hide out
with. I don't want to have to shoot nobody."

Prairie dragged himself and Son to their feet. "Looks like the
situation is under control. Let's book." He hooked his arm through
Son's and began pulling her away.

She resisted at first, drawn back by the magnetism of the man
she believed to be her father. But she saw the sense in his strategy.
"Let us withdraw now and return to fight another day. And get to
know Papa without a mob." She flagged El Marinero a dazzled
little wave, then allowed Prairie to pull her away.

"Yeah, right."

They were beating a highly satisfactory retreat—chip truck
within sight, Domino safe where he was for the time being—when
Casey Dakota, disgusted beyond all endurance hurled a fateful
curse: "*Scheisse!*"

Son stopped dead, frozen by the memory of Tinka, dwarfed by
her plumed bridal finery on the steps of the Dorfburg Lutheran
Church, uttering the last word she had spoken to her daughter:
"*Scheisse.*" Son turned slowly and focused instantly on Dakota's
giant paw of a hand lashed to his side by El Marinero's rope. Aside
from a patina of dings and gouges, the top knuckles of his right
index and middle finger were missing. Roper's hands.

"But he shoots blanks," Son protested.

El Marinero hissed out a long sigh and let the rope around Dakota go slack.

Son advanced on Dakota, her pink fiesta blouse slipping off her shoulder. "You're sterile, right? Isn't that what you tell everyone? You're sterile."

The translation "*estéril*" buzzed around the *vaqueros*, who nodded as if the pieces of this puzzle were finally starting to fit together.

Dakota glowered. "This is not exactly the time or the place, peanut."

Dewey bounded forward. "Yeah, Dad shoots blanks. Why else'd he adopt me?"

Son slapped her hand over her heart, beating out a grunt of relief. "Thank the Great Spirit. I thought for a moment . . ."

Dakota's wiener dog poked her nose out of the RV. Seeing that the angry noise had apparently come to an end and that the big human who fed her Livasnaps was available, she jumped out the door and twinkle-toed up to Dewey, who bent down and let her leap into his arms.

"Naw," Dewey said, rubbing his little pet's ears, "if Dad coulda had his own, he wouldn't never have needed me or little Tinka."

"Tinka?" Son shut her eyes tight as a sudden wave of nausea rolled through her. "Your dog's name is Tinka?"

"I think we all better go inside." El Marinero pulled the Appaloosa's head around. The men beside Javier parted, and El Marinero started for the house. Son and Prairie glared at the Dakotas, who glared back.

"After you," Prairie said, shooting his hand out.

"In a pig's eye," Dakota snarled back.

In the end the two men marched into the house side by side, a wary arm's length apart, with Son and Dewey leading the way. Dewey was still holding the dachshund. The dog scrambled up his chest, poked her long nose over Dewey's shoulder, and whimpered when she saw Casey Dakota, the other potential provider of Livas-naps.

"Shut up, you four-legged turd. I'm oh put you in a skillet with some sweet peppers."

Son shuddered.

Chapter 28.

As they all sat around El Marinero's dining room table, Son noticed that it was nearly identical with the front door, massive planks of mahogany held together with studs of black iron. Casey Dakota sat across from her. Occupying the mom and dad spots at the end of the big table were Prairie and El Marinero. Dewey Dakota lurked around in the background. Son prayed that she was moments away from finding out that Casey Dakota had named his dog Tinka because he was a mad Teutonophile with a passion for all things Germanic. That he had a chalet-style bird feeder in his front lawn, the complete works of Karl May on his bookshelf, and every version of *Der Ring des Nibelungen* ever recorded.

Dakota lifted his lip on the side of his mouth like a mongrel baring a fang and launched a brown comet of tobacco juice into the Big Red can El Marinero had provided him. Son abandoned all hope that Casey Dakota might be a closet Wagner devotee. She wanted to end this inquiry immediately and simply leave with the vision of El Marinero astride his mount, radiant with the kind of natural aristocracy she would have loved to claim as her heritage.

Dakota dabbed the back of his wrist at the brown-stained corners of his mouth and initiated the proceedings. "What's the deal here?"

El Marinero and Prairie traded glances across the table, then looked at Son. It was up to her. If she wanted to walk away right now, they'd see to it that she could. But Son had committed herself, her life, to one thing from an early age: truth. That dedication had been her badge of shame and her greatest glory, her scarlet letter. She had always refused the illusions that insulated the lives of those around her, the Dorfburgers. She faced life, she embraced it, without benefit of stone-washed jeans or hair mousse or any of the other emollients offered by the merchandising monolith. She had to know.

El Marinero stood. "Prairie, why don't we disappear for a while?"

"Son, you gonna be okay?" Prairie asked.

Son nodded without speaking. That worried Prairie, but he followed El Marinero out of the room, stopping at the door. "Dewey, you want to step into the kitchen with us, get something to eat?"

The boy, mesmerized by the spectacle of his father in a state close to cowed, shook his head. "Ain't hungry."

"Yeah, you are," Casey Dakota corrected him. "Get outta here."

Dewey reluctantly left. Son and Casey Dakota faced each other across the planks for several long moments before Son finally made herself ask, "Why did you name your dog Tinka?"

Dakota folded his arms across his chest. "I think I'm oh be the one asking the questions here. Why'd you want to know?"

"Because Tinka is my mother's name."

"So what?"

"Tinka Getz."

"Getz!" Dakota slapped his hand on the table. "That's it! I been trying to remember that name for thirty years. She's your mama? Tinka? Man, always wondered what happened to her.

Damn, you don't look nothing like old Tinka. Had that hair like, what's that stuff they put on Christmas trees?"

Son felt ill. "Angel hair. I think you mean angel hair."

"Tiny. Lord, she was a tiny little thing. Could put my whole hand around her—"

"Please! I do not care to hear where upon my mother's anatomy your hands have been." Son was overwhelmed. "This is not possible; you're sterile. You are sterile, aren't you, or is that just a lie to lure women into your bed."

" 'Lure? Lure?' Beat 'em off with a stick's more like it. There's something about my body chemistry. Flat drives the ladies into rut. 'Lure.' They'da had me standing at stud hadn't been for them shitty-pants dependents on the boat home. Mumps ain't nothin' if you're five years old. You get it after your nuts drop and it's a whole 'nother smoke."

"Boat home from where?"

"Alemania. Home of the Huns."

"So you were viable when you met my mother."

Dakota narrowed his eyes. *Viable.* He didn't like the sound of that. He'd be consulting his lawyer before he answered any more questions.

"Against my will, I am being forced to a very unhappy conclusion."

"How's that?"

"You are my father."

"*You're* unhappy? You ain't exactly what I would have picked out of a catalogue. Naw, no way. Forget it. If I'da had a daughter, she'da been one of them super-petite models. Little button nose. I'da bought her some size-two pink Tony Lamas and carried her around like a doll."

"I don't suppose either one of us, then, is quite what the other would have wanted."

"Life'll do you like that. Every time." Dakota tipped back his chair and studied Son. "Goddamn, maybe that's why I get a crawly feeling every time I see you. You're the spitting image of my grandmother. Hated that old bitch and, Jesus, did she hate me. Kept telling Ma it wasn't too late to leave me out when it froze. So you're my daughter."

Dewey Dakota bounded back into the room the instant his father admitted that this might be possible. "A sister! I finally got me a sister just like Harlan Joe's sister!"

"No, shithead, not 'just like Harlan Joe's sister.' I ain't gonna have the entire Winnie junior varsity lined up outside *my* house. Now get your dumb ass out of here."

"But Da-a-ad."

Casey Dakota pretended to lunge out of his chair, and Dewey vanished. Chuckling, Dakota sat back down and fell into a reverie. "Tinka Getz. Damn, those frawleins were hot for cowboys! Like the frogs for coloreds. They was paying to get at us. None of them like Tinka, though. All them jerries were hard-headed, but that woman! Lord! She could teach a mule. Decided she was going to America and that was that. Worked out the whole stowaway plan herself. Not that it was all that hard a deal on a troop transport hauling back half the American families in Germany and an entire Wild West show. Horses and everything. You know what really turned me on about Tink, though?"

The vision that had sustained Son through all those barren years in Dorfburg, the picture of Gray Wolf, her aboriginal father, as aloof from the mainstream as she was, began to fuzz over and break up like an image beamed from a satellite that was moving irrevocably out of range. "What?"

"Her legs. She shaved them. Man! I'll tell you what, you coulda been at the monkey house at the zoo with most of the frawleins and they ain't all natural blondes either, believe you me."

"That was it? That was what attracted you to my mother?"

"Yeah, we was hottern' a couple of boar minks there for a while. Until she tried to kill me."

"Tinka tried to kill you?"

"You don't need to sound so by-Jesus happy about it. Woman attempted murder. After I stowed her away and everything. Waited until I was down to kick me. Got those mumps. Must have had something else, sick as I was. Didn't have the strength to get out of bed. Begged her to bring me some water. She'd a-let me die. Brought me something to drink, all right. Regular angel of mercy, your mama. I know it wasn't water. She'd buddied up with that witch doctor Cootie Ramos, so Lord only knows what he pounded up for her. I thought I was sick before; I didn't know what sick was until I drank that. Like to died. I was out of my head with fever. Come to, all my money and Tinka was gone. Never saw either one again. Ought to turn them both in to Immigration."

Son absorbed this information with outward calm. What astonished her even more than learning the identity of her father was discovering the surprising person her mother turned out to be. Son felt acres of new common ground with her mother solidify beneath her feet.

It did not take any great leaps of imagination to envision what Dakota might have done that would have inspired a spoiled, tough-minded girl like Tinka to such loathing. She certainly wouldn't have waited around for Casey Dakota to pull out his radiator hose. If nothing else, Son had always admired her mother for that; like those Tuba City boys, she didn't take crap from anybody.

"So you're my kid." Dakota let the front legs of his chair fall heavily to the floor.

"It would appear so."

"Well, at least you got a brain in your head. You gonna be contesting my will, looking to get a piece of the company, wanting me to buy you your own vehicle?"

"I don't want anything from you." Which was not strictly true. Son wanted so much from Casey Dakota, from a father, *her* father, that the immensity of her unfulfilled desires dwarfed even her ability to put it into words.

"You know, I always hoped my kid would say those words to me just like I said to my pa: 'I don't want nothing from you, you sorry sack of shit.' " Dakota, having finally accepted his paternity, closed his eyes and shook his head, amazed at the concept. "So you're my kid."

Son, who had grown up devoting so much of the sound track on her inner monologue to responding to that exact statement, could only give a frozen nod.

All of a sudden Dakota stood, clapping both hands down on the table. "Gotta motate! Gotta beat the shit out of Prairie James and get my money back." The heavy chair scraped against the tile floor as Dakota pushed it back. "You be good now, hear?"

He started to leave. When he was halfway out the door, Son jumped to her feet and yelled, "Wait!"

Annoyed, Casey Dakota glanced back.

"You are not leaving!" Son announced. Filled with the power of a message finally grand enough for the mighty delivery she had spent her life perfecting, she intoned, "You are my father and you cannot leave."

"That a fact?" Dakota asked with casual contempt.

"Yes, that is a fact. Come here immediately."

A dicey blend of menace and curiosity narrowing his eyes, Dakota sauntered back. "You pretty used to getting your way, huh?"

"I have not gotten my way once in my entire life. All I have ever gotten is a way no one else wants. You, however, are my father and you will give me my way. You owe it to me."

"How do you figure?" In spite of himself, Dakota was intrigued.

"You started my life, Casey Dakota."

"Sounds like you owe *me* for that little transaction."

"I did, I did owe you. But I paid. I paid every time I dreamed that my father was a man to eclipse all other men. That the gift of his blood running in my veins was enough to elevate me above the common herd. I paid. I paid with the first thirty years of my life. I put them on an altar and offered them to the father I did not know as if he were a god."

"A god, huh?" Casey Dakota had never met another human being—aside from Dewey, who didn't count—whose opinion of himself coincided so closely with his own. "We could get to like each other, precious."

"Not in a million years. But I have paid and you owe me and you will give me my way."

Dakota watched this curious creature, and Ina Jane, his grandmother, came to life. Grumpy, pissed-off every minute of her life, mouthy bitch, but smart. Smart and strong. His brains came from her; he knew that. His own father was too stupid to see his way out of a lard-and-beans life, tramping from one trashy oilfield to another. His grandmother was the only one with enough upstairs to know there was something better. His grandmother and him. But he was the one strong enough to go after a better life and get it. So here it was again, that same pissed-off, sulled-up intelligence that had sprung him from a loser's life. Blood will tell. If a lifetime spent around horses hadn't taught him another damn thing on this earth, it was that: blood will tell.

"And what do you figure I owe you?" The more of himself, his brains, that he saw in Son, the more he liked watching her work.

"You will let Prairie keep the money that you owe him."

"Me and Prairie, darlin', that's history. Pretty soon it's going to be *legal* history. But that, that's a whole 'nother deal."

"All right, then. Give me fifty-three hundred dollars with which to compensate the guide who helped me to find my father."

Dakota barked a sharp, delighted laugh. "Too bad you didn't get a dick to go along with them balls." He liked it that she didn't smile. They both possessed the first ingredient for success in business: they didn't care who liked them and who didn't. Actually that was the second ingredient. Loving money was the first. "I'm oh take your proposition under advisement. But first I got a little deal for you. You still want to announce for me?"

"Would that offer include lodging at a Best Western motel?"

"No, *that* offer involved rolling over on Prairie James, which you failed to do. This offer involves doing something with your rat shit life and making certain that everybody you ever meet on the circuit knows who your daddy is and exactly where your brains come from. It also involves never again dressing like a Tijuana whore going square dancing." Dakota jutted his jaw toward the bedraggled hot pink outfit.

"I have much to consider. This has been a day of surprises."

"Yeah, life. More turns than Chinatown. You want me to hug you or anything?"

"No, I don't think so."

"Naw. Okay. Well! Some folks got to work. There's still a rodeo in Gallup needs to be produced. Come see me. Dewey!" The boy materialized instantly, still holding the dachshund, Tinka.

"Yes, Dad."

"We gone; get into the RV."

"Ain't we gonna rip Prairie James a new asshole first?"

"Did I issue that order? Did I direct you to rip Prairie James a new asshole?"

"No, sir, Dad, sir."

"Get in the RV."

"I still can't believe it," Son muttered as Dakota made for the front door.

"Can't believe what?"

"Oh. That I'm not Indian."

"Oh, you ain't off that hook yet, doll baby. You got a grand-mother was full-blood Jicarrilla Apache. Meanst sons of bitches ever to bash a rock onto a kernel of corn."

"Really? Apache? The Apaches were the only tribe never to be subjugated by the European invaders."

Dakota had his hand on the wrought-iron latch of El Marinero's front door. "I'da like to have seen someone try and subjugate Ina Jane." He opened the door, and the sun of a new day blinded him.

"Wear these," Son said. She handed him the pair of vintage sunglasses.

"Always wondered where these went to." Dakota put the glasses on, stepped outside, and was lost in the dazzle of a day of surpassing brilliance.

Chapter 29.

Prairie gave Son the wheel of the chip truck when they reached the highway, then went back to the plank and passed out. Son's silence had exhausted him more than the wake he and the Sailor had conducted the previous night for all the rope men missing in action. If he'd been the prying type, he'd have asked her how bad it was messing her over, finding out that the world's biggest blowhole was her father. More than that, he wanted to know how he'd gotten out of Tres Caballos without Casey Dakota whomping him. But he wasn't that type. Instead, he'd asked her if she wanted him to drive or if she'd like to hole up somewhere. Get some rest.

But Son had just shook her head so hard that she'd flailed her cheeks with her braids and said she wanted to push on and that she wanted to drive. She had a lot to figure out. He couldn't argue with that and turned the wheel over to her with instructions to head north by northwest to Las Vegas, Nevada, where he fully intended to set up a short-term investment plan with the best-looking black-jack dealer he could find. Then, even though Domino was snorting down his neck, he passed out.

When Prairie came to and looked out on a world turning khaki beneath a nuclear late morning sun, he figured he'd been out a few hours and they were closing in on the giant waffle grill that was Phoenix, Arizona. Muscling Domino out of his way, he staggered to the passenger seat. "You want me to take over?"

Son still had that shell-shocked look on her face and shook her head.

"You hungry?" Prairie asked, hoping to see a Denny's materialize.

Son shook off another *no*, eyes locked on the asphalt.

It was eerie, her not talking. After a couple of minutes of staring out at sorghum fields with central pivot irrigators circling above, Prairie felt pushed to start babbling himself. "Hey, Poke, since it turns out I'm not your old man, you want to keep the team together? You can be my regular, official announcer."

"And who's going to hire us?" she inquired, but she didn't look over.

"I've got contacts. I've worked for every producer in the business. Casey Dakota isn't the only game in town."

"You are finished, Prairie James. You will never again earn your living as a trick roper."

Not exactly the morning chat show Prairie was looking for, but it was marginally better than stone silence. "Shit, you think I don't know that? Hell, I was finished ten years ago. Just couldn't stop that good loop from buzzing. Might as well go out on top. Retire while I'm still the best in the world. Don't tell anyone that the trick to being the best in the world is doing something no one else cares about."

"A life's work must be it's own reward."

"Hey, that's fine for your cerebro types bending over your illuminated manuscripts and shit, but it takes a little more juice for me to get off. Can you believe I shit away my life on fugging rope tricks?"

"The artist does not choose his art; it chooses him."

"You want to know how it'll play out? I'll tell you. Twenty, thirty years from now some pencil neck making a documentary'll track down my wheezing ass and haul me out to spin a few loops that I would have been ashamed to pop off at a kid's birthday party.

He'll talk about another tradition of the Old West dying and I'll kick a month or two later and he'll dedicate the deal to me. Maybe all those cornballs who like to get together and mourn the passing of the Old West will splash a few salty wet ones for me."

"I would share more fully in your grief except that I am too preoccupied with my own."

"Yeah, you're right. I just got *fired* by Casey Dakota, not sired. I did what I could to keep you from finding out."

"Yes, I see clearly now what a friend you tried to be, and, though you were misguided, I truly believe that your intentions were good."

"Hey, you know, a lichen'd be depressed to have Dakota for a father."

"Thank you."

"Don't mention it."

"I am depressed."

"Figures. Listen, look at it this way. Think of all the dominoes that had to fall to get you squirted out."

Hearing his name, the wonder horse poked his head out between Son and Prairie.

"Not you." Prairie tried and failed to push him back. Leaning far forward so that he could see Son, he continued his attempt to cheer her up. "I mean, for most of us the big event is a hole in the rubber. Jesus, a president had to get assassinated to give you your shot."

"What?"

Prairie lunged around Domino and grabbed the wheel, since Son seemed to have undergone a seizure that caused her to stare at him blankly and ignore the semi whose lane they were drifting into.

"Oh, yeah. Didn't I tell you?" Prairie got the truck back into its prescribed lane and replaced Son's hands on the steering wheel.

"You never told me anything. You actively kept me from learning anything."

"Oh, yeah. Well, the deal was, the reason they put the tour together in the first place, was on account of Kennedy getting killed in Dallas. They wanted to do this thing reaffirming American values. Some happy horseshit like that. That's how they were able to pull the strings to get us all together. Yank me and the Sailor out of the merchant marine. Get Dakota out of the army. I honestly think they dug Ramos out a federal pen somewhere. Never could get the truth out of that guy."

The assassination of a president. Son pondered for several long moments the fateful import of this newly revealed circumstance of her birth. "So that's what it took to bring my progenitors together."

"Nothing less."

"Epoch-making," Son decreed, her spirits rising noticeably as she contemplated the grandeur of the stage that had to be set for her entrance. It almost compensated for having a vulgarian lout for a father.

"You know that stuff about Tinka trying to kill Dakota . . ."

"Impressive, isn't it?" Son answered.

"Yeah, well, maybe. Anyway, that's not strictly true. I was the one tried to . . . well, not kill him, just not help him get well. I gave Tinka something Cootie pounded out on his metate. Some roots. I don't know what all. He deserved it's all I can say."

"So you knew my mother."

"Tinka? Yeah, I knew Tinka. Formidable woman. Formidable. And stubborn. What Tinka wanted, Tinka Getz. One minute I'm sitting at the NCO Club watching her eat a cup of Hershey's syrup with a spoon, next minute I'm helping Dakota build a false bottom into his rope trunk to sneak her onto the troop transport. Customs guys never even checked it. All those sick kids, crying and throwing up. They wanted us out of the country as quick as we'd go. What did that sign back there say?" Prairie craned around for a glimpse of the highway sign disappearing behind them.

"It said Hereford, seven miles."

"Hereford? Please, God, tell me there's a Hereford, Nevada."

"No, we're in Texas. We've been in Texas since I crossed the state line two hours after dawn."

"You're telling me that it's already tomorrow morning? I slept around the clock?"

"Yep."

"Yep? What the hell are we doing in Texas? I told you Las Vegas. Las Vegas, Nevada. Didn't I tell you Las Vegas?"

"You did. I chose to ignore your order in favor of a more enlightened plan for your future."

"This is not happening."

"After you fell asleep, I had a lot of time to think about both of our futures. You are a relic, Prairie. A relic of two lost ages. Of the great age of shipping and of cowboying. You have been overtaken by time—"

"Thanks."

"Trick roping is a doomed enterprise—"

"Listen, this day and age, being a white male is pretty much a doomed enterprise."

"And I considered what you could do with your life that would be of value and I came up with an obvious niche that you could fill most admirably."

"Yeah? And because you yourself are such a shining example of your skill with career counseling, I'm going to bite. What have you got for me? Strip show barker? Towel boy at a bathhouse? No, no, I got it. I can get into FAMILY FARMING. That way, I can be a relic of *three* lost ages."

"Should I continue?"

"Yeah, yeah, tell me, Son, what is my niche?"

"Father."

"What? What are you talking about, 'father'?"

"Father to Tuffie's children. You will return to Tuffie and make her tribe into a family. It is enough to justify a man's life."

"You have lost it, Poke."

"Though I have no proof other than that presented by my own eyes, I believe that you are Jonathan's biological father."

"Jonathan? Listen, I've asked Tuff about that. She swears he's not mine."

"The estimable Ms. Branch is nothing if not proud. She has taken the very wise position of excluding from her life any man who might feel bound to it by obligation."

"*That's* why she never tells who the fathers are? I thought she just wasn't sure." Prairie considered. "Jonathan?"

"If we have learned nothing else from my odyssey, surely we have learned that biological fatherhood is a mere technicality. Your charge will be to accept all of Tuffie's children as your own."

"Whoa! Whoa! Whoa! Has Tuffie even said she wants me around the place?"

"She has not. You shall have to prove to her that you are worthy. It is a mother's duty not to bog down her children's lives with worthless fathers. I see clearly now how significant it was that my own mother performed that service for me."

"So what are you suggesting? I just sort of lurk around the property and sweep up or something until Tuffie accepts me?"

"You are a useful man. You will find ways to help. Mothers need help. Mothers always need more help than they ever get. Jonathan needs a father and you need a son. All Tuffie's children need a father and you need someplace to belong."

Prairie had no answer. At least not one with any snap. He worried because this lunatic idea was beginning to sound not only possible but inevitable.

"Don't turn! Don't turn! I've got to think this over!" Prairie barked as Son disobeyed his order and wrenched the wheel of the chip truck to the right to make the sharp turn off of the main road onto the long drive up to Tuffie's dilapidated house. A deep bass grinding sound rumbled through the truck as it bumped onto Tuffie's potholed road.

"That sounded expensive," Prairie commented.

The front right tire lurched over a small bomb crater and the bass grinding jumped several octaves to a falsetto shrieking.

"Now *that* sounded fatal."

Prairie's diagnosis was verified an instant later when the truck dipped gently to the earth, the front bumper plowing through the crumbling asphalt, as the once-proud flagchip of the Lay's empire ground to a halt.

Prairie, Son, and Domino all got out to assess the damage. They were still nearly a fourth of a mile from Tuffie's front door. At least one member of their party was completely content with their destination. Domino ambled off toward a waist-high clump of weeds, throwing his head to the side as he cropped off a thick wad. Still chewing, he sauntered up the road.

Though Tuffie's pickup was parked in front, the house seemed to be empty. No dogs barked, no screen doors swung open, no tribe of children swarmed out into the yard.

"U-joint," Prairie concluded, glancing nervously from the truck to the house.

"The hand of fate," Son countered.

"Poke, here's the straight stroke on this. I come from a long line of shitty fathers and there is no reason to believe that I will be any better."

"But you already have been a good father. To me. Dakota may have started my corporeal existence, but you started my real life. You placed my interests above your own. You would have sacrificed yourself for me."

"What? I was supposed to let that douchebag fry you?"

"It seems to me that the major reason anyone decides to have children anyway is so that they can get it right."

"There is that. My old man certainly left plenty of room for improvement." Prairie kicked the truck. "Piece of shit. What's the big debate here? I'm not going anywhere. What about you, Son? You sticking around? We can drag the truck off the road, use it as a guest cottage."

"I may stay briefly. Long enough for Jackson to come and get me."

"Jackson?"

"Yes. Jackson. Piercing the mystery of my paternity has released a great store of energy within me. My life now spreads before me like an enchanted forest I have but to wander through in perpetual delight. I believe that Jackson will make a fine companion with whom to embark upon my journey of ceaseless wonder."

"He's a good choice."

"We'll come to visit as often as possible."

"I'm sure Tuffie'd like that. Should we go on up?"

"I have one more thing to say."

"Why does that not surprise me?"

"I want to thank you—"

"You don't have to—"

"I *want* to thank you. I have learned much from you. You did not like the father that fate assigned to you and made the courageous decision to choose another, more admirable one, the noble El Marinero. If I knew him better, I might choose him as well. But, since I don't, and for all the reasons I enumerated earlier, I am designating you to be the father I wish I'd had."

"Poke. Son, I don't think you really want—"

"You may hug me."

Prairie opened his arms and Son buried herself in them.

Up at Tuffie's house, Domino poked his nose in through one of the screens that Prairie had repaired and a high, reedy voice screeched, "Domino!" A second later, the front door flew open and Jonathan burst out.

Son peered up at Prairie, who was studying the skinny little boy, naked except for his signature Batman underpants, his Tony Lamas, and a length of clothesline coiled across his chest, race down the long hill. She saw something stir in his face she had not seen before. Something buoyant and proud and hopeful.

Prairie caught Son squinting up at him. "I'll give you this, Miz Getz: you make the most incredible things happen."

She looked away. The sun was making her eyes water.

"Don't choke up on me now. The good part's just starting." Prairie clapped her to his side in a one-armed, comradely embrace. "Who would have ever thought I'd have a daughter I could call Son!"

"Do me a trick! Do me a trick!" Jonathan accelerated down

the hill until he was careening out of control. Prairie swept up the
little boy into his arms just as Jonathan's feet began to slide out
from under him.

"Do you a trick, huh?" Prairie put the boy down and unwound
the clothesline from around his bony chest. "Okay, I got one for
you. This one's called El Zopilote."

Prairie opened his hands and the rope seemed to soar out of
them, taking off for the sky like a flushed bird. El Zopilote was pure
beauty hanging there in the air above their heads, just like a turkey
vulture riding a thermal without putting a single beat of his great
black wings into the trip. Just sliding through eternity on good
grace and bad looks.

Prairie stared up and knew that there wasn't another man on
earth who could put it up in the sky like that. Not even the Sailor.
Sure as hell not his wormrod son, Heriberto.

Son stared up and saw the turkey vulture of her vision hovering above her like a guardian angel. Her quest had been completed.

The other Branch children poured out of the house. The
twins grabbed at each other's T-shirts, the trailing one pulling back
the leader. Spur charged out with one leg covered in white lather,
the other newly shaven. Boots came last. She wore a dingy pair of
baby doll pajamas and a broad smile filled with her new, even,
white teeth. Tuffie, hair flat on the side she'd had against the pillow, face pale and still wrapped in dreams, stood at the open screen
door.

When Son looked back down, the Texas morning had been
bleached white as old bones. The only spots of color that remained
were the copper heads of Tuffie's five fatherless children running
toward her and Prairie.

For a second, maybe less, those heads bobbed in slow motion
coming down the hill just like a handful of pennies tumbling
through silver water as Mickey carefully washed his change. They
gleamed like that in the sun, like pennies waiting to be spent.